BLOOD OF IAX

BLOOD OF IAX

ROBBIE MacNIVEN

BLACK LIBRARY

For my granddad, Dennis. You'll always be loved.

A BLACK LIBRARY PUBLICATION

First published in 2018.
This edition published in Great Britain in 2019 by
Black Library,
Games Workshop Ltd.,
Willow Road,
Nottingham, NG7 2WS, UK.

10 9 8 7 6 5 4 3 2 1

Produced by Games Workshop in Nottingham.
Cover illustration by Marc Lee.

A CIP record for this book is available from the British Library.

ISBN 13: 978 1 78496 892 2

See Black Library on the internet at

blacklibrary.com

Find out more about Games Workshop
and the world of Warhammer 40,000 at

games-workshop.com

Printed and bound by CPI Group (UK) Ltd, Croydon, CR0 4YY

It is the 41st millennium. For more than a hundred centuries the Emperor has sat immobile on the Golden Throne of Earth. He is the Master of Mankind by the will of the gods, and master of a million worlds by the might of His inexhaustible armies. He is a rotting carcass writhing invisibly with power from the Dark Age of Technology. He is the Carrion Lord of the Imperium for whom a thousand souls are sacrificed every day, so that He may never truly die.

Yet even in His deathless state, the Emperor continues His eternal vigilance. Mighty battlefleets cross the daemon-infested miasma of the warp, the only route between distant stars, their way lit by the Astronomican, the psychic manifestation of the Emperor's will. Vast armies give battle in His name on uncounted worlds. Greatest amongst His soldiers are the Adeptus Astartes, the Space Marines, bioengineered super-warriors. Their comrades in arms are legion: the Astra Militarum and countless planetary defence forces, the ever-vigilant Inquisition and the tech-priests of the Adeptus Mechanicus to name only a few. But for all their multitudes, they are barely enough to hold off the ever-present threat from aliens, heretics, mutants – and worse.

To be a man in such times is to be one amongst untold billions. It is to live in the cruellest and most bloody regime imaginable. These are the tales of those times. Forget the power of technology and science, for so much has been forgotten, never to be re-learned. Forget the promise of progress and understanding, for in the grim dark future there is only war. There is no peace amongst the stars, only an eternity of carnage and slaughter, and the laughter of thirsting gods.

Strike Force Fulminata
'The Lightning Brotherhood'
Ikaran Intervention Demi-Company

Captain Demeter
Lieutenant Tyranus
Lieutenant Samson
Ancient Skyrus
Chaplain Kastor
Apothecary Polixis
Techmarine Tiberon

Intercessor Squad Nerva
Sergeant Nerva
>   Brothers Ovido, Priscor, Spurius, Tarquin, Plinus, Quintillius and Sergius

Intercessor Squad Valorious
Sergeant Valorious
>   Brothers Vespasior, Gallus, Cassians, Vito, Albanius, Dynator, Cypran and Caius

Intercessor Squad Faustus
Sergeant Faustus
>   Brothers Servio, Drusus, Cnaeus, Atilius, Avit, Tiberius and Sextus

Intercessor Squad Klastis
Sergeant Klastis
>   Brothers Fadius, Aeneras, Quiris, Lucarius, Clovens and Cellus

Hellblaster Squad Domitian
Sergeant Domitian
> Brothers Ennio, Trajo, Gratian, Junarius, Lorens,
> Luco, Marius, Otho and Victus

Aggressor Squad Tiro
Sergeant Tiro
> Brothers Torr and Uxis

Reiver Squad Severus
Sergeant Severus
> Brothers Fobus, Stryx, Scaris, Pulo, Tarkus and Vorr

Repulsor Grav-Tank *Extremis*

CHAPTER ONE   TO THE GORGON

KASTOR

The Fulminata had come to Shebat Alpha, and none could stand before them.

Kastor, Chaplain of the Dioskuri, roared. It was an expression of pure rage, fuelled by piety and stoked by righteous hatred. The noise, amplified by his vox-vocaliser, made the bellows and grunts of the greenskins surrounding him sound pitiable by comparison.

Salve Imperator shattered an ork's skull. It then snapped the neck of a second, hurling the beast back into its kindred. Energy crackled around the skull-topped crozius arcanum, blackened blood evaporating from it with every searing strike of the power mace. Bones cracked and flesh was pulverised. The towering Primaris Chaplain was a whirlwind of furious judgement, his leather cassock and vestments snapping around him, his pitch-black power armour splattered with a patina of alien viscera.

He had moved too far ahead. He was cut off. The realisation made him smile.

An ork attempted to headbutt him. It rammed itself

impotently against the stylised ribcage that encased his breastplate. Kastor snatched the beast by the throat with his free hand, hauling it from its feet so that its piggy eyes were level with the deep ruby lenses of his skull helm. The beast bellowed at him, spittle spraying from its maw, but the Chaplain silenced it with a headbutt of his own, bone cracking and tusks snapping as he caved in the alien's face.

He dropped the ork, his armour registering the strikes of crude cleavers and fists from all sides. None penetrated. He spun in a tight arc, vestment scrolls whipping around him, and cleared a semicircle of space with a single swing of Salve Imperator.

'See how easily the alien falls before the weaponry of the righteous,' the Chaplain boomed. 'Praise the Emperor for giving us this chance to enact His will!'

His slaughterous euphoria was interrupted by the familiar, battering thunder of bolter fire. Blood and sinew burst around him as a hail of mass-reactive bolts shredded the mob attacking him, their remains splattering his armour. Already the runtier greenskins at the rear of the melee had turned tail and were fleeing back up the street, perhaps unwilling to engage something that could bellow louder than one of their warbosses. Kastor let them go, the battle fury draining abruptly from his genhanced body.

'Too far again, Salve,' said Captain Demeter. The commander of the Fulminata was clad in his Gravis plate, the proud heraldry of the Ultramarines befouled by blood and grime. Behind him was Intercessor Squad Nerva and Ancient Mars Skyrus, who bore the lightning standard of Fulminata. Its blue-and-white silk rippled in the smoke shrouding the embattled street, the weak sunlight glinting from the wings of the golden bolt-and-aquila that tipped its crosspiece.

'The xenos exist to be purged,' Kastor responded. 'And *I* exist to perform that purging.'

The deafening report of a battle cannon interrupted Demeter before he could respond, the shell shrieking over the heads of the Primaris. It detonated further up the street in a great storm of broken masonry and ork remains. Kastor turned to survey the Imperial forces behind the Ultramarines – a squadron of Voitekan Leman Russ battle tanks grinding forwards in single file, supported by a platoon of Astra Militarum infantry from the same world. They paused, crouched on the pavement as they stared up in undisguised awe at the Primaris who had broken the ork mob. Kastor raised Salve Imperator, the crozius still wreathed with lightning.

'See how the beasts run, soldiers of the Throne,' he said, his voice booming over the growl of engines and rattle of nearby gunfire. 'This is *our* city, the *Emperor's* city, and we will reclaim it one step at a time. Press on. Crush these alien remains beneath your boots and the treads of your mighty tanks. The Emperor protects!'

The advance continued.

'Watch the manufactorum colonnades to the right,' Demeter ordered over the vox, highlighting a series of towering industrial pillars on the shared tactical display. The huge rockcrete structures had once been testimony to Shebat's productivity but now lay cast down in rubble and ruin, a metaphor for the city's fall. It had been great once – the foremost manufactorum of Ikara IX's Adamantium Belt, a refinery for the vast deposits of ore mined in the Tombstones, the mountain range within whose barren flanks the city nestled. Four millennia of industry had created a sprawling hive of smokestacks and smelter-scrapes, surrounded by a thicket of prefabricated habitation blocks and a further sprawl of slums and shack dwellings.

Then the green menace had come to the Ikara System, and Shebat's productivity had ended.

Kastor blink-acknowledged Demeter's directive via the visor display and drew his Absolver bolt pistol. Its heavy-calibre rounds made a mockery of even the tough hides and thick bones of the orks, each detonating shell bursting apart chests and skulls in gouts of blood and pulverised organs. He forced himself to check his pace so he didn't begin to outdistance his battle-brothers once more.

'With the support of the Astra Militarum, we've already succeeded in pushing the greenskins back,' Demeter continued. 'The xenos currently fester in a refinery square overlooked by the industrial plants' ruins.'

The map of Shebat overlaid on Kastor's visor display showed that they were less than a mile from the day's primary objective – the Excelsior Arch.

It had been more than a Terran year since war had engulfed Shebat. For a while, when the port city of Melu burned and the greenskin forces had reached the outskirts of Ikara IX's capital city, Kroten, it had seemed as though the planet would fall to the alien invasion.

Then the Fulminata, a Primaris demi-company of the Ultramarines Chapter, had been despatched, alongside the primary Imperial Navy subsector battlefleet, three Astra Militarum army groups and a *conroi* of Imperial Knights from House du Frain. Within five days, Kastor and his brothers had driven the xenos from the capital's outskirts, then followed up by breaking the greenskin siege lines encircling Merkoro.

Two weeks ago the brotherhood had arrived outside

Shebat. The Astra Militarum's Third Army, commanded by Field Marshal Stefan Klos, had secured the slum sprawl and established three beachheads into the city proper. Now the drive to the Gorgon was underway.

'Maintain fire protocols,' Demeter said over the vox, his voice as calm and measured as it was during the company's firing rites on board the *Spear of Macragge*. Intercessor squad Nerva had secured the main thoroughfare leading into the square, laying down bolt rifle fire as the orks charged them from all four corners. The open space allowed the trio of Voitekan battle tanks to spread out, their heavy bolters and battle cannons hammering shells point-blank into the oncoming mobs.

'See how the Emperor's wrath cuts them down!' Kastor bellowed to the Astra Militarum infantry squads advancing out between their tanks, adding their las-fire to the barrage. 'Keep firing! Not a single greenskin is to leave this place alive!'

'Kastor,' Demeter said, his tone full of warning. The Chaplain had begun to advance again.

'They will not stand, brother-captain,' he said.

'And you will not present them with an easy target,' the captain responded. Return fire broke out from the ruins around the square's edges, more mobs of greenskins armed with crude sidearms flocking to join the battle spreading through the refineries. Their shooting was worse than inaccurate, but there was enough of it for Kastor to take two hits to his breastplate and another to his left greave in quick succession.

'Lieutenant, bring your weaponry to bear on the refineries,' Demeter said, the order routed to the commander of the Voitekan armour. A clipped affirmation coincided with the whine of turret hydraulics as the battle tanks switched targets.

They never got a chance to fire. The enhanced aural units of Kastor's armour detected a high-pitched whistle, growing rapidly louder.

'Incoming!'

Sergeant Nerva was the first to shout the warning, issuing it over his external vocaliser for the benefit of the Guard infantry.

The first shell hit the space between the leftmost and centremost of the three Leman Russ battle tanks. The Voitekan infantry squad there simply vanished in a hail of metal and rubble that battered the sides of their tanks, spattering the vehicles with tattered human remains.

Another five shells struck the square within three seconds of the first. Fire blossomed, the detonations ripping indiscriminately into greenskins and Imperial soldiers alike. One hit the ground barely a dozen yards to Kastor's right. He felt his auto-stabilisers lock as the blast wave struck, accompanied by a storm of rubble and dirt. His armour blared with alarms, the auto-senses indicating shrapnel damage to his right pauldron and knee joint. When the smoke settled, however, he stood unmoved, his crozius shining bright with destructive energies amidst the haze.

'Xenos artillery,' Demeter voxed. 'Coming from across the river. I'm routing the coordinates to Serxis, but it will be at least twenty minutes before the bombardment cannon is locked.'

'Priscor and Quintillius have been hit,' Sergeant Nerva added. 'If we stay here, we die. We either go back or we go into them.'

'Into them then,' Kastor snarled, feeling his battle fury surging to life once more.

'As the Brother-Chaplain says,' Demeter responded calmly,

as the air filled with the shriek of more incoming shells. 'Primaris, advance.'

POLIXIS

'Medicae!'

Polixis was already moving up along the street's left-hand pavement when he heard the scream. Ahead, he could see a platoon of Namarian Imperial Guardsmen caught in a barrage of crudely aimed ork firepower, coming from a bombed-out residential block. He watched as the Namarian's colonel went down.

Polixis kept to the side of the street, instinctively knowing that it was unlikely any of the orks' shots would be coming his way when there were so many targets out of cover ahead of him. In just a few seconds, the Namarians had taken a slew of casualties. He saw the platoon's medic – caught sprinting towards the fallen colonel – collapse in a burst of blood as he in turn was hit in the side of the head.

'Medicae!' came the scream again.

Polixis cursed. He considered carrying on through the haulage work yards to his left, to link back up with Squad Valorious. But with the Namarian colonel down, their entire advance was stalling, and the wider spearhead couldn't afford that. Against his better judgement, Polixis cursed and broke from cover.

He ran from the street's edge and crossed to the downed colonel, using his bulk to shield the man. Shots came cracking his way, but he was too busy assessing the Namarian's injury to even notice. The man had taken a hit to the leg, probably an artery shot. Polixis spent precious moments slicing away his blood-drenched fatigues, trying to decide how to deal with the wound. His own equipment was far superior to anything carried by the Guard, but he had forgotten just how incredibly fragile humans were. It was only at times such as these, kneeling over the wounded soldier, that he properly appreciated the gulf between the Imperium's fighting forces.

Arterial spray painted Polixis' white gauntlets red. The Primaris Apothecary let out a slow breath as he tied off the torn femoral artery, applying a coating of counterseptic powder to the bloody gash in the colonel's thigh. The Namarian screamed.

'I have nothing for your pain,' Polixis said gruffly. 'Everything that will fortify my brothers would kill your kind.' Polixis bound the wound tightly with a bandage pad taken from the man's supplies and looked across at the Namarian platoon's corpsman. He was kneeling on the pavement, hands and forearms as red and soaking as the Space Marine's. His expression was an all-too-familiar rictus of concentration as he fought to tourniquet a leg torn almost in half by an ork slug round.

More hard rounds cracked past, one grazing Polixis' shoulder. Namarian infantry were supporting a combat team from Intercessor Squad Valorious as they secured the haulage work yards of the refinery district, a slow, grinding battle that had been going on since dawn. It had put their sector of the assault behind schedule. Polixis had been drawn from the main spearhead by two injuries to Valorious, Brothers Vespasior and Gallus. Neither were fatal, but the same could not be said of the wounds the Namarians were sustaining.

The Apothecary's heads-up tactical display lit with new information. The spearhead of the Primaris assault, driving directly for the Excelsior Arch, had suffered three casualties.

The log scrolling past identified heavy shelling, and the guns' thumping reports were audible from where he stood. He blink-clicked the company command channel.

'This is Helix. Do you have need of me, captain?'

'If not now then we will soon, Brother-Apothecary,' crackled Demeter's voice, overlaid by the crash of detonations. *'Redeploy to our coordinates with all haste.'*

Polixis sent an affirmation and moved to the side of the Guard corpsman struggling nearby. He bent down and grasped the bloody limb in one hand, yanking the tourniquet into place with the other. The wounded man wailed, slick with sweat, his face a wretched mask. He had the white eyes of a beast in pain, stripped of the intelligence and dignity of the human race. It was difficult to resist an impulsive sense of disgust at such a display. *He is only a man,* Polixis found himself thinking. Now was no time to consider the contrast between the Guardsman's desperate, agonised expression and his own stark white battleplate and helm. He wondered whether the man's terror was magnified by his presence. It would not surprise him.

'I must go now,' he said to the corpsman, who was looking at him with wide eyes. 'Check to make sure it's tight enough and tie off the popliteal. As far as I can judge your kind, the colonel is stable, but you must get him to cover. Remember your training and you will save lives here today.'

The man visibly struggled to find a response, staring at the giant, white-armoured warrior, but Polixis was already moving off, breaking into a run as he left the humans behind and headed south.

He checked the visor display again as he went. One of the three wounded sigils – Ovido's – had flashed from yellow to red. He was flatlining rapidly, the vitae signs on Polixis' diagnostor helm fading. The Apothecary picked up speed, servos whirring, boots pounding debris-strewn streets as he used the burst map uploaded to the shared tac-display to navigate along the rear of the ground taken in the morning's assault. The orks had been driven from their positions across the city, yielding four miles in barely an hour and a half.

The Gorgon was almost within touching distance.

Polixis' map turned him westwards, back onto the leading edge of the assault. Staying behind the immediate front line would take too long – he would have to skirt through it. Passing a trail of injured Astra Militarum troopers and stretcher-bearers in the pelts of the Tmaran Scalp-takers, he headed down a side street away from a gunfight that appeared to have broken out in the smelter work yard of a refinery primus. The tribal warriors cringed back at the Space Marine's passing, averting their eyes from a being Polixis knew they likely deified. He barely even acknowledged their presence, instead activating the vox.

'Prime Tertiary, be advised, I am inbound on the rear of your position.'

'*Acknowledged, Helix,*' came the reply from Lieutenant Samson. Polixis pounded into the work yard, taking a sharp right into cover behind a conveyance belt for mega smeltry blocks. Terrified-looking Tmarans scrambled to make way for him as heavy slugs cracked overhead. As he entered, he saw that the far wall had been demolished and appeared to be acting as a strongpoint for a greenskin mob that had entrenched itself in the neighbouring ore warehouse.

There were two other Primaris in cover behind the heavy conveyance belt, Brothers Cypran and Caius.

'The lieutenant?' Polixis asked over the external vox. Caius gestured towards the doorway of the main manufactorum building. Outside it a haulage lifter had toppled over, providing a length of reinforced plasteel that sheltered more Guardsmen. Samson was among them.

Polixis broke from behind the conveyance belt and vaulted the lifter's fallen crane, slamming into the gravel beside Samson. The lieutenant didn't look up from the fresh ammunition drum he was clipping into his auto bolt rifle.

'Just passing through, Helix?' he asked, using the Apothecary's battle cant signifier.

'Yes. Your situation is stable, lieutenant?'

'Keeping the beasts' attention on us,' Samson said, nodding to Cypran and Caius, the latter of whom leant over the conveyance belt to ease off a burst of bolt rifle fire. 'Faustus is taking a combat team north around their flank. We should be moving on within the next ten minutes.'

'I'm needed with the captain,' Polixis said, glancing once more at the tactical display. Brother Ovido's vitae signs were crashing.

'Fastest way is to the right,' Samson said, nodding to the work yard's north wall. 'Covering fire on my mark.'

Polixis broke from behind the crane as the thunder of bolters filled the work yard. The sudden fury seemed to only encourage the orks, who returned fire with a chorus of howls and roars. Shots sparked around Polixis, but none touched him as he hammered pauldron-first into the red brick wall. The masonry gave way with a crash. He carried on through the broken rubble and dust, finding himself in an alley running parallel to the work yard, presumably the same one taken from the manufactorum by Faustus en route to the greenskin's flank.

He took the first right, into a grimy, deserted inner-city hab street. An ork scrap-truck lay at the far end, burning, surrounded by an indiscriminate litter of greenskin and Guard dead. The bodies were brutalised, the full savagery of the two races' antagonism clear in eviscerating blows and point-blank weapon blasts.

The air filled with a familiar, furious shriek as a cruciform shape shot overhead, dangerously close to the jagged tops of the ruined refinery stacks. The Imperial Navy Lightning fighter was pursued by a crude ork aircraft, its autocannons blazing. The contrast between the two races could not have been clearer – the sleek, war-ready Imperial machine and the brute, ramshackle xenos engine, its ugly form riveted and bolted together in haphazard fashion. The mere sight of it stirred Polixis' disgust. Both flyers were out of sight again in an instant, a scattering of hot brass falling around Polixis as ejected cartridges sprayed across the street. The Apothecary paused briefly to assess his map, continuously updated with feedback from the linked auto-senses of the rest of the company spread across the city. The distant shellfire was now altogether closer, and he could see a haze of smoke rising above the hab units directly ahead.

He sped down a side alley, over a carpet of blackened, shrivelled bodies that had been caught in the promethium gout of a flamer. Ahead of him, the refinery square opened up. It had been reduced to a wasteland, pockmarked with craters and the strewn wreckage of human and alien corpses. He passed over a female Voitekan with her ribcage split open by shrapnel, side by side with a greenskin whose head had been half-demolished by a bolt-round. Beyond them, another human and alien lay intertwined, a Voitekan's bayonet impaled through the beast's eye while its fists remained clamped around the dead man's throat, both bodies frozen in their death throes.

The battle had swept through the open space and continued now on its western side – Polixis could see Ultramarines and Voitekan infantry to his left fighting together, engaged in a close-quarters firefight with greenskin mobs that had spilled over into a violent melee on the corners of adjoining streets. To his right, a Leman Russ battle tank lay near the start of a street leading off to the east, gutted by what looked to have been a direct shell strike, flames blazing from the twisted wreckage. Another had made it halfway across the square before a further hit had thrown one of its treads, leaving it slewed to one side and immobilised.

Brother Priscor lay against the tank's flank. Polixis crossed the square at a run, the air around him resounding with the fury of the combat playing out barely fifty yards to his left. Priscor's vitae signs were dropping steadily. The Apothecary saw why as he approached – the Primaris had lost both legs, presumably to a close-range shell strike. They'd been severed just below the knee plates, two nubs of ripped muscle and skin, blood and stubs of bone. A smear of red on the sooty flagstones of the square marked where he'd dragged himself to the battle tank's protective bulk.

Polixis dropped down beside the wounded Ultramarine. Priscor's helmet turned towards him.

'Brother-Apothecary. You're a welcome sight.'

'Remain still, Brother Priscor,' Polixis said, speaking with the brusque tone he fell into automatically during field surgery. 'This will not take long.'

He plugged a prognosticator into Priscor's left tasset dermal node, linking his armour with that of the wounded Primaris. Polixis' visor display blinked as it updated with fresh data, the diagnostor helm providing him with a full readout of Priscor's body readings.

'Your Larraman cells are working to cease the blood flow,' he said as he uncapped the plasma node latched to his backpack and linked it through the port in Priscor's vambrace. 'But you will bleed out before they are able to heal the wound sufficiently. I am providing you with a transfusion, followed by a cell acceleration stimm to hasten the process. That will stabilise you until you can be moved.'

'Bastard greenskins,' Priscor spat, but said nothing more. Polixis noted the strain indicated on his visor display from the Intercessor's left gauntlet, where Priscor was still gripping his bolt rifle.

The Apothecary activated the transfusion pack, the clear plastek of the plasma node turning a deep red. As it pumped fresh blood into the downed Adeptus Astartes, he slipped the multisyringe from his medicae webbing and flicked the adapter to the coag-stimm. Priscor made no sound as Polixis jabbed the needle into the port in his right tasset and depressed the plunger. Not for the first time the Apothecary wondered at the strange torture entailed in the existence of a Space Marine – while his genhanced metabolism meant that pain was more often than not reduced to little more than a dull ache, the changes wrought also ensured that he would remain fully conscious and coherent except in the direst of circumstances. A human warrior who had suffered similar injuries would have been left barely conscious, but Priscor would be afforded no such respite.

'Your vitaes are stabilising,' Polixis told him, glancing at the display readings as the stimm set to work. The pulse of blood from both stumps had been reduced to a slow ooze, congealing around the great scabs that had begun to blotch the hideously torn muscle tissue.

'Your secondary heart should provide sufficient circulation,' he went on. 'But do not try to move. I have tagged your armour with a retrieval sigil. Provided we do not lose this position you will be evacuated within the next half an hour.'

'You have my thanks, Helix,' Priscor said, helm turning to look towards the battle raging along the square's western side.

'I know what you're thinking,' Polixis said. 'But you will not leave the side of this tank. Consider it under your protection until its crew can refit. I will not lose any more of the Fulminata on this campaign.'

'I'm no use here,' Priscor growled.

'You are,' Polixis said. 'You can tell me where Brother Ovido is.'

Priscor pointed towards the melee, his voice shot through with an angry regret.

'He was still with Nerva when I saw him last. If he has fallen, it will be in amongst that.'

'Then I am needed elsewhere, brother,' Polixis said, removing the plasma node and capping it, cutting off the transfusion. 'A week in the *Spear of Macragge*'s medicae bay and I will have you fully fitted with bionic substitutes. You'll be back down here with the rest of Nerva before the last of the xenos have been purged.'

'I'll take that as an oath, Brother-Apothecary,' Priscor said sternly as Polixis stood. 'For Ovido's sake.'

'For Ovido,' Polixis agreed. He turned west, towards the edge of the square and the battle still raging there, and broke once more into a run.

As he went, he unclamped his Absolver bolt pistol.

It was clear to Polixis that the greenskins were on the verge of breaking. He saw a detonation rip through the rear of the aliens' mob, wicked metal slicing thick green flesh and sending blood and limbs skywards. He realised that their own artillery across the river had attempted to shift its target zone to account for the Imperial push across the square, but with typical orkish inaccuracy, was overcompensating and now hammering the mobs in the rear still trying to force their way to the front. At the same time, Intercessor squad Nerva and the single Leman Russ that was still fully functional had been reinforced by a company of Voitekan infantry, who were now pouring las-fire down the streets branching from the western side of the square. Faced with the choice of dying beneath their own barrage or throwing themselves at the steadily advancing Imperials, the greenskins had chosen the latter.

As Polixis ran he located the company banner of the Fulminata. Its blue-and-white silk fluttered proudly exactly where he'd expected to see it – at the point where the greenskins had reached the Imperial line on the rubble-choked corner of one of the refinery blocks, unleashing a swirling melee that threatened to drag in the Voitekan platoons on either side. Amidst the flashing blades and churning bodies, the Apothecary caught the actinic flash of power weapons and heard a familiar bellow ring out, audible even over the crash of the nearby shelling.

He very nearly smiled as he ran.

Then the fury of close combat hit, and the honed skills of a warrior bred for nothing but total war took over. Ahead, a greenskin hefted its crude axe to cleave the skull of a wounded Zoitekan Guardsman. Polixis fired, his bolt detonating inside the creature's guts, shredding its lower torso. It went down with a bellow next to the Guardsman, and Polixis finished it with another shot to the skull. Directly ahead, Brother Tarquin grappled with another greenskin, the Primaris' gladius lodged in the beast's chest. Despite this, it tried to grind its own cleaver deeper into the space where the Space Marine's pauldron met breastplate. Polixis shoulder-charged the ork, throwing it back with a grunt and dragging both weapons free. Before it could recover its balance, he fired again, blowing away half its face in a spray of foul alien gore.

'Brother Ovido?' he demanded, half turning to grasp Tarquin's shoulder.

'The captain,' he grunted, opening fire with his own bolt pistol, aiming past the Apothecary as another ork rushed at them, bellowing.

Polixis pressed on. All around him men, beasts and the Adeptus Astartes grappled and hacked, stabbed and spat, but it was a blur even to his hyperactive senses. His eyes were fixed on the company banner, grasped high in the fist of Ancient Skyrus, lit by the lightning of Captain Demeter's power sword and the blazing crozius arcanum of Chaplain Kastor. As he broke through to them, he noticed a crumpled body at Skyrus' feet.

'Ovido,' the standard bearer said.

Polixis didn't require his prognosticator to know that the Primaris was dead – two heavy slug rounds had punched through his breastplate, cracking the Space Marine's fused ribcage and almost certainly rupturing both hearts and lungs.

'Brother-Apothecary,' said Demeter. The captain was half facing away from him, dragging his power sword from another greenskin corpse. 'Kindly perform your rites.'

Polixis knelt beside Ovido. He activated his narthecium, the advanced medicae tool that encased his left gauntlet, muttering the Litany of Recovery as he did so. A glance told him the sternal progenoid, the gene-seed buried in Ovido's chest, had been damaged beyond recovery by the two shots that had killed him. The secondary cervical progenoid, however, was not beyond saving.

He accessed the emergency sealants around Ovido's gorget, unclamping his helmet with a quiet prayer to the armour's machine-spirit.

'Blessed battleplate, yield your fallen brother to me now.'

The fallen Ultramarine's face was revealed – wrathful in death, pale and stony-eyed, as though still damning the xenos that had shot him. Mag-locking his bolt pistol to his thigh, Polixis used two fingers to close the Ultramarine's eyelids, before triggering his narthecium's carbon alloy chainblade.

Combat recoveries were unpleasant at the best of times. The reverence and care that the body of any fallen member of the Chapter deserved had to be set aside in favour of measured haste. Polixis sliced the tip of the chainblade along Ovido's throat, cutting the white flesh with a practised stroke. Blood welled bright from the small incision as he deactivated the chainblade and extended the narthecium reductor's extractor tube and flesh hooks, sliding it into the cut and keeping the wound from sealing. The thumbnail-sized pict-caster above the tube's tip linked with his helmet display, showing him the grey, fleshy gland he sought in Ovido's neck. With a blink-click he triggered the extractor tube's scissor end after it had slid over the progenoid, neatly severing the gland from the connective tissue embedding it into the larynx.

With the gene-seed disconnected, Polixis activated the reductor's suction valve. There was a whirring noise as the land was dragged free from Ovido's flesh and shunted up the extractor tube into one of the sealed cryo-receptacle vials at the narthecium's rear.

As Polixis worked, the slaughter around him continued. His transhuman senses were aware of it, capable of splitting focus between the probing of the extractor and the surrounding thump of axes and the clang of steel on ceramite. He pulled a mortis tag from his plastek medicae webbing and inserted it into Ovido's primary breastplate port, just to the left below his fused rib-plate, providing a beacon to locate the body later now that the battle-brother's auto-senses were offline. As Polixis stood, a spray of blood splattered his white armour, a greenskin's severed head flying past him from the direction of Captain Demeter.

'He is recovered,' the Apothecary said, speaking the rite of the fallen. 'His legacy endures.'

'Brother Priscor?' Demeter asked.

'Stable.'

'Then let us press on,' Demeter continued, switching to address both the Primaris and the Guard over the vox. 'The Gorgon lies just ahead, my brothers. Forward!'

KASTOR

An hour since first entering the refinery square, the Fulminata secured the eastern end of the Excelsior Arch. Kastor caught sight of the great bridge ahead, scarred by the bombing runs of Imperial Navy Marauders, craters riddling its broad expanse. Still it stood. Greenskins packed it from span to span, the mobs thrusting individuals through the holes and over the bridge's sides in their bestial eagerness to reach the east embankment and join the battle raging through Shebat Alpha.

The final phases of the day's objectives were at hand – they were to secure the eastern bank of the river. Demeter led the final drive to the bridge. Kastor strode to his left and Polixis to his right, their bolt pistols thundering, the Intercessors of

Squad Nerva forming a wedge around them, while Ancient Skyrus' banner fluttered at the centre of their formation. Voitekans kept their flanks clear with volleys of las-fire, the Guard maintaining their discipline in the white heat of the close-quarter combat that had been grinding on ever since the refinery square. Reinforcements pressed in from the north and the south – a squadron of Namarian Leman Russ battle tanks and two companies of Kelestan Stormers, relentlessly driving the greenskins towards the banks of the river.

That river was the Gorgon, the great, sluggish expanse of polluted water that curved through the heart of Shebat, two thousand paces from one embankment to the other. The Excelsior was the greatest of six bridges that had once spanned it, from Saint Collum's Crossing in the north to the adamantium mag-lev line in the south. A week of Imperial bombing runs in the build up to the offensive had reduced all but one to broken stubs and rockcrete rubble heaped in the foaming sludge below. Only the Excelsior endured.

The bridge's entrance archway lay before the Primaris. Kastor could tell that it must once have been an ornate affair, a great stone monument engraved with images showing the industriousness and toil of the city of Shebat. It had been scarred by the brutalities of war, and was now further defiled with the crude iconography of the greenskins: huge skull effigies and totemic devices had been bolted to its front and sides, and a rickety-looking ork crane had heaped wrecked battle spoil – weapons, armour, even parts of a burned-out Leman Russ – on top of it. The transformation of humanity's great works into a bestial mockery of their former glory sent fresh fire blazing through Kastor's veins.

'Drive them into the Gorgon, my brothers!' he bellowed, charging forwards into the press. Shells fell from across the river, indiscriminate detonations ripping through the embankment zone. Kastor realised he was grinning with a rictus of frenzied passion as he set about once more with Salve Imperator, the crozius crushing skulls and cracking shoulders and ribcages. Demeter joined him, both his power sword and his boltstorm gauntlet ignited, a crackling tempest of destruction. Kastor was partially aware of Polixis on the other side of the captain – the Apothecary had drawn gladius and Absolver bolt pistol, medicae tools exchanged for the implements of butchery.

A battle cannon shell pounded into the press of greenskins beneath the archway in front of them, dangerously close to the advancing Primaris. The shock wave battered the Space Marines, accompanied by a hail of shattered rockcrete and body parts. The blast cleared a space ahead, affording the Ultramarines a break in the melee. It was then that word crackled over the captain's earpiece.

'The *Spear* strikes,' he relayed to those around him. The words had barely been uttered when the heavens parted.

A spear of light lanced down from above. Its brightness imprinted itself even on the lumen dampeners of the Ultramarines' visors, searing a perfect circle in the ashen clouds. The light struck the ground directly across the river, the point of impact obscured by the warehouse blocks lining the opposite bank. There was a burst of brilliance, followed by a thunderclap like the closing of the Eternity Gate. The warehouses shuddered, and seconds later the shock wave hit the east side of the river, buffeting man and ork with the fury of a gale. Kastor lowered his head into the storm, stabilisers activating once again. He felt debris striking his armour, ricocheting off his legs, torso and pauldrons and making his vestments whip about him. The rockcrete underfoot shuddered, the city shaken to its very core.

The shock wave passed. The light blinked from existence, replaced now by a great pillar of black smoke that began to rise towards the torn sky. The *Spear of Macragge* had struck, an orbital bombardment that had obliterated the ork artillery positions firing from across the river. The shellfire ceased.

The stunned hush that followed didn't last long. There was a cracking sound, and the ground shook once more. The crack rose to a crash, echoing back from the ruins bordering onto the river and overlaid by the howling of thousands of alien throats. Kastor realised that the Excelsior Arch, battered for days by munition payloads, was finally breaking in the aftershock of the *Spear of Macragge*'s strike.

He lowered Salve Imperator and watched as the great bridge began to collapse. The arch closest to the west bank gave way first, plunging hundreds of greenskins into the broken rockcrete and toxic slurry of the river below, the xenos struggling and clawing at one another as they were slowly dragged under. The rest of the great bridge followed arch by arch, the air filling with the sound of ruination as the city of Shebat was split in half. The destruction only ended a hundred paces from the east bank's defiled entrance archway, the last of the bridge's masonry crumbling away to leave behind a jagged stub of stonework, the last remnants of Excelsior's majesty.

As the echoes of the collapse began to fade, the Imperial forces redoubled their assault. The surviving greenskins trapped on the east bank were cut down, bolt-rounds and las-bolts bursting apart their toughened hides and crude scrap armour. Kastor strode ahead of the advance, unheeding now of the orks dying around him. He entered the shadow of the archway, the stonework soaring above him, and turned back the way he had come. Before him were his battle-brothers, stained and scarred by the day's fighting, and either side of them the stern-faced men of the Guard, bloodied but with victory gleaming in their eyes.

'Brothers!' the Chaplain bellowed, voice amplified to a thunderous exhortation. 'The day is ours! In the Emperor's name we have purged, and by His will we shall do so again! Today we have reclaimed half of this great city. Tomorrow, we retake the other half! *Ave Imperator!*'

The response, issued from human and transhuman throats alike, was deafening.

CHAPTER TWO   FALLING SKIES

KASTOR

By late afternoon, the aquila was flying once again above the Basilica of Saint Albarak the Smelter. The echoing, decrepit Ecclesiarchy headquarters had been the primary objective of the northernmost Imperial salient assault. According to the after-action reports being logged on Kastor's display, it had fallen almost without a fight, largely abandoned by the greenskins as they had flocked to engage the Fulminata's drive to the Gorgon.

Now it was the headquarters of the combined Imperial command in Shebat Alpha. Kastor watched as a harried-looking Ministorum deacon hurried from pillar to pillar, applying tinctures of blessed oil and muttering the Canticles of Purification. Orderly staff officers began flooding the nave and apse, setting up the paraphernalia of military command. A humming power generator was inserted into the ambulatory, fussed over by red-cowled tech-adepts. Thick clusters of cabling led to a holochart assembled in the chancel, beneath the remains of the altar. More lines were tacked to the narrow stone casements leading to the basilica's belfry, where the headquarters' communication hub had been established, hardwired in case signals became blocked or scrambled. Physical charts, troop rosters and orders of battle were pinned up to the bullet-scarred walls of the apse, and the whole echoing space was soon illuminated by jury-rigged lumen strips that buzzed with electrical charge. A flakboard sentry post was being constructed outside and sandbags and ablative shielding heaped around the broken windows and entrances.

Kastor lent his own prayers to the work of the Ecclesiarchy, seeking to reconsecrate the old stonework around him. As night fell, Field Marshal Klos arrived with his senior staff and a detail of Tempestus Scions, who took up security rotations around the former place of worship. Captain Demeter was present as well, a giant in his blue Gravis armour, dwarfing the humans scurrying about his feet. An extensive debrief of the day's engagements began, along with final planning and preparation for the next day's push.

Kastor and Polixis removed themselves early and passed together down into the vaults. The space was being converted into a reserve armoury bunker, stocked with crates of supplies to be used should shelling force the headquarters staff underground. The Primaris had passed through the echoing, dank spaces to a familial offshoot, a branch of alcoves owned – according to the crumbling lettering – by the great Shebat industrialist family, the Fazals. There, on one of the tomb slabs not yet occupied, they laid out the body of Brother Ovido.

Kastor lit the stone alcove with the wan light of a trio of electro candles. He watched in silence while Polixis worked. Techmarine Tiberon had already removed the Intercessor's blessed Mark X power armour and armaments, for repair and reuse. Polixis now harvested his body. Those organs that could still be implanted into future generations of the Ultramarines Chapter were extracted one by one before being placed carefully in white cryo units stamped with the helix sigil of the apothecarion.

'Spirit of the Emperor's righteous servant, accept your removal from the flesh of your warring vessel,' Polixis murmured. 'Stay true, that you may imbue the future of the Chapter with vengeful purpose.'

Kastor listened as Polixis continued to recite the Rites of Recovery, his brother's gauntlets and narthecium red with Ovido's blood. The crumbling old tomb space filled with the soft rending of flesh and the surgical buzz of chainblade and drill bit.

The final organs were removed, joining the precious, lone progenoid that had already been sealed into the main cryo unit. Ovido lay like a demonstration piece for Space Marine physiology, his ribplate split open, remaining organs exposed to the cold, dank air. Polixis set to work sewing the sliced flesh back together, working with a speed and precision that none but the most experienced human surgeons or mortuary attendants could have matched. Eventually, with Ovido's remains bound by rows of neat black stitching, he nodded wordlessly to Kastor. The Chaplain, his skull helm even more sinister in the flickering candlelight, took a step forwards to stand over the slab and the body that lay atop it.

'Blessed Emperor of Man, saviour of our race, look down upon us now as we recall the deeds of a brother fallen in your service.'

The words sounded through the old crypt, as dark as the shadows that stretched and yawned around the Space Marines. Polixis bowed his head while Kastor intoned the Chapter's funerary rites, commending the soul of Ovido to the Emperor and to the honoured forebears who had fought for mankind's pre-eminence for over ten thousand years.

'He held the breach at Ktar alongside Scaevola and Tulio for eight Terran hours, until reinforcement could be made,' the Chaplain said, listing the fallen's greatest achievements. 'At Lorenzis he destroyed a dozen heretical war engines single-handedly. Against the Cult of the Fivefold he was grievously wounded while ensuring the safety of Brother Ronus. Who else among the assembled recalls his deeds?'

'I remember him at Patricius Lorn,' Polixis responded. 'I remember him at the Kab Pass. He helped me to stabilise Brother Tars from then-squad Drusus. Tars would have fallen that day without him. Now he is an honoured sergeant in the Second Company. That is just one of Ovido's many legacies.'

Ovido's brethren from Squad Nerva should have been present to recount their personal memories of the fallen. Such a thing was not possible, with the Intercessor squad holding the east bank of the Gorgon through the hours of darkness, and in truth to receive a full remembrance while the company was still combat-effective was rare. The Codex Astartes called for honour and reverence but also practicality, as far as the dead were concerned.

Ovido had been a Mars-born Primaris, like many still among the Fulminata, so his body would have no resting place within the realm of Ultramar. Once back on board the *Spear of Macragge* it would be cremated and its ashes fired into the void, a last tribute in an uncaring and brutal galaxy.

Kastor closed the small ceremony with the Final Rites, making the sign of the aquila over the pale corpse. Afterwards the two Primaris stood in silence for a while, the only noise the distant scrape and thud of more supplies being hauled down to the adjacent crypts by Guard orderlies.

'Priscor lives?' Kastor asked eventually.

'Yes. He's been shuttled to the *Spear of Macragge*. Artema is tending to him until I can relocate. She reports that he is in a stable condition.'

The comm-piece in Kastor's ear blurted, a sudden, jagged spike of static overlaying a few incoherent words. After a few seconds, it returned to silence. The signal in the crypts was almost non-existent.

'Squad Nerva will want vengeance,' Kastor went on. 'I must be careful to channel their hatred towards its proper end.'

'That is your prerogative,' Polixis said.

'I sense there is more you wish to say,' Kastor continued after Polixis went no further. 'Speak your mind, my brother. You have seemed reticent these past few days. Our brothers may not notice, Polixis, but we came from the same womb. You cannot hide this from me.'

'Every squad bar the Reivers has now suffered at least one fatal casualty since making planetfall,' Polixis said, looking from Ovido's body to his blood brother, the Chaplain. 'The xenos have been driven back on all fronts, but they still control vast swaths of Ikara. Even this city is only halfway to being cleansed. At the current rate, our casualties are only just sustainable.'

'I am sure Captain Demeter is aware of that,' Kastor said.

'But it would be remiss of me not to mention it,' Polixis said. 'You are the guardian of this company's spirit, my brother, but I am responsible for their bodies. It is my duty.'

'You wish for me to mention it to the captain,' Kastor surmised.

'He will be expecting me to take issue with our losses. That is part of my role, after all. Hearing it from you will carry a greater weight.'

More static chopped in over the vox. Both Primaris ignored it. Kastor went on.

'You know him as well as I, brother. He does not take the death of a single Ultramarine lightly. Our mode of warfare on this world is dictated by circumstance. We have no intelligence pertaining to the xenos warlord leading the aliens here, and without the ability to land a single, precise blow our place is bolstering the Guard. You saw what we achieved out there today. How many weeks would be required, and how many thousands more would have fallen, had the humans been forced to fight their way to that river street by street without us?'

'We are bred for war, and losses are inevitable,' Polixis said, the words sounding tired and heavy. 'I long ago accepted that. But if we cannot find a means to shorten this conflict, few of us will leave this world.'

'I will speak with the captain,' Kastor repeated. 'As should you. I am certain the matter is already on his mind.'

There was yet another jagged spurt of static over the vox. A cold feeling settled over Kastor, a foreboding instinct born of more than a century of combat. He could tell from the slight shift in his brother's stance that he had felt it too.

'Something's wrong,' the Apothecary said.

Without another word the two Primaris strode from the alcove, Polixis motioning to the four Chapter-serfs in their blue shifts waiting outside to enter and seal Ovido's remains in the black plastek body bag they carried between them. They made for the stone stairs leading back up to the basilica, supply orderlies in the uniform of the Departmento Munitorum hurrying to get out of their way. It was only when they emerged into the ambulatory behind the basilica's apse that the vox signal cleared, and the full weight of what was unfolding became apparent.

The sudden surge in vox traffic was originating from high orbit. From the snatches of ongoing conversation that the Space Marines' vox-beads were picking up, it sounded as though there was a full-scale stand-to among the Imperial Navy fleet anchored above Ikara IX.

They rounded the ambulatory and entered the chancel, where the holochart had been set up. Bodies crowded around it, sweat-streaked and pale in the unforgiving brightness of the makeshift lumen arrays. There were Guard corps commanders in the field dress of their respective regiments, signals officers, the Munitorum Quartermaster Primary and the commander of the local Ikaran elements, all chattering nervously while two Adeptus Mechanicus adepts bent over the chart's regulator relay. Kastor noted the presence of Field Marshal Stephan Klos, son of Lord General Helgar Klos, one of the Heroes of Cadia, a decorated Astra Militarum commander whose face bore as many jagged scars as Demeter's.

The captain was also among them. He had cleaned and anointed his Gravis armour in the hours immediately following the day's engagement, and now he towered over the officers and staff aides gleaming and untouchable. His helm was mag-locked to his hip, and his viciously scarred features were stern and silent, thrown into strange contrasts by the lights from the lumens above and the glow of the chart below. The humans nearest him hurried to make way as Kastor and Polixis joined him on either side.

'Brethren,' he said. 'Brother Ovido has received the Final Rites?'

'He has, brother-captain,' Kastor said. Both the Chaplain and the Apothecary had removed their helmets as they approached the chart, conscious of Demeter's orders that they present their faces as often as possible around their human allies. Being seen as anything other than unyielding automata was not something that concerned most Adeptus Astartes, but like many of Guilliman's favoured, the captain of the Fulminata seemed to be as much a diplomat as he was a soldier. According to Demeter, showing the human soldiers and citizens of the Imperium that they were flesh and blood had a multitude of morale benefits. Polixis understood the reasoning, though he knew that Kastor considered it a foolish affectation. The Chaplain respected Demeter enough, however, to adhere to the ruling in his presence.

Without their helms, Kastor knew he and the Apothecary's shared lineage was laid bare. Both had the same firm jawline, accentuated by the natural bulk and solid bone structure of all Primaris, though Kastor bore the scars of a tyranid's claws that marked him out from his brother. Both had the same hair, as golden as a full Iaxian harvest, though Polixis wore his cropped closer to the scalp. Most clearly of all, both had the same pale grey eyes, wintery and discerning. In the face of a human being they might have been described as thoughtful, even sad. There was no denying that, even accounting for the transitional similarities common to the genetics shared by all Ultramarines, Kastor and Polixis had been brothers before the beginning of their first initiation rites.

'There is a situation, captain?' Kastor asked as both Primaris surveyed the holochart. It had been beaming a sea-green projection of Shebat and its surrounds – the great, polluted sweep of the Gorgon and the arid peaks of the Tombstone mountains that lay immediately to the west and south. Parts of that map were dissolving now and being replaced with a star chart showing the Ikara System, its constituent planets and moons, and the positions of Imperial fleet elements. Sections of the display continued to blink and update as augur and sensorium data filtered through, overseen by the two tech-adepts labouring to keep the hololithic chart connected.

'*Situation* is an understatement,' said Field Marshal Klos, speaking for the first time. He smacked one palm into the holochart's glassy surface, causing the entire three-dimensional display to flicker.

'They've caught us cold, Throne damn them. How many times have I told high command not to underestimate these beasts?'

'A xenos fleet has just completed a warp jump into Ikaran real space,' Demeter explained to Kastor and Polixis. 'Dangerously close to the system core.'

'How close?' Kastor asked, eyes on the chart. Green skull runes – no doubt representing ork capital ships – were starting to appear amidst the stellar cartography.

'You heard the Ultramarine,' Klos snapped at a bald, corpulent Navy attaché in the starched green dress uniform of the segmentum battlefleet. 'How close?'

The man jumped, all but cringing beneath the sudden, intense scrutiny. His eyes darted over the chart readings.

'I… I think perhaps four hours, my lords, if they maintain their initial heading and speed–'

'*Perhaps?*' Klos snarled, smacking the chart again. 'Perhaps just about sums this all up. Throne damn it all. Morelin.' He snapped his fingers at a white-uniformed man with the heavy aural augmetics of a Guard vox-chief. 'Have you got Lord Commander von Klimt on the line yet?'

'No, sir,' Morelin said, one hand going up to the device sutured into the side of his skull as he filtered the communications traffic reaching the headquarters. 'His aide claims he's *still* in an emergency holo-conference with Rear Admiral Corran.'

Demeter had said nothing since Klos' arrival, but as the field marshal opened his mouth to utter another string of invectives, the Space Marine raised his right gauntlet. The motion was slight, yet it caused even the gruff Cadian to pause.

'Captain Spalding,' the Ultramarine said levelly. 'Can you offer us a professional opinion on the size of the enemy fleet that has just entered real space?'

'The numbers are still updating,' the Navy officer replied hesitantly. 'But the system's augur station and the fleet's sensorium arrays have confirmed at least five capital ships, with between three and five more currently being assessed. Escort numbers remain unverified, but it is undoubtedly a major incursion. The subsector battlefleet elements anchored in high orbit are probably outnumbered a little over two to one.'

'It can only be the fleet of Warlord Urgork himself, then,' Demeter said. 'He has brought the forefront of the Waaagh! to this system.'

'It's as I feared,' Klos said. 'I warned von Klimt about this. Two weeks ago the greenskin offensive in the Arden System stalls. Two weeks ago we retake Priscilia and secure the Ior Salient. Why? Because they've shifted their centre of power. They've moved their focus, their strength of mass, to here. To this system. Two weeks is a short warp jump from Arden. Two weeks and they redeploy their primary elements here and crush us, turning the flank on the whole subsector defence. Sometimes I think those damned xenos could teach our high command a thing or two.'

Kastor growled, a gauntlet on the haft of his mag-locked crozius. 'Careful, field marshal.'

To his credit, even Klos appeared to immediately regret his words, blanching at the black-armoured Space Marine's ire.

'If Urgork's fleet is approaching, our own in-system elements will be overwhelmed,' Demeter went on. From anyone else around the chart, it would have sounded like defeatism. From the Primaris it came across merely as carefully considered fact. He continued. 'An evacuation would also be impossible before they reach orbit.'

'So we engage the bastards,' Klos said, recovering his brashness. 'At the very least we can give the neighbouring systems time to readjust, maybe even dispatch reinforcements. We can sell our lives dearly here.'

'I suspect that will be our fate, field marshal,' Demeter agreed. 'But it is pointless to sacrifice that which can be saved. I recommend the subsector battlefleet conducts a fighting retreat to the edge of the system, to either hold there for reinforcements or complete a warp jump withdrawal.'

'You want to yield orbit to the xenos?' Klos said incredulously. 'That would give them immediate planet-wide air superiority. They'd fill the skies with their scrap bombers and launch orbital strikes with impunity.'

'That is the situation we will find ourselves in when our own fleet elements are destroyed,' Demeter pointed out. 'How long do you believe Rear Admiral Corran can hold out for? A Terran day, at the most? The sacrifice of significant elements of the Imperial Navy would provide us with almost no tangible advantage.'

Klos said nothing, eyes fixed on the holochart as he digested the Ultramarine's words. Demeter continued.

'I will be transmitting instructions for a fighting withdrawal to my own flagship within the next thirty minutes. The shipmaster will recommend the same course of action to the rear admiral.'

'I doubt von Klimt will suggest anything similar to Corran,' Klos said. 'The fool will probably want him to attack head-on.'

'Then he will find himself without the support of the *Spear of Macragge*,' Demeter replied.

'Lords,' said Spalding tentatively, gesturing at the holochart. A new sigil had blinked into life on the display, an ork glyph, larger than the others clustered around it.

'What is it? Urgork's flagship?' Klos demanded, peering at the data readouts accompanying the marker designate.

'No,' said Spalding. 'It's worse. Much worse.'

SERXIS

Shipmaster Serxis broke the vox-link and sat back in his command throne. Beneath him the bridge of the *Spear of Macragge* lay in silence, the faces of a hundred deck officers turned up towards him in expectation. The spartan work surfaces, cogitator banks and vox-relays gleamed in the light cast by the lumen strips and pict screen stands. Even the servitors ranking the gantries that ringed the command dais had gone into standby, awaiting the fresh bursts of coding cant that would give them purpose. Serxis gestured towards the augur banks and spoke.

'Diagnosticator, bring me the latest sensorium readout from quadrant nine, sector thirteen. Remove all incomplete variables prior to transference.'

The order was not the one the bridge serfs had expected. The *Spear of Macragge*'s augur staff hurried to obey, filtering the data and transmitting it directly to the shipmaster. Serxis swiped and enhanced the slates built into the arms of his command throne, his genhanced mind analysing it all in just a few heartbeats.

The augur returns didn't lie – Serxis saw his fears confirmed in the first grainy pict scans of the target area. There was a behemoth at the heart of the ork fleet that had just torn itself from the warp and was now approaching the system's core at full steam ahead, plasma drives blazing. Going by the designates Imperial strategos attempted – often in vain – to apply to the ramshackle alien void vessels, it was a battle-ship, longer and bulkier than even an Emperor-class capital vessel of the Imperial Navy. That was not what gave Serxis pause, however. It was the thing attached to the ork craft.

'Heavy customisation,' he murmured to himself. 'Extra armour bulk and engine housing. It's a transport...'

He trailed off. The scans showed that it was coupled to what appeared to be a large sphere of void-born rock, a meteorite of fused and scarred stone. Its craggy surface was studded with more ork structures and plasma drives of its own, which blazed in sympathy with those of its carrier. A great skull glyph in its underside seemed to glare at Serxis through the grainy images he swiped through, full of alien malice.

'A rok,' Serxis said. It was a method of planetary invasion so crude and so mindlessly brutal that only the greenskins could possibly have conceived of it. An asteroid or meteor-ite would be seized by an ork fleet and mined, installed with plasma drives that would enable the aliens to steer it to their own course. Thus directed it would be flung at a target world, crash landing with enough force to annihilate any planetary defences. Those greenskins within that survived the impact would then disgorge and slaughter the stunned defenders.

The roks' only weakness was the fact that they rarely, if ever, were capable of warp travel. They could be detected far out on the fringes of a system, engaged and neutralised. They possessed no warp drives.

This one, however, did. The battleship had acted as its

carrier. It would deliver it directly to Ikara, of that Serxis had no doubt.

The soft voice of the *Spear of Macragge*'s signals officer disturbed Serxis' thoughts.

'Rear Admiral Corran is awaiting a connection, lord.'

'Put him on the throne vox,' Serxis ordered, activating his personal earpiece. The static-chopped voice of the Navy admiral crackled in his ear.

'Word from downstairs, shipmaster,' he said. *'Lord Commander von Klimt has given my fleet discretion to engage or withdraw as I see fit.'*

'My company commander has ordered me to mount a fighting retreat to the system's edge,' Serxis replied. 'If we attempt to hold this anchorage we will likely be surrounded and destroyed in detail.'

'Agreed,' Corran said.

'I sense a degree of reluctance, rear admiral,' Serxis said.

'Leaving one of the God-Emperor's worlds undefended before a ramshackle conglomerate of xenos scum doesn't sit well,' Corran admitted.

'I agree. Perhaps a compromise. From their current speed I don't believe the main body of the xenos fleet will be able to overtake us. We should be able to engage their vanguard and still withdraw without becoming committed to a full fleet action. And while we're at it, perhaps we might attempt to strike a blow at that monstrous payload they have bound for Ikara.'

'Agreed,' Corran said. *'If you wish to take the lead, the* Pride of Macaroth *and* Lance of Vengeance *will support you.'*

'We have been given discretion to conduct a fighting withdrawal,' Serxis said. 'So let's fight, rear admiral.'

'Good hunting, Ultramarine.'

The connection ended. Serxis looked out across the bridge once more, taking in the expectant silence before issuing the order.

'All hands, clear for action.'

URGORK

Morkopalypse was ready. Urgork bashed his skinnin' blades together, the huge, wickedly serrated weapons clanging out over the bridge of the *Worldhammer*. Slyboy, the ork warboss' blind seer, cringed back from his master's exuberance.

"Ere we go, Sly, ya git,' Urgork bellowed, grinning from tusk to tusk. He thumped one of his great blades into the decomposing squig corpse sagging beside his trophy-laden chair and snatched the ork psyker by the throat with his now-free hand, hauling the runty greenskin close.

'Y-you betta have got dis one right,' he snarled, gristle-flecked spit splattering the weirdboy. The smaller ork squirmed and choked, nodding vigorously in the warlord's grasp.

'T-t-tell me…' Urgork trailed off into incoherent stammers, tusks grinding together. His body seemed to freeze up, a twitch tugging at his scarred face, one eye rolling back into its socket while the other dilated. Slyboy's legs beat the air in panic as the warboss' grip continued to tighten, slowly choking him.

'Grok,' Urgork managed to growl from between his locked jaws, foam building around his maw. A greenskin scurried up the ladder to the boss chair dais, a hunchbacked, wheezing creature clad in a greasy white smock, black leather glove-gauntlets and grimy goggles. He fumbled with a dirt-encrusted syringe as the warlord started to spasm violently, shaking the near-unconscious Slyboy back and forth like a rag doll. The bent-over painboy, syringe finally readied, lunged forwards with a yelp and stabbed it into the meat of the warboss' thigh, using both hands to inject a huge load of viscous-looking yellow liquid.

Urgork's head snapped back. He let out a shuddering gasp as both eyes refocused. His hand unclenched and Slyboy clanged to the deck, choking and retching. Grok yanked the syringe out and backed away, twitching nervously.

The warboss lowered his head again, slowly, flexing his neck and shoulders. Bones crunched and popped. The savage seizure that had gripped him was gone. He nodded to Grok.

'My thanks, doc.'

Slyboy had used the few seconds' respite to attempt to crawl away, feeling his way blindly through the detritus littering the command deck. Urgork grunted and snatched him by the scruff of the neck.

'Tell me again, Sly,' he growled. 'Tell me of da vision.'

'They's all down there, boss,' the pitiful ork mewled. 'All the 'ard boys, in their big ruin city.'

'And da one in white too?'

'Yeah, boss, 'course!'

'And you got Big Mek Cogkrusha da propa coordinates?' Urgork demanded.

'Yeah, boss, I swears!'

Urgork grunted again and released the weirdboy.

'Den it's time,' he said, yanking his second skinnin' blade from the squig corpse.

'Grok, stand close,' he barked. When the hunched painboy was crouched next to his boss' chair, he slammed the hilt of one of his blades into a huge red button that was wired crudely into the arm of the seat.

Nothing happened. Urgork sighed and hit it again. There

was a violent lurch and a scream of rusting gears as juddering motion seized the chair. It began to descend, disconnecting from the circular dais around it, sinking down into the deck with an unhealthy rattle. Urgork's grin returned as he was carried down, down from his flagship, through its refuse-clogged holds, and then on into *Morkopalypse*. The great, hollowed-out meteorite was packed full of the boys, its multiple decks resounding with the chanting of individual mobs and warbands as they worked themselves into a battle frenzy.

The platform on which the boss chair sat passed each open level one by one. As it went by Urgork bellowed and slammed his long knives together. Each passing deck roared back its approval, driven into a mania by the presence of their warboss. He watched as an ork knocked down another in one of the mobs, a fight breaking out instantly as individual boys vented their mounting battle-frenzy in the only way they knew how.

This was gonna be a right propa scrap when it all kicked off.

Finally, the platform clattered to a stop, the crudely modified grav-lift levered into the control room at the rok's heart. Stabskar and his chief nob, Grimtoof, were waiting for Urgork, in among Big Mek Cogkrusha and his tinkerers. Urgork gestured to the kommando boss with one claw. Stabskar forced his way to the chair's side and bowed low, his soiled camo cape draping the mesh decking plates.

'You and your boys know your job, Stabba?' the warlord demanded.

"Course, boss. We won't let ya down again.'

'Den let's go!' Urgork bellowed, slamming the pommels of both knives into the flanks of his chair. 'What we waitin' for?'

'Orbital entry,' Cogkrusha said after a moment's silence, the Big Mek's voice like the rattle of rusty gears. Urgork glowered.

'Fine,' he grunted.

'Won't be long now, boss,' Cogkrusha clattered, bionic optics clicking as they focused on the control room's plethora of cracked, mismatched viewscreens.

'The humies' ships is comin' for a scrap.'

POLIXIS

The evening sky above Ikara IX was riven by fire as new stars burst into brief, furious life overhead. Most of those on the planet's surface saw little but indistinct flares amidst the grey smog that blanketed the polluted atmosphere, but the wind that sometimes knifed down from the Tombstones was blowing a gale as night fell, affording Polixis a view of the full fury of an orbital engagement playing out.

He watched the silent flashes and flares light up the dark from the steps of the Basilica of Saint Albarak the Smelter. Demeter and Kastor were still inside. The feverish activity of the headquarters had entered overdrive, with an immediate planet-wide stand-to being issued. Orders coming out of Kroten seemed to be rudderless, sometimes contradictory. Demeter had passed on word that Shipmaster Serxis and Rear Admiral Corran were going to engage the vanguard of the xenos fleet before withdrawing, an act that Demeter had left to Serxis' discretion. With nothing to contribute to the command and control of the developing situation, Polixis had taken his leave.

The basilica square lay before him, quiet and wrapped in night-time shadows. The broken remains of a Chimera armoured personnel carrier sat where it had been gutted by an ork rocket earlier in the day. Alien bodies had been heaped in one far corner and burned by flamer-armed purification teams, their stinking, charred remains now smouldering in the dark. Much of the rest of the square had been taken up by mortuary orderlies, who had laid out row after row of dead Imperial Guardsmen, clad in the black plastek wraps of Munitorum-issue body bags. Bar a few off-duty troopers smoking lhos and talking quietly near the foot of the steps, and an Ecclesiarchy preacher moving along the dead ranks sprinkling blessed salve, the square was empty. Polixis briefly pondered the curious similarities between the dead below and Ovido's body lying in the crypt beneath him. The sheer scale of the Astra Militarum's losses made it tempting to think of their deaths as more impersonal, almost meaningless, but in truth Polixis knew the difference between the fallen was more slender than it seemed. All had fallen in the cause of mankind, all had received a blessing over their remains, all would live on in the memories of their battle-brothers. As far as Polixis was concerned, the sacrifice was one and the same.

He turned his eyes once more to the distant, deadly beauty of the unfolding high orbit engagement, his mind continuing to wander. The litanies he had memorised as an initiate spoke so often of the importance of legacy and heritage, of how through his gene-seed an Adeptus Astartes could live forever. Once he had doubted such claims – no conscious memory remained, all else was mere metaphor. Future battle-brothers learned the names of those who had gone before and their many deeds, and perhaps their breasts swelled with pride knowing they bore a part of them inside, but it was all so much history. But such doubts had only plagued Polixis when he had still been young, still grappling with his new existence. He knew better now. Individuality meant nothing.

'The purpose of us all is to fight and to sacrifice ourselves when we can fight no more,' Polixis murmured to himself as he watched the sky, letting the induction litany of the apothecarion ease his thoughts. 'To pass on our own gene-seed so that another can serve the Chapter when we no longer can.'

There was perhaps extra poignancy in the fact that Ovido had been Mars-born, among the first of his kind. A little over half of the Fulminata were the same. They had come to Ultramar, to Macragge, and painted their Mark X power armour the blue of the Ultramarines. They had learned the Chapter's doctrines by rote, fought and bled and died beside their new brothers, but they had not been from Ultramar, nor even from the Five Hundred Worlds. They were the first of their kind, the first Primaris, forged on a distant, red planet by a being far beyond the understanding of any of them.

Polixis was not Mars-born. He was from the Realm of Ultramar, a son of the agri world of Iax, the first Primaris Ultramarine to be recruited from the worlds the Chapter called home. One of the first, he corrected himself silently, as his blood brother came out onto the basilica's steps to join him.

Polixis nodded. Kastor said nothing, looking to the sky. The occasional, silent flash of a macro-cannon broadside or the blink-beam of a lance strike reflected from the glossy black sheen of his power armour. Neither of them spoke.

A memory intruded as Polixis watched his brother. He remembered looking up at the spread of stars, lying on his back, limbs aching from a long day's toil. The night air had been warm and quiet and full of the sweet musk of the harvest cycle. The medicae in him explained the sudden recollection easily enough – it was nothing more than the firing of brain synapses, a shadow in an abandoned room that vanished with the coming of light.

Such flashes were not unheard of among the first genera-tion of Primaris born within the Realm of Ultramar. Polixis understood better than most that, for all their prowess as warriors, the creation of new Primaris was not a perfect pro-cess. Kastor could sometimes summon up what appeared to be perfectly clear memories of their shared childhood. For Polixis it was far harder – his past was relegated to these half-moments, so slender and so fine that they felt unreal. His training as an Apothecary helped him rationalise them as a simple, minor failing in his induction process. Once, per-haps, he had reclined in the agri fields of Iax, maybe close to the collective that he called home, with his brother at his side, watching the night sky.

It didn't matter. He told himself that whenever the shadow-memories stirred. Those agri fields were long gone now, and that starry sky had been ripped in half by the stuff of nightmares.

'What news, brother?' he asked Kastor, deliberately break-ing the contemplative stillness.

'From orbit?' Kastor replied, eyes still on the starry vault. 'Serxis has engaged. He is attempting to target the rok, but the xenos have it well shielded. He will be forced to with-draw within the hour.'

'And from high command?'

'Von Klimt is demanding reinforcements for Kroten. He expects that to be the rok's target. Klos has agreed to send his reserve. Two corps, they're mobilising as we speak.'

'This will be bloody,' Polixis said, eyes on the Guardsmen in the square below.

'It is a blessing,' Kastor replied, his voice low but tinged with relish. When Polixis said nothing, he went on. 'The xenos' supreme warlord will be among their fleet. He has come here to fight, of that there can be no doubt. He presents us with an opportunity – slay him, and his dominion over the greenskin tribes he commands will end. They will fragment as they always do, and this war will turn at a stroke. Kill Warlord Urgork and the subsector will be cleansed before the year is out.'

'You are fortunate, my little brother, to always be able to find a bloodthirsty positive among our dire circumstances. Were a whole company at our side I may share your optimism. We have here only half-strength, and we have suffered losses.'

'The captain knows how to use what he has,' Kastor said, his voice full of certainty. 'Once the xenos leader commits himself, we shall strike.'

'It is already decided then?'

'It is. Word is being passed to Lieutenants Samson and Tyranus – we are preparing to move with the dawn. Kroten is presumably their target, so we will go there too.'

'Has the captain told Field Marshal Klos?'

'He is doing so now. I doubt there will be many objections. The field marshal is brash, for a human. His ire is focused on his commanding general and the fact that he is expected to send his reserves to support him.'

'He will need them here, I imagine,' Polixis said. 'As soon as the warbands across the river realise their fleet has seized orbit, they will attempt a counter-attack.'

'It is only a shame that we will not still be here to greet them,' Kastor growled.

'You seemed eager to purge today, brother,' he said, smiling knowingly. Even now, after so long, seeing his younger brother roused to ire brought him a mixture of amusement and something akin to awe.

'The xenos here are weak,' Kastor said without any hint of levity, and Polixis could sense the fire that forever smouldered in his brother stirring once more. 'Even by the oafish standards of their degenerate race. We can see why now. This was only a second front for them. Well, now it has become their primary focus. When the xenos warlord comes, he will bring his best with him.'

'A challenge, if nothing else,' Polixis said heavily.

'As the Emperor wills.'

Polixis nodded but said nothing more as, overhead, a great flash lit up the sky, illuminating everything beneath for a few seconds, like the birth of a second sun.

Somewhere high above, the Apothecary knew, an entire ship had just died.

SERXIS

To a casual observer, the quiet that had reigned over bridge of the *Spear of Macragge* had been totally subsumed. The multi-tiered command decks rang with the clatter of proximity alarms and incoming munitions warnings. The communications pits were filled with the hissing, crackling urgency of dozens of vox messages, and cogitators chimed and pinged with reports from weapons systems, the enginarium, the shield generators and the astrocartography bay. Blue-uniformed runners and rating officers hurried from workstation to workstation or up the flights of narrow spiral stairs to the upper tiers, polished boots ringing off the mesh rungs and decking plates.

Serxis reigned over it all from his command throne, like a graven colossus in the midst of a bustling town square, immovable, largely silent, his occasional commands issued in clear, measured tones.

The bridge of a ship of war as large and as powerful as the *Spear of Macragge* was never a truly calm place during a full void engagement. The scenes unfolding around the ship-master were a prime example of a well-drilled and highly dedicated command crew carrying out the tasks they had all performed many times previously. The engagement with the xenos vanguard seemed to be going well, and the Ultramarines warship was running at optimum efficiency.

But it did not take all of Serxis' experience to be able to see that unfolding events presaged disaster. His eyes narrowed as he watched the data displays, already anticipating the turning of the tide.

The Imperial Navy Avenger-class grand cruiser *Lance of Vengeance* was out of position. It had taken up station starboard of the *Spear of Macragge*, and it had closed relentlessly with the oncoming vanguard of the xenos fleet. Real Admiral Corran, in tandem with Serxis, had changed the course of his flagship, the *Pride of Macaroth*, to engage the ork escorts from range. Too close and the trio of Imperial capital ships ran the risk of becoming entangled with the main xenos fleet bearing down on them – and nor did Serxis want to risk an ork boarding action when his battle-barge was bereft of its complement of Adeptus Astartes and had only half of its Thunderhawks and none of the Overlords on station. Keeping the orks at distance for as long as possible also slowed their arrival to the anchorage point above the city of Kroten, the expected target of the alien flagship and its rok payload.

'You've drifted,' Serxis said to himself. He didn't have a vox-link established with the *Lance of Vengeance*'s commander, and he already knew that transmitting anything now would be in vain.

Without stasis anchor or a new heading, the *Lance of Vengeance* was turning on its port broadside, close to the ork fleet. Serxis knew that its captain, Marro, had a record of high-risk manoeuvres and close encounters, a past that explained his position in charge of an aged, largely outdated grand cruiser like the *Lance*. Marro had already complained that the short-range batteries of the Avenger would be completely wasted if unleashed from distance.

Serxis tapped in to the vox traffic between Marro and Admiral Corran, expression grim as the scale of the approaching disaster became more apparent.

'*I will have you before the admiralty board if you don't disengage immediately, Marro,*' Corran shouted. Marro's response was a sound of weak affirmation. Serxis had heard that sort of noise enough times before during void combat, where a man's fate was sealed long minutes before death's slow reach caught up with him. He already knew it was too late.

A trio of greenskin escorts, little more than brute conglomerations of welded-together scrap, were triggering their hyperthrust, burning out their oversized plasma drives in violent bursts of sudden speed. Serxis could only watch the holochart mapping out the movement of the ships around the *Spear of Macragge* as the outmanoeuvred grand cruiser struggled to turn, Marro caught in panic between the desire to finish bringing his port batteries to bear and the sudden need to escape.

Whichever he chose, his fate was sealed. A point-blank storm of fire from the *Lance of Vengeance* ripped apart one of the oncoming escorts, dwarfed by the grand cruiser's bulk, but the other two made it through. They rammed themselves directly into the Imperial ship's flank. The *Spear of Macragge*'s prow pict-casters caught the collision, and Serxus watched with a dark expression as the first alien warship slammed home.

They had been built with just such insanely brutal tactics in mind. Both were wedges of reinforced detritus, created to shield the larger ork ships from incoming fire and, when the time was right, plough indiscriminately into enemy vessels. Serxis saw bulkheads and the *Lance*'s macro-cannon batteries buckling in slow motion, a ripple of tearing adamantium rupturing the hull and collapsing deck after deck. He knew he was watching the deaths of thousands. He had experienced the same numerous times during void combat, but the remoteness, the silence and the almost languid slowness of the collapsing capital ship still rendered it all deeply disconcerting.

Then the second ork escort hit, this time towards the *Lance*'s aft, and the grim spectacle reached a crescendo. The impact of the alien vessel against the reinforced plating beneath the grand cruiser's bridge tower deflected it, slamming it into the side of the enginarium block. The plasma drives buckled, then detonated. The blast travelled in a wave of broiling blue flame along the length of the *Lance*, consuming both it and the battered remains of its killers. As the sunburst flash of total annihilation lit the void, the *Spear of Macragge*'s augur systems overloaded, the pict-feeds shorting out before blinking back online.

The *Lance of Vengeance* was gone. All that remained was a scattering of debris, flickering with fires that died out in the vacuum of space.

'Gunner, maintain your rate of fire,' Serxis ordered, then switched to the communications pits. 'Get me a link to the *Pride of Macaroth*.'

'Shipmaster Serxis,' came Corran's voice over the vox. He sounded strained.

'I believe the time to withdraw has come, rear admiral,' Serxis said. When his words were met with silence, he carried on. 'We have already suffered a blow here for little gain. We must not compound Captain Marro's mistake.'

'*You're correct,*' Corran replied, though Serxis could sense the rage that burned in every word, the desire to avenge the loss of the *Lance of Vengeance* by throwing the entirety of the battlefleet against the oncoming greenskins. '*I will… issue orders for an immediate disengagement.*'

'The *Spear of Macragge* will hold station until you have set a course,' Serxis offered, knowing the admiral's ponderous flagship would need some time to come about.

'*My thanks, Ultramarine,*' Corran responded. The link went dead.

'Shipmaster, the xenos are changing formation,' one of the augur attendants called up from the sensorium banks. Serxis turned his gaze from the *Pride of Macaroth*'s representation on the holochart back to the alien fleet. The augur analysis was correct – the sigils were shifting across the display. Until that moment the alien fleet had remained clustered around its flagship, denying the Imperial long-range bombardment the opportunity to target the warlord's vessel. Now, however, they were spreading away from it, their cumbersome drives adopting new headings that carried them wide across Ikara's orbit. For a moment Serxis thought they were trying to outflank and envelop the Imperial ships before they could pull away. Then the icons that represented the alien fleet blinked. Another had been added by the augur arrays, adjacent to Urgork's flagship but pulling away rapidly.

Serxis realised what he was looking at. The flagship had released the rok. Moreover, it had done so early, long before it was positioned in an orbital arc above the capital city of Kroten.

'Link to Captain Demeter, immediately,' he ordered the vox-seneschal. 'Signal to the surface. The sky is about to fall.'

POLIXIS

Polixis saw it first, as a twinkling amidst the fiery sky. It grew rapidly, a star burning white as it fell from the war-wracked firmament, a herald of annihilation. The vox-network burst into frantic chatter, garbled orders, reports and requests for clarification flooding the channels. All eyes in the basilica square stared heavenwards as the light grew to a furious intensity.

'May the Emperor and the primarch be with us all,' Kastor murmured when he caught sight of the white blaze.

The scream of the plummeting rok filled the air, a roar of bone-shuddering intensity vibrating through every brick and girder in Shebat. Polixis could do nothing but watch as the light filled the sky, the whole world, its rage like the primordial awakening of a new god. It howled overhead, framed by the basilica's spires, eclipsing the city's ruinous skyline. The strength of its passing threw the Guardsmen across the square down to the rubble-littered flagstones. It almost shook even the Space Marines from their feet.

The rok struck. It hit south of the basilica, amongst the remains of the slums near the eastern bank of Gorgon. The impact sounded like the death knell of the whole world, coupled with a flash of light even more brilliant than the destruction of the capital ship in orbit above. Polixis saw the skyline of the city to the south caught like a snap-pict in a moment of perfect clarity, backlit by the fire of the collision. He braced himself.

As the report of the meteorite's impact echoed through Shebat, the shock wave struck. The buildings on the south side of the square, already reduced to bullet-scarred walls and mounds of rubble, crumbled. The blast slammed debris into the square, throwing up the corpses lying there alongside those still living. Both Kastor and Polixis were picked up and flung, despite the efforts of their power armour's servos and stabilisers, directly back into the wall of the basilica. Polixis grunted, his genhanced body stopping the blow from stunning him or driving the wind from his lungs, even as he felt a section of his armour's backpack unit crumple. He fell to his knees alongside Kastor as the wave passed on, the sounds of the rok's impact still ringing in his skull, his Lyman's Ear failing to cancel out the thunderous noise.

The Basilica of Saint Albarak the Smelter still stood. Its foundations had been laid deeper and stronger than any other building in Shebat Alpha, and though its crypts quaked and stones were shaken from its belfry, the walls remained intact.

Polixis regained his feet. The scene of destruction that would undoubtedly have played out before him was lost, completely obscured by the dust cloud that had accompanied the blast wave. Even with his auto-senses stripping out the haze and boosting what little light there was, he could barely make out the bottom of the basilica's entrance steps. The vox had also gone silent, the landlines to the main communications hub broken, the impact and the dust distorting the remote channels. For a moment, Polixis felt he and Kastor were the only beings left on Ikara, perhaps the only two left in the whole of existence. There was nothing, nothing but the swirling of the dust and the low hiss of the vox, a dreadful, languid peace left in the wake of the terrific destruction. It was the quiet of near-total extinction.

'The rok,' Kastor said, jolting his brother from the surreal reverie he'd slipped into. 'How far to the south do you think it came down?'

'Within the city limits,' Polixis said, starting to move down the steps.

'Where are you going?' Kastor demanded.

'I'm needed elsewhere,' the Apothecary replied, pausing and looking back up at him. 'See to the captain, brother. He will need you now more than ever.'

'Go carefully,' Kastor warned. 'The xenos are upon us.'

Polixis forced himself not to respond to the obviousness of his blood brother's instructions. He knew that he tried to advise Kastor just as frequently. The difference between them was that the Chaplain would more than likely snap something back at him, whereas Polixis usually managed to hold his tongue and accept the advice. Somehow he knew this had always been the case.

Polixis ran across the square. The auto-senses shared by the Primaris were still online, still connected. His diagnostor was reading half a dozen injuries, all from squads along the southern edge of Shebat. Scroll-data indicated damage caused by collapsing buildings.

Shadows loomed at him from out of the impenetrable dust, limping and stumbling. Anyone in the city not blessed with the genhancements of the Adeptus Astartes had undoubtedly been left stunned by the rok's landing, ears deafened and movements sluggish. The sky itself had come down, and death had followed.

Polixis did not stop to assist them. There was worse coming. He knew that thousands of greenskins would be disgorging from the rok, flooding its crater and storming the flattened streets around it. What was worse, they had come down on the Imperial side of the Gorgon, effectively out-flanking the gains made by the Guard and the Primaris the day before. With a single, great blow the greenskins had all but reclaimed Shebat Alpha.

The Apothecary carried on into the rubble beyond what had once been the edge of the square. There were no more streets to follow, only an undulating wasteland of wreckage, spars and twisted girders jutting through mounds of broken masonry, the thousands of hab blocks, refineries and manu-factoria south of the basilica reduced to complete ruination. The dust still hung heavy in the night air, so that he had only his armour's inbuilt compass and the blinking burst map to navigate by.

It was slow, hard going. He came across more survivors as he went, mostly rear echelon Guard units.

'Help us, my lord!' one man pleaded, stumbling from the darkness cradling a broken arm. Others bore injured com-rades, crying out for the Space Marine's aid or for orders amidst the confusion.

He stopped for none. He had no instructions for them, and no time to help them tend injured friends or dig others out from under the collapsed ruins. If he did pause, more would die when the orks struck.

After a while his vox-bead crackled back to life. Deme-ter had managed to re-establish the link to the rest of the demi-company, and his instructions went out to all squads, his voice as calm and level as ever.

'*Field Marshal Klos has ordered a complete withdrawal from Shebat. We will be facilitating that retreat. The dust cloud from the rok is still too thick to risk a full aerial extraction, so it will be on foot. All squads are to hold their current positions for thirty minutes so that the Guard can conduct a staggered, overlapping move eastwards, towards the ash wastes. There they will seek to establish a new front line. All units, confirm.'*

Polixis blink-acknowledged the fresh orders as he went. Even disregarding the fact that there were now thousands of greenskins on the eastern bank of the river, the devastation wreaked by the rok's impact had shattered Imperial command and control. Units were scattered, dazed and struggling to deal with thousands of casualties from the collapsed buildings. Some were cut off, others had simply vanished, buried by the sudden, violent tremors that had shaken apart most of the city. From the reports trickling in on the other frequencies, it seemed as if the main combat forces stationed along the newly taken line of the Gorgon's east bank were largely intact, but spotters were reporting increased activity from across the polluted river, including what looked like crude barges and rafts – the xenos on the western bank had clearly been preparing to cross en masse for some time, and now that reinforcements had arrived they were seizing the opportunity. Combined with the assault expected from the rok itself there was no practical means for the Guard to resist for long, even with the Primaris at their side.

Polixis paused to check his visor display beside a street lumen whose wrought-iron post had someone survived the demolition of everything around it. The nearest squad, Klastis, was a mile to the west, overlooking a stretch of the river docks. They weren't reporting any casualties. The second nearest, Squad Domitian, was.

According to the vox, Brothers Ennio and Trajo had been buried by the roof of a collapsing manufactorum, and the rest of Domitian were still working to extract them. They were the most southern of the Primaris squads – when the greenskins from the rok first encountered Imperial forces, it would be Domitian's Hellblasters.

'I am approaching from the north-east, watch your targeting matrices,' Polixis said over the vox. A few minutes later he discerned shapes in the gloom ahead – the familiar bulk of Mark X power armour.

'Well met, Brother-Apothecary,' Sergeant Domitian called out as he approached. Like everyone else, the Ultramarine's proud blue armour was now a uniform grey, caked in the dust that had shrouded Shebat. Four of Domitian's Hellblasters, Brothers Gratian, Junarius, Lorens and Luco, were standing watch over the rubble that had once been a manufactorum side-row, while three more – Marius, Otho and Victus – worked to haul debris away from one of the numerous mounds that had formed where one of the refinery city's workhouses had once stood.

'Ennio and Trajo were still inside when the shock wave hit,' Domitian said. 'As were Gratian and Luco, but they were able to work themselves free.'

'You have contact with them both over the vox?' Polixis asked.

'Yes. I'll patch you through.'

'*Brother-Apothecary,*' crackled Ennio's voice over the link. He sounded calm and unhurried, apparently untroubled by the fact that he was buried beneath tonnes of rubble.

'Can you describe your injuries to me, brother?' Polixis asked, assessing the remote vitae readout as he spoke.

'*Left arm shattered,*' Ennio said tersely. '*It is unresponsive.*'

'*Both legs,*' Trajo added, the pain audible in his voice. '*You should leave me, brothers, I will only be an encumbrance.*'

'Cease such foolish chatter,' Polixis ordered, checking the rubble underfoot. The armour of the two Primaris had clearly taken the worst of the collapse – any unaugmented human would have been immediately crushed by the building's fall.

'We shall have you up soon, brothers,' he added.

'We are to withdraw when they are recovered,' Domitian said.

'So it seems. The Guard are retreating eastwards.'

Domitian didn't answer. After a pause Polixis realised why. His genhanced hearing, further magnified by his power armour, had detected noises in the darkness, out beyond the small perimeter established by the squad. Bestial bellows and roars, and the pounding of iron-shod boots.

'Xenos,' Domitian said.

'From the south,' Brother Gratian added, plasma incinerator raised.

'We must hurry,' Polixis said, unclamping his Absolver bolt pistol.

'Prime incinerators,' Domitian ordered, the words followed by a low whine and the blue glow of charged plasma, suffusing the dust-choked night. Otho, Marius and Victus has redoubled their efforts to drag aside the rubble, working down towards the locator tags triggered by Ennio and Trajo.

'Are there no Guard units nearby?' Polixis asked as the raucous sound of the approaching mob grew louder.

'None that survived,' Domitian said, facing south into the night. 'We rescued about a dozen men, all injured. They're on their way to the rear.'

There was a thudding burst of bolter fire, muffled and distorted by the dust. Polixis half turned, checking the designator on his display. The squads further along the Gorgon, including the nearest – Klastis – had begun to engage the greenskins that were attempting to cross the river. Any hope of support was rapidly evaporating.

'Fire at will,' Domitian ordered. The bellowing from the darkness had reached fever pitch, seeming to resound from all quarters, filling the night with the chilling promise of bloodshed. Polixis felt his twin hearts rising to the tempo of the approaching battle, and realised a snarl of adrenaline-fuelled anticipation was splitting his lips.

In that moment, he understood once again where Kastor's burning passion for the thunder of war came from.

A shout went up from Victus. Polixis saw he was dragging battered, grime-encrusted plate armour from the rubble at his feet. The Tabran campaign markings were visible around the gorget – it was Ennio.

Polixis started towards him. At the same time, hunch-backed shapes came lumbering from the dust-swathed night, their roars filling the darkness.

'Open fire!' roared Domitian.

CHAPTER THREE EVACUATION

DEMETER

Captain Demeter and Ancient Skyrus were joined by Chaplain Kastor as they departed from the basilica. Field Marshal Klos and his staff were packing away equipment they had set up mere hours before, burning what couldn't be taken in promethium drums in the remains of the square outside. Preparing to evacuate, one of the marshal's aides had recommended blowing the munitions stockpiled just that evening in the crypts beneath the basilica, but Klos had denied the request, mindful of the propaganda defeat that would be inflicted on Imperial forces if they were seen to demolish one of the only buildings still standing in Shebat, and an ancient place of worship at that.

Demeter had done what he could to assist the Imperial Guard's withdrawal. Amidst the disaster's fallout, the captain had noted that a small piece of good fortune could yet prove decisive. Adhering to the orders to reinforce the capital of Kroten in expectation of the rok's landing there, two of Klos' eight corps had already been on the move and were largely clear of Shebat when the meteor had struck. They were now busy preparing a new defensive line on the edge of the ash wastes to Shebat's east, just beyond the remains of the slum outskirts. If Klos could extract even a few more corps, Demeter believed there would be sufficient numbers to pin the greenskins in the city until further reinforcements could be brought up.

Saving just a few divisions, however, looked like it would be a tall enough order, let alone several corps. Communications were still choppy, and the wasteland the city had been reduced to was combining with the night and the dust to confound attempts at an orderly withdrawal. What was worse, the xenos were now attacking along the length of the Gorgon in concert with those pouring from the rok. All contact with the southernmost Guard brigades had long been lost, and Demeter began receiving reports from his southernmost Primaris, Squad Domitian, that they were coming under sustained assault. All along the line the Primaris were holding on while they could, giving the Astra Militarum the precious minutes they needed to disengage. Demeter's gut told him they'd need more time.

'Bring up *Extremis*,' he ordered Techmarine Tiberon over the vox. 'And Squad Tiro. We are taking the fight to the xenos.'

'We are to counter-attack?' Kastor asked as they passed down the basilica's steps and into the square beyond.

'The xenos must be focused,' Demeter said. 'They will be drawn to the area of most resistance. *I* will provide that resistance.'

'The rest of the demi-company–' Kastor began.

'Lieutenant Tyranus will take command,' Demeter said. 'His orders are to continue the extraction and support the Astra Militarum for as long as possible.'

'Allow me to accompany you, captain,' Kastor said. 'Together we shall stem the tide of alien filth long enough to bring righteous fire back to this city.'

'No, Kastor,' Demeter said. 'The company will need your presence and inspiration now more than ever. You are to link with Tyranus and provide leadership for both the Fulminata and the Guard.'

'Captain Demeter,' Kastor said, coming up short. Demeter stopped with him.

'We cannot lose you,' the Chaplain said. 'The company needs your leadership. The Guard needs it. Any one of us would die at your side, beneath the banner of the Fulminata. Its sacred folds cannot be allowed to fall into the hands of xenos savages.'

'None of us will leave this city if a stand is not made,' Demeter said. 'There is no time for debate, Kastor. You will go now and link with Lieutenant Tyranus. That is an order.'

Kastor bowed his head briefly, clearly swallowing a bitter protest.

'Until we meet again, brother-captain,' he said, making the double-gauntlet salute of the Primaris.

'Courage and honour,' Demeter replied.

POLIXIS

The Hellblasters opened fire. Four beams of blue brilliance lit up the darkness, the sunburst flare of plasma weaponry further enhanced by the reflective properties of the dust cloud. The leading orks were reduced to swirls of ash and burning embers, the stench of atomised innards immediately filling the clogged air.

The aliens' roars redoubled as those behind realised they'd finally found opposition in the ruined city. The crack of plasma was answered by the crude hammer of slug weapons as the greenskins returned fire, an inaccurate hail of hard rounds filling the air and ploughing the rubble around Polixis. He ignored the fusillade and ran to the side of Victus and Ennio.

'I've had worse,' the latter said as Victus helped pull him to his feet. His power armour was battered and scarred, but his left arm from the vambrace down had taken the worst of the impact – it had been crushed while shielding his head from the workhouse's collapse. Polixis didn't need to run a diagnostor scan to know it would require complete restructuring, perhaps amputation.

'See to Trajo, Brother-Apothecary,' Victus said, unclamping his bolt pistol with his right hand. Behind him, Polixis saw that Otho and Marius had finally dug down to the last of their trapped battle-brothers.

'Both legs,' Trajo said, his tone not quite masking the pain in his voice. He was seated, and blood was oozing from half a dozen ruptures in his thigh and shin plates. Polixis knelt swiftly and stabbed an adrenaline shot into his tasset port.

'That'll keep you going, for now,' he said, motioning to Otho and Marius. 'You'll have to lift him clear.'

'We must withdraw, Brother-Apothecary,' Domitian said. The Hellblasters covering the rest of the squad had set their incinerators to rapid fire, dangerously close to the overcharge setting that would unleash searing destruction at the risk of fatal malfunctions to the volatile plasma cores. Streak after streak of blue light whipped away the oncoming greenskins, their scrap armour, furs and hides as impotent a protection as their thick skin and bones. There were too many, however, to hold back for more than a few moments. The brilliant bolts unleashed by Gratian, Junarius, Lorens and Luco were also serving to draw more orks towards them, threatening to overwhelm their flanks or, worse, cut them off entirely.

Otho and Marius had Trajo lifted between them, signalling their readiness with blink-click confirmations. Polixis stood by them as they worked their way down from the mound of excavated rubble to more stable ground.

'Formation Ardent,' Domitian said, ordering a defensive withdrawal focused around protecting Trajo. The rest of the Hellblasters closed smoothly around their wounded comrade, paying no heed to the hard rounds whipping the dust-choked air and cracking from their power armour. Ennio joined Polixis, his incinerator hefted in his remaining good arm. Domitian and Victus took up the rear, laying down rapid, accurate bursts of fire from their assault plasma incinerators.

The squad didn't get far before it became apparent that it was too late to disengage. The greenskins coming from the rok hadn't arrived in a single group as expected, but moved northwards like a bloodthirsty tide. While Squad Domitian had stemmed it for a hundred yards just east of the Gorgon, the rest of it had flowed on around them. Now, as they tried to pull away, it threatened to come crashing in from either side. Greenskins were closing from almost every direction, and the air itself vibrated with their battle-frenzy.

Polixis fired to his right as he kept pace with the rest of the squad, moving at an ungainly half-run while they ensured Trajo was shielded at the centre of their small phalanx.

'*Squad Domitian, we are inbound,*' crackled the voice of Sergeant Klastis. The Intercessors were withdrawing from the riverbank, and Klastis' route to the east would carry them close to the Hellblasters as they tried to force their way northwards. A glance at the tactical display told Polixis they'd be too late. It would take at least ten minutes to link up, minutes they no longer had.

The first greenskin broke through to them. It threw itself at Brother Luco with a howl, a huge cleaver slamming into the Hellblaster's right pauldron and lodging there, splitting the dust-caked Chapter crest.

Luco fired with barely a yard between him and the greenskin. The plasma bolt turned the ork to ash and fused the whole right side of the Primaris armour's ceramite. Luco tugged the cleaver free in time to fling it deftly into the chest of the second beast to run at him.

By then, a third was grappling with Junarius. The squad was overrun.

Polixis slipped his gladius from its black plastek sheath and turned it, point downwards, continuing to fire with his bolt pistol into the onrushing aliens. One directly ahead of him collapsed with its throat torn out by an explosive round; another had its thick skull blown apart in a shower of grey matter. The pistol's chamber clicked empty. There was no time to reload.

He spun the gladius once more and lunged into the charge of the next ork to come at him, the world around him seeming to slow as the full force of his enhanced combat biology took over. Everything became smaller and simpler. Existence was reduced to nothing but his blade and the bared weak points of the aliens' vile physiology.

The first ork to die by his sword did so with it rammed up through the soft palate of its jaw, the wicked tip of the razored vibrosteel punching into its small brain. A twist of the wrist and a violent tug, and the short blade was free and swinging once more. An opened throat to his right, a short, sharp jab through an eye socket to the left, two more twitching, dead greenskins at his feet. The Apothecary's motions were little removed from the way he slit flesh and sawed bone on the operating table – conservative, precise, powerful, unlike the wrathful hammer blows delivered by his younger brother.

He sensed dark alien blood splattering the dust already caking his white battleplate, creating a foul patina, and the stink of the ork's opened innards penetrated the filters of his armour. A chill part of his mind, far detached from the adrenaline-fuelled bloodletting, observed the emotions that drove each killing blow. It found little of the passion and fury, the fire and zealotry, that put strength into Kastor's arm. Instead there was a cold disgust, coupled with a juxtaposition – the desire to protect.

Kastor, like many of the Adeptus Astartes, killed the xenos because he hated them. Polixis killed the xenos because, first and foremost, he wished to preserve the lives of his brothers and those they had come to protect.

Something hit the Apothecary's backpack, hard. He grunted, taking a step forwards and allowing the blow to jar right along his pauldron. As it did so he turned sharply to the left, gladius a blur.

A greenskin brought down Brother Lorens, cleaving his helm and skull, and smashing its way to the centre of the Ardent formation. It parried Polixis' gladius with the haft of its bloodied battle axe. Polixis took another half-step back, giving him room to turn the swing into a thrust that dug into the scarred meat of the alien's upper arm. It grunted and drove itself against the Apothecary, its stinking, solid bulk cracking off his breastplate, the spikes adorning its rusting armour gouging marks in the ceramite.

Polixis shifted his grip on his gladius and tried to cut left, sawing into its trunk-like neck, but the beast was too close and the blow only gouged deeper into its shoulder. The thing was in his face, snapping its tusks just inches from his visor, the butcher's stench of its maw filling his senses. He couldn't get his gladius clear to stab for a vital point, so he forced it deeper into the alien's shoulder, driving it into tough xenos muscle, trying to angle for its throat.

The ork grappled with him, seemingly impervious to the blade digging into its flesh. Polixis' armour began to flash warning sigils as it was locked in a death-grip, ceramite and servos straining against the alien's iron-hard muscles. The Apothecary released his gladius and blink-activated his narthecium. Both the reductor chainblade and the drill bit buzzed to life. He plunged them into the ork's flank, teeth gritted. The beast roared and loosened its grip as it tried to grapple with his arm. Polixis used the opportunity to rip himself away from the ork and, lightning-fast, whipped the reductor's chainblade across its throat. Blood burst, and the alien stumbled, choking and snarling as its lungs filled with fluid.

Polixis delivered a short, hard kick to its left kneecap, bringing it down as it died. He deactivated his narthecium, blood spraying from its chainblades, reloaded his pistol and dragged his gladius from the dead ork's shoulder.

The slaughter continued. Around him, he could see Squad Domitian was almost overrun. All bar Trajo, Otho and Marius were fighting hand-to-hand now, gladius, chainswords and pistols drawn. Greenskins were coming from the darkness on all sides, bellowing for blood, heedless of the ork corpses that already lay thick around the Primaris. Lorens was still down, and his vitae signs had turned red on Polixis' visor. He pushed past Marius, Otho and Trajo, all three now firing one-handed, point-blank bursts of plasma into the surrounding xenos, searing them away even as more charged into the melee.

The Apothecary cut down two more orks standing between him and Lorens' prone body, bolt-rounds hammering fist-sized holes in the aliens' torsos. More rushed in, their boots grinding over the fallen Primaris' body.

'Stand fast, Apothecary,' Domitian's voice rang out as he pushed past with his plasma pistol raised. Its vents were glowing white-hot, steam rising from its coils as they overheated. More orks were blown away, but it made no difference. They kept coming, the broken city resounding with their animalistic frenzy.

A sudden rage gripped Polixis. The icy detachment that had driven him before melted, and he lunged into the press, firing his reloaded bolt pistol left and right. Something far closer to the emotion channelled by his brother was rising up inside him as he discharged round after round into the aliens surrounding him, eyes fixed on Lorens' body just ahead, and on the boots that trampled and defiled it. His mind locked on to the desire to reach those sacred remains, to defend and preserve the precious flesh within. If the progenoids were not safely retrieved he would not only have failed Lorens and Squad Domitian, but all future generations that could have been spawned from the warrior's genetic inheritance.

A light lit the gloom, the blaze of fire rather than the actinic blue of a plasma discharge. Too late, Polixis realised one of the greenskins mere feet away was hauling a crude flamer, the rusting tanks strapped to its back sloshing with some form of volatile chemical. It had a blackened metal visor lowered over its face, and Polixis could hear its manic cackling even over the thump of blades and the hammer of weapons discharges all around. The pilot flame on the nozzle of its weapon flared.

And died. The greenskin's laugh turned to a grunt of annoyance as it gave the tanks on its back a heavy blow with its fist, but the light didn't reignite. The brute turned in a half-circle, then bellowed with anger when it realised something had cut the greasy pipelines running between the canisters and the weapon's nozzle, spilling stinking fuel around its feet.

A shadow loomed in the darkness behind it. A long blade slashed, like a flicker of lightning, there and gone again in one precise motion. The ork's bellow was cut abruptly short and blood gouted from its severed jugular. It swayed for a moment, apparently unable to comprehend that it had just been killed, then collapsed into the spreading puddle of fuel still gushing from its flamer tanks.

The shadow was gone. For the first time Polixis became aware of a shift in the melee around him. There was a new dynamic, the thud of heavy bolt pistols and the keening, razored whisper of combat knives parting flesh and muscle. More dark shapes darted to his left and right, and abruptly the press began to lessen – the rush of greenskins had been reduced to a scattering, orks turning in confusion and firing blindly into the dust as members of their mob dropped with opened throats and torsos shredded by point-blank heavy bolt-rounds.

'Brothers,' Sergeant Domitian voxed as simultaneous realisation reached the Hellblasters and the Apothecary.

One of the shadows materialised in their midst. It was as tall as any of the Primaris around it, and by all rights should not have been capable of such stealth. Its armour, while bearing many similarities to that worn by the other Ultramarines, was more streamlined and form-fitting, eschewing the heavily plated bulk of the standard Mark X for silent, black servo bundles and shaped ceramite plates that hugged thighs, torso and arms. Most striking of all was the warrior's helmet – the visor had been moulded into the likeness of a grinning skull, painted white to match, the two eye sockets glowing with the ruby redness of probing autosense lenses. It reminded Polixis of his brother.

'Brother-Sergeant Severus,' he said. The Reiver inclined his head slightly, his voice a cold whisper issuing from his death mask's vocaliser.

'Brother-Apothecary. I am here to extract you.'

'Through happy coincidence? Or did Chaplain Kastor send you?'

'I have my orders,' Severus replied levelly. 'We must move, before the xenos encircle us once more.'

Polixis looked to Trajo, still held up by his battle-brothers. He was sure that even with the Primaris' advanced biology, the Hellblaster was struggling with the pain of his shattered legs. The Apothecary turned to Domitian. The sergeant had hefted Lorens' body in his arms, servos grinding as they accommodated the Primaris' great weight.

'We are ready,' he said.

'I can extract his progenoids here–' Polixis began.

'He comes with us, Apothecary. Let us be gone from here, before an even greater sacrifice is required.'

Severus' Reiver brethren were still only half-suggested shapes in the surrounding shadows, backlit occasionally by the flare of their heavy bolt pistols. They watched over the Hellblasters as they withdrew to the north-east, veiled, half-glimpsed figures who brought swift death to everything in their path. Severus himself had departed once more from the Hellblasters without Polixis noticing, simply disappearing from the midst of the battered Ultramarines. The sound of bolter fire from off to their right intensified, followed by the whip-crack of lascannon discharges.

'Is that *Extremis?*' Domitian wondered aloud. Polixis tapped into the visor map's sigil overlay. A glance told him that the demi-company's Repulsor grav-tank was indeed just to their east, and heading in the opposite direction.

'Captain Demeter is with it,' he said aloud. 'It seems he's… counter-attacking into the horde.'

'That is madness,' Domitian said. 'He'll be overrun.'

'*Our orders are to continue the withdrawal,*' Severus interjected over the vox.

'The captain is buying us time,' Polixis said. 'The orks will flock to him, and especially *Extremis.*'

He could sense Sergeant Domitian's struggle. The Hellblasters were now the closest Primaris to the captain. They could support him. But the reasoning behind Demeter's counter-attack was obvious – it was to allow them to withdraw. They all had their orders.

'We continue north-east,' the sergeant said eventually. 'Maintain formation and watch the flanks. And may the primarch and the Emperor be with the captain.'

STABSKAR

Stabskar watched the big beakies withdraw into the cover of the dust shroud. He said nothing, but the expression on his blunt, scarred face was clear enough – anger mixed with a rare degree of uncertainty.

The ork kommandos had sniffed out the beakie ambush seconds before it had been sprung – never had either Stabskar or his biggest nob, Grimtoof, witnessed the blue boys act so sneaky-like before. Luckily Grimtoof had sniffed out the counter-ambush at the last minute, and Stabskar had ordered the lads to restrain themselves. Stabskar wasn't going to waste lads against any old beakie band – that was what the footsloggin' mobs were for.

So the kommandos held back, and now their prey was slipping away into the rubble and the night.

'I reckon dat was 'im, boss,' Grimtoof growled from where he was kneeling atop the nearest mound of debris, peering through the spottin' tube after the withdrawing figures. 'I reckon dat's da one in da white bits.'

'You don't know what you're talkin' about,' Stabskar huffed, unwilling to admit that the target set for him by Urgork was potentially escaping. 'Could be any git out there. We'll find da one da boss wants, and soon.'

The crump of a large explosion followed by a swelling roar to the east drew the kommandos' attention away from the receding Primaris.

'More beakies,' Grimtoof hypothesised, peering through the dust. 'Comin' this way.'

'Probably just tryin' ta distract da mobs,' Stabskar said. 'Let's take a look.'

The kommando boss led his band around the rubble mounds, moving low and fast, soot-smeared stabbin' knives unsheathed. A hellish glow lit the darkness ahead, the flicker of promethium flames, suffused with occasional flashes of actinic blue. The bulky forms of other greenskins became visible the closer the kommandos drew – multiple mobs, roaring and bellowing with battle-lust, stampeding through the city's wreckage towards some sort of spreading combat.

'High ground,' one of the kommandos, Lugin, grunted, gesturing to the toppled remains of what had once been one of the humie's habitation blocks. It stood as a pillar of shattered masonry and twisted girders, jutting out of the rubble a little further north.

'Stay 'ere,' Stabskar said to the rest of the mob, and gestured at Grimtoof to follow him. The two kommandos sheathed their wicked blades and began to climb the steep mound, hand over hand, scarred green fists gripping the remains of jagged stonework and bent plasteel struts. They scaled the ruins like burly simians, coming to a crouch side by side at the collapsed block's pinnacle.

Beneath, to the east, a savage brawl was playing out. Fire lit the night, gouting from the fists of a trio of heavily armed beakies. They were wading into the mobs charging them like slow-moving machines, surrounding themselves with an expanding wall of blazing heat and leaving a trail of burning, blackened corpses behind.

Even more killy-looking was the war machine advancing behind the flamer-armed blue boys. It was a great battle tank, but what immediately drew Stabskar's' attention was not its heavy, sloping blue armour plates, or even the dakka blazing from its many weapons sponsons. What made the kommando stare was the fact that it was floating. It moved with a heavy, leaden grace, its flanks and rear engines throbbing with some sort of anti-gravitic thrust. Even more impressively, the space beneath its bulk was not simply open and clear – a downward force was crushing everything the tank was moving over, grinding rubble and pulverising corpses, leaving a trail of completely flattened destruction in its wake.

'Ain't neva seen da humies using somethin' like dat before,' Grimtoof said, peering through his spottin' tube.

'Cogkrusha would love to tinker with dat,' Stabskar said

thoughtfully, chewing slowly on a scrap of old flesh he'd extracted from between his tusks.

'Looks like they got a boss pole too,' Grimtoof added.

'What?' Stabskar demanded, grasping the spottin' tube from his subordinate. He peered through the grimy lens, past the mobs of torched boys, until he was focused just ahead of the big, hovering tank. There he saw what Grimtoof had spotted – a banner rippling in the fire-licked dust, blue and white, a winged lightning symbol topping it. Even better, there was another beakie warrior besides the one carrying it. His armour was like the three with the burny bits, but instead of fire he was wreathed in lightning that cracked from one great gauntlet and from the sword shining in his other fist.

'Humie boss boy,' Stabskar growled, tossing the spotter back to Grimtoof. 'If he's 'ere, the white one could be close. Let's get down there.'

The two orks clambered back down the hab block's ruins. They'd barely rejoined their mob when a fresh bout of roaring swelled from the darkness. Stabskar and Grimtoof exchanged a glance. They knew that sound.

Urgork and his boss nobs had arrived.

DEMETER

Extremis had spearheaded the Fulminata's counter-attack throughout the night. Demeter and the three Aggressors of Squad Tiro followed in its crushing wake, beneath Skyrus and the silkweave of the Fulminata's standard. They had continued south from the basilica until word from *Extremis'* commander, Techmarine Tiberon, crackled over the vox. There were contacts ahead.

As the Repulsor's lascannons spat beams of blue energy into the dust and its heavy bolters began thundering, Demeter and the others moved to secure the grav-tank's flanks, keeping their formation tight on the sides of the heavy vehicle. Moments later, as the first greenskins came scrambling over the rubble, Squad Tiro ignited their flame gauntlets.

The blaze of promethium kept the xenos at bay for long, heat-washed minutes, and those aliens that stumbled aflame through the inferno were smashed to bloody wreckage by Demeter's boltstorm gauntlet or power sword. The auspex read thousands of contacts, closing from the south, east and west. Just as Demeter had hoped, the prospect of such a vicious combat – not to mention the presence of the Repulsor – was dragging the greenskin assault towards them for miles in every direction.

'All units, continue the withdrawal,' the captain voxed. Communications were getting choppy thanks to the increasing distance between himself and the rest of the Fulminata. Those locator beacons still being transmitted showed squads pulling back to the north and east, bound for Shebat's outskirts. How many of the Guard had already got out was impossible to say, but the flash of combat engagements across the burst map was rolling steadily eastwards from the Gorgon. Only in the south had it stalled, locked around the bastion of Demeter's resistance.

'Anti-armour to the east,' Brother Torr's voice crackled over the link. The words had barely registered before a battered-looking rocket corkscrewed up through the black smoke and flames, detonating above the Repulsor and showering its blue hull with a burst of metal fragments. A second rocket followed almost immediately, slashing just past the tank's prow and away through the smoke.

'Brother Uxis,' Demeter voxed. The Aggressor's icon blinked with an affirmative as the heavily armoured Primaris widened the cordon to the east, bringing the ork tank hunters into range of his ever-hungry flamers. The blackened nozzles of the weapons were glowing white-hot now, and the air was almost unbreathably heavy with black smoke and the stench of charred flesh and liquefied organs. The captain's auto-senses were reading an external heat approaching a thousand degrees, and even the proud blue heraldry adorning the Aggressor's resistant ceramite plates had started to blister and blacken.

An ork stumbled through the fire, ablaze from head to foot, howling with fury even as its lungs choked with fumes. A short, hard slash of Demeter's blade sent its head tumbling from its shoulders, and the rest of its body thumped from his armour, sprawling on the ash-darkened debris underfoot. Skyrus was behind the captain, between him and the Repulsor's frontal glacis, the artificial material of the company standard ensuring it didn't combust in the infernal temperatures. The captain felt a sudden, fierce upsurge of pride as he half turned towards the rippling blue and white, the golden lightning bolt of the Fulminata topping the banner. Every minute that it continued to fly preserved more lives. There was no greater purpose the proud standard could serve.

As though in answer to his thoughts, a series of bestial howls rose above the pulsing of the Repulsor's grav-engines. A glance at his gauntlet's inbuilt auspex told Demeter that a fresh wedge of contacts were approaching rapidly from the south.

Shapes came charging through the fire wreathing the front of the spearhead formation, heedless of the heat that engulfed them. Demeter realised immediately that they were the bodyguard of some powerful greenskin leader – each was a muscle-clad brute wielding weapons their lesser kindred would have struggled to lift. The captain's thoughts were confirmed when, seconds later, an even greater shape came charging through the inferno, the earth shuddering beneath it.

The captain recognised it immediately from the intelligence dockets and briefing sessions undertaken when they'd first arrived in the Ikara war zone – it was Urgork, the freakish lord and master of the Waaagh! that had brought devastation to the surrounding systems.

The Aggressors' fires picked out its nightmarish body – the patchwork limbs and jagged stitches that criss-crossed its mostly exposed flesh. It had a great, wicked blade in each fist, and as it burst through the flames its small, cruel eyes locked with Demeter's visor. It gestured at him with one of its skinning knives and barked something in its alien tongue, as either side its bodyguards threw themselves at the Aggressors, choppas and chainaxes battering flame-scorched Gravis plate.

'Face me, xenos,' Demeter snarled, raising his boltstorm gauntlet. Urgork answered with a grunt. Head down, the hulking alien charged, barging lesser greenskins aside. Amidst the roaring flames and the crackle of raw, destructive power, Demeter met it head-on.

CHAPTER FOUR   THE ASH WASTES

POLIXIS

Polixis and Squad Domitian linked up with a trio of Zoishen Leman Russ battle tanks about half a mile west of Shebat's outskirts. The Zoishen commander, a captain named Chao'li, had already lost half of his armoured company fighting scattered rearguard actions along the banks of the Gorgon, as greenskin barges and rafts had poured across the sluggish, toxic river. The remaining tanks were accompanied by little more than a single ragged platoon of Voitekan infantry, who stared at the Primaris as they emerged from the night, caked in dust and congealed alien blood.

'Is there anything left further south of here?' Domitian asked Chao'li, whilst the battered column paused amidst the remains of what had once been the city's main mag-lev line, now broken and twisted beneath the mass of debris thrown down by the rok's impact.

'We're the last,' Chao'li said from the cupola of his Leman Russ Punisher. 'I had a Demolisher half a mile south-east of us, but I've not heard anything over the vox for twenty minutes. If he's not already out, he won't be getting out.'

'Keep moving,' Domitian said, the Hellblasters falling in either side of the tanks as they began to trundle along the mag-lev line's remains. Severus and his pack of Reivers had already dropped away, disappearing with as little notice as they had first appeared, presumably moving to help extricate another squad from close contact with the xenos still pouring across the river.

Polixis checked the dispersal runes on his visor – nearly all of the demi-company had progressed east and were nearing Shebat's edge. All except Captain Demeter, his Aggressors and the Repulsor, *Extremis*. They remained to the south, utterly surrounded now by icons representing enemy contacts. Every instinct demanded Polixis turn and go to the aid of his captain and brothers. To lose the captain, the company standard and the likes of *Extremis* was a dire blow for the Fulminata, but to also lose all of their progenoids as well was almost unconscionable. He tried to focus his mind on the matters that defined him – duty, the willingness to serve and save. He had to follow orders. He had to follow the Codex.

'Without the seed of our warriors, the Chapter dies,' he reminded himself, voicing one of his Apothecary pledges. 'But without me few can extract it. I will put my own duty above all else.'

To have stayed at Demeter's side or gone back to him once he was engulfed would have been an outrageous dereliction of his own duties and a break with numerous salient tenets of the Codex Astartes. Worst of all, it would have rendered the captain's sacrifice in vain. He would not go back.

He busied himself with reviewing his charges as he trudged alongside the Zoishen tanks. According to their readouts both Trajo and Ennio were suffering, but their vitaes had stabilised and the chances of a fatality had now reduced to almost nil.

Trajo would have joined Brother Priscor aboard the *Spear of Macragge* for bionic refits and an intensive period of bonding therapy, but the xenos fleet now controlling orbital space had denied such a possibility. The crippled Primaris would have no choice other than to remain with the rear echelons, once they were eventually re-established. Ennio at least would still be capable of fighting once the crushed remains of his left forearm were amputated. Guilliman knew, it looked like the Fulminata would need every Primaris still capable of lifting a bolter soon enough.

Eventually they broke free of Shebat's eastern flank and past the slums that had been flattened by the rok's blast wave. Dawn light was attempting to break through the pall of dust and ash kicked up by the impact, creating a dull grey tinge that the auto-senses of the Primaris picked up and amplified. Polixis mounted a final mound of masonry on Shebat's edge as the armour and their weary support squads trudged past, the passage of the tanks making the rubble underfoot vibrate. The Apothecary looked east, to where the ash wastes spread out beyond the refinery city, undulating dunes and barren tundra whipped by an eye-stinging, throat-parching wind. The many miles between Shebat and the great, brutalist sprawl of the capital city of Kroten would have appeared truly desolate were it not for the thousands of figures now making their weary way out into the expanse.

Polixis watched as the Imperium withdrew from Shebat. The miserable grey light picked out dozens of columns – insubstantial, faceless masses in the half-darkness, winding away from the city's edge. Armoured vehicles, tanks and cargo 8s interspersed lines of bent-backed, respirator-clad infantry moving with the weary tread of those who had just come within inches of a violent death. Company and regimental pennants fluttered in the caustic wind, their ash-caked fabric acting as rallying points for the scattered units that had dragged themselves from the ruined city after command and control had broken down. Less than half a mile away Polixis' enhanced eyesight picked out the struggles of a labouring Adeptus Mechanicus enginseer and his dead-fleshed servitors as they fought to repair a Leman Russ that had broken down just off one of the rockcrete roads leading from the city. Nearby, a Departmento Munitorum flatbed was dispensing water canisters, the quartermaster standing on the back of the trailer bellowing furiously for order at the mob of parched Guardsmen that had surrounded the vehicle. The entire expanse before the Primaris was a disorganised, demoralised vista, the personification of defeat.

Domitian clambered up onto the runners of Chao'li's battle tank, the vehicle pausing before it rolled out into the ash wastes. They were consulting the Guard officer's pocket chart. Polixis descended from his mound of rubble and rejoined the squad. Trajo had been mounted on the rear of one of the Zoishen tanks, and Polixis applied another salve-shot to him via his armour's interface port. The Hellblaster was silent, his mood grim. It looked as though bionics were going to be the only feasible treatment.

'Soon you'll contain so much metal that Helix won't be able to operate on you any more,' Gratian joked gruffly, looking up at his fellow Hellblaster. 'Techmarine Tiberon will be the one to oil you.'

'At least it won't be difficult for me to kick you to death when you make more ill jests, brother,' Trajo replied from between gritted teeth. Despite himself, Polixis smiled.

'Fifth and Eighth Corps have established a cordon three miles further east,' Domitian voxed as he dropped back down from the Leman Russ. 'Along a ridgeline past the waste dunes. The tanks will continue following the mag-lev. There's still no contact with Lieutenant Tyranus, so we'll do the same and link with the new front once we reach it.'

They moved on, joining the rear of a straggling column of Namarians already using the mag-lev line to move out into the grey expanse beyond the city. Even behind the glassy film of their respirator lenses, Polixis could recognise the looks they gave the towering Ultramarines – fear coupled with shame and raw exhaustion. It was easy to forget that even the most experienced soldiers of the Astra Militarum lacked the fortitude of the Adeptus Astartes – in the past twelve hours these men had successfully driven the xenos menace from half of Shebat and achieved all their objectives, only for the sky itself to come crashing down on them. Comrades had been crushed and buried alive in their thousands, and an enemy they had thought beaten, at least for one day, had come surging at them once again with renewed ferocity. Now they were retreating, abandoning wounded friends and the streets they had fought and bled for, all reduced to rubble. These men were beaten.

They could be rallied though; Polixis knew that much. He had seen his brother do it enough times to be in no doubt about the resilience of mankind's fighting spirit. He just hoped it could be done before the greenskins followed up on their victory.

The vox clicked, a few words cutting through before the link degenerated into static again. Contact with the rest of the Fulminata had been almost wholly lost, and most of the squads were only appearing occasionally now on the map interface. There was no sign whatsoever of Demeter or the battle-brothers who had made their stand to the south. Polixis forced their fate from his mind. There was nothing that could be done now. They had to reach the newly established line out in the wastes, then ensure it was capable of receiving the next greenskin attack when it inevitably came.

As the column trudged on, the Apothecary glanced back towards Shebat. The ruination that had descended on the city was only just becoming apparent as the day's light spread, and the worst of the dust cloud began to settle. A moonscape of craggy stone, rockcrete and broken girders stretched away, as desolate and bleak as the ash dunes ahead. In the distance, the Primaris thought he could pick out the defiant spires of the basilica, still standing tall amidst the destruction. He wondered whether the orks had reached it yet.

Polixis did not put a great deal of stock in battle oaths and pledges of vengeance. He had more vital duties to attend to than matters of personal honour. But in that moment, surrounded by defeat, he swore that he would return and reclaim those distant spires, for the primarch and the Emperor, and all those who had fallen in their defence.

Today had been a bloody reckoning. There would be another, soon.

KASTOR

The nexus of the new Imperial defensive line east of Shebat Alpha was a long, low ash dune labelled Ridge 1. It had only just acquired the moniker, courtesy of some departmento cartographic analyst attached to the Eighth Corps. Whether the primitive ash waste dwellers had a name for the rise running between the mag-lev line and the main highway to Kroten, nobody seemed to know. On the Fulminata's strategic displays it remained a nameless, largely featureless stretch of barren grey soil.

By the time Kastor reached it, defensive preparations were well underway. Two batteries of Vostroyan mobile artillery from the Eighth Corps had been sited just back from the ridgeline – Basilisks and Manticores mostly, interspersed with Hydra anti-aircraft guns. Initially the Guard had attempted to establish trenches along the ridge's length, before quickly realising that the shifting ash-soil would make the task impossible. Instead sandbags had been filled, and raised redoubts were taking shape, interspersed with battle tanks acting as makeshift strongpoints. The air was filled with the thud and scrape of shovels and the growl of engines as the Ultramarines Chaplain climbed the slope to where the corps commander's skull pennant was fluttering in the bitter morning breeze.

Lieutenant Tyranus was at Kastor's side. The Fulminata's second in command had assumed leadership of the demi-company since contact had been lost with Demeter. He had spoken little to Kastor since the Chaplain had linked up with him just east of the basilica. He could sense the lieutenant's thoughts were the same as his – both seethed over the defeat they had suffered. Multiple times during the withdrawal from Shebat it was all Kastor could do not to turn on his heel and stride after Captain Demeter. Each time he had reminded himself that the role of the Chaplain was not only one of fiery vengeance. He was a guide, an exemplar for all his brethren, and to be seen to abandon reason and go against direct orders in the name of zealous fervour was a sin against the Codex that he refused to commit.

They climbed Ridge 1. All the Fulminata's squads had reached Imperial lines, though most had done so further north – it would take time to gather them all once more. Ahead of Kastor, amid a sandbag redoubt being slowly assembled by labouring, ash-caked Kelestan Stormers, lay the forward command post of Major General Chevik. It was a prefabricated enviro-dome reinforced by flakboard and sandbags and studded with vox-uplink masts. The respirator-masked Tempestus Scions standing guard at the main entrance didn't try to stop the two Ultramarines as they ducked inside.

Within they discovered a cramped space housing little more than a camp desk littered with charts and data-slates, and a bulky vox-system, wired up to a wall formed at the rear of the dome by a row of departmento-stamped flakboards.

General Chevik himself was standing to one side, an aide helping him out of his heavy, brocaded red uniform while another vainly tried to dust the cloying grey ash from the thick fur of his tall papakha hat.

The commander of the Eighth Corps was a short, bluff figure, typical of the Guard regiments of Vostroya. His heavy grey moustache was impeccably waxed and curled, and a jagged scar running down the left side of his face caused one eyelid to droop lower than the other. The aides continued to try dusting ash from the fine lace and furred collar of the general's uniform while Chevik, now in his shirtsleeves and boots, made the sign of the aquila towards the two Primaris.

'My lords,' he said, flinty eyes taking in the towering armoured warriors without any hint of trepidation. 'Welcome to Eighth Corps command. How can I be of service?'

'Our thanks, major general,' Tyranus said, mirroring the Guardsman's salute. 'We have come here directly from Shebat. We no longer have contact with Captain Demeter, so I have assumed leadership of the Fulminata for the time being.'

'Then my men and I are at your disposal, lord,' Chevik said, inclining his head slightly.

'You have received word from Field Marshal Klos?'

'Not since I was ordered to establish a new defensive line here. From what I can gather, the field marshal is with Fifth Corps, six miles to the north.'

'Show me your dispositions,' Tyranus ordered, moving to the chart-littered camp table. Kastor remained near the post's self-sealing entrance flap as the lieutenant discussed the strength and location of Chevik's sixteen divisions. In truth the Chaplain's mind was elsewhere.

Severus had reported back to him in person. His brother lived. He had already given silent thanks for such a blessing. To have lost the captain and ancient, alongside the Repulsor and the Fulminata's standard, was a grievous blow. To have also lost the strike force's only Apothecary would have spelled disaster. Kastor did not feel the need to further rationalise his orders to the Reivers. Polixis would no doubt be angry with him – if there was one particular fault they both shared, it was the fact that neither found it easy admitting when they needed help, least of all from the other. It had been the same ever since they were children, not that Polixis remembered much of their lives pre-induction. The privilege of being haunted by those memories seemed to have been reserved for Kastor only.

He watched as Tyranus listened to Chevik's reports about the situation of the new front. The lieutenant had mag-locked his helm, and his expression was open and engaged – like Demeter, interacting with others seemed to come naturally to him. He had consciously moulded himself in the captain's image, striving to achieve the ideals of the Codex, a rounded warrior-strategist with an eye for the diplomacy required whenever the disparate wings of the Imperium's armed forces fought side by side. Objectively, the Fulminata couldn't have found itself with a better commander. That didn't ease their loss, though.

'We're still receiving columns from Shebat,' Chevik was saying, indicating three points along the ridgeline displayed on one of the maps. 'Mostly elements of the First and Third Corps. Organisation is minimal. We're admitting them through our lines here, here and here. The rear echelons have been opened up, and they're being regrouped. Major General Hunley is still in command of the Third, First is under the acting command of Commissar-General Vrenk.'

'Are both corps still combat-capable?' Tyranus asked.

'You were with them, my lord. You probably know better than I do. The collapse of so much of the city and the chaos of the retreat has left some units at less than fifty per cent of their starting strength. How many of those reported missing will straggle in over the next few days is impossible to say. There seem to be a great deal of walking wounded too, again courtesy of the city's collapse. My corps' aid stations are already overburdened, and we're working to establish better triage all across the line.'

'If the greenskins mount a concerted attack across the line within the next few hours, we will not be able to resist them,' Tyranus said simply. It looked as though Chevik was going to argue, his Vostroyan pride stung. Eventually though, he nodded.

'I cannot deny that. Not only would the line collapse, but any breach would likely see the whole front overrun. I doubt those units still regrouping to our rear would hold for long. We are not ready.'

'Then it is my duty to make you ready,' Tyranus said. He turned towards Kastor.

'I will need a transport,' the Chaplain said before the lieutenant had spoken.

'You may have my personal command Chimera,' Chevik said. 'Its vox-systems should help you coordinate more closely with the commanders on the ground.'

'I will dispatch Sergeants Klastis and Nerva to the corps immediately north and south of us,' Tyranus added. 'With the Emperor's blessings, we will be ready by nightfall.'

'May His light go with you, brother-lieutenant,' Kastor said. 'And with you, General Chevik. I will return as soon as I am able.'

He made the sign of the aquila and pushed out through the enviro-dome's flap. Outside the wind was rising, whipping up an ash cloud to further clog an atmosphere already choked with the dust of the rok's fallout. Though midday was fast approaching, the world seemed locked in a perpetual twilight, the figures labouring at the sandbag redoubts below Kastor reduced to indistinct, bent-over spectres in the grey gloom. Though he'd been outside for mere seconds, already ash was starting to heap around his boots and cake his vestments.

There was a sudden, supersonic bang, reverberating like a thunderclap across the ridgeline. Kastor looked skywards, but even his skull helm's lenses were unable to pick out whatever had passed overhead through the dust storm. It seemed hard to believe that any aircraft could be aloft in such conditions, but nor did he find the idea of greenskin pilots braving the choked atmosphere hard to believe. Once the worst of the ash settled, the ork's crude air fleet would surely descend on the Imperial positions en masse. As long as the aliens controlled orbit, they controlled the skies.

Instinct told Kastor that the fighting in Shebat had only

been a prelude, that there was more slaughter to come. He hoped he was right.

The xenos scum were crying out for vengeance, and he would deliver it.

STABSKAR

The kommandos were the first greenskins to reach the humie shrine-place. Under Stabskar's directives they approached cautiously, using the flanks of the square laid out before the looming structure. There was no movement from up ahead – the ruins stretched away in the grey half-light, and the humie corpses and wrecks that littered the square remained motionless.

Stabskar signalled for the point-boys to move in through the great building's front doors, peering after them as they disappeared into the darkness beyond. His gut told him the humies were long gone – he'd never heard of them abandoning big, fancy, spikey buildings like the one in front of him without a fight unless they'd decided to leg it. He hadn't reached his current rank, however, by taking unnecessary risks. That was what the footsloggas were for.

After a few tense moments one of the kommandos re-emerged on the building's entrance steps and waved the thumb and little finger of one hand above his head – all clear.

'Move, gits,' Stabskar grunted at the rest of the mob, iron-shod boots cracking off the stone steps as they hustled up and into the great building. Beyond the doors, the kommando boss found himself in an echoing, vaulted space that rose on thick stone pillars and swooped overhead in a series of vast arches.

He had seen such structures on several previous occasions – they always made for good looting. He'd never understood why the humies spent such time and effort building them, much less why they then packed such wastes of space with all sorts of shiny gubbins. But what mattered most of all was that they usually gave a good scrap trying to defend them.

'Where's all da humies, den?' one of the kommandos, Gritt, demanded sullenly. Stabskar didn't deign to answer, but it was a struggle not to show his own disappointment. Taking one of these buildings without a fight felt wrong.

'Zorg,' the kommando boss snapped at the smallest, runtiest greenskin in the mob. 'Get movin' and find da warboss. Tell 'im da humies is definitely gone, and we've got their big spikey place.'

As Zorg scampered off Stabskar drew his ragged camo cape around him and sat heavily on one of the carved wooden benches occupying the building's open floor, the timber groaning beneath his weight. If nothing else, he hoped taking the vast structure would make Urgork forget about the fact that his kommandos had failed to find the beakie in the white armour.

POLIXIS

The Voitekan on the operating table was unconscious again. Polixis watched the orderlies working over him, marvelling at their struggles. To see the difficulty human medicaes had in keeping their patients stable always led Polixis to reflect on the blessings of Adeptus Astartes physiology. Here men screamed. They lost control of their bowels. They flatlined. They bled out, and the Apothecary had been forced to remind himself that a normal mortal's wounds didn't clot within seconds of their own accord. Men looked to their battlefield exploits to claim that Space Marines were a long step removed from humanity, demigods of war, but the differences were even more apparent here, beneath the harsh surgery lumens, amidst the blood and the sweat and the screaming and the thump of bone saws and slitting of scalpels.

He dragged himself from his thoughts and turned away from the operation he'd been watching, heading instead for the medicae dome's entrance. The large space was packed with the wounded and the dying, and stank of counterseptics and blood. Most of the injuries were fractures, breaks and crush wounds, all related to the sudden collapse of so much of Shebat's infrastructure when the rok had struck. Many of the Guardsmen confined to the ward had been carried in the arms of their exhausted squad mates, or had limped in themselves. The staff – the rear echelon medical contingent of the Eighth Corps – had barely set up that morning before the casualties began flooding in. They were wholly out of splints and were running short of plast-wraps and caster braces.

And this was only one of the larger casualty wards. Polixis had parted ways with Squad Domitian at one of the forward triage stations near the base of Ridge 1's reverse slope. It was nothing more than a large, open-sided tent with some jury-rigged tarps keeping the worst of the ash storm at bay. Medicaes and corpsmen were working in their respirators, and simply keeping wounds clean was nigh-on an impossibility. Body bags were stacking up outside, many almost submerged in the drifting pall of ash that befouled everything in the wastes.

Polixis had operated on Trajo with what little equipment

he had to hand. When he'd arrived at the facility, a separate compartment outside the main ward featured hoses and decontamination units for those entering the sterile environment beyond. Polixis had begrudgingly permitted the servitors to remove the worse of the battle grime from his white plate, but a far more thorough job – and the correct benedictions to the armour's venerable spirit – would be required before it was free of the day's bitter legacy.

As he stepped out through the sealant flaps and back into the wind and ash, he tried to quell the frustration that still simmered at the back of his mind. He had seen enough of the galaxy and its horrors to know just how badly mismatched individual servants of the Imperium were against their foes. The reality of mankind's struggle was something he knew he would never be comfortable obscuring. It was difficult to give hope when there was so little to go around.

Ironically, it was his brother whose words could uplift. Polixis had seen him bring purpose and resolve to planetary governors and underhive savlar-militia alike. To him, the words he spoke were not lies or manipulative half-truths; they were the fuel that kept the candle in the dark aflame, that stopped the light that gave humanity hope from guttering out. And Polixis couldn't deny that hope was their surest weapon, especially in times such as these.

He turned to follow the eastern flank of the ridge, towards the rally coordinates newly uploaded by Lieutenant Tyranus. The Fulminata were to regroup at Eighth Corps' headquarters, near the centre of the ridgeline. From there they would oversee the preparation of the new defensive positions. At best they would be largely completed by the time the greenskins coordinated their inevitable offensive.

At worst, the Fulminata would be the only ones standing

between the rampant xenos and the complete collapse of Imperial forces west of Kroten.

KASTOR

Kastor moved among the Imperial Guard like a vision of death. Men cringed away, gasped, even cried out as he passed by. The barked commands of officers and sergeants died on the wind as the spectre materialised from the ash and dust, the storm snatching at his vestments and the cowl that shrouded his nightmarish skull. The wounded were the most afraid, for some no doubt believed he had come for their souls. They clutched aquila tokens and lucky charms and turned their eyes away, not daring to breathe through their respirators lest the rattling inhalation drew the glowing red gaze of the phantom.

Kastor strode the eastern slope of the ridgeline, amidst those Guard units newly arrived from Shebat. He spoke to some, and it was always the same message, a single word – *follow*. And follow they did, some out of fear, some out of awe, some because of the hope that, when their time came, the reaping spectre would remember them kindly. They followed, moving from the clogged trails being used by the other retreating columns towards shallower paths, almost lost amidst the ever-shifting wasteland. They went together, disparate men and women from the far corners of the galaxy, Voitekans and Kelestani, Faeburn Vanquishers and Vostroyans, flame-troopers from Pyr and marksmen from the snow forests of Lorek, first united under the aquila and now again in the long shadow of the great, grim figure who led them through the wind and ash.

Kastor took them to the tribal rock that jutted close to

the northern extent of Ridge 1. It was a gathering place for the nomadic scavenger peoples that inhabited the ash wastes, evidenced by the totemic remains heaped around the base of the stony protrusion. The dust-caked skulls of great ash-fangs and greymaws, and all manner of rusting detritus and trinkets, heaped the sides of the jagged outcrop. Amongst the litter the Astra Militarum gathered, hundreds of respirator-clad faces staring upwards in silence.

The Chaplain climbed the flank of the ridge and then turned along the top of the outcrop, his heavy boots grating slowly on stone. The wind was even stronger on top of the rock, making his robes and purity parchments flutter and snap. He drew back his cowl, revealing the full morbidity of his skull helm. Below, the human soldiers of the Imperium waited, more straggling in by the minute, drawn by the single, rasped command of the black-armoured giant.

The Chaplain of the Fulminata raised Salve Imperator in one fist, slowly. Deactivated, the skull mace gleamed coldly in the grey light, its empty eye sockets seeming to glare down at the weary, ash-covered congregation. Kastor held the weapon before them in silence before he finally spoke.

'We have all failed,' he said. 'We have all fallen short of the devotion our Emperor requires of us.'

The words were not delivered loudly or forcefully, only amplified enough by his helmet's vox-unit to carry over the worst of the wind. It brought a murmur back to him, the half-voiced disbelief of those whose denial was finally coming undone.

'A day that started in glorious victory was seen out in the totality of abject defeat,' he went on. The murmurs rose.

'Perhaps your officers have told you otherwise. Perhaps they have sought out hope in what has befallen us – a tactical withdrawal, and massed redeployment. That is to their credit, for it is their duty to maintain your resolve. But be under no illusions here, soldiers of the Emperor. We have failed Him. Amid that defeat, who here has not lost a brother or squad mate? In among a city brought to ruination, who has not abandoned brethren trapped and crushed by the weight of Shebat's destruction?'

Someone shouted from the assembly, the words lost but the anger clear.

'You are not alone,' Kastor said, still holding up his crozius arcanum. 'I am condemned with you, I and all my brothers. We, too, have failed. We too have been driven out by xenos filth, cast into the wilderness by beasts that have no right to share this galaxy with us. Some of you will even have witnessed my brothers fall, brought low by the savagery of the greenskin menace. Yes, for we are not immortal on the field of battle. We die also, and the Ultramarines Chapter has suffered a grievous blow amidst the ruins of Shebat.'

There were more shouts, a swell of shock and outrage among the huddled congregation, rising like a tide over the fear the Guardsmen felt towards the towering Primaris.

'This loss is no easy thing to take,' Kastor went on, voice amplified above their protestations. 'Failures like these haunt the memory and breed doubt and fear among those not staunch in mind and soul. And yet, my brothers, and yet...'

The murmuring below trailed off as the Guardsmen waited on the Chaplain's words.

'Yet there is a strength in such a defeat, for the few who have the courage to find it. There is an awakening. New resolve, new understanding, a purpose that is clearer and firmer than what came before. Not all rally to it. Not everyone stands again after they are struck down. But I do. And by your presence here, I know that you do too.'

This time there was only silence. The Chaplain's voice continued to rise, reverberating now through the ash storm, bass and unyielding as iron.

'We were defeated yesterday, but we were not broken. We failed, but we have not been destroyed. We are still standing, every one of us. And if we stand, we can fight, and if we can fight, we can win. Avenge our losses, wipe away the stain of our failure and reclaim this world.'

'For Voitek and the Emperor!' came a shout from someone close to the front of the assembly.

'For Shebat and Ikara!' added another. The voices in the crowd returned, rising, no longer in dismay but in pride and defiance.

'The xenos will come again,' Kastor boomed. 'But this time when they do we will be ready! This time we will meet their savagery, and we will break them with lasgun and with bayonet!'

The crowd began to cheer. Kastor continued.

'Do not be dismayed by their violence or their numbers. Stand by your squad mates, listen to the orders of your commanding officers and, above all, remember that you are soldiers of the God-Emperor's Astra Militarum, the defenders of humanity and the vanquishers of its darkest foes. No failure, no defeat. After today, we will know only victory! For the Emperor!'

The final words were punctuated by the activation of Salve Imperator – lightning surged up the mace and crackled about its skull tip, a sudden, searing affirmation that the Chaplain's words were not mere oration. The cheering went on for long minutes, during which Kastor privately narrated the

Seventeenth Admonishment in his own head, a penitence canticle that reminded its reciter that their only worth was in their service to the Emperor and the Chapter. The cheers of men had turned many of the Emperor's chosen from the path of righteousness before.

Afterwards, he led the assembly in the singing of 'Imperator Gloriam', that old Guard battle-hymnal. In the meantime, fresh runners had arrived for the units Kastor had gathered, bearing deployment and disposition dockets.

The congregation started to disperse, moving now with less weariness and more purpose. Officers barked orders, and men rallied to platoon and company standards that streamed in the ash-heavy wind. Columns began to set off as their new orders were checked and confirmed. The pause had put steel and vigour into what had previously been a mass of tired, confused and directionless men and women.

Only one figure remained, formerly hidden amongst the crowds near the base of the rock, close to the old rubbish heaped up by the wastes' tribespeople. Kastor descended from his promontory and paced through the rusting detritus, to where his brother stood and waited.

'Why here?' Polixis asked him.

'Because I can be seen,' Kastor replied, gesturing towards the rock. 'And because it pulls units away from the congestion on the main tracks. Moving them here means they can disperse more effectively, especially with the storm slowing everything down.'

'Practicality as well as fervour,' Polixis said. 'You do the Chapter honour, as ever.'

For a moment, neither Primaris spoke. Kastor offered his arm. After the briefest hesitation, Polixis took it in the warrior's grip.

'It is good to see you once again, brother,' Kastor said.

'And to see you,' Polixis said. 'I thank the Emperor that you left Shebat unharmed.'

'I felt the hand of Him on us both. Likewise with Squad Domitian. Brothers Trajo and Ennio will fight again?'

'They will, though Trajo not for some time.'

'I shall visit him as soon as my duties allow. Knowing him, he will rail against anything that sees him removed from the front line, no matter how grievous the wounds.'

'The Emperor knows, we will need every battle-brother soon enough.'

There was silence between the two of them before Polixis spoke once more, and this time there was iron in his voice, as unyielding as Kastor's when his words to the Guard had reached their crescendo.

'You sent the Reivers to see me safely out of Shebat, didn't you?'

'I did,' Kastor said, without any hint of hesitation. 'The Fulminata suffered enough last night. I could not countenance the loss of its Apothecary as well as its captain, ancient and all those battle-brothers who perished fighting to give the Astra Militarum time. Lieutenant Tyranus approved the deployment of Severus and his brethren.'

'He could have been elsewhere. He could have been securing the captain.'

'Captain Demeter's orders were in no way uncertain. He wished to draw as many xenos to himself for as long as possible. He did not intend to leave Shebat.'

'I hope you at least counselled him otherwise,' Polixis said.

'Of course I did,' Kastor replied, fire now in his own voice. 'What would you have had me do? Disobey his orders? Go after him? Bring the rest of the Fulminata to his side? You know that what he did was perfectly within the bounds of the Codex, and more importantly, it saved lives. The defences on this ridge would not be enough without the evacuation of so many men from the city. He has given us a chance to stem the xenos here when they come.'

'You think these men who heard you today will stand when the greenskins come again? You cannot be everywhere at once, Kastor. What will your congregation say now that they disperse? Will enough men take heart from the stories that spread from your words?'

'They will say they saw one of the God-Emperor's chosen,' Kastor replied simply.

'And that doesn't bother you?'

'Should it?'

'Are we the Emperor's chosen, brother? I have certainly never found any particular divine spark to us, not when I have studied the physiology of our kind. There is no noble grace when I saw off limbs and suture flesh and try to restart twin hearts. We are brute meat, my brother, changed beyond recognition to fulfil a single purpose – the role of the warrior. We are no different from the vat-grown of Mars, or any machine that is crafted and optimised to fulfil a single, specific purpose. We are certainly no more divine than those men around us. In fact, perhaps we are less so. Do you not teach that mankind's glory is in the very nature of its humanity? As a medicae, I would hesitate to call either of us human. Not any more.'

'You are angry,' Kastor said, his voice growing quiet. 'And that makes you churlish, brother. I will forget what you are saying here, for both our sakes.'

'You think I am saying this only to annoy you, little brother? You think me so petty?'

'I think you normally have a clearer mind than I, Polixis. I invite you to use that mind to question where these words are coming from. Turn your thoughts inwards, and consider that it is this past day's pain and loss that is speaking, not you.'

Polixis drew in a deep breath rather than reply and forced himself to consider the Chaplain's counsel. A part of him already knew Kastor was right. Another part wanted to refuse that realisation. He wondered how often they had done this as children, arrayed in frustrated opposition to one another.

'The loss of the brother-captain has affected me,' Polixis admitted, speaking slowly now as the anger drained from him, little by little. 'The loss of all the battle-brothers on this campaign has been a hard burden to bear. You know that none of them sit quietly with me. I have sought to better honour my role as this company's Apothecary by distancing myself, but even after all this time...'

He trailed off. Kastor picked up the words.

'You would not be a better Apothecary if you did manage to distance yourself from those under your charge, that much I can assure you. Your very nature is what has led you to this role. It is a blessing and a curse – a curse because you feel each and every loss so acutely, but a blessing because you will never stop striving to help those in need. Your role is the hardest of anyone in the brotherhood. We are all warriors. As you say, we have been bred for it. Yet you alone are expected to set aside the mindset of a trained killer to help and to heal. It is your protective nature that allows you to do that. Never feel the need to quash that. If you felt nothing for our fallen, I would be far more concerned.'

Polixis nodded. 'My thanks, brother. I had to say that.'

'You are not alone,' Kastor replied. 'Do not forget that. We all feel the past day's losses. It is to be expected – each of the fallen was an exemplar of the Chapter. It is my duty to ensure that we all continue without surrendering to darker passions – bitterness, guilt, unchannelled rage.'

'I do not envy you your position, Brother-Chaplain,' Polixis said, offering his arm once more.

'Nor I yours, Brother-Apothecary,' Kastor answered, taking him by the vambrace. 'The xenos will come again, and soon I fear. When they do, go with care. I was speaking the truth when I said we cannot afford to lose you now as well.'

'I would demand the same of you,' Polixis said. 'But I know I will find you wherever the fighting is hardest.'

'We all do the Emperor's will, one way or another,' Kastor replied, and Polixis had known him long enough to be certain that there was a smile playing out behind the death-grin of his skull helm.

'I will see you again soon, brother.'

URGORK

Urgork looked around at the vaults and statues that constituted the humie's shrine-thing. Cogkrusha had told him they called such a place a 'kathedral'. Supposedly, it was the place where their big boss watched over them. There was no sign of him now though, much to Urgork's chagrin. No humies at all, in fact. They'd all run, like the weak, pink little runties they were.

The warboss was standing with one boot on the side of the overturned stone slab that had formerly held pride of place in the echoing chamber. Beneath him the mobs were already busy turning the structure into a place worthy of their warboss' presence. The statues were being hauled down and

BLOOD OF IAX

smashed, and the walls and pillars were being daubed with blood and dung. Nob Scabit's lads were erecting a great ork skull glyph over the shattered windows at the rear of the chamber – Mork only knew where they'd scavenged it from.

Most important of all were Urgork's own trophies. The stone slab was being refashioned by Cogkrusha and his tinkerers, the arching ceiling above resounding to the noise of chisel-drills and welding hammers as they drove spikes and staves into the defiled white stone, fashioning a new throne for Urgork. Already the great red-daubed squighide of his personal banner had been draped above it, and his trophy rack had been laid out before it, the dead eyes and empty sockets of the warboss' vanquished challengers afforded a fine view of the greenskin occupation of the great building.

Even more important were the latest additions to Urgork's spoils. The blue beakies had fought long and hard – whole mobs had been immolated by their blazing fires, and Urgork's own body still ached from the wounds he had suffered at the hands of their boss. If his own nob bodyguards hadn't outnumbered the beakies by so much, the fight may have even gone against the warboss. In the end, though, it was the big beakie lying dead, and not the other way around. The corpses of the defiant warriors – each as big and tough as the largest of Urgork's mob leaders – had been dragged to the warlord's new lair, their blue armour caked in dust and blood and defiled by markings carved in by their killers. Urgork was still deciding what to do with them, but for now they made a fine display at the foot of his new throne.

He'd also ordered part of the kathedral's wall to be demolished to make room for the huge tank the humies had been using – the machine bits that had allowed it to float seemed to have failed, but some makeshift runners fashioned from girders dragged from the city ruins, combined with the exertions of a trio of ork Deff Dreads, had hauled the thing through the rubble all the way to Urgork's headquarters. The warlord had told Cogkrusha in no uncertain terms that he had to complete the new throne before he would be permitted to lay hands upon the captured war machine. He could practically feel the big mek's excitement buzzing in the air around him.

'Boss?'

Urgork grunted, tearing his eyes away from the stone slab and the welder-masked grots labouring around it. Stabskar had approached unnoticed, as he so often did. The kommando's second in command, Grimtoof, was hovering close behind him, eyes darting between the warlord and his more immediate boss.

'You wanted me, boss?' Stabskar went on. He was trying to act unconcerned, but Urgork could smell the fear on him like the stink of grot piss.

'Stabskar,' the warboss growled, straightening up to his full height, so that he loomed over the two kommandos. 'You done good securin' this place. It's gonna be the 'eadquarters til the last humies outside the city has been crumped.'

'Tha–' Stabskar began, but Urgork carried on over him.

'I didn't tell ya to find dis place though, did I, Stabba?'

Again Stabskar tried to speak, and again Urgork continued without listening.

'What did I tell ya to find, Stabba? Tell me what I sent you after?' Stabskar went silent, his eyes now on his spiked boots.

'The beakie, boss,' he said quietly.

'Which beakie, Stabba?'

'The beakie in white, boss. You wanted da beakie in white bits.'

'Exactly,' Urgork said, smacking one hand down on Stab-skar's shoulder, making the kommando grunt. 'Ex-actly, Stabba. I gots me plenty of beakies in the end…' He paused to gesture expansively at the mound of corpses dumped at the base of his slowly forming throne. 'But what colour is they all, Stabba?'

Stabskar hesitated, choking on his words as he tried to avoid the obvious.

'Oh look,' Urgork said, taking his hand off the ork's shoulder and bending to drag one claw through the dust and blood caking one of the humie's armour, leaving a clear trail. He turned sharply back and bellowed in Stabskar's face, a wad of phlegm splattering the stunned greenskin.

'They's blue, Stabba! All of 'em! No white 'uns!'

'W-we looked, boss,' Stabskar managed, cringing back.

'And you found 'im, didn't you?' Urgork demanded. Stabskar had no reply, and the bigger ork went on. 'You found 'im and you let 'im leg it. Yeah, I was told all about dat.'

Stabskar turned towards Grimtoof, still lurking behind him, sudden anger replacing the fear in his eyes. Urgork snatched him again before he could fully round on his subordinate and dragged him in close.

'I gave you one job,' the warboss snarled. 'So now you gets the reward comin' to you. Doc!'

The final word echoed through the vaulted chamber. It was followed by a scampering noise as Grok emerged from behind the apse, hauling his squig-satchel full of saw blades and needles.

'My injekshun, doc,' Urgork demanded, holding out one hand while keeping Stabskar clamped in the other. The kommando began to struggle, but it was too late – without pause Urgork snatched the heavy syringe Grok offered and plunged it into Stabskar's thick neck. Grinning darkly, the warboss jabbed the plunger down.

The effect was instantaneous. Stabskar gasped and choked, both hands gripping Urgork's arm as his eyes began to bulge. A mewling noise escaped his throat, and foam started bubbling from between his tusks. Urgork released him and pushed him towards the steps of the raised stone slab. The kommando fell to his knees on the edge, hands now clutching his throat, and released a great heaving explosion of vomit. It hit the steps and the flagstones below, making the nearest orks beneath push and shove one another to avoid it. The bile darkened rapidly, and the lumps floating in it thickened – Stabskar's eyes were wide with agony as he continued to throw up parts of his liquidating internal organs, blood and mulched stomach following pieces of lung and his intestines. He voided his bowels as well, and the flood from his maw lessened abruptly as his throat gave way beneath the acidic flow, disintegrating and drenching his chest.

Finally, the greenskin collapsed forwards, rolling down the stairs, covering himself in his own dissolved innards. He came to a stop at the bottom, face down in the steaming, slowly spreading slurry, twitching as the syringe's contents ate away the last of his guts.

Silence reigned. Every greenskin in the chamber had stopped and was staring at Stabskar's corpse as it slowly became still.

'Can't take 'is medicine,' Urgork grunted, smacking the empty syringe back into Grok's satchel and shoving the painboy away. The warboss glared at the mass of orks below, and kicked a boot against the corpse of one of the blue beakies, the clatter making everyone jump.

'Who said you could stop workin', ya gits?' he demanded.

The orks hurried to look busy again as Urgork turned towards Grimtoof. The kommando had been trying to slink away unnoticed, but froze under Urgork's gaze.

'Got somewhere betta to be?' the warboss demanded.

'No, boss,' Grimtoof replied, shaking his head vigorously. Urgork grunted and moved down the steps to the side of Stabskar's corpse, boots splashing in the foul, steaming patina that had drenched the flagstones. He yanked the ork's soiled camo cape from the body and tossed it to Grimtoof, who caught it with a grimace. He then gripped Stabskar's remains by the scruff of the neck and dragged him back up the stairs, through his own fluids, until he was slumped over the stone slab. Urgork waved Cogkrusha and his grot workers away with one hand, drawing one of his skinnin' blades with the other.

'This is a good way to break da new boss chair in, ain't it?' he asked Grimtoof. The kommando simply nodded, dripping cape in one fist, staring as the warboss plunged the blade into the flank of his erstwhile boss and began slowly peeling back a layer of tough green hide.

'You is da boss of Stabba's mob now, Grim,' Urgork went on, working his blade slowly and methodically just beneath Stabskar's flesh, stripping it away little by little as he flensed the torso back to oozing, part-liquefied muscle.

'Yes, boss,' Grimtoof said quietly, watching with horrified fascination as the warboss worked.

'Same orders,' Urgork said, not taking his eye from his blade's progress. 'Find da white beakie. Bring 'im here, alive. Reckon you can do dat?'

'Yes, boss,' Grimtoof said again.

'Send out grots,' Urgork said, gripping a section of flesh with his free hand and dragging it back. Blood and jellied matter was drenching the white stone slab beneath Stab-skar's now-ragged corpse, running down to pool beneath the mound of beakie dead piled before it. 'Use your sneaky lads. You know 'em. I'm sendin' Zograk to attack the humies outside the city tonight. Go in wiv 'is lads and get me dat zoggin' beakie. If you don't… don't come back.'

'Gotcha, boss,' Grimtoof said, still staring at the gruesome work. Urgork half turned the corpse over, continuing to slide his long blade with a short, firm skimming motion. The warboss paused and looked up, glaring at the remaining kommando.

'You still 'ere?'

Grimtoof turned and left hastily, boots splashing in Stab-skar's effluvium, as the great skull glyph being erected by Scabit's mob finally thumped into place.

GRIMTOOF

Outside the warboss' new lair, more greenskins were gathering, filling the ruined square with raucous tribal chants and the growling, revving engines of the war trucks that now choked what remained of the adjacent streets. The rest of the kommandos were crouched on the steps close to the big spiky building's broken-down entrance, and they gathered around Grimtoof as he stepped out.

'Where's da boss?' Krulkil asked.

'Dead,' Grimtoof said, baring his tusks. 'He failed da big boss too many times. I'm in charge of dis 'ere mob now. Big Boss' orders. Any git what complains can take it up with 'im, right once he's done makin' a new banner from Stabba's hide.'

There was no response from the assembled greenskins. Grimtoof looked at each in turn, but none met his gaze – even without knowing the exact details of what had happened to Stabskar, the threat of Urgork's displeasure was enough. He wrung the stinking bile from the former boss' ragged cape and, with all due ceremony, draped it over his own shoulders before speaking again.

'Same job as before. He wants da white beakie boy. Dis time we're gonna get it done. I ain't endin' up like Stabba.'

'How we findin' 'im though, boss?' Urgin asked. 'All the humies are gone. He could be anywhere by now.'

'Humies is just to da east,' Grimtoof said. 'We'll send out da grots. Dorken and Krulkil, you make sure they do it right. All these lads are 'eaded for a scrap tonight.' He gestured at the mobs filling the square. More were still pouring in, drawn to the new seat of power now established by their warboss. They'd won a great victory the day before, and now they were hungry for more. Grimtoof could feel the power of the Waaagh! suffusing the very air around him, making it practically crackle with energy. The sound and fury of so many good lads gathered together made the very stones of the ruined city vibrate. The urge to get stuck in was almost overwhelming. They were kommandos, though. They played it cleverer than the footsloggas.

'We'll go in under cover of da assault,' he went on. 'Probably be dark too, so dat'll help. Once the grots have 'im fixed, we're in an' out sharpish. Big boss wants da git alive, so no mistakes, or we's all squigfood. Stick close and keep a good eye out. Got it?'

The rest of the mob grunted their affirmation. Grimtoof turned his gaze back to the mobs below, as the chanting and bellowing reached a bestial, heart-pounding crescendo. Despite himself, he realised he was grinning.

One way or another, they were headed for a right good scrap.

CHAPTER FIVE   THE BATTLE OF RIDGE 1

HANLON

Darkness was falling, and with it the storm had died. Lieutenant Hanlon shifted the focus ring on the bulky Munitorum-issue magnoculars she carried, zooming in on a shallow depression in the ash dunes directly ahead of her position. Something was moving out in the gathering dusk, a black mark on the featureless grey ashscape. The Namarian pressed her comm-bead's transmission stud.

'Possible contact, twelve o'clock, one thousand yards out. Standby.'

The rest of the six-man reconnaissance team acknowledged with silent double-taps of their bead mics. Hanlon shifted slightly, her body pressed against the warm, dry earth, settling her grip on the magnoculars. They'd been in position for three hours, Terran standard, ever since relieving the last of the day's piquets – a platoon of Faeburn Vanquishers. The six Namarians were flat to the earth and spaced out over a hundred yards, capes draped over their bodies and doused with liberal amounts of the ash surrounding them. In the lengthening shadows and dust-hazed air, they were almost totally indistinguishable from the ground they occupied.

They'd had over a dozen minor contacts already, all of them small, wiry greenskin slave-creatures scurrying through the wasteland ahead. Sergeant Rakin, Hanlon's second, thought they were just scavengers come from the city, but Hanlon suspected their presence was more sinister – to her, their activities looked like the work of spotters or scouts.

She shifted the magnoculars back over the zone where she'd spotted movement, seeking out a hard fix. Behind her, a sound like a thunderclap rang out, followed by two more. A series of distant thudding noises followed, and light flared briefly across the wasteland. She didn't look back. She knew she was hearing the sound of aircraft and the detonation of their bombs along the ridgeline to the recon unit's rear. The moment the worst of the ash storm had lifted, the dust-choked heavens had filled with crude ork planes. Hanlon had heard rumours that the Navy had abandoned Ikara's orbit to a xenos armada, and half of the aircraft that should have been denying the greenskins air superiority were still in the launch bays of void warships now on the other side of the system.

All of which was why Hanlon had been relieved when Colonel Ruthers had assigned the recon company to piquet duty. Even if it took them closer to the alien horde that had stormed Shebat, at least they were no longer stationed on Ridge 1 while the bombs rained down. The aerial attacks were little more than a distraction down among the scrap and ash that stretched out between the ridge and the edge of Shebat's ruined slums.

The gretchin were an altogether more immediate problem. She caught sight of the thing she'd seen earlier thanks to the magnoculars' light-amplifying filter – it was diminutive and hunched over as it scurried from one rock to the next. It also appeared to be carrying something. Hanlon was sure she caught the glimmer of a lense. She cursed softly. They were definitely scouts.

'Contact confirmed,' she murmured into the comm-bead. 'Markel?'

'Target acquired,' the sharpshooter responded over the link. 'Take the shot.'

A crack echoed out over the ash. Hanlon saw the greenskin runt twist as it ran, a puff of blood and viscera – curiously devoid of sound at such a distance – flashing across the lieutenant's view before the thing went down. It didn't move again.

'Target eliminated,' Hanlon breathed. 'Good shot, Marks.'

'Notch another one up, Vorn,' Markel murmured in response. Hanlon felt Vorn, the squad's other marksman, bristle. They were both armed with Mark VII Zerstran long rifles, hard round, silenced. Both had turned the piquet duty into an unofficial competition over who could pick off more of the little hook-nosed aliens.

'More ammunition expended per killshot,' Vorn grumbled. *'I could take out a dozen green runts as well if I blew through five magazines at a time.'*

Hanlon hushed Markel before he could respond to the accusation. She wanted to check in on their transport.

'*Battlewrath*, this is Viper One. Are you still in position, over?'

'Viper One, Battlewrath. *Still holding in sector five. Just say the word.'*

The voice of *Battlewrath*, the unit's Chimera armoured personnel carrier, was some sort of comfort at least. If things went south, they could withdraw back to the ridgeline at speed. They'd need to, if the artillery newly sited along the long ash rise started dropping shells.

There was another thunderclap, and Hanlon's ears filled with the sudden, aching roar of supersonic engines. She allowed herself to half turn and caught a glimpse of a trio of cruciform shapes whipping through the darkening skies further east. Imperial Navy Thunderbolts, climbing into an interceptor run on the greenskin bombers speckling the dust clouds higher up. Earlier she'd seen an ork fighter peeling away, one engine ablaze, pluming foul black smoke as it twisted into a death-dive south of the recon team's position. It had struck the ground amidst a blossoming fireball, the explosion reaching Hanlon's ears long seconds after the distant flash of light. She hadn't spotted a chute. She doubted the greenskins fitted their aircraft with any sort of escape precautions anyway.

More Imperial fighters rocketed overhead, Lightnings this time, lower and faster. They were there and gone in a bang of displaced air, and it took a great deal of effort for the Namarian not to sit up to see their targets above the ridge to her back. She could hear the distant staccato thudding of Hydra anti-aircraft batteries intermingled with the deeper notes of the bombing run detonations – despite the onset of night, it seemed like the greenskin's aerial bombardment was only intensifying. She checked her wrist chrono. They only had fifteen more minutes before sundown, and then the last of what little light was penetrating Ikara IX's dust-shrouded atmosphere would be gone.

Another greenskin aircraft ploughed into the wasteland, further north. This time it was a bomber, and the detonation when its payload went up caused a small mushroom cloud of flame and black smoke to flare into existence. Hanlon felt the earth beneath her tremor as the shock waves from the impact travelled through the shifting, unstable ash. She caught more movement, this time a little to the south, on the edge of the sector being watched by a tribe-team of Tmaran Scalp-takers. Another damned greenskin spotter. She was about to call it in when she realised something was out of place.

The tremors from the downed bomber hadn't dissipated.

She paused, making sure she was right, then tapped the comm-link.

'Anyone else still feeling that?'

'*The ash is shifting,*' Wylk, the team's vox-operator, responded.

'*Subterranean activity?*' Vorn said.

'*Wait, listen,*' Crevin replied. Hanlon paused and held her breath, straining for whatever sound the team's pathfinder had picked up. It didn't take her long to hear it too – beneath the distant thudding of flak guns and the bass crumps of explosions, a noise like a swelling ocean was steadily rising. As it continued to increase in volume so too did the tremors running beneath the Guardsmen. She felt a shudder slip up her spine as she realised what she was hearing.

The roaring of thousands of throats, and the pounding of thousands of boots. It was the sound of an army of savages on the move, and it was drawing closer.

She snapped her magnoculars back up and trained them directly west of the recon team's position. Darkness had shrouded the vague, jagged line that demarcated the ruins that had once been Shebat's most easterly slums, but with the viewfinder set to maximum Hanlon could see shapes moving out beyond the city's remains. Not the lone, skittish motions of one or two gretchin, but the churning mass of a wall of bodies, stampeding east. Directly towards her section.

'Great Namara's golden hair,' she cursed. 'Wylk, get on the vox and get me the officer of the watch. Now!'

KASTOR

The commanders of the Fulminata – those who yet lived – had gathered in the shadow of General Chevik's headquarters to assess their new position. Kastor had seen Field Marshal Klos arrive at the fortified enviro-dome two hours earlier, coming from Fifth Corps' dispositions further north. Tyranus had already spoken with the field marshal and Chevik again in private. Now, as Klos called a general briefing of all his remaining corps commanders, Tyranus did the same with his brother Primaris.

Besides Kastor, four of the brotherhood's five surviving sergeants were present – only Sergeant Nerva was elsewhere, left in command of the squads holding the short stretch of the line at the heart of Ridge 1. Severus was there too, the grim skull helms of both the Reiver and Kastor ensuring those Guardsmen stationed close to Chevik's tent gave the transhuman assembly a wide berth. Polixis had been offered a space at the briefing, but had elected to continue working back at the main medicae hub set to the ridge's rear.

The others were gathered in a circle, helmets clamped to their hips, bolters locked across thighs or chests, waiting on the word of Lieutenant Tyranus.

'There has been no word from Brother-Captain Demeter,' he said.

'May the Emperor guide and watch over his worthy soul,' Kastor said.

Tyranus nodded before continuing. 'That being the case, it is my duty to assume complete command of the Fulminata until such times as the captain is recovered, or his death is confirmed.'

'The Codex supports your appointment,' Lieutenant Samson said firmly, nodding across the circle to Tyranus. 'The captain's final orders were clear, and his sacrifice will not be in vain. Our new defensive lines here will allow us to check this fresh xenos invasion.'

'Agreed, lieutenant,' Tyranus said. 'Nonetheless, we must prepare for the worst. I am ordering the rest of the demi-company to maintain its cohesion from now on. We were weakened in Shebat because we spread our strength too widely. Even if it helped us preserve the Guard during the withdrawal, we were unable to land a telling blow against the xenos. That will not be the case when they come again.'

'But for how long are we expected to maintain these positions?' Sergeant Valorious asked. 'High command must be aware of the situation here. We are overextended, still disorganised and heavily outnumbered.'

'There are reinforcements coming from Kroten,' Tyranus said. 'But it will be at least a day before they arrive, and a number more before they are fully deployed. We must be the bulwark until then.'

Kastor assessed Tyranus as he briefed his sergeants. He had few doubts about the lieutenant's new command, and yet it was inevitable that it should feel strange, almost sacrilegious. Demeter was not long unaccounted for, and beneath the veneer of a standard situational briefing, Kastor could sense the pain of each and every one of the Ultramarines present. All wished they had been at the captain's side when he had taken his stand.

'Do we know the strength of the reinforcements on their way?' Domitian asked.

'Von Klimt has not been forthcoming with exact figures. I suspect the numbers will not be sufficient to launch a counter-attack, but they should be enough to stabilise the front. Simply put, that is our primary strategic objective. If we stop the greenskin warlord here it will give Imperial forces on Ikara the time to redeploy, and if that is achieved it in turn allows the rest of the subsector to shift its weight to this system. At worst, Urgork's new momentum will be halted, at best he will be trapped and killed. But first we must hold this ridge.'

'What about the situation in orbit?' Sergeant Klastis asked. 'Is it true the fleet has completely disengaged?'

'It is. To the best of our knowledge, the Imperial Navy are currently holding station on the system's spinward edge. The *Spear of Macragge* is with them. They are waiting on reinforcements before contesting orbit. That means the xenos are in complete control of Ikara IX's anchorage for the foreseeable future. It's a reality we are simply going to have to accept for the time being. Expect them to assert their air superiority over the next few days.'

'They've withdrawn for now, though,' Domitian pointed out, glancing skywards. There had been no sign of the alien aircraft that had first fallen on them just a few hours earlier.

'They are likely refitting,' Tyranus said. 'Let us pray that remains the case.'

'Do we have a holding point for our own casualties now that extraction to the *Spear of Macragge* is impossible?' Valorious asked. 'And are our own Thunderhawks and Overlords going to continue to operate out of the Korten airfields?'

As the others spoke, Kastor watched Samson. Aside from his opening support for Tyranus, the lieutenant hadn't spoken since the start of the briefing. His endorsement had been fit and proper – Tyranus' seniority was unambiguous, and the character of both officers suited their new roles. Tyranus had always modelled himself after Demeter. Now that respect could help mould him into the commander the Fulminata needed.

For his own part, Samson had never progressed beyond the role of a competent second, and Kastor wondered sometimes whether he ever would. He was large and stoic, and few could best him gladius to gladius in the sparring pits. He was the very image of a praetorian of ancient Macragge, with his heavy features and short, curled blond hair. His silence, however, betrayed the truth behind his deference – he preferred enacting the orders of others rather than issuing them, at least on a company-wide level. Kastor didn't doubt he would be an excellent second for Tyranus, but if the first lieutenant were to become a casualty, the situation might warrant Kastor's own intervention.

'Communications from the piquet line to the west,' Sergeant Faustus said abruptly, interrupting Tyranus' response to his sergeants. The Ultramarines had unrestricted access to all the channels and frequencies being used by the Astra Militarum. Faustus automatically pinged the correct signal to the rest of the assembled Ultramarines. Kastor listened as a thickly accented Namarian voice blurted over the priority communications band.

'Repeat, greenskin incursion from the west! They're coming!'

More voices overlaid it, confirmation from the piquet units all along the line pouring in. A full-scale xenos assault was rolling from the city towards Ridge 1. Kastor turned west, towards Shebat. The dusk and the ash obscured his view, but he swore he could detect a tremor in the earth and a tidal roar on the air. His fist clenched unconsciously around his crozius arcanum's worn grip.

'The piquet line is withdrawing,' Faustus said. 'Field Marshal Klos is issuing a full stand-to.'

'Assemble with your squads, battle-brothers,' Tyranus said, unclamping his helm. 'This time there will be no retreat.'

HANLON

Hanlon and her recon team ran for their lives.

The pounding of their boots against the dry earth was punctuated by the whip-crack of multilaser fire as the Chimera they were racing towards sent covering fire streaking over their heads, punching pursuing greenskins off their feet and splattering the ash with dark blood. Hanlon smacked her palm against the shoulder of Sergeant Rakin, the Namarian crouching just feet from the transport's open rear hatch, blazing away at the charging xenos with his rifle on semi-automatic.

Transports from the forward observation posts had raced up, ash and dust churning from their tracks, providing a means of exfiltration. It was as Hanlon and her men had raced for their Chimera that things had started to go wrong – the lead elements of the onrushing ork wave began blazing away with their inaccurate firearms, and shells from the artillery positions embedded into Ridge 1 began hammering down just a few hundred yards from the withdrawing piquet line. Great blossoms of ash and dirt, scattered with gory shreds of xenos meat, burst across the line, the initial impacts throwing the whole recon team to the ground.

It was carnage, and Hanlon's team were in the midst of it.

'Go!' Hanlon bellowed at Rakin, her voice barely audible over the Chimera's engines and the frenzied bellowing of thousands of onrushing aliens. Rakin rose and ran alongside her, both Guardsmen pounding up the Chimera's access ramp and into the tight, bare metal troop compartment.

'All in, *Battlewrath*!' Wylk was already shouting into the vehicle's intercom unit. 'Get us out of here!'

The rear hatch began to rise even as the armoured personnel carrier turned sharply east, the recon team inside flung unceremoniously against the fold-down benches to one side of the hold.

'On the las arrays,' Hanlon shouted over the roar of the transport's engines, grabbing the overhead rail before she was thrown down. The rest of the squad snatched at the stocks of the lasguns built into the Chimera's hull, the troop benches acting as a low firing step as they angled them downwards and started to fire.

Hanlon peered out of the armourglass vision slit in the Chimera's rear. The narrow view showed only a horde of greenskins and the ash cloud kicked up from the transport's tracks. Gunfire flared in the gloom, and she heard the sharp crack of rounds ricocheting from the vehicle's ramp and rear armour. A flurry of bright las-beams streaked back into the oncoming mob – the turret multilaser had been rotated a hundred and eighty degrees.

For a second, the lieutenant felt a surge of relief. They were pulling away from the ork charge now, and the dust was beginning to shroud them. Just a few more minutes and they'd be hitting the base of Ridge 1, under the cover of Imperial lines.

The moment of reprieve didn't last long. The panicked voice of the Chimera's driver blurted over the intercom.

'*Contact right, contact right!*'

Hanlon just had time to register the words before she heard a loud clang from the right-hand side of the hull.

'They're right outside!' Vorn screamed, still firing his hull lasgun. 'Throne! Where did they come from?'

Nobody answered. The Chimera pitched suddenly to the left, hard. Hanlon lost her grip on the overhead rail and grunted as she slammed into the side of the hold. At the same moment, a detonation slammed through the transport, like a hammer striking an anvil, shuddering the whole vehicle and making the Namarian's ears ring. Hanlon reached for the troop bench, trying to right herself, dazed and sluggish. She touched her brow and realised she was bleeding from a gash above her left eye. Smoke was filling the hold, stinking and black.

'We're not moving,' Markel said groggily. 'Why have we stopped?'

Only then did Hanlon, her head spinning, realise that they'd come to a standstill.

Wylk found his feet first. He banged the exit rune, coughing as more smoke poured into the hold. The rear ramp dropped, thudding down into ash churned by the Chimera's tracks. Hanlon saw immediately that those tracks were no more – the blast had scattered broken links from the right-hand runner across the dusty earth.

'Out,' she managed to bark, scrambling to her feet and down the fallen ramp. Initially, she could see nothing amidst the churning ash. Her world had been reduced to the filmy lenses of her goggles and the rattle and scrape of her respirator mask. She spun back towards the Chimera and saw the scorch marks all along its right side. Something had clamped on to its flank and detonated, leaving the vehicle useless and immobile. That wasn't Hanlon's most immediate concern, though.

There were greenskins attacking the Chimera's crew compartment. Even at a glance Hanlon could see they weren't like regular orks. They moved hunched low to the ground and were clad in what looked like the ragged, dusty approximation of her team's recon capes and spotting goggles. One had used what looked like a lascutter combined with a welder to sear a hole in the flank of the Chimera's forward section, and now others were dragging the hapless crew out into the ash.

Battlewrath's commander was screaming horrifically as one of the grunting aliens crudely butchered him with a huge cleaver, and two others had grasped the driver and were physically tearing him limb from limb. Hanlon stared in horror as she saw flesh and blood-sodden fatigues rip, exposing still-pulsing organs and white bone. As she stood rooted to the spot, one of the greenskins turned to her, peering through its heavy scrap goggles.

It pointed a claw at her and bellowed.

'Go!' Hanlon shouted. 'Go, go, go!'

The recon team ran, past the opposite side of the Chimera. The orks came bounding after them, letting out bestial cries and firing their slug weapons indiscriminately. One round thumped into the ash just ahead of Hanlon and another plucked at her camo cape as she ran. A part of her – drilled by the memory of her commissar's furious orders – wanted to turn back and open fire. She thrust the suicidal thought aside. *Battlewrath*'s crew were dead, and the rest of the greenskin attack was bearing down on them. She wasn't even sure exactly which way she was running any more.

'We're dead,' Vorn was panting over the link. 'We're *dead.*'

'Keep going,' Hanlon snarled. 'Or I'll kill you myself.'

Another shell screamed down and detonated nearby, showering them with dust and dirt. Hanlon forcing herself to focus through it all, kit bouncing as she ran, breath rasping through her rebreather mask. If she got just one member of her team out, she decided, her own death would be worthwhile.

Hoping for anything more now seemed like asking for a miracle.

KASTOR

Kastor paced the redoubt line. The firing step beside him was manned by ranks of Guardsmen, lasrifles laid out across the sandbag parapet, file after file rendered faceless and identical by the pall of ash kicked up by the artillery. The Chaplain could sense the heady mixture of emotions that so affected mortal men about to enter a combat situation – the stiff, quivering postures that betrayed anticipation, terror and a nervous, infectious excitement.

For his own part Kastor felt no such emotions. His thoughts ran two parallel paths. One was cold, firm, a subconscious focused on an overly familiar pre-battle cant – his bolter was blessed and loaded, Salve Imperator had been anointed, his armour's servos and power plant were functioning at optimum levels with a full integrity readout, and the displays running across his auto-senses – the burst map, vox transcriptions, chronometer, ammunition counter, vitae signs and squad location and status markers – were all activated.

The other path, his more conscious train of thought, was fiery and filled with the bitter taste of revenge. He could feel the combat stimms and adrenaline pumping through his limbs, making them ache with readiness. The thudding of his twin heartbeats, battering at the back of his breastplate, was a potent reminder of both vitality and mortality. While even one continued to beat he would fight on in the name of the Chapter and the Emperor. Memories from the day before, of

Demeter's sacrifice and the ignominy of withdrawal, made the Chaplain's hold on his weapons tighten. They had known the xenos would come again. Today would be the reckoning every Ultramarine here prayed for. His armour's servos grated with the strength of his grip, and it was all he could do to stop himself from unleashing a bellow of battle-lust.

Control. He was an Ultramarine, a loyal and humble servant of his Chapter and the Imperium. He would not sully his rank or his brotherhood with the savagery and mindlessness so often exhibited by lesser warriors. Though he had been forged for war, it would not consume him. He would channel it instead.

'Look to your weapons, soldiers of the God-Emperor,' he called out, his powerful voice booming through the redoubts and sandbag embankments. 'Recite the litanies of loading, readiness and accuracy. Listen for your officers and sergeants, and if they are lost, trust in your bayonets and the guidance of the Emperor.'

The words came easily. He sensed the soldiers he passed standing a little taller and firmer as they faced out towards the foot of the ridge. A few even dared snatch a glance back at the skull-helmed giant in the black battleplate. Kastor did not rebuke them. His armour and vestments were in themselves a sacred symbol of the Emperor's vengeful judgement, and to witness them on the brink of combat was a blessing that those who fought in His name were worthy of. He had no right to deny them.

'Yesterday we were dishonoured,' he continued as he walked. 'Yesterday we were defeated. But today, our absolution is at hand. Now is the time for vengeance. Now is the time to cover our shame with xenos blood, to crush it beneath the weight of alien corpses. We will make yesterday a footnote in the annals of Imperial history. Today we break the greenskins, here, on this ridge. Today is the victory future generations will speak of.'

He passed in front of an artillery section, the Earthshakers embedded just to the rear of the secondary redoubts. The whole world seemed to shudder every time they fired, causing dust to leap from the sandbags all around. Kastor didn't delete the percussive thunder with his Lyman's Ear, instead using it to modulate his helm's vox-speakers. Not even battling directly beneath the thunder of the artillery would drown out the words of one of the Emperor's Chaplains.

'Soldiers of the Imperial Guard, do not take a backward step. With your lasguns you will slay the alien, but with your faith and your courage you will reconquer this entire world. The Ultramarines will be there with you when you do. Stand and fight with us, for the glory of the Emperor and the Imperium, for the honour of your regiments and for the future of Ikara.'

On he went as he walked the line, slowly and firmly, voice clear over the crash of the big guns. The litany only ceased when he came to a section of redoubt manned by the Intercessors of Squad Faustus. The sergeant acknowledged him with the Primaris salute, two gauntlets across his chest. His battle-brothers stood on the redoubt's floor, each with one foot up on the firing step steadying them, their height allowing them to see over it without needing to leave the ground.

'We didn't have time to heighten it after we took it over,' Faustus said, indicating the sandbag parapet.

'It will be enough,' Kastor said. 'I am more concerned about the rest of the line. Our spacing is short.'

Faustus said nothing, glancing along to the next Ultramarines position. It was held by Domitian's Hellblasters, and there was less than a hundred yards of redoubt between it and Faustus. Kastor had no doubt the Zoishen infantry in between them would hold, but he was less sure about the long reaches of the ridge where there were no Primaris to bolster the Astra Militarum soldiers. Tyranus' decision to concentrate the demi-company's remains at the heart of the Imperial defences would create an unassailable bulwark, but supporting the flanks would be almost impossible.

'Reinforcements are inbound from Kroten,' Faustus said. 'If we can maintain the integrity of the line's centre through the night...' he trailed off. Kastor slapped a gauntlet against his pauldron and nodded.

'Not a backward step, my brother. I will see you again soon enough, I am sure.'

The Chaplain carried on down the line, while around him, the first spotters dotted along the redoubts identified contacts out in the ash haze.

POLIXIS

'Great father of the endless skies, if I should this day die, see me to your holy side, that I may bring Tmara pride.'

Polixis stood with Squad Valorious on the western extreme of the section of ridge held by the Ultramarines, and listened to the traditional death poems being murmured by the Tmaran brigade holding their flanks. Behind them was a regiment of Voitekans stationed in reserve, and then a battery of Kelestan Manticores that were sending shrieking hails of rockets overhead into the haze, detonating among unseen targets below.

'Contacts,' Brother Gallus said over the vox. The Ultramarine's auto-senses had detected motion amidst the ash shroud, stripping it back and identifying movement patterns long before the humans on either side were capable of spotting anything.

'Good eyes, Gallus, standby,' Sergeant Valorious replied. Polixis moved to Gallus' side, looking out at the open expanse of grey tundra stretching away from the foot of the ridge. There was something out there, but his own visor couldn't get a fix. The slowly gathering Ikaran night was making visibility even worse.

He glanced at Gallus. The Intercessor had taken a heavy ork slug round through the shoulder in Shebat just before the final push for the Excelsior Arch. Polixis had removed it, and the Primaris showed no signs of impairment a day on. Only his pauldron indicated that he'd been wounded – there had been no time to patch the jagged, silver rent punched in the curving blue ceramite.

The throaty voice of a Tmaran tribe-officer crackled over the vox, indicating that they too had finally spotted something.

'Hold your fire,' Valorious urged them. 'Follow my directives, Guardsmen, and the day will be ours.'

The primal, swelling roar of the approaching greenskin horde was now audible over the thunder of the ceaseless artillery barrage, fuelling the anticipation of the Ultramarines. Kastor had already passed by on his way along the line, exchanging a few words with Valorious and several other Intercessors. He had said nothing to Polixis, though they had exchanged a warrior's handshake, hand-to-vambrace. After Kastor's sermon earlier that day there was nothing more to be said between them. Polixis' enhanced hearing could still hear his brother's distant words, carrying faith and fury over the storm of war that was gathering along the ridgeline.

'Contacts identified,' Gallus said. 'Astra Militarum.'

'Confirm?' Valorious said. Polixis turned his gaze back out towards the tundra, searching for what Gallus had already seen. After a few seconds it became apparent – figures were visible running through the ash, five in total, clad in the combat capes and light flak-plate of the Namarians.

'A piquet team?' Brother Cassians enquired. All of the other reconnaissance units watching the front had already withdrawn up the ridge to their parent units. For some reason this one had been left behind.

'Their transport must have been hit,' Valorious surmised.

The running Guardsmen hadn't got far before more shapes materialised from out of the darkening pall behind them. These were hunched, brutish. They emerged first in dozens, then hundreds. As Polixis watched, yet more joined them, charging out of the drifting ash bank barely a hundred yards behind the fleeing humans.

'Enemy contacts,' the voice of the Tmaran commander clicked over the link. *'Approaching maximum range. Make ready.'*

'Hold your fire,' Valorious interjected. 'You'll hit those men.' He switched to addressing Lieutenant Tyranus on the command channel, speaking with rapid, clipped efficiency.

'Forward units still in the open in sector thirteen, approximately three hundred yards from the base of the ridgeline. I am taking a detachment to bring them in, pending your orders.'

Waiting only for confirmation that the message had been transmitted, Valorious blink-selected two of his Intercessors – Brothers Vito and Albanius – over the visor display.

'Without those piquets we wouldn't have known about this attack until it was too late. We shall not abandon them. On me.'

The three Primaris pulled themselves up over the parapet

and dropped down on the other side. Polixis went with them. Valorious turned, a warning hand going up to the Apothecary's breastplate.

'Do not risk yourself, brother. This needs to be done quickly.'

'As I recall, I beat your most recent time in the training runs, sergeant. Some of those men are likely injured, and even if they are not, what will you do if you or a member of your squad falls while recovering them? I am coming with you.'

There was no time for debate. Valorious chambered a round in his auto bolt rifle and set off down the slope, voxing that Brother Gallus had command until he returned. Polixis, Vito and Albanius followed, fanning out either side as they went. Their armour struggled in the yielding ash, the stabilisers working hard to keep them upright as they moved as swiftly as possible downhill. Polixis unclamped his Absolver pistol as he went. Beneath him the full weight of the greenskin assault was becoming apparent, spreading left and right as far as the ash cloud permitted him to see.

All along the rest of the line, heavy weapons teams and battle tanks embedded into the ridge opened fire. Heavy bolters and autocannons began battering out streams of tracer-guided hard rounds into the darkening gloom, while missiles, mortar shells and battle cannon rounds tore gaps in the onrushing tide in sudden bursts of dust, steel and ripped green bodies. The section directly ahead and around Squad Valorious, however, remained eerily silent. It felt as though they were descending into the pit of a cauldron, or some sheltered valley removed from the thunder and flashes of the storm that raged amidst the peaks all around.

Polixis heard Valorious give the order to open fire, and the trio of Intercessors either side of the Apothecary began to shoot on the move, their bolt rifles bang-clicking with a steady stream of controlled bursts. The Guardsmen ahead had spotted them and redoubled their efforts, stumbling through the ash as bolt shells whipped past with lethal precision. The greenskins closest behind tumbled down in the dust, skulls and chests pulverised by the detonating rounds.

There was some return fire, but even stationary orks were horrific marksmen – on the move their shots sprayed the air and twitched bursts of ash from the ground, but nothing came close. The Primaris reached the foot of the ridge, the space between them and the recon team closing rapidly.

Then the infantry lining the redoubts on the ridge above opened fire, and the night dissolved in an eye-aching blaze of death.

HANLON

Hanlon knew Wylk was struggling. The vox-operator, weighed down by his kit, had begun falling behind as they ran.

'Give him cover!' Hanlon shouted, forcing herself to slow her pace. She'd barely uttered the words when a crack from the ash swirling about them was followed by the sight of half of Wylk's skull bursting open in a mist of brain and bone.

'Throne damn it!' Hanlon panted, waving for the rest of the squad to keep going.

They carried on, lost in the dust, deafened and disorientated as they stumbled and gasped for breath in their rubbery respirator masks. The pounding of her heart had grown painful in Hanlon's chest, and her muscles burned with unrelenting strain. A little part of her just wanted to collapse, to lie down and let the oncoming beasts trample her. The memory of the Chimera crew's gory fate kept her going.

If not for herself, she had to carry on for the rest of the team. She'd already lost Wylk. She wouldn't let the others down.

Shells screamed from out of the darkness, each detonation shaking the earth underfoot and throwing up more ash to shroud their surroundings. One struck so close that it threw them all to the ground, and Hanlon heard the whicker of shrapnel as it whipped past. A piece of undistinguishable flesh, the blasted remains of one of their pursuers, impacted into the dust beside her as she stumbled back to her feet. They were right behind them.

Then the ash cleared, like a sign from the God-Emperor Himself, and they were out past the worst of the barrage's dust cloud. Ridge 1 reared up before them, bristling with defensive works and weapon emplacements and lit by spotter lights. From somewhere deep inside, Hanlon felt fresh vitality power her limbs, throwing her towards that yearned-for slope and the safety of sandbags and brothers in arms.

As she ran, she could see heavy weapons on the ridge either side opening fire on the wave of orks pouring from the dust, but the positions directly above remained silent. She began to panic, thinking that they'd been abandoned and the recon team would reach the redoubts seconds before the orks punched through an empty gap in the Imperial line. Then she spotted movement, and her mind surged with fresh hope.

Four figures had clambered over the parapets of one of the redoubts. Four giants, clad in heavy armour. Even as she saw them her mind refused to believe what it was witnessing – four members of the Adeptus Astartes, Ultramarines, the God-Emperor's praetorians. They were real after all.

The Space Marines began to move down the slope as the

Namarians neared its base, and Hanlon realised that they were coming to give them close-range covering fire. She threw herself on, vaguely aware of the rest of her squad doing likewise around her. They couldn't falter now, they just couldn't.

Then, less than a hundred paces from the foot of the ridgeline, with the Ultramarines' covering fire whipping past, the rest of the Imperial forces defending Ridge 1 joined the battle.

There was a spectacular crack, like the shattering of worlds, as the lasgun-armed infantry all along the line unleashed their first volley. The new night was lit up by thousands of darts of brilliance – red, green, blue – as the regiments holding Ridge 1 poured small-arms fire into the rising tide. Xenos went down, their bodies riddled with dozens of cauterised las wounds, flesh blown to atoms by higher megathule shots. Those behind trampled their erstwhile kin as they closed on the foot of the ridge.

The Guard above Hanlon fired as well, and the sudden blaze of light momentarily blinded her. She tripped and fell, no breath to cry out as she thumped into the ash and heard the familiar whip-crack of las-bolts – thousands of them – searing overhead. She scrabbled in the grey dust, panting, spots flaring before her eyes as her sight slowly returned. For long seconds she didn't know where she was or what she was doing.

She realised something was standing over her, its broad shoulders blocking the blizzard of illumination that had descended on the space between the ridgeline and the edge of the ork attack. At first Hanlon thought it was a greenskin. She gasped air into her lungs, scrabbling among the soft, dry ash for her rifle.

A hand stopped her. It gripped her beneath one arm and, seemingly without effort, hauled her up onto her feet. She found herself staring into burning red eyes and an unyielding white helmet visor, caked with dust.

'You can run?' scraped a voice seemingly forged from iron.

Hanlon only managed to nod. Her heart was racing and she could barely breathe. It seemed impossible that she could be standing so close to something so vast and so implacable, and yet still be permitted to live. The mere hum of its active battleplate was making her teeth ache.

'Then go.'

The huge figure thrust her towards the ridgeline. She stumbled but carried on, half bent over, no longer even aware of whether or not the rest of the team was still with her. All that mattered was the slope, the damnable, exhausting, seemingly endless slope, and reaching the top of it before the las-bolts flying overhead or the monsters charging from behind reached her.

POLIXIS

'Maintain covering fire,' Valorious ordered. The three Intercessors stood like a blue bulwark amidst the rising green tide, auto bolt rifles rattling as they cut down the waves that threatened to crash over them. The greenskins were close enough for Polixis to have opened fire too, his power armour compensating for the recoil of the Absolver bolt pistol as he snapped shots off into the seemingly endless morass of savagery stampeding towards him.

From the glance that he was able to snatch left and right, it looked to Polixis as though the ork charge was at its furthest extent directly ahead. The fact that the Astra Militarum holding the ridge above had been forced to hold fire for so long had allowed the greenskins to gain more ground than anywhere else along the line. They'd followed hard on the heels of the retreating Imperials without the threat of the barrage being laid down on either side. Valorious himself hadn't authorised the Tmarans to open fire – clearly one of their commanders had panicked. So far, however, their shots had all whipped over and past the Ultramarines and the small band of battered, exhausted Namarians now slogging up the slope.

None had been carrying obvious wounds, and Polixis had sent them on while the Primaris gave them covering fire. They had only a few seconds more before they too would have to turn or risk being overrun.

Thunder rolled across the ridgeline, separate from the continuous hammering of the artillery and the heavy weapons emplacements. A ripple of detonations burst close to the base of the slope, just north of where Polixis stood. He caught a darting light streak overhead, followed by another. More explosions flared amongst ork hordes, snapshots of light silhouetting disintegrating bodies and wrecked equipment. The Imperial Navy's air support had arrived from Kroten, scrambled the moment the piquets had reported massed movement in the evening shadows.

'Grenades,' Valorious snapped. 'Then fall back on the Apothecary.'

The Intercessors sent a trio of fragmentation grenades arcing into the horde, while Polixis began to move backwards up the slope, reloading as he went. Blasts ripped open the nearest greenskins, and the Ultramarines used the few seconds' respite to move back after the exhausted Namarians. Valorious was last to begin moving, unloading clip after clip from his weapon's drum magazine as he went. An ork with a primed stick grenade in one fist went down just before it could lob the explosive, the blast adding to the decimation of those around it.

Still the orks came. They hit the bottom of the slope and rushed up it without pause, iron-shod boots digging into the soft earth. Still the Imperial Guard poured in their las-fire, mowing down rank after rank with a latticework of blazing energy bolts. Some of the orks charged head first into the coils of razor wire that had been hastily dragged out before the sandbag redoubts. Those that hit it were snared and dragged into the vicious wires, and those behind simply trampled over them, even as their kindred roared and writhed, tough bodies slowly shredded, dark blood drenching the ash. The attack bore no hallmarks of careful consideration or tactical nuance. It was an animalistic stampede, and it seemed as if nothing was going to be able to stop it.

Valorious paused a little over halfway up the slope and now stood his ground, still firing, silhouetted against the charging horde by the flare of his bolt rifle. Teeth clenched, Polixis doubled back and snatched his pauldron, dragging him half around.

'No more sacrifices, sergeant, not while I'm here. Get back.'

Valorious turned back to the xenos and started to shoot once more, but he also began to move again, backwards up the last hundred yards, firing his assault weapon from the hip with a degree of accuracy far beyond unaugmented humans. The air was heavy with return fire, but Polixis paid it no heed. Amidst the storm of las and hard rounds, a warrior could do little more than put his faith in his battleplate and the hand of the Emperor.

The Namarians were at the redoubts, scrambling up over the parapets and dropping onto the firing steps beyond. The thunder of the rest of Squad Valorious' bolt rifles had joined the fire of the Tmarans around them, and the edge of the ork assault seemed to come apart before Polixis' eyes as he finally reached the safety of the Imperial lines. He accepted the offered gauntlet of Brother Gallus, servos whirring as he pulled himself up and over the defensive works and down onto the other side. As Valorious, Vito and Albanius joined him back in the redoubt, he became aware of the crack of auto rifles amidst the familiar thunder of the Intercessor's bolter fire. He realised that the recon team they'd just rescued had taken up positions on the firing step alongside the hulking Primaris and, almost without pause, were now adding their fire to the fusillade being poured into the onrushing greenskins. Despite coming within feet of being torn apart, the soldiers hadn't hesitated to continue to do their duty.

Polixis stood alongside one and began firing his pistol, a sudden, unexpected surge of pride rising within him. It was not just for his brothers or the Chapter that he fought, but also for all mankind. As long as a human fought on Ridge 1, he would not abandon it.

KASTOR

Kastor watched in silence as the orks charged up the slope towards him. There were thousands of them, brute savages clad in rough leathers, pelts and scrap metal, wielding cleavers and axes and slug guns that they fired indiscriminately at the redoubts or skywards into the ash clouds. Some scrambled up the shifting slope on all fours, like mindless animals, while the bigger ones actively pushed and shoved their smaller kin into the dirt so they could be at the forefront of the assault.

Kastor despised them. He had done so since he had first

heard of them, in the stories told in the haylofts or around the shepherd campfires of Iax's agri collectives. They were mankind's ancient enemy, the most common antagonists in the tales of the mighty Ultramarines that coloured the native folklore of his home world.

That initial hatred had only grown after his induction, and their full, savage nature had been laid bare before him. They were the bane not just of humanity but of civilisation itself. They sought only endless war, tearing down all that was ordered and anything that was peaceful, from one end of the galaxy to the other. Like an infestation they would spring up, and only righteous flame could truly eradicate their barbarism. Everywhere mankind went, the greenskins fought them there. There were few things Kastor yearned for more than the annihilation of their alien race.

For that reason, the more he saw pouring from the dust and darkness below, the more he silently rejoiced. More to slaughter, more to eradicate. He would see their bodies butchered and their spores burned. No trace of their existence would be left on Ikara by the time he was finished.

His twin hearts leapt in his breast when the Imperial line opened fire, and his optics saw the leading edge of the horde savaged in righteous detail. He watched as las-bolts in their thousands ripped, punched and burned into green flesh, liquefying organs, searing away brain matter and sending bodies tumbling and rolling through the ash. Nearby, Squad Domitian's Hellblasters were adding even more glory to the blaze that was lighting up the night, the eye-achingly brilliant bolts of their plasma weapons turning whole mobs of alien warriors to just more blackened ash in a few seconds of concentrated firepower. The heavy weapons of the Imperial Guard did even more egregious slaughter – heavy bolters and autocannons mowed down the oncoming ranks, while missiles and mortar shells, and the greater munitions of battle tanks and artillery, rent great gaps in the alien masses.

It was butchery, unadulterated and raw, and it made Kastor's hearts soar and his voice break out in praise of the Emperor. Below, the green tide faltered, and for the first time since they had come storming from Shebat's ruins the aliens' offensive stalled.

'See how they falter beneath our righteous fury!' Kastor intoned, beginning to pace the line once more, voice thundering over the fury of the barrage. 'Load and fire, soldiers of the Emperor. Load and fire! They will not stand!'

He forced himself to check his own rising passion long enough to review the Fulminata's tactical display – all squads were holding their positions, ammunition was being expended at a manageable rate and the kill counters were soaring. He frowned when he saw the automatic log showing that Polixis had accompanied three members of Squad Valorious down the slope moments before to cover a retreating piquet unit, but it seemed their gamble had worked, for they were now shown as safely back within the defences of section 13. Kastor growled. He would have to have words with his brother again following the night's engagement. The Chapter could not risk losing him.

He could not risk losing him.

'Pick your targets, soldiers,' he said as he carried on, through a section held by a battalion of Faeburn Vanquishers. 'Aim for their legs. Bring them down and they will be crushed by those behind. Do not waste a single shot.'

Klastis' squad, the last section of the Fulminata to the north, were holding the bulwark just past the Faeburns. Tyranus was with them. The lieutenant had unclamped his power sword and now stood with it point-down, gauntlets resting on its hilt as he analysed the damage being done to the ork assault.

'They will break soon,' Kastor said as he joined him.

'They are bringing up armour,' Tyranus responded. Greenskin scrap-waggons and looted battle tanks were beginning to emerge from the ash cloud to the rear of the ork lines, and a few had even started lobbing shells into the ridge's forward slope. They were being destroyed almost as swiftly as they emerged, though, an easy target for the lascannon teams and embedded Leman Russ squadrons lining the area just below the crest.

'Fifteen more minutes,' Tyranus estimated.

'I pray they hold for longer,' Kastor replied. 'By the Emperor's will, I hope every xenos in Shebat throws itself at us, here and now.'

'I should not have doubted the Astra Militarum,' Tyranus said. 'They are standing their ground.'

'Thanks to your directives,' Kastor said.

'And your sermons, Brother-Chaplain.'

This time, Kastor didn't respond. An explosion tore through the redoubt he had just passed through. He felt the blast wave hammer into his back, followed by the battering impact of debris and shrapnel. He turned as smoke and ash shrouded Klastis and the other Ultramarines in the bulwark.

The position occupied by the Faeburn Vanquishers was no more – the sandbags and flakboards had been shattered, and the scorched, churned-up earth was littered with the remains of eviscerated Guardsmen. Wounded and dazed soldiers were stumbling through what had formerly been a disciplined firing sector. In an instant, the barrage that had been tearing into the ork assault from that part of the line was gone.

The greenskins below roared and renewed their charge, pounding up the slope towards the open wreckage left in the detonation's wake. Kastor began to run at the breach, instinct taking over, but even as he did so an even more immediate threat registered with his genhanced senses. Over the sounds of the oncoming greenskins and the renewed thunder of Squad Klastis' bolt rifles, he could hear a noise as dire as it was familiar – the shriek of more incoming munitions and the rattle of crude engines in the night sky above.

CHAPTER SIX   CODEX COMPLIANT

POLIXIS

'Repeat, the line has been breached. Guard reserve units are inbound.'

Polixis heard Klastis' report over the vox just before the detonation ripped through their section of the line. Something went off just a few yards to the rear of the sector held by Squad Valorious, toppling a heap of sandbags and showering the position's defenders in a rain of dirt and ash.

'Cover,' Valorious barked, more for the benefit of the Astra Militarum than the Primaris around him.

More explosions followed. A mortar redoubt to the rear took a direct hit, and the next wave of debris that came raining down included thick strings of gore and torn flesh.

'Xenos bombers,' Valorious growled over the link. 'Where in Guilliman's name is the Navy?'

The question remained unanswered. More detonations ripped their way across the ridgeline. Polixis saw a redoubt less than a hundred paces to the south take a glancing hit, concussed Guardsmen flung against their own defences, the shooting faltering as the line buckled and men clambered, dazed, back towards the firing step.

A Namarian mobile artillery battery five hundred yards back towards the rear of the ridge was the next position struck. The dugout blew up spectacularly, levelling a portion of the slope and decimating a Kelestan battalion holding in reserve nearby. Another ork bomb struck dangerously close to Chevik's command dome, gutting a Chimera and horribly wounding a clutch of staff officers. A third almost wiped out Squad Nerva. It hit directly ahead of their dugout, killing a mob of the orks charging the position, along with almost all of the Guardsmen holding it with the Ultramarines. The smoke cleared to reveal the Primaris, their armour battered, scarred and splattered with ash and blood, standing amidst an expanse of mangled human and alien remains, splintered flakboard and ripped sandbags.

Polixis began to move north towards Nerva's position, his visor lighting up with four separate minor wounds requiring treatment. How they hadn't suffered more grievous injuries when all else around them had been reduced to ruin spoke as much of the durability of Mark X power armour and the strength of Primaris physiology as it did the guiding hand of the Emperor, not that Polixis would have admitted as much to Kastor.

He moved in among the Tmarans holding the section between Nerva and Valorious, just as Ridge 1's aerial defences began to hit back at the airborne attack. Hydra flak batteries interspersed among the rear line started to thud as they sent streams of tracer-guided shot into the night sky, seeking out the greenskin aircraft rattling over far above. The darkness, already lit by las-bolts and the flare of detonations, was further illuminated by laddering pillars of flak and bursts of flame where the Hydras found their mark.

One of the first greenskin aircraft to be hit came apart in

the sky directly north of Polixis. He stopped as he saw the aircraft's remains, wreathed in fire and black smoke, hurtling towards his position. His genhanced senses slowed the moment down, and he witnessed every detail in perfect clarity – the remnants of the still-turning rotor blades, the greenskin skull glyph mounting the prow of the disintegrating cockpit section, the one wing spinning slowly away like debris leaving a planet's orbit, riddled with flak damage. He saw it all, his mind calculated angles and trajectories, and he realised in the time it took for one of his hearts to beat that in all likelihood he was about to die.

Then training, reinforced by a century's experience, took over.

'Down!' he bellowed at the pelt-clad Tmarans around him. He snatched the nearest two by their shoulders and hauled them onto the duckboards at the redoubt's base. Everyone else seemed to move with an aching slowness, and the world was filled with the roar of the destroyed alien aircraft as it came plummeting in to meet the ridge.

At that moment, kneeling amidst the tribesmen, his head bowed and his eyes closed, Polixis realised his last thoughts were of home. He had never seen it so clearly. Another boy was at his side, stood amidst fields of golden corn that stretched in every direction, undulating gently beneath a pale blue sky. He realised that the boy was Kastor, young and smiling once again. He'd forgotten that vista until that moment, until the point of death. To his own surprise it brought a small, private smile to his lips.

The aircraft hit. The world seemed to turn and spin, and he allowed his Lyman's Ear to bring him blessed silence, cancelling out the horrid fury of the impact and the explosions which followed.

His mind reset, like a newly initiated cogitator block running through its basic systems. He was aware that he'd been thrown onto his side against the redoubt's rear wall, and that part of it had collapsed on top of him. He was aware of a body, ripped and bloody, striking him after he landed. He felt pain in his left wrist and right thigh, and his visor lit with warnings – penetrative wounds, neither serious.

A regular human would have been left stunned and grievously injured, but the mind of a Primaris could not be impaired by shock or trauma. Even as he landed, Polixis was aware that the wreckage had come down directly in front of and behind where he'd been crouched. Fire and metal had ripped through the redoubt, shredding the lightly armoured Tmarans and pulverising the defensive works. The Apothecary was back up just seconds after the initial impact, throwing aside the debris that had covered him and shrugging off the gory remains of the Guardsmen who'd been beside him when the plane had hammered through. He paused briefly to tug the sliver of twisted metal that had sliced into his left vambrace free – the pulse of blood over the white ceramite clogged immediately, and he felt the sudden pain dull as his body blocked it out.

He half turned to assess his situation. Flames and black smoke had engulfed this section of the line. The remains of what looked like part of the ork plane's fuselage lay embedded in the dirt barely a dozen feet away, fire licking from its wrecked husk. There was nobody alive in the immediate vicinity. Nobody human, anyway.

There were orks in the remains of the redoubt. The mobs attacking the Tmaran positions had taken advantage of the destruction unleashed by the wreckage just as they'd done all along the line, using the reduction in Imperial firepower to cover the last few yards.

Polixis stood alone. He didn't hesitate. His gladius was in his fist in an instant, spearing through an ork's throat as it ran blindly through the smoke and ash, leaving it impaled and twitching as hot, dark blood jetted over the Ultramarine's forearm. He ripped the blade free and put two bolt-rounds into the torso of a second ork scrambling into the redoubt. The lack of visibility made Polixis feel as though he were the only one left defending the entire ridge line. The thought sent fresh determination surging through his mind. He would hold this place alone if he had to.

'Come and die, xenos scum.'

Two more orks came at him out of the smoke, bellowing, cleavers raised. He tore open the stomach of one with a point-blank bolt-round, then turned aside the swing of the other with his gladius. The first came on despite its hideous injury, seemingly oblivious to the thick intestinal strings spilling from its split gut as it tried to hack off the Apothecary's right arm. He took the hit on his pauldron and drove the greenskin back with his superior height and bulk, a haymaker swing of his gladius keeping the second ork at bay as it recovered from its first strike.

Behind them he could see more rushing from the pall, tusks bared and weapons raised. There was no sign of any sort of Imperial reserve to his rear.

Teeth gritted, he fought on.

KASTOR

The first ork to breach the Imperial defences on Ridge 1 had its skull split open by Salve Imperator.

Kastor roared and kicked the broken corpse squarely in the stomach, sending it slamming back into the other greenskins scrambling in its wake. Either side of him Klastis' Intercessors had switched to bolt pistols and their chainswords or gladii.

'In the name of the immortal Emperor and the restored primarch, strike them down!' Kastor roared as energy wreathed his crozius. The mace's skull tip slammed through the haft of an axe wielded by the next ork to scramble up through the ash and blood. The swing carried on, pulverising its face and shattering its tusks even as it howled in mindless, alien fury.

Kastor brought his Absolver up as he recovered from the killing strike – the heavy bolt pistol bucked in his gauntlet, its booming report every bit as fearsome as the Chaplain's roared battle prayers. Still the orks came, though, trampling their dead and their wounded, seemingly unable to do anything other than fling themselves against the human's defences.

Kastor would have had it no other way.

A crude chainsword struck the Chaplain's right pauldron, juddering off the black ceramite with a screech of metal and a shower of sparks. At the same time a stray round struck his helmet, ricocheting away and snapping his head to the left. He recovered immediately, snarling an oath of vengeance on behalf of his power armour as he brought Salve Imperator crashing down again. More orks broke beneath his fury – grey brain matter and shattered bone befouled his vestments and dripped from the stylised rib bones of his breastplate. He pressed forwards to the edge of the redoubt's remains, planting himself amidst the torn sandbags and broken bodies of the Faeburn Vanquishers as he reaped with his crozius arcanum. Still the xenos came, bellowing and grunting, eyes filled with manic fury. They thought nothing of death, nothing of pain or injury. All they desired was to fight. Kastor welcomed each and every one, a litany on his lips.

In the end it was the Imperial Guard, and not the Ultramarines, who sealed the breach.

A squad of Pyran veterans, including a trio of heavy flamer teams, pushed up from the south, spears of liquid flame engulfing those mobs still trying to force their way into the opening. Greenskin roars turned to howls of agony as flesh sloughed off and innards liquefied, and billows of black smoke brought the gut-turning stench of charred alien meat with it.

Kastor snapped the neck of an ork that was ablaze from head to foot, half lifting the alien as flames licked around his black gauntlet before flinging it back down the ridge. Ahead of him the breach had been turned into a wall of fire, filled with the writhing, blackened forms of burning xenos. The urge to burst through the flames and carry the fight to those beyond was almost more than Kastor could bear. He forced himself to take a step back and deactivate his mace. Either side of him Klastis and the Intercessors who had held the breach with him – Fadius, Aeneras and Quiris – were all befouled with alien blood, their armour battered and rent. They'd carpeted the redoubt's scarred remains with ork corpses, their gladii and the teeth of their chainblades dripping with thick strings of xenos viscera. The Imperial Guard moving in to secure the position were forced to tread on the bodies of the greenskins as they moved to set up a new firebase.

'Section five is secured,' Kastor voxed to Tyranus, pinging the message through the Astra Militarum's command channels. 'I am relocating.'

He turned his attention to Klastis and his three Intercessors, briefly grasping the forearm of each in turn.

'Well fought, brothers,' he intoned. 'We have done the Emperor's work here today. Hold this position.'

While the flames had bought a respite around him, a glance at the state of the burst map on his visor told the Chaplain that the opposite was true across the rest of the line. The chaos of a full pitched battle was never adequately represented on charts or displays, even in real time, but what data that was available showed that well over half of the Imperial reserves had been committed at breach points all along Ridge 1. Four of the Fulminata's five combat squads had been or were currently engaged in close combat. Only Domitian's Hellblasters were keeping the greenskins storming their section of the line at bay, the raw firepower of the plasma weapons decimating the mobs as rapidly as they gained ground.

It was carnage, brought on by the destruction wreaked by the greenskins' aerial attacks. The worst of the bombing runs seemed to have passed – those aircraft not brought down were likely returning to their fleet to refuel and rearm – but they had done more than enough damage. The ridgeline was close to breaking point.

'*Salve, redeploy to sector one*,' crackled the voice of Lieutenant Tyranus over the private link. '*Prime Tertiary requires immediate close support.*'

Kastor was about to confirm the redeployment orders when a sigil on the burst map caught his eye. It was his brother's, and not only had it become separated from those belonging to the nearest squads – Nerva and Valorious – but the scroll-feed indicated that the Apothecary was engaged in hand-to-hand combat. Kastor immediately turned south, keeping the channel to Tyranus open as he went.

'Prime Alpha, Helix has been isolated. I am moving to support.'

* * *

POLIXIS

This time there were too many. The wreckage of the dug-out was flooding with greenskins, trampling over their own dead as they poured into the gap torn in the Imperial line. Polixis stood firm in their midst, fighting with a cold, brutal efficiency. His focus was on his gladius, his every motion dedicated to its use as a death-dealing tool. It tore jugulars and carved open faces, sliced hamstrings and took out eyes with clinical precision. Greenskins were hideously difficult beasts to kill – their natural toughness and near-immunity to both pain and fear was almost on a par with the Adeptus Astartes. Polixis made clean, hard killing blows where he could and disabled those he could not, leaving them clawing the ash, blind or unable to stand. Alien blood ran thick and black down the vennel of his short sword and pattered against his armour like foul, hot rain. On he fought, letting his armour take the inevitable blows that pierced his guard, trusting in the heavy Mark X plates.

'This is Polixis, my sector is breached,' he snapped between blows, checking the vox's transmitter in the corner of one eye. It was unresponsive. He fought on.

It could only last so long. More orks came for him, drawn as much by the cold, bloody resistance of a single determined warrior as by their desire to overrun the fracturing Imperial line. Polixis' subconscious, still assessing the situation beneath the endless, tireless work of his sword arm, registered a difference in the greenskins surrounding him. A flurry of fresh blows fell at him from behind, and he turned in a tight, vicious circle, gladius swinging, to find another wave of orks rushing the redoubt. These ones were coming from the rear of the ridge, though, rather than the front slope, and they were clad in grimy camo capes and spotting gear. Worse were their blades – they were slick with fresh blood. Polixis realised why the Imperial Guard hadn't flooded the section with reinforcements. The orks now rushing him had used the breach to outflank and cut off whatever reserves had been moving up from behind.

More blows rained down on the stranded Apothecary. He turned aside the cleaver of one greenskin and slashed the throat of another before returning to the first, driving it back into the press with a trio of strikes towards its lower torso before flicking the gladius up to take it in the thorax. In the four seconds it took to do so, his armour registered another three hits, two ringing off his backpack and another nicking the rear of his knee, piercing the joint seal but not drawing blood.

The vox finally ticked active on his visor. He managed to say a single word.

'*Kastor.*'

A slight overextension into a thrust and one of the xenos' serrated blades cut up and under his right pauldron. A jab of pain and fresh blood stained his white armour red. He grunted and twisted into the stab, using his superior bulk to smash the alien back and break its grip on its knife at the same time as he ripped his sword free from the skull of another. Bisected brain matter splattered those around as he stabbed once, twice, three times into the ork's gut, hard and fast, no room for finesse or broad, sweeping blows. He ploughed his sword into another's skull as he kicked the first ork down, trying to make more room, trying to force his way through the press as more strikes pounded from his backpack, pauldrons and helmet.

There was a hissing sound, followed by a violent crack.

Polixis turned in time to see one of the cape-clad green-skins ramming what looked like a grox prong at him. Electric charge surged when its wire-coiled tip struck the Apothecary's left pauldron. Power burst through his battleplate, searing through his black carapace and into his flesh and bones. He cried out, his muscles going into spasms before his jaw locked. His armour answered his pain – servos shrieked and his visor flared with a dozen critical warnings before its display blinked offline.

The greenskin pulled the prong away, but energy continued to crackle across Polixis' armour. He shuddered, his body still struggling to function in spite of the shock it had sustained. As the electricity that sparked across his battleplate started to short out, he tried to move, tried to force his aching muscles to obey. They wouldn't. At first he thought his whole body had been paralysed. Then he realised it was something worse.

The xenos prong hadn't only overloaded his auto-senses, but had also burned through his servos, locking and immobilising them. His armour had become a prison, and he was trapped in it, utterly helpless.

The orks rushed him. The first to lay its claws on his battleplate received the full force of the charge stored up in it, flinging it back against the bodies of its kin. The others came on regardless, bellowing with bloodthirsty excitement. Polixis tried to blink-click his visor display, but it remained blank and unresponsive. He braced himself for a rain of blows. Instead a trio of greenskins slammed themselves bodily into him. Unable to react, he fell, hitting the bloody ash just as the ork with the prong reignited the electrodes. As pain flooded his body once again and he felt hands gripping him, the terrible truth dawned.

They weren't trying to kill him. They were trying to take him alive.

KASTOR

Kastor ran at full tilt, the platoon of Kelestan Stormers he'd requisitioned struggling to keep up. It was roughly five hundred yards from the breach the Chaplain had held to the locator marker representing his brother on the burst map. To get there he had to pass through another melee next to Squad Nerva's redoubt. The Primaris burst in amongst the orks who had fought their way over the parapet like a righteous thunderbolt, a storm of lightning-wreathed destruction that annihilated the greenskins in a matter of seconds. As the Namarians who'd been battling to hold the redoubt scrambled back up to the firestep, he carried on, passing the Hellblasters of Squad Domitian. Their plasma weapons were steaming, vents white-hot, dangerously close to overheating. Still they fired, though, laying down a curtain of actinic blue energy that turned mob after mob of charging greenskins into more ash to carpet the slope. Theirs was one of the few parts of the line where no xenos had yet penetrated the defences.

Beyond Domitian, Kastor found a stretch of redoubts completely overrun by orks. He charged them without any hesitation. Salve Imperator was a tool of annihilation, coursing with power. Scrap armour buckled and axe shafts splintered; cleavers shattered and helmets were staved in with relentless, hate-fuelled efficiency. The Chaplain's boots ground broken alien bodies into the dirt and ash as he carried on and on, splitting skulls and breaking necks with each unstoppable overhead swing.

For their own part, the orks threw themselves at the rampant

Ultramarine without hesitation, their every thought bent towards their desire to fight and kill. The gigantic, skull-faced warrior held no fear for them, even as he smashed his way implacably through their mobs. All he was to them was a challenge – victory meant power, while death to them held no meaning. Their mindless tenacity was what made their race so deadly.

Their blades and slug rounds had torn his vestments in half a dozen places, and almost every plate of his black armour was scraped silver in one part or another, the ceramite cut right down to the plasteel beneath. Some of the blows penetrated, but Kastor didn't notice the pain before his body blocked it out. His mind was a sea of fury, driven by the need to reach Polixis. Everything else – rallying the Guard, holding the ridgeline, driving back the endless xenos tide – had been consumed by the fires of his rage

He could not fail now. To do so would spell disaster on every imaginable level. The Guard didn't so much support his attack as simply follow the trail of brutalised xenos corpses he left behind.

It felt like an age, but finally the Primaris Chaplain found himself without any enemies before him. He had smashed a path of destruction through the xenos attack. Behind him, the Namarians and Kelestani secured the remains of the redoubt, driving into the orks amid a flurry of rapid las-fire. Kastor ignored them, pressing on past the Zoishen infantry holding the next section. The fire-streaked dust and darkness rendered visibility infuriatingly low, but the burst map sigil put Polixis just a hundred yards ahead.

Kastor was almost there when the marker blinked from existence. It displayed neither injury warnings nor a death signifier. It simply vanished.

For the first time in his life, the Chaplain swore. He followed up with a roared battle litany as more greenskins appeared on the edge of the sandbagged tunnel connecting the Zoishen's position and the next section. His charge, pauldron first, slammed the first ork clean off its feet, his boots snapping its throat as he carried on, bolt pistol blazing in one fist and crozius ignited in the other.

He rounded the corner into the next dugout, and instead of more redoubts found himself presented with a barren expanse of devastation. It looked as though a greenskin aircraft had crashed directly into the section of redoubt ahead. He'd been aware of one of their fighters, riddled with flak, roaring overhead earlier, but his mind had been too focused on repelling the assault on his own section of the line to consider exactly where the plane had come down. Now it was obvious – burning wreckage and twisted metal had decimated the churned-up ash, and the sandbags and flak-boards that had once constituted the defensive works had been scattered and torn to pieces.

The area was also crawling with greenskins.

The nearest turned as Kastor came round the corner into the remains of the position. The Primaris took in what lay before him in a single second – not only the carnage that had broken apart the defences, but the dozen or so green brutes struggling to heft something over what was left of the redoubt's parapet. It was a body, seemingly inert. Through the blood and grime, Kastor caught the flash of white ceramite.

'Helix!' he roared, the name amplified by his helm to such a degree that even the greenskins cringed back. He flung himself in the direction of his older brother, the last vestiges of restraint scorched from his mind by the need to reach the Apothecary. The orks that stood against him were an indistinct blur, blood and broken bone, the Chaplain's whole body blazing with combat stimms and raw adrenaline as he pushed himself to his limit.

Kastor understood failure in that moment. Even as roaring alien warriors broke and died beneath his weapon, he saw more hauling his blood brother beyond his reach. His mind slowed the entire situation down as his body went into overdrive, and everything was rendered with a surreal degree of clarity. He saw the skull of the ork in front of him splinter, brain matter bursting slowly upwards around Salve Imperator's head, shattered bone and broken tusks spinning away. He saw the flare of a slugga muzzle beating out a tattoo as its owner sprayed shots inaccurately over his head. He saw las-bolts searing into the press around him, punching through green flesh and rusting armour, wounds sizzling as they cauterised.

He saw Polixis, his brother, being dragged like so much loot out over the parapet and down the corpse-littered slopes beyond, his captors bellowing and gesticulating triumphantly. The Apothecary seemed incapable of movement, immobilised. The realisation twisted Kastor's gut, and sent a fresh metabolic surge of adrenaline through his veins. He had to reach him.

The orks struggled with the Apothecary's weight, but there were enough of them – they were hauling him away faster than Kastor could force his way through their kin. For every beast he broke another pressed itself into him, bellowing and snapping its foul maw, pounding impotently on his ribbed black armour with fists and clubs, cleavers, axes and chainblades.

'Emperor give me strength!' Kastor roared, knowing even as he did so that neither his zeal nor his transhuman body would be sufficient.

He was still fighting and still praying as the Imperial Guard stormed in around him with las-bolts and bayonets, while the body of his brother disappeared out into the darkness of the ash-shrouded night.

The end came with the dawn. It was a miserable, uncertain thing, a grey pall beneath an ugly orange star, its light weakened and tainted by the dust that still hung heavy in Ikara's atmosphere.

As the new day bled weak, watery colour back into the world, the last acts of violence played out along Ridge 1: a few las-bolts snapping away into the lifting ash shroud; the rattle of a slug weapon somewhere out in the half-dark; the detonation of a final shell, its payload twitching corpses and furrowing dirt out on the slope-side. Silence followed, like the quiet that came after the last pattering raindrops of a storm.

Kastor knelt amidst the wreckage. The blood on his armour and vestments had congealed, leaving encrusted streaks and stains on the ancient plate. Though Imperial forces had long since retaken the breach in which he had fought, none of the mortals nearby dared approach him. Most probably assumed he was in prayer.

In reality, he was searching for something.

He had seen his brother taken. He had seen him incapacitated, somehow, and dragged away by xenos savages. But he hadn't seen his gladius, until now.

The short sword was embedded in the skull of a greenskin half-buried by a mound of its dead kindred. Kastor looked into its sightless eyes, into a face forever twisted into a bestial rictus of mindless hatred. Eventually, he placed one gauntlet on its thick jaw, another on the gladius' grip, and pulled.

The weapon came free with a crunch, grey brain matter oozing down its length. Kastor stood and looked around.

The defenders of Ridge 1 were blinking and sluggish in the wan light, like men awakening from a nightmare. Piquet teams and skirmish chains were being thrown out down the slope, bone-weary, while officers with raw throats pressed bloodshot eyes to the rubber cowling of their magnoculars. All reports Kastor could hear over the vox said the same thing – the ork tide had receded, pulling back with first light to the eastern edge of Shebat, where they continued to fight amongst themselves and lick their wounds.

Kastor watched in silence as flamer teams were deployed to the forward slope to clean the mounds of xenos dead piled there, and soon a thick pall of stinking black smoke hung over the remains of the Imperial line. There were no unengaged reserves left to be brought up to relieve those units still in position, but Chevik had approved a corps-wide order – Kastor assumed without consulting Field Marshal Klos – allowing commanders to stand down every second man on a rotating basis throughout the morning. Guardsmen slept where they had fought, sitting on their firesteps with their backs to dugout walls, cradling their lasguns. A few tugged aside their respirators long enough to chew down ration bars, risking greythroat and eyerot for the sake of easing the ache in their bellies. Many more just sat in silence.

The Chaplain checked the location markers still winking across his visor display. The Fulminata remained at their posts. Tyranus and Samson were touring the line together, speaking to each sergeant in turn. All the squads had been reduced to combat teams to cover as many of the breaches as possible. These had been further decreased by casualties sustained over the course of the night's storm assaults.

According to the reports, three brothers were dead – Spurius from Nerva, Dynator from Valorious and Lucarius from Klastis. Three more had been badly injured. Brother Clovens had lost an arm and Cellus a hand, both from Squad Klastis, while Servio of Squad Faustus had suffered a mangled leg following the destructive work of an ork bomber's munitions. All three were stable. The bodies and equipment of the three fallen had been taken to the rear.

Kastor assumed that the ranking sergeant, Nerva, had overseen the removal of their progenoids. It would have been difficult work with Polixis gone.

The thought brought a cold anger with it. Kastor's fists clenched, and it took long seconds to master himself, to not cry out in rage or vent his fury on the alien corpses heaped beneath him.

Eventually, he stirred himself. He forced his thoughts back to the importance of his duties, murmuring a blessing to his brother's gladius and mag-locking it before moving down the line. As he went from one squad to another, he paused and led the assembled battle-brothers in brief prayers of thankfulness, his voice low and level as he offered up veneration to the primarch and the Emperor. He anointed the armour and brows of those who wished for it with sacred unguent from one of his sanctus-vials, and offered additional prayers of guidance and strength alongside those who had been badly injured. Last of all, he stood over the three bodies of Brothers Spurius, Dynator and Lucarius, laid out side by side near the rear of General Chevik's command dome and guarded by Brother Marius. The words of the funerary rites were whipped away by the rising wind, each utterance as cold as the wasteland chill that bit through to bone and marrow.

When the service was ended Kastor waited alongside the

bodies. Ordinarily he would have returned to the forward positions and looked to the faith of the Astra Militarum – at times even the iron will of the Adeptus Astartes required guidance following battle's tempest, and there were thousands of warriors across the ridgeline without the strength lent to them by genetic enhancement. Hundreds would have benefited from the Chaplain's pastorship, but he didn't move until Tyranus returned from the redoubts and completed his debriefing with Chevik and Klos. The Primaris lieutenant saluted Kastor, clenching his fists to his breastplate. The Chaplain returned the gesture but remained silent. Tyranus spoke first.

'The reinforcements from Kroten are approaching. Their outriders are a little over two hours from our rear echelons.'

When Kastor remained silent he continued.

'Klos is rotating the Fifth and Eighth Corps into reserve come nightfall, when the main column comes up. We will hold our positions here. Aerial scans show that the greenskins are massing for another attack amidst the slum ruins, and we expect the bomber wings to return from low orbit before the end of the day.'

'He was still alive,' Kastor said. It was Tyranus' turn to remain silent as the Chaplain went on, as though the lieutenant hadn't been speaking.

'They'd disabled him somehow. Locked his armour. But he was alive. Of that I'm certain.'

'I believe you are correct, Brother-Chaplain,' Tyranus said slowly. 'But they have him now. It is likely he is deep within the city's ruins, and whether he yet lives...'

'He does,' Kastor said, a hint of fire flickering behind his softly spoken words. 'I would know if he had passed on.'

'His loss is a grievous blow,' Tyranus said. 'The Fulminata have suffered enough on this world already.'

'I will recover him. I will go myself, and I will return him to the Chapter, dead or alive.'

Kastor knew it would have been easy for Tyranus to respond immediately. It would have been natural for him to order the Chaplain to abandon his plan straight away, to demand he adhere to the Codex's chain of command and focus on his duty towards the rest of the Fulminata. But he was Demeter's protégé, and he knew Kastor. Instead of interrupting the Chaplain, he held his silence while Kastor continued.

'The Fulminata need him. The Chapter itself needs him. He is our Apothecary, and he holds the legacy of us all in his hands.'

'He is also your blood brother,' Tyranus said in a tone that, anywhere else, would have sounded almost conciliatory.

'I will not deny that,' Kastor admitted. 'I will not claim that I am motivated by duty alone. My heart burns for him, for what he is assuredly suffering, even now. That is why I will go alone. I will not risk any of our brotherhood in this task. And that is why I pray you also see fit to release me.'

'You are presumptive, Brother-Chaplain,' Tyranus said. 'I understand your desire to retrieve your blood brother, and I acknowledge too that rescuing him would greatly benefit the Fulminata, regardless of your familial bond. But I reject your insinuation that losing you also would have little further consequence. In the past few days, we have suffered the deaths of Captain Demeter, the company's ancient and Techmarine Tiberon. We have lost our standard, *Extremis* and now our Apothecary – not to mention almost a third of our battle-brothers who have been killed or grievously wounded. To lose our Chaplain as well would amount to something not far removed from a death blow.'

'You honour me, brother-lieutenant–' Kastor started, but Tyranus continued over him.

'Every member of the Fulminata values your spiritual guidance and your knowledge of the Chapter's creed. Every engagement we have fought has involved your presence on the front line, whether you have employed your oratory or fought in the melee itself. And I myself find no shame in admitting that I have need of you, Kastor. I have been thrust into a position of command during the white heat of a fully active combat zone. It is a duty I have long prepared for, but that does not mean I am happy to simply discard you or the advice you have to offer. You are now the most senior member of this brotherhood – none of those still fighting have held their current rank for as long as you have held yours. Regardless of my position as first lieutenant or acting captain, you are as much a commander of the Fulminata now as I am.'

Kastor didn't have an immediate response. He let Tyranus continue.

'You place me in a difficult position. I do believe Polixis still lives, though what foul purpose would lead to the xenos taking him alive I can only guess. I do wish to see him rescued, both for your sake and for the sake of the Fulminata. We need him, and that will only become more apparent the longer we remain on the front lines. All that being said, allowing you to seek him out runs the risk of committing a basic Codex error – compounding pre-existing failure.'

'This is the nature of command, brother-lieutenant,' Kastor said. 'You will rarely find yourself with an easy decision. Savour them when they come.'

'Brother-Captain Demeter taught me the importance of finding peace with every new course,' Tyranus replied. 'Sound analysis followed by firm commitment to a decision is one of the core tenets of command. For that reason,

I have concluded that you will not go to find Polixis. You will remain here, with the demi-company.'

Silence followed the lieutenant's words, interrupted only by the low moaning of the ash-wind and the ruffle of Kastor's vestments and scroll-pieces. Tyranus carried on.

'You are too valuable to risk in an operation that offers such little chance of success. Permitting you to leave would be a dereliction of my role as leader of the Fulminata. You will not go into Shebat Alpha seeking Helix. Instead, I will dispatch a Reiver team under Severus' command. They will seek his trail and, if possible, extract him, dead or alive. They are ideally suited to this sort of mission.'

'Their loss would scarcely be less of a blow to the company than my own,' Kastor said.

'That is correct, but I consider the likelihood of their return to be far greater. They are under orders to maintain their covert protocols at all times. They will be air-dropped into the Tombstones, and from there work their way into Shebat from the south-west over the next few days. If they cannot locate Polixis, or if they deem his extraction untenable, they will withdraw and return to us here.'

'I see,' Kastor said, forcing his voice to remain level. 'I pray the Emperor has guided you to this decision, brother-lieutenant. I will ask His blessings on both you and our Reiver brethren.'

'My thanks, Brother-Chaplain,' Tyranus said, inclining his helmeted head slightly. 'And my thanks also for your understanding. I will not be surprised if the xenos return before nightfall, and when they do I will have need of you more than ever before.'

'I will visit the squads once more,' Kastor said. 'And what Guard regiments I can.'

'No,' Tyranus said, the word catching Kastor by surprise. 'You have given much these past few days, Brother-Chaplain. I believe it would be best if you sought a moment of personal reflection. The xenos will take some hours to build their strength once more, and I have seen to the rest of the Fulminata. Go and quieten your mind. We will have need of you soon enough.'

'Very well, brother-lieutenant,' Kastor said. Though the urge to continue walking the line and venting his anger was strong, he realised the lieutenant's suggestion was a good one. He needed peace, if only for a while.

Tyranus dismissed him, and he passed out towards the rear of the Imperial lines. It felt strange to be suddenly alone, after the cramped environment of redoubts and bulwarks, flakboards and sandbags. The ash wastes stretched away from him, flat desolation interspersed with thickly coated boulders and wiry, grey-caked rot-roots.

He pressed on into it, his boots sinking heavily into the soft, shifting soil. The targeting matrices of his visor bounced across his display, seeking hostile contacts, seeking anything at all that it could lock on to. The only interesting thing it found to highlight was Kastor's destination – the smoking wreckage of an ork aircraft, brought down the night before and left burning out in the wastes.

It had ploughed a long furrow when it had crashed. Both its wings were gone and its tail section had come away, buried in the grey soil a hundred yards away. What remained of the fuselage lay at the end of its destructive ditch, burned out, smoke still coiling from its half-buried nose grille.

Kastor circled the mangled cockpit. He found three bodies within, charred and blackened beyond recognition, the skeletal fists of one still clamped around the aircraft's flight stick. He mounted the fuselage, the metal groaning under his weight. Once atop it he sat, his legs folded, the wind tugging at his vestments.

Once seated he reached down and pulled his copy of the *Lectato Ultramar* onto his lap, along with its iron key. Both hung from the heavy, consecrated chains wrapped around his waist, fastened there even in the heat of battle.

The *Lectato* itself was a mighty tome, its covers protected by a layer of flak-plate stitched into the red leather, its pages bound by an ornate plasteel lock-clamp. An ordinary human would have struggled to even lift it, but Kastor could carry it easily enough in the crook of one elbow, and had long grown accustomed to its unwieldy bulk whether in or out of combat. It had broken the skulls of a number of heretics and xenos in the six decades since he had finished inscribing and binding it.

He slotted the key in and unlocked the cover clamp, opening the weighty vellum pages to the place marked by a black strip of velvet. It felt like an age since he had consulted the book. He found himself missing the dark, weighty stillness of the Chapel of the Dioskuri. It was the place of worship he tended to aboard the *Spear of Macragge*, and it remained the closest thing to home he had left in the galaxy.

He banished such thoughts, silently chiding himself for his weakness. Sentimentality was a sin, at times a grievous one. It dulled the honed blade and softened minds that were required to remain forever battle-keen. It had no place in the hearts of a Primaris.

He looked down at the last passage he had marked, one digit following the words, as it had done ever since his days as a notary. It was a sermon from the Twelve Nights of Absolution, by Past Master Antonio Polaris. The short homily stressed the importance of the acceptance of failure and the need for salvation – the acceptance that none were perfect in the Emperor's sight and none could truly live up to the tenets of the Codex without spot or blemish. Acceptance did not mean that a warrior of the Chapter acknowledged any lesser effort, but it guarded against the multitude of heresies that could stem from the frustration that so often haunted brothers of the Adeptus Astartes. Anger, confusion and bitterness all reared their ugly heads when a genhanced champion accustomed to victory suffered a severe or sudden setback. Accommodating failure was one of the hardest lessons, especially for a Primaris.

Kastor pondered the words, confronting his own failures since his arrival on Ikara – the loss of first Captain Demeter and then Polixis, and his own inability to help either of them. He exposed the white heat of his rage and disappointment and allowed it to cool. Attaining detachment, removing himself from the present and analysing his own thoughts and actions were skills that had always come more naturally to Polixis. Kastor envied him that. His own mind only seemed to function in the present, driven on by instinct and reflex. He found it easy enough to offer up advice on the trials of others, but when it came to his own difficulties he so often found himself enslaved to his passions.

He finished the passage, uttering the short catechism that closed Polaris' teachings. The next page offered a tactical sermon on Codex-standard protocols for a battalion to division-level combat withdrawal, summarising the salient aspects with a series of skull-headed bullet points. He read over the long-memorised words without really focusing, his mind still on the previous passage and on the book as a whole.

'Thank you for the instruments of your will,' he murmured as he read, drawing a slow, steady reassurance from the heavy tome. At times, a warrior was guilty of only venerating his arms and armour. The *Lectato* was proof that a true servant of the Emperor required more.

The book itself was one of half a dozen texts held in reverence by the Ultramarines. It had been the magnum opus of Master of Sanctity Balthazar Quillex, arguably the Chapter's greatest spiritual leader of the 34th millennium. Using his vast knowledge and indomitable faith, he had set out to transcribe a condensed copy of what he believed to be the core tenets of the Codex Astartes. He had combined these with the foundational teachings of the Chapter's Reclusiam to create the *Lectato* – a blend of the Chapter's doctrine and faith.

Of course, Quillex's undertaking had been controversial at the time, and remained so to the present day. Some believed the Codex – the sacred writings of their own blessed primarch – could and should not be reduced or distilled in any way. There were others, however, who had always pointed out that the Codex itself frequently stressed adaptability and a suspicion of dogma. The view of the Codex and its teachings as more malleable had become increasingly commonplace since the return of the great Guilliman. It was a view often associated with the Chapter's Primaris contingent, and while both the primarch and the likes of Chapter Master Marneus Calgar had been clear in their demands for cooperation between the hardliners and the adaptionists, there had been a great deal of impassioned debate over the past few decades.

Kastor had always been a believer in Quillex's philosophy. That which was rigid, broke. That which bent, endured. He was living proof of that, he and every Primaris who now fought throughout the galaxy. The Imperium's dogmatic teachers would never have sanctioned his creation, would likely have destroyed his kind in their cryo-tanks if they had discovered them. But without the Primaris, and without the blessed primarch's foresight, the Imperium would no longer exist. To adhere for dogma's sake alone was in itself a sin. Dogma was why the Imperium suffered now as it did.

Kastor knew that dogma demanded he obey Lieutenant Tyranus. It demanded he stand with his brothers on the ridgeline and leave the salvation of his blood brother to Severus and the Reivers.

'I do not serve dogma,' he murmured to himself. 'I serve the living primarch and the living Emperor.'

The Fulminata would bend, but they would not break, of that much he was certain. He knew each of his brothers; he had spoken to them in turn in the aftermath of the previous night's storm. They were vengeful and resolute. They did not need his guidance. What was more, they were being reinforced. The dust cloud to the south was testimony to the weight of the Astra Militarum forces moving up to the ridgeline from Kroten. As much as Klos would be struggling to admit it, von Klimt was delivering on his promise to back up the ragged forces driven from Shebat, shifting the weight of Imperial efforts on Ikara to the new front. Within a week the tenuous line along Ridge 1 would be the epicentre of sprawling defensive works sixty miles long. The Fulminata would be withdrawn and utilised in their traditional role whenever they found themselves deployed to a grinding war of attrition – as a mobile reserve used to stem breakthroughs or spearhead the counter-attack, when it eventually came. Such an operational stance had little need of Kastor's oratory skills, at least in the short term.

That was what he told himself as he turned to another passage, 'The Losses of Captain Marcus Draido', a cautionary tale about the struggles of a former commander of the Second Company, who had found his duties impeded by his desire to preserve lives. Ultimately his decisions had only resulted in more death and misery among those he had sought to save. It served to teach the Adeptus Astartes the truth of their condition, that time and again they would be called upon to abandon those who looked to them for protection or, even worse, turn against them for the greater cause. Like all Space Marines, Kastor knew the extent of the timeless evils that stalked humanity. Combating them required sacrifice – not the easy, honourable sacrifice made in the heat of battle for a brother in arms but the desperate deeds that tried the soul.

'Is that the sacrifice I am being required to make now?' he asked aloud, the book still open before him. 'Am I to be tried for hypocrisy? For espousing the necessity of loss among others only to abandon everything to ease my own pain?'

Was he truly going to disobey Tyranus and leave behind the Fulminata on a mission that would almost certainly end with his own death?

He realised that his hands had clenched into fists, resting on the *Lectato*'s pages. The insidious ash had already covered them in a thin, dusty layer. Angrily he swiped the residue away and closed the book, the clap of the heavy cover echoing out over the wasteland.

There were no easy choices, but he had made his. He dropped down from the ruined aircraft's fuselage, boots thumping in the dust. In the distance his auto-senses picked out a familiar thudding sound, followed by a dull crump. More followed, a far-off, staccato ripple. He recognised the report of artillery, greeting the oncoming evening.

The afternoon was wearing thin. He would have to hurry. Checking that the *Lectato* and its key were chained securely around his waist, he began to jog back towards the distant ridgeline, servos whirring, thoughts ignited once more.

CHAPTER SEVEN   DOCTOR'S ORDERS

POLIXIS

Why he still lived, Polixis did not know.

They tried to knock him out, as they dragged him to the foot of Ridge 1's slope. They beat his helmet with cudgels and the flats of their cleavers, grunting furiously. Polixis endured each ringing blow, unable to resist. It was almost impossible to knock an Adeptus Astartes unconscious, and doubly so with a Primaris. His helmet held, though a crack had appeared over his right eye-lens, splitting his visor. The display remained blank and inactive, his servos unresponsive.

After a while, his captors gave up and hauled him up once more, six of them struggling with his weight. They were all clad in the soiled camo capes and patchwork infiltration gear of the mob that had attacked him from behind in the redoubt. As they moved downhill and back towards Shebat, they forced their way through the warbands still headed towards the battle raging across the ridgeline. Some greenskins tried to get at Polixis, roaring excitedly, but his captors beat them away with grunts and balled fists.

They reached one of the rickety flatbed engines greenskins

commonly used for transportation, parked a few hundred yards from the base of the slope and protected from the greedy gaze of nearby mobs by several more of the cape-clad orks. Polixis could do nothing but snarl with frustration as he was hoisted up into the truck's rear end, most of the mob clambering up after him. The vehicle's abused engine revved, and the tyres bit ash and grit as they spun, sending the transport skewing in the direction of Shebat. Polixis was shifted to the left but kept largely in place by the hobnailed boots of his captors. They were shouting over the throaty sound of the engine, partly with exhilaration at the breakneck ride, partly due to the nature of their prize.

Why he had been spared, let alone snatched in what seemed to be a premeditated plan, Polixis had no idea. He could only assume he was going to be used as some sort of trophy, or perhaps enslaved, put to work in a gladiatorial pit. Intelligence claimed that the xenos were running an expansive slave trade west of the Gorgon, mostly dealing in captured citizens and waste nomads and supplemented by those Imperial Guardsmen foolish enough to allow themselves to be taken alive. If the xenos filth thought he would allow himself to be used in such a way, they would soon regret their mistake.

He tried to move again, but still his armour wouldn't respond. His visor remained blank and the servos inert. He spat a string of expletives that would have made Kastor snarl a reprimand at him.

The greenskins sensed his frustration. One of the brutes hanging on to the stanchion along the edge of the flatbed bellowed angrily over the excitement of its kindred, gesticulating at him. The one with the prong stepped unsteadily over the boots of the rest of the mob and lunged downwards.

Polixis braced himself, teeth gritted, just in time for the surge of pain from the prong that arced through his body.

It felt like a long time before the truck screeched to a stop. They'd left Ridge 1 behind, the thunder of battle fading away until it was consumed by the roar of the transport. The ride became more juddering as they reached Shebat and began to career across rubble-choked streets. Polixis was slammed back and forth in the foot of the flatbed, his armour scraping its sides. The greenskins kicked him at every opportunity and let out bestial laughs, even as they struggled to keep their own grip on the bouncing truck. At one point, as they surged over a heap of broken debris and all four wheels left the ground, one of the runtier greenskins slipped and tumbled out of the open rear end. The others just laughed all the harder, gesturing crudely as the unfortunate ork picked itself up from the rubble, receding rapidly into the distance.

'Emperor give me strength,' Polixis murmured to himself, struggling once more against his unresponsive armour. In that moment, he wished that Kastor were there, if only because he would know the right words to ease his fury. His struggles were impotent, and the xenos knew it.

The truck braked violently, throwing both Polixis and most of the orks hard against the drive compartment. The engine cut out, whether killed on purpose or because it had finally broken from the strain, Polixis couldn't tell. All he could see was the low, grey Ikaran sky, paralysed as he was. The greenskins started manhandling him once more, heaving him like so much deadweight out of the truck's back. He immediately recognised where they had taken him.

The Basilica of Saint Albarak the Smelter.

The great, gothic structure still stood, looking sadly out over the ruination of the city that had built it. Polixis wondered whether it would have been better to have seen the place of worship reduced to rubble – the fact that the greenskins had claimed it seemed like a far worse fate. The square beyond its front steps was now choked with refuse, while the great aquila doors had been broken open and cast down, the gold cladding bent out of shape and befouled by greenskin dung. Blood, paint or both had been used to daub crude glyphs across the basilica's stonework, and a ragged banner depicting a wicked, curved blade and leering half-moon fluttered above the open entranceway.

The sight of the basilica's defilement made Polixis' heart burn with a fresh surge of fury, far removed from the detached, forensic mindset he was accustomed to. It was his own impotence that did it, as much as the thought of alien filth defiling mankind's great works. He was a warrior, modified and then honed for nothing less than eternal war. To be rendered entirely unable to fight, to even resist, as he was dragged like a trophy-corpse towards the basilica, enraged him beyond reason. The fact that it was his own armour, brutalised by xenos cunning, that had left him incapacitated only completed the irony.

'You will suffer for this,' he shouted. 'I will see you all slaughtered like the animals you are!' The orks around him mirrored the shout with crude grunts and bellows, mocking him as they heaved him in through the basilica's open doors.

The inside was a scene of bedlam. Greenskins had infested the place of worship in its entirety. They had hung their ragged banners and skull glyphs from the balconies and buttresses, while others had smashed the carved rustwood pews to splinters and heaped the remains as kindling around the nave. More dung and indiscernible debris covered every surface, along with stacks of trash and rubble that seemed to have been dragged inside as loot. The greenskins themselves were everywhere – orks, gretchin and even the bulbous maw-beasts called squigs, leashed on rusting chains, slavering and snapping at anything that got close. They argued and scrapped, ate rancid meat and drank foul brews across the nave and on the balconies, amidst the cloisters and right to the back of the annexes. A place that had once resounded with the diligent praise of mankind's faithful now echoed with the raging, raucous, manic madness of total alien supremacy.

At its epicentre lay what had once been the basilica's apse. The semicircular space had been transformed into the throne dais of the beast that had come to conquer Ikara. Polixis was hauled towards it, and as he was taken down the nave, the noise of the greenskins intensified. They flocked to him from all sides, howling, their spit befouling his armour as he was moved by his captors to face the monstrosity that awaited him.

It was seated upon a chair of stone, darkened by blood and filth and surrounded by what looked like piles of wreckage hidden beneath heavy squig skins and hides. It took several seconds for Polixis to realise the base of the throne was in fact the remains of the basilica's altar block. Crude metal spikes had been riveted into it to form a barbaric resting place. The outrage he felt at such blasphemy didn't last long – his eyes fixed on the creature that lounged atop it, the beast that rose as he was dragged onto its dais.

As befitted all ork warlords, it was gigantic in size – even though it was hunched, it towered over its surrounding attendants. Its incredible musculature and trunk-like body held neither surprise nor fear for Polixis. He had spent the past century killing beasts just like it.

But there was something different about this one. That became apparent when the Apothecary was finally thrown down before it. For a creature so high in the esteem of its kind, it wore relatively little in the way of armour or customised weaponry – hide clothes and furs adorned it, and two long, serrated blades hung from its hip, along with a collection of yellowing skulls. What really caught the Ultramarine's attention, however, was the nature of its flesh. It did not take Polixis' extensive knowledge of anatomy to recognise that the thing he was looking at wasn't one creature, or at least it hadn't been originally. For a start it was misshapen – an arm and a leg were shorter than their counterparts, giving it a lopsided stance, and the hunch of its back was even more pronounced than usual. One eye was notably larger and more dilated than the other, and its jaw jutted forwards so much that thick wads of drool seemed to constantly dangle from its tusks.

It might simply have been a particularly ugly xenos, were it not for the evidence of the flesh itself. It was marked all over by savage, wilful surgery. The thing was a mass of mismatched green flesh, criss-crossed with crude sutures and thick stitching. Deep surgery scars ran from the base of its skull down the centre of its face, binding together the paler and darker halves of its skin. It wouldn't have taken an Apothecary's eye to discern that the individual dermal patches were foreign to one another – the shades and textures varied massively. The thing that ruled the orks on Ikara and the surrounding systems, the thing that called itself Warboss Urgork, was a freak of diabolical science, and testimony to the unnatural hardiness of its race taken to the nightmare extreme. It was a patchwork horror of sewn-together ork skins and body parts, and the very fact that it was alive and conscious sickened Polixis.

The thing leered at him, a drooling, tusked grin, one of its mismatched yellow eyes blinking while the other remained glazed. It gestured at the greenskins still holding him and barked a string of commands, spittle spraying the apse's grime-smeared flagstones. They dragged him to one side, to where a rack of thick metal struts and coiled razor wire had been bolted to the floor. Again, Polixis tried to force action into his limbs, straining against the prison that his armour had become. He felt a few servos tick and grate, but beyond that, nothing. The orks slammed him against the rack and dragged clamps and wire around his limbs, snaring him.

Only then did the warlord approach. It did so with a pronounced limp, a hand fingering the hilt of one of its wicked blades, its leer replaced by the focused expression of a curious animal. It stopped a few paces from the bound Primaris, its minions flocking round, silence settling slowly across the riotous space.

'Da w-white beakie,' Urgork rumbled. He spoke in a hideous, stammering bastardisation of Low Gothic, but it was intelligible. Polixis said nothing in reply.

'You's da boy I've been lookin' for,' Urgork continued, moving a little closer. 'Da b-big b-beakie git I've 'eard all about. They tell stories about you lot, ya know? You's da lad dat patches 'em all up. My weirdboy's s-seen it.'

Polixis still refused to respond. Urgork pointed a claw at the sea of ugly green faces around them.

'These lads all came 'ere to fight. Didn't ya, boys?'

The orks roared their agreement, the sound rebounding thunderously from the vaults high above. Amidst it Urgork leaned closer, his voice lower.

'But I didn't. Sure, I wanted to scrap wiv da big new beakies, but I gots somethin' else on my mind too. You's gonna help me, git, and when you's done I'll give you a good, quick death. Won't even strip ya skin.'

The creature tapped one of his long blades.

Polixis tried with all his might to move his limbs. His muscles clenched and strained and his jaw locked. A slow, hissing breath escaped from between his teeth as he focused everything into trying to wrench his arms free from their bonds.

There was a low grating sound, the misery of locked servos being forced against their will. The barest hint of movement followed, as both arms inched forwards slightly before coming up against the resistance of the clamps. Urgork looked at him with what could have passed for a quizzical expression, a wad of saliva drooling from between his tusks. He leaned close to the clamps as Polixis struggled in silence, as though inspecting them. As though he hoped to see them bend and break beneath the fury of the Primaris.

Instead they held firm. The ork grunted and motioned to the mob surrounding them.

'Zap 'im again, Morglum.'

The smaller greenskin with the electro prong pushed itself to the fore and plunged the crackling rod into Polixis' flank without hesitation, the bolts of lightning picking out its rictus grin. The Apothecary's struggles ended and a cry of agony was ripped from his throat as the powerful electrical charge surged through his body, channelled directly into his flesh by his dermal nodes.

'I like it when you big humies struggle,' Urgork said over the crackling sound. 'But I also likes watchin' ya fry as well. So why not 'ave both?'

The charge cut off, bolts of lightning still arcing and sparking across Polixis' armour.

'You's a quiet one, ain't ya?' Urgork demanded. 'Don't g-go all shy on me, beakie.'

The warlord stepped close and placed one great hand on Polixis' helmet. Energy danced and snapped from the white ceramite and up the greenskin's stitch-crossed arm, but if the ork felt any pain he didn't show it. He held Polixis' head in the palm of his great, scarred fist. Then, with sudden, savage motion he reached up with his other hand and snatched the helmet between them. He locked fingers behind Polixis' head and started to pull.

Ceramite and plasteel groaned. Polixis felt a hideous pressure on his neck and spine, and his breath caught. He knew that ordinarily such an assault on his battleplate would have caused warnings to burst to life across his visor display, but there was nothing – it remained blank. His auto-senses were dead and his servos locked.

It would have been natural for a human mind to give in to panic or despair. An Adeptus Astartes was immune to the former, but the latter was not unknown. In that moment Polixis realised that he was almost certainly going to die – if not in that moment, then very soon – and that he would likely do so in pain so excruciating that even his transhuman body would be unable to block it out. Far worse were the realisations that his blessed armour and equipment would fall into the grubby, defiling hands of the xenos, and that his own progenoids would be left to rot with his corpse, abandoned and forgotten.

'Kastor, give me strength,' he said from between gritted teeth. He said it without thinking, intoning Kastor's name as readily as the primarch's or the Emperor's. He had always been there, always ready and willing no matter the task. To be taken and used like this wasn't only bringing shame upon the Chapter. It was bringing shame to Kastor.

Urgork gripped and twisted his helm all the harder. The plasteel's groan became a tortured shriek as the gorget finally broke and the seal was ripped open. Polixis let out a gasp as air flooded his lungs again, and the unbearable tension on his neck lessened. Even a Space Marine would certainly have had his head torn from his shoulders by the ork's brute strength – only the incredible durability of Primaris physiology had saved him. He blinked as his eyes adjusted automatically, exposed now before the assembled aliens.

Urgork dropped the helmet. It cracked from the flagstones before rolling down the steps from the apse, not even reaching the bottom before a bickering mass of gretchin descended on it. Urgork leaned in close to Polixis, the ork's vile stench engulfing the Ultramarine, wicked tusks and mismatched, cruel eyes just inches away.

'Now we can look at each uvva, one pretty face ta anuvva,' Urgork growled. Polixis met the ork's gaze, but said nothing. His brother would probably have snarled a prayer of purging or spat in its face, but the Apothecary did not see the point in either action. He would not converse with xenos. The warlord grunted, half turning away.

'Maybe dis w-will get ya interested. Grok!'

There was a scrabbling sound, and another greenskin wormed its way to the front of the assembly. It was a bent-over creature, clad in what Polixis realised was a hideous mockery of a human medicae's uniform – a soiled white smock and black rubber gloves, complete with an optical cluster strapped to its bald head. The strange greenskin came up short when it latched eyes on Polixis, its jaw hanging slack.

'Told ya I'd get one, didn't I?' Urgork demanded. The runty creature nodded, not taking its own greedy eyes off Polixis.

The Apothecary recognised its expression, but it took long seconds for him to properly place it – it was staring at him in veneration. The ork was looking up at him the way so many humans had done before, with a heady mixture of awe and fear. The realisation made his skin crawl. He found himself looking away, where moments before he had held the gaze of a beast perfectly capable of tearing his skull from his spine.

'You t-t-two good lads is gonna help each uvva,' Urgork continued, clapping one hand on Polixis' pauldron and the other on the small ork's shoulder. 'You is gonna help each uvva ta help me.'

'I would rather die a thousand deaths,' Polixis said, unable to hold his tongue any longer. 'If you think I would even consider helping you then you know nothing of my kind.'

'I know a fing or two,' Urgork said, grinning at the Primaris. 'We'll see if you's still talkin' so tough after we is done wiv you.'

'There is no torture that you could devise that would turn me against my own species.'

'Y-you boys is 'ard lads, n-no denyin' dat,' Urgork said, his stammering appearing to grow worse. 'I c-could put my skinnin' blades ta work, and I could use my painboy 'ere and my weirdboy, maybe even old Big Mek Cogkrusha, and I r-r-reckon all togetha we could cook s-somethin' up dat'd make you squeal event… eventually. Could take some time though. A-ain't no point either, n-n-not when I's already got a betta idea.'

'It will do you no good,' Polixis said. 'The weight of Imperial retribution will be upon you soon.'

Urgork laughed, a wet, ugly, hacking sound. The laugh gave way to a bout of coughing, and a sudden rigidity took hold of the greenskin's posture. A hand shot out, snatching for the hunchbacked medic as the warlord's distended jaw locked and his eyes widened. Foam began to bubble around his tusks.

The thing called Grok stuffed a hand in the hide satchel it was carrying and dragged out a wicked syringe filled with a foul-looking yellow liquid. Without pause it slammed the needle into Urgork's flank and rammed down the plunger. The warlord spasmed, shuddered, and the surrounding orks pushed and shoved against one another as they tried to back away.

Polixis stared at the warlord in morbid fascination, automatically picking up on details without really registering them fully – the dilated eyes, the spasming movement, the muscular contractions and locked jaw. A low, keening sound escaped Urgork's throat, curiously at odds with his towering bulk. Then, abruptly, his head snapped to the side, and he spat a great wad of bilious phlegm at Polixis' feet.

'Dat's… betta…' the warlord wheezed, bones and sinews popping and crunching as he flexed his arms and took a few deep, rattling breaths. He rounded on Polixis once more, and a feral madness blazed in his yellow gaze.

'Not seen one of da lads do that before, 'ave you?' he demanded, brutish expression caught somewhere between anger and amusement. 'But I can tell you's never met a boss like me neither. I'm one of a kind, and you's gonna help me out whether you likes it or not.'

Polixis said nothing, simply held the ork's mismatched glare. The greenskin grinned more broadly and gestured at him.

'Zap 'im again.'

KASTOR

Kastor left as evening drew near, and mankind went to war once more against the green menace. Ork artillery had been brought up and bedded down in large quantities along the edge of Shebat, and as the shrouded sun began to dip towards the Tombstone's saw-toothed peaks they started an indiscriminate bombardment of Ridge 1. The Astra Militarum's big guns, which had until that moment remained silent to avoid triggering another massed assault, returned fire.

According to Kastor's visor display, Fifth and Eighth Corps were being fully stood-to once more, as shellfire blossomed and great clods of ash and dirt showered down on newly repaired sandbag redoubts. The first large-scale reinforcements from Kroten – a spearhead division of Moskatin Light Infantry – was arriving at Ridge 1's rear echelons and receiving their deployment orders, bellowed to them over the hammer of Basilisk mobile artillery pieces and Griffon heavy mortars.

Kastor was only vaguely aware of it via the tactical updates logged on his visor. He departed with Task Force Marilus just before the light started to fail.

The air war – dormant all day – was beginning to come alive once more. The vox was reporting a massed daytime air raid on Kroten, and augur systems had picked up more waves bound for the skies above Ridge 1. The day before, the greenskins had focused their aircraft on one target and then the other. Today it seemed as though they were using their vast numerical superiority to strike at both with simultaneous, equal force. Kastor suspected there was nothing Flight Marshal Roggens could do but deploy a few token wings to contest them.

One of those wings flew cover with the Thunderhawk *Dromidas*. Its pilot, Brother Quilo, took it hard and low for sixty miles south of Ridge 1, arcing slowly westwards as they swung wide around Shebat Alpha's southernmost remains.

The Thunderbolts sent to chaperon the Ultramarines flyer stood off, maintaining an operational altitude ceiling in order to avoid drawing attention to their charge. As evening drew in, a flight of greenskin heavy bombers were spotted heading northwards. For a while it looked as if their fighter support was going to sweep away from the raggedy formation and give chase. Whatever beast commanded the wing, however, clearly knew better than to allow its escorts to leave the bombers exposed. After a brief detour the greenskin fighters rejoined their heavier cousins, and the Thunderbolts resumed their south-westward course, roaring far above the rattling Thunderhawk.

Kastor sat within *Dromidas'* hold, strapped to one of the restraint benches. His helmet was mag-locked to his belt, revealing the features he shared so closely with his blood brother: the golden hair, firm jawline and soft, discerning eyes. Those eyes were on the other occupants of the transport as it juddered through a fresh patch of turbulence.

There were three of them, Primaris Ultramarines seated across from the Chaplain. They wore the customised, form-fitting power armour and death's head masks of the Reivers, and their own bowed heads and silence mirrored that of the Chaplain.

Kastor contemplated them without speaking, knowing they were all aware of his gaze. Severus himself sat opposite Kastor, flanked by his two death-brothers. Their names were Fobus and Stryx. All three had removed their helms, though the skull masks remained in place, obscuring their lower faces. Not for the first time, the Chaplain pondered the similarities between his own office and those who followed the path of the Reiver.

Some called them a cult. It was a false accusation – Kastor

had examined the beliefs of each one of the Fulminata's death-brethren in detail over many decades. Their actions and attitudes set them apart. Kastor could understand how their fellow Ultramarines – especially non-Primaris – found them a strange and potentially dangerous addition to the Chapter. They were taciturn in the extreme, and when they did interact with their battle-brothers, they usually displayed either a high degree of morbidity or a vicious, bloodthirsty streak that seemed far removed from the balance espoused by the Codex. Their mode of warfare required them to be ruthless, efficient and, when necessary, uncompromisingly brutal. Such attributes were far from uncommon among the Adeptus Astartes, but among the Reivers they were ampli-fied, sharpened to an edge as wicked as the long blades they wielded with such chilling ability.

Severus exemplified them – taciturn at best, with the grace and poise of a hunting larix. His every move was consid-ered, his every pronouncement precise. Where Kastor's eyes were a soft blue, approaching grey, the Reiver's were like ice, cold and unyielding. His shaved head was criss-crossed with ridges of thick white scar tissue, and Kastor could count on one hand the number of times he had encountered him without the skeletal leer of his skull mask fixed in place. His grim demeanour would likely have seen him treated as an outcast by the brotherhood, were it not for the fact that there was barely a single member of the Fulminata who did not owe their lives to the intervention of his Reivers at some point or another. No other squad came close to their kill tallies, and even the likes of Lieutenant Samson would have thought twice before coming between them and their designated kill-target. Demeter used to describe them as his hunting hounds – give them the scent, and they would not stop until their quarry had been tracked down and brought to heel.

The Reiver sergeant's eyes had been fixed unblinkingly on the Thunderhawk's deck, but they rose abruptly, meeting Kastor's. The Chaplain found himself recalling the cold, predatory gaze of the crophound that had come for the grox herd he'd been watching over one night, the memory dredged abruptly from his youth. He'd known that to break contact with the starved animal would mean instant death, yet the urge had been overwhelming. He'd hesitated, standing his ground, torch in hand, the grox behind him lowing in distress as they caught the predator's scent. He decided later on that the encounter had surely lasted only seconds, and yet it had felt like so much longer, his young heart hammering in his chest, his skinny limbs trembling, breath held, as though to even emit it would be to risk the savagery of claws and fangs.

Polixis had saved him that night. The older boy had come running with another torch in hand, shouting at the top of his lungs. The beast had taken fright and loped back off into the darkness.

But Polixis wasn't here any more. Severus looked away, turning his eyes to the deck again. Kastor realised he'd been holding his breath.

'One hour out, brethren,' the voice of the pilot, Quilo, crackled over the intercom. Kastor forced himself to take his eyes off the Reivers and glance at the locator auspex wired above the hold's disembarkation ramp. It showed their latest fixing, just east of the Tombstones and south of Shebat. Ostensibly the plan was simple. Insertion into the mountains around the city followed by infiltration into its ruined heart. Whatever purpose Polixis had been taken for, it was almost certain the warlord of the Waaagh! would demand such a potent trophy. Finding Urgork would lead to finding Polixis, and discovering the location of a greenskin leader was rarely a difficult process. That was what he had impressed on Severus, when he had caught the Reiver's reticence at allowing the Chaplain to join his brethren.

The hard part would be living long enough to get Polixis out.

Severus had run over the operation with Kastor immediately after take-off. He had spoken only briefly to the Chaplain when he had first arrived, jogging through the swirling ash cloud just as the three Reivers were climbing the Thunderhawk's rear ramp.

'If you are to accompany us, Brother-Chaplain, you will follow my directives to the letter,' he had said. Kastor had sworn he would do so. No questions about his inclusion were asked. Kastor had no doubt the Reiver was aware Tyranus had not approved his place in the mission. Nor, however, had the lieutenant specifically forbade him from going. There had been neither binding oaths nor orders. Had he been a part of the demi-company's direct command structure there was no doubt he would have been forced to remain on the ridge, but his position as Chaplain afforded him the autonomy he needed. Those were the conclusions he had drawn during the afternoon's meditations.

Had Captain Demeter ordered him to stay, he would have stayed. As it stood, though, only the strictest reading of the Codex would have indicated that he had no other option than to follow Lieutenant Tyranus' directives and remain on the ridge.

The letter was clear, the moral was not – did the brotherhood still need him, and would a renewed greenskin assault right now push them beyond breaking point? He doubted it. The truth was he had been at peace the moment he had stepped down from the wreckage of the ork fighter's fuselage. He was going to find his brother or he was going to die trying. If there were any consequences he would face them unflinchingly when he returned.

'You are concerned, Brother-Chaplain,' said Severus over the sound of *Dromidas'* engines. Kastor realised he was looking at him once more.

'Is that why you so rarely remove your mask, sergeant?' he replied. 'So no one can discern your true feelings?'

'The masks are not for our benefit but for those we hunt,' Severus said humourlessly. 'We are their death made manifest. Regardless of whether they fight or flee, we will come for them. They must be made to understand that.'

'Two covers of the same book,' Kastor said, looking down at his own skull helm, locked to his hip. 'I am a reminder of mankind's mortality, the revelation that all shall stand before the Emperor and be judged, vengefully if need be. You bring that same lesson to mankind's enemies.'

'We do,' Severus said, his eyes still on the Chaplain. They had conversed before about the particular beliefs of the Reivers, and their place within the Chapter. Even the hardliners had accepted that the Codex Astartes supported their mode of warfare – covert infiltration and brutal shock tactics were already at the heart of many Space Marine combat doctrines. It was the Reivers' more unconventional trappings that had caused concern outside their brotherhood. The skull masks and the morbidity, the closed nature of their squads and the rumours of blood rites and cult-like inductions. Kastor knew such stories for what they were – unsound gossip – and was sure to stamp them out wherever and whenever they reared up in the sparring blocks or barrack dorms.

Appearances aside, the Reivers were no death cult. Perhaps Kastor's respect for their insular aspects was part of the reason Severus hadn't refused him. Or perhaps he understood better than anyone else in the Fulminata the terrible urges that took hold when a brother fell or was captured. Perhaps that was why he hadn't questioned him when he had appeared from the ash with a look as cold as his own in those pale eyes.

POLIXIS

Polixis slept the half-sleep of the Adeptus Astartes, his thoughts sluggish and distant. The catalepsian node, the sixth of the glands, organs and nodes that made a Space Marine, allowed its bearer to enter a meditative state when regular sleep was not an option. Parts of the brain were rested in turn, allowing Polixis to maintain a degree of consciousness and readiness.

Without it he would not have been able to sleep at all. The urge to continue his attempts at escape had only increased as Urgork had left him and darkness had descended on the basilica. It had to have been days since he had last slept, and while a Primaris was more than capable of remaining combat effective for long periods at a time, Polixis understood better than most the importance of rest. The pain of torture and the mental and physical strain of his unique form of imprisonment had worn him down – he was resistant to hardship, but not immune.

The cold, clinical part of his mind told him as much, even as the rest of his thoughts continued to burn with an anger he was sure his younger brother would have approved of. The mere fact that the xenos thought it could use him to its own ends was enough of an affront, even before he considered the defilement of the basilica around him. He did not need Kastor's battle rites to feel an unaccustomed surge in his hatred for the enemies of mankind whenever he came across their blasphemies against the Imperial Creed. Perhaps it was simply his brother's nature finally rubbing off on him.

'You taught me more than you know, little brother,' he growled.

Eventually he was able to quell his thoughts and reassert his detachment enough to find a degree of rest. Around him the basilica had largely fallen silent – it seemed even the greenskins needed time to recover from their near-constant scrapping. Dozens lay sprawled across the bare stone floor, most of them intoxicated by the vile-smelling fungal brew they seemed to imbibe so much of. Even the squig beasts were unconscious, rocking gently on their backs, their warty tongues lolling from open maws and stubby, upturned limbs twitching the air.

Where Urgork had gone, Polixis didn't know. His altar throne was now vacant. The Apothecary had last seen the deformed greenskin limping down into the basilica's undercroft accompanied by his gaggle of flunkies and minions. Presumably the orks had already discovered the munitions abandoned in the crypts beneath, left behind by the Guard during their hasty evacuation. Polixis didn't doubt the shells were already being lobbed back at the artillery pieces they had been forged for, all along Ridge 1. He could hear the distant rumble of the guns on the heavy night air.

In his own absence, Urgork had left the greenskins that had first captured Polixis to guard him through the night, surely as much from their fellow orks as to stop any escape attempt. The Apothecary had encountered their kind before, albeit on only a few occasions. They seemed to style themselves after the covert units of the Astra Militarum and Tempestus Scions, engaging in crude and basic sabotage, assassination and the penetration of rear-line cohorts. While their raggedy capes and rugged night-vision goggles could appear incongruous, Polixis had witnessed their work first-hand – the ambush in the Karsin Delta on Mira III and the great hunt through the Solek jungles. They could be extremely deadly. They were a reminder that while Imperial propaganda worked tirelessly to portray the green menace as crude, oafish and savage, such a view was disingenuous. The orks could not have infested vast swathes of the galaxy with their brutish spore without being highly adaptable and cunning. That was something too many good soldiers of the Imperium – officers and men alike – had discovered to their cost.

Polixis realised he too had made the same mistake. He had allowed himself to be drawn into the fury of the breach assault during the battle on the ridge, and had become snared. That the ork kommandos appeared to have been sent specifically for him was an even more disturbing revelation. Urgork still hadn't described exactly what he wanted from the Primaris, seemingly content to let the question prey on him during the long, dark hours. While Polixis could conceive of nothing he feared that would break him either mentally or physically, every moment he remained in captivity created a further moment of risk – what if the xenos used him to draw in the Fulminata, or tried to bargain with the likes of Field Marshal Klos? How many men might be lost if he was utilised as bait?

What was worse, how would Kastor react? He had no doubt

his brother believed he was still alive. Had Tyranus managed to convince him not to embark on a rescue attempt? Would his rage allow him to pause long enough to reflect on the madness of risking his own life in some hopeless effort, now that the Chaplain's leadership and guidance was needed by the Fulminata more than ever before?

From the sounds of the distant artillery, it seemed as though another offensive was already underway – were his battle-brothers even now fighting against the onrushing green tide, suffering their blows without their Apothecary at hand to aid them?

'Guide my blood brother,' Polixis muttered, reaching out once more to the Emperor and the primarch. 'For the sake of the Chapter, don't let him do anything foolish.'

The thought of Kastor engaged in an effort to save him made Polixis' captivity intolerable. He had to try to get out, but escape was impossible if he was immobilised. As time elapsed he drifted in and out of his subconscious, allowing his catalepsian node to engage and fade out his bleak surroundings.

How long he remained in a fugue state was difficult to tell. With his auto-senses offline and his helmet gone he had no access to a chronometer, and the darkness within the basilica remained near-complete, lit only by a few red embers amidst the piles of trash and broken pews the orks had been roasting their food over. At some point, motion disturbed his languid thoughts, triggering a gland-impulse that returned him immediately to full consciousness.

His guards had drifted off to sleep, but there was one greenskin in the defiled basilica still awake.

The greenskin medic was back. The creature was still clad in its dirty hospital garb, the plastek material of its black gloves crackling slightly as it moved up onto the apse dais. It took a while for Polixis to realise what it was doing. He watched with growing surprise as it moved from one sleeping greenskin to the next, one of its grubby syringes in a gloved hand. With a care rare in such beasts, it injected each of the six orks sprawled about Urgork's throne and Polixis' rack, its ugly face a focused rictus of concentration. Only when the final dose had been administered did it place the syringe carefully back into its satchel and approach the Primaris.

Polixis looked down at the hunched creature but said nothing. Wordlessly it reached up with its gloved hands and ran them along first his breastplate and then his outstretched left arm, the plastek squeaking slightly as it dragged over the ceramite's white surface. The thing's fingers came to rest on the bulky apparatus of his narthecium, still attached to his left gauntlet. It stood on its tiptoes, squinting as it inspected the device in the near-darkness, its claws probing the wicked edges of the chainsaw, the drill bit's spike and the blank screen of the diagnostor panel. Last of all it touched the cryo-vials at the rear of the device. It paused, and something approximating a smile split its tusked maw.

'Dem lads won't be wakin' up anytime soon,' it hissed, one hand still on the narthecium as it gestured with its other back towards the guards lying unmoving across the apse. 'Thought I'd come visit ya. Compare notes, one doc to anuvva.'

Polixis didn't reply. The thing's smile became an angry grimace. It slid a thick, rusting saw blade free from the pockets stitched into its surgical gown, and placed one boot on Polixis' left knee guard, gripping his right pauldron and using it as a brace to drag itself up to eye level. Its stinking breath engulfed the Apothecary, and its mad little eyes were suddenly just inches away.

'You ain't gonna be quiet with me, humie,' it snarled.

The ork pressed its rusting saw against the bare flesh of Polixis' throat, just above his broken gorget seal. The Space Marine didn't flinch. He met the greenskin's ugly, squinting gaze as it began to force the jagged metal against his trachea, letting out a grunt of effort as it did so. It had clearly never encountered the durametallic coil-cables that lent Primaris a layer of subdermal resilience – its expression became one of confusion and then anger as the vicious edge of its misappropriated surgical tool only succeeded in drawing the most slender line of blood from the Apothecary's bared throat. The greenskin clearly considered putting the weight of both its hands behind the blade, before thinking better of the danger of losing its grip on his armour. Instead it drew the saw back, glaring, and spoke again.

'What's da point of you humie docs? You save da runty ones. You don't even stitch 'em up wiv new body bits. Some of da boys you save don't even fight no more after. Why save 'em if dey can't fight?'

'Saving the life of a servant of the Emperor is a goal, regardless of whether or not they can still fight,' Polixis said, the disgust he felt at the mere presence of the creature forcing the words from his lips. 'We are not enslaved to war, like you. You are a disgusting breed of beasts, and your concept of healing reflects that.'

'So you's sayin' ya got somethin' betta ta be doin' than crumpin'?' the doc sneered, baring its small, pointy tusks in an approximation of amusement. 'I ain't neva heard of beakie boys doin' anything uvva than crumpin'. What, do ya herd squigs when you ain't scrappin'?'

Polixis ignored the creature's crude mockery. The smile melted once more from the greenskin's face, its manic mood oscillating dangerously.

'Da big boss is well pleased Grimtoof and 'is gits snatched you. He's been lookin' for one of youse for a long time. I blame dat pophead Slyboy for it. He's da one dat got all dem ideas into da big boss' head. Tellin' him da white beakies would fix 'im all up. Dat git. He don't need no fixin'. I made him, and he's perfect as is!'

The ork's voice had risen steadily through the diatribe. One of the unconscious guards sprawled next to the rack twitched and grunted. The medicae froze, still gripping on to Polixis. After a few seconds of silence, it grinned its vile grin once more, speaking again in a sibilant whisper.

'Dat's why I've been makin' sure ol' Sly has been takin' his medicine good and propa. Give it another few weeks and he'll be spewin' his guts out. Den we'll see how good 'is visions are for da boss.'

The ork let out a sickly little giggle, the gloved claws of its right hand scraping Polixis' pauldron as it gripped him tighter.

'Your warlord is a freak experiment,' Polixis said. 'Does it not anger you that your own mad creation is now your master?'

The ork returned its saw blade to Polixis' throat, so suddenly it almost lost its grip on his armour.

'You don't speak about da big boss like that,' it hissed. 'He's da greatest warlord wot ever existed.'

'And also dying,' Polixis added. 'Your insane surgeries may have given him life, but how much longer does he have? How much longer before your injections rot his insides?'

'You don't know nothin',' the ork snarled. 'Da big boss has got it in his 'ead that you's gonna fix him up, but he don't need fixin'. You understand? You's not gonna say anythin' to him. I'm his doc, not you.'

203

'Even by the standards of your race, you are a weak and pathetic creature,' Polixis said slowly.

'We'll see who's weak after da boss is done with ya,' the ork hissed back, withdrawing its impotent saw blade once more. It dropped back down to the floor and tapped the rusting tool against Polixis' breastplate.

'Remember what I said, beakie. You don't tell da big boss nothin'. If you does, I'll be back when da boys is all asleep again, and we'll see how tough ya skin really is.'

CHAPTER EIGHT   THE TOMBSTONES

KASTOR

When they were three minutes to the drop zone, Severus slapped his gauntlet against Kastor's left pauldron, confirming his glider was ready. Kastor had replaced his backpack with one provided by the Reivers during the flight, as dawn had broken out across the wasteland below. Its slightly greater bulk felt cumbersome, and the rest of his armour still had not accepted it as its new power source. The supply reading kept blinking on and off, and occasionally a system overheat warning would appear on the overlay and remain frozen until Kastor blink-deleted it.

He would make the necessary apologies to his blessed armour later. The pack was required, because it incorporated the grav-glider fins utilised by the Reivers for silent aerial insertions. He had also removed his robes and vestments, folding and locking them in the little reliquary clamped to the small of his back, beneath his backpack. They would only be an encumbrance, both during the aerial drop and in the covert operation to follow. Both the glider backpack and the vestments were points Kastor had conceded to Severus before take-off – the operation would be conducted just as the taciturn sergeant had originally planned, and the Chaplain's inclusion in Task Force Marilus would not change that.

'Thirty seconds,' crackled the voice of the pilot. Stryx hauled back the Thunderhawk's side hatch, exposing the world scudding past below. The featureless expanse of the ash wastes had given way first to the arid foothills of the Tombstones, then the rocky slopes and gullies of the great mountain range itself. The drop zone chosen by Severus was deep in the heart of the mountain range, far from the prying eyes of xenos patrols or air cover. It would allow them to initially traverse the easier routes along the valley bottoms and sparse waterways that wound between the peaks, before approaching the edge of the city itself under the cover of darkness, just east of the Gorgon's winding, toxic expanse.

'Drop zone reached, green light,' the pilot's voice clicked.

Fobus was first out, stepping into space without hesitation. Stryx followed, then Kastor stepped up. For the briefest moment he was on the edge, jagged yellow slopes and knifeback ridges whipping past beneath him. Then he went over, his ears filled with the roar of the Thunderhawk's engines, sudden weightlessness tugging at his stomach.

He forced his body into a descent pattern position, battling the whipping wind and gravity's angry pull. A quick glance at his chronometer, then he triggered his grav-glider. The fins engaged, snapping out and locking. Immediately his descent was slowed, tugged back as his armour absorbed the shock of the arrested plummet. He looked down, taking a few seconds to assess the drop zone.

Fobus and Stryx were a hundred feet below and peeling off to his left, dots of blue against the ochre backdrop of the Tombstones' newly dawned majesty. Directly beneath, the blue waters of a nameless mountain tributary glittered, the ribbon winding away through the lower valleys and gorges until it reached the Gorgon. The earth around it provided a rare dash of green amidst the dusty yellows of the arid mountains, clusters of shrubs and small trees hugging the thin strip of fertile soil provided by the tributary. The view as the sun rose – from the jagged peaks set against the low, grey sky to the greener earth directly below – was spectacular.

Kastor didn't pause to savour it. Severus – dropping a hundred feet to his right and further up – had marked a stretch of ground close to the riverbank via their shared visor uplink. Kastor locked his own viewfinder into the coordinates and used the rudimentary glider stick attached via the backpack to steer his controlled descent towards it.

As he dropped, he caught sight of *Dromidas* banking round, white streamers inscribing an arc in its wake. The pilot signed off over the vox as he headed back east, the Thunderbolts having already peeled away to avoid detection.

Kastor and the Reivers were alone.

The ground rushed up with surprising speed. Fobus impacted first with a brutal thud, followed by Stryx, both off in the low undergrowth to Kastor's left. For the briefest second he was worried he would overshoot and come down in the river itself. He pressed hard on the glider stick, speeding his descent as he arched his back and brought himself round to a landing position. He hit the ground near the riverbank with far more force than he intended, whipping through the branches of a clutch of low bushes and then cracking his right foot against the rocky earth. He skittered along, the vanes attached to his backpack clacking, until both boots struck true and his armour was able to give him enough shock absorbance and balance to run the last few yards.

He skidded to a halt just before he hit the embankment. The stream before him was swift and clear, fed by springs further up the mountainside, a far cry from the nightmare toxicity of the great Gorgon, which the waters would eventually join.

He turned, his bolt pistol and crozius unclamped in an instant as the vanes of the glider pack automatically folded away. Nothing stirred in the undergrowth around him. He was alone, lost in what felt like a small paradise, far removed from the choking grey wastelands of the plain below and all the blood and death and muscle-aching, heart-pounding strain of desperate combat.

He snapped out of the moment, barely holding back a curse. His half-botched landing had wasted enough time as it was. He locked Salve Imperator and advanced into the undergrowth, following the location markers of the Reivers on his display.

He found them gathered a hundred yards further north, crouched around the fuzzing blue projection of a handheld holo display, laid out in the underbrush between them. Severus looked up as Kastor approached, eyes cold as ever above his skull mask.

'Congratulations on your landing, Brother-Chaplain,' he said. If the remark was meant humorously, it didn't show in his voice.

'I can't say I recall my last glider insertion,' Kastor grumbled, kneeling down beside the Reivers. Severus said nothing more to him, pointing instead at the projection.

'Shebat Alpha lies to the north. We should be on the approach routes not long after nightfall, and nearing the outskirts by middle-dark. That will greatly assist our infiltration. Reports from the wastes indicate another xenos assault on the ridge was repelled last night. If another doesn't come this afternoon then it will tonight. All their focus should be eastwards. We follow the bank of the Gorgon once we pick it up and use it to penetrate as deeply as possible. That means submersion if necessary. All clear?'

It was. Stryx deactivated the projector and folded it away. Wordlessly, they moved out.

POLIXIS

Urgork returned with the dawn. The misshapen greenskin approached Polixis as he rose once more from his half-sleep, the medicae-thing that had come to the Apothecary during the night trailing behind. Weak sunlight was filtering in through the basilica's shattered windows, and the orks filling the place were rousing themselves with bleary grunts and growls. Polixis' guards seemed particularly hard hit – they stirred only sluggishly, unaware of the after-effects of whatever drug had been administered to them the night before. For his own part, Urgork seemed in a fine mood. The beast gave Polixis one of his ugly half-grins as he mounted the apse steps.

'Mornin', doc,' he exclaimed. 'Hope you s-slept good and propa. Got plenty of work to be gettin' on wiv today.'

He stopped in front of the Apothecary, fists balled on his hips, looking the Primaris up and down.

'You's probably thinkin' I'm gonna start crumpin' ya right about now,' he said, his tone verging on conciliatory. 'C-crack dat big white shell open and start stickin' you wiv all dis and dat. Maybe Morglum's zap stick again, or Cogkrusha's big saw? Can't lie to ya, beakie, I'd like ta see how much of all dat stuff you could take. Maybe later. But for now, we is gonna keep it nice and simple. You'll tell my doc how ta fix me up. If you does, I promise I'll chop ya quick an' hard when da time comes.'

The closest greenskins laughed darkly, clearly aware of their warlord's lies. The medicae greenskin hunched over behind Urgork just glared at Polixis, fingering the handle of one of its saws.

'You are a monstrosity, without any right to life,' Polixis said. 'All the medical science in the galaxy could not extend your existence by a second. Even if it could, I would not tell you of it.'

Urgork moved, the motion sudden and violent, the speed belying his deformed body. He snatched Polixis by his hair and slammed his skull back against the rack's frame, snarling in his face.

'You still talkin' tough, beakie. Time to change dat for good. We'll see how tough you really is soon enough.'

The ork stepped back and clicked his fingers at a gaggle of minions clustered around his throne. They scrambled to comply, snatching and tugging at the raggedy hides that had been drawn over whatever was heaped at the throne's base. As they were dragged away, Polixis felt his body surge with a fresh dose of adrenaline and stimms. His fists clenched and his face flushed with rage.

Before him lay the remains of Squad Tiro, Ancient Skyrus and Captain Demeter. Their corpses had been dumped around Urgork's throne like so much trash, their proud battleplate rent and bloodied, frozen in their death throes. Demeter held pride of place at the foot of the throne, slumped over, helmet bowed as though he had been greeted by the Emperor in his final moments. His right arm was missing, and his ancient power sword, Justicier, lay discarded in the debris and dried blood at his feet.

The sight of his brothers' defiled corpses enraged Polixis beyond words. He flung himself against his restraints, but still his own armour resisted him, subverted by the unknowable xenos technology that had killed its machine-spirit.

'Guessin' ya knew these gits,' Urgork said, his voice now low and mocking. 'They put up a right propa scrap. Well, some of 'em did. They all squealed in da end though. Especially this 'un.'

The warlord aimed a kick at Demeter, causing the body to slump to one side. Polixis redoubled his efforts, snarling. Urgork just laughed.

'This must be yours too, den?' he said, bending down beside Skyrus' remains and tugging at something caught under the battleplate. A long strip of blue-and-white silkweave emerged as Urgork dragged at it, accompanied by a ripping sound as a section remained trapped beneath the body.

'You humies love ya bits of cloth,' the ork said, holding it up in one fist for Polixis' benefit. The Primaris found himself looking at the white crest of the Chapter, just discernible through the blood and dirt that caked it. He realised he was seeing the ragged remains of the Fulminata's standard, now held in the clutches of the filthy alien.

'I will kill you,' Polixis said. 'I will carve your head from your shoulders, and see your body turned to ash!'

'Dat's da s-s-spirit. We gots ya big tank, too,' Urgork said with casual disdain, pointing towards more hides flung across a great, bulky object that had been hauled through a gap smashed in the basilica's flank. 'Gonna let my big mek tinka wiv it. Make it bigga, stronga, fasta. Da usual. And you's gonna see it all, beakie. Unless ya help me.'

'May the Emperor's burning blade take you, and all your vile spore.'

'Thought you'd say somethin' like dat,' Urgork said, holding a hand out for one of the painboy's syringes. 'Don't ya worry though, beakie boy. We's just gettin' started. P-plenty of time ta change ya mind.'

KASTOR

It would have taken several days' travel for anyone else to approach from the drop zone to within fifteen miles of Shebat's southern edge. It took the Primaris until nightfall. They moved at the double, following the comparatively easy path taken by the stream as it sought out the Gorgon amidst the crevasses and gullies of the Tombstones' depths. Their stamina was barely tested – even without the servos of their armour enhancing their speed and poise over the rugged terrain, their endurance was unmatched. Following such a bloody battle, even a fellow brother of the Adeptus Astartes would have shown a degree of weariness by late afternoon, and would doubtless have benefitted from a pause to maintain efficiency and area awareness.

The Primaris needed no such respite. The Reivers were accustomed to such pace and distance when tracking quarry, and for his own part Kastor knew such exertions were well within his own limitations. He was far stockier than the typically lithe Reivers, and his armour and its systems were not as optimised towards long distance movement as theirs, but he adapted his mind to it, knowing ultimately that his heavily enhanced body would follow. He sunk part of his thoughts into a recital of the Third Teaching of the Master of Sanctity, even as he continued to automatically scan the landscape they passed through, constantly aware of the most optimal pathways, potential ambush points and areas where they could be observed from. All the while he maintained a determined gait, armour whirring, his systems stable now that the battleplate seemed to have finally, grudgingly, accepted its new power source.

They picked up the Gorgon towards early evening, as the shadows along the peaks lengthened and the darkness sitting in the valley bottoms deepened. The stream led them down skittering slopes and short, tumbling waterfalls, until their enhanced hearing detected the rushing of the great river, followed soon after by the toxic stink of its pollution. They found it wending its way between two great scree slopes, its sluggish passage hastened only slightly by the inflow of fresh water from the mountain stream. Its banks were scummed with foam and nameless slurry, and vapours rose from patches of its crusted surface like the fumes of a rotting corpse. The slopes either side of it were barren and dry, offering nothing in the way of concealment.

'We take to the ridgeline for now,' Severus said, indicating the nearest crest. 'And follow it north.'

The Primaris mounted the rocky slope, spreading out as they went. The elevation afforded them a better view, both of the valleys below and the peaks that still stood between them and Shebat. Black smoke was visible climbing from the location of the ruined city, a slow, lazy coil set against the red of the dipping sun.

They'd been following the Gorgon for an hour when Severus, on point fifty yards ahead of the others, detected something. It was a sound, bouncing along the gorges and crevasses further north-west – the growl of engines. The auspex confirmed the noise moments later. There was a column of some sort moving north towards Shebat, also running parallel with the Gorgon. As they drew closer more noise became apparent – raucous shouts and the occasional thudding burst of gunfire.

'Greenskins,' Severus voxed. 'One valley across. The auspex is struggling to get a dedicated fix.'

'We go around?' Fobus replied.

'If they are moving on Shebat they will cut across our route, and if they stop for the night they will have blocked the most direct path. It would require a substantial detour.'

'If they're coming up from the south that needs to be confirmed,' Kastor interjected. 'We were unaware of any route through the mountains sufficient to allow xenos reinforcement of Shebat from that direction. Lieutenant Tyranus needs to know if they are reinforcing the city. We should run reconnaissance on them while we have the opportunity.'

Severus was silent for a while, crouched along the ridgeline further ahead, and Kastor wondered whether he was struggling with anger at the Chaplain's interruption. When he spoke again, however, his voice was as emotionless as ever.

'Perhaps. It depends where they stop for the night. There are several lesser approaches to the city they might use – if their choice carries them out of our path, it would be foolish to divert and risk detection. Besides, we are too deep in among the Tombstones now to send a message back to the Fulminata. The communications link has been lost.'

'And if the xenos halt right along our route?'

'Then we improvise.'

They moved off once more, keeping to the ridgelines as they wound their way north. The sound of the greenskin column receded as the evening wore on and they drew away from the Primaris, dropping off the edge of the auspex's range finder.

The separation didn't last for long. As darkness fell lights became visible ahead, the flickering red glow of campfires in the valley adjacent to the route they were following.

It seemed the greenskins were set to obstruct them after all, whether they knew it or not.

Severus called another halt. He scanned their immediate surroundings, as well as the numbers of the orks ahead. To the east, a mountain peak rose to a wicked tip, now lost in the darkness, a nigh-unassailable pinnacle of jagged, dry stone. Westwards the Gorgon snaked out, bending around another spine-like promontory. Between them lay a series of narrow, small valleys, ripped from Ikara's earth by age-old geological disruption. They would take them either through or directly past the gorge where the xenos column had made their camp.

'At this stage, a detour isn't feasible,' Severus said. 'According to the readings the encampment ahead isn't large – I estimate between seventy and a hundred xenoforms, a dozen vehicles, light armour. Infiltrating through their lines offers the best outcome-to-time ratio. Assuming, Chaplain Kastor, that you remain at my side at all times.'

'I swear it,' Kastor replied, not pausing to question the Reiver's words. Now was no time for churlishness.

'If we press on, we will be amongst Shebat's slum ruins by dawn, probably before the column is on the move again,' Severus continued.

'If we're that close to Shebat, why have the xenos halted for the night?' Fobus wondered. 'If they carried on, they'd reach the outskirts before middle-dark.'

'Fuel efficiency, breakdowns, superstition,' Severus said. 'Until we get closer it is impossible to say. I will move up and conduct reconnaissance. Hold this position until I return.'

The Reiver sergeant headed off into the darkness once more,

servos silent, disappearing even from Kastor's auto-senses almost immediately. He waited, scanning the surrounding darkness for anything untoward, feeling his own heightening sense of anticipation. He suppressed it, refusing to savour the possibilities. If Severus was correct about the numbers of the greenskin encampment then it was entirely possible that four Primaris – especially three Reivers and a Battle-Chaplain – would be able to wipe them out without sustaining serious injuries. The desire Kastor felt to do just that didn't stem solely from the anger still smouldering in his heart.

All Adeptus Astartes were shock troopers first and foremost. They disdained camouflage in favour of proud heraldry that declared their presence to friend and foe alike. They preferred the fury of sudden, violent assaults and lightning frontal attacks that, had they been conducted by lesser troops, would have seemed like suicidal madness. Only in rare cases – as with the Reivers – did they favour covert undertakings and careful infiltration.

Kastor focused his mind on the Codex. The blessings of the Emperor were not to be squandered by adherence to a single, stifling style of warfare. His only objective was to return his brother to the Fulminata, and at the moment infiltration was by far the optimal strategy. Following Severus' lead and maintaining a low profile was improving his chances of reaching Polixis, and giving in to the natural desire to bring vengeful justice to the nearest xenos would not help either of them.

Severus returned twenty minutes later, materialising as rapidly as he had vanished.

'My original scans were correct – I estimate eighty xenos and counted nine trucks. It appears several of them have broken down. They have paused for now, but they may depart at any moment, with or without those engines that have failed.'

'So do we wait?' Kastor asked. 'Or press on? If dawn comes and we remain anywhere near here, we run the real risk of being compromised.'

'I know,' Severus said. 'Their security is unusually high – I was forced to eliminate two gretchin just to attain an effective overwatch position. I doubt they will be missed, but the same cannot be said once we start terminating the orks themselves.'

'Then let us not concern ourselves with the difficulties of infiltration,' Kastor said, his anger rising. Every moment they delayed left him feeling as though his blood brother were slipping further and further away. 'You have seen them for yourself, they are not numerous. Between us, and with the blessings of the Emperor's wrath, we can slay them all and be underway again within the next half an hour. At this point any other course of action is a waste of time.'

'Breaking cover this early into an operation is not what the Codex advises,' Severus said. 'Nevertheless, it champions flexibility above all else during covert infiltrations, and on this occasion my instincts agree with your bloody nature, Brother-Chaplain. With me.'

The four Primaris advanced through the night, to where the knife-backed ridgeline they'd been following turned sharply east, leaving them on the edge of a rocky promontory overlooking the gorge below. Kastor mimicked the Reivers' movements, dropping down onto all fours and approaching the gorge's edge in a crouch. He was forced to bite back another curse, this time at the faint whirring made by his power armour's servos, ear-achingly loud compared to the perfect silence of the stealth suits worn by the other three.

'That's far enough,' Severus cautioned, switching to his mask's internal vox to hide the sound of his voice. Kastor raised his head slightly, his visor lighting up with target locks as the encampment below came into view.

Severus was right – the greenskins were on alert. Two ramshackle ork trucks had broken down halfway along the gorge and were now in various states of disrepair, greenskin mechanics bellowing at one another as they pulled away wheels and cracked open drive sections. The remaining vehicles in the column had circled in what little space the gorge allowed, and while most of the aliens were now idly scrapping or slumped in their trucks, asleep, a few were manning their pintle weapons and peering out into the darkness. Headlights and the flames of a few delusory campfires lit up the rocky space, and Kastor realised that there were gretchin up on the gorge flanks with them, further left and right – none had yet noticed the Ultramarines almost in their midst, but it would only be a matter of time.

'We shall have to be fast,' Severus voxed. 'Moving into their lines before striking will be impossible, and we lack the ranged weaponry to begin the assault from the gorge's flanks. Speed and fury shall be our watchwords.'

'We are the bane of the xenos,' Kastor said. 'So let us strike them from above. The space between the edge of the gorge and the bottom should be sufficient to allow our grav-gliders to engage.'

Severus looked towards the point where the cliff above the greenskins was at its highest, assessing their chances. He nodded.

'I believe you are correct, Brother-Chaplain. Such an attack would be unorthodox, but it would dramatically reduce the time we were exposed to xenos fire. It seems we've already got you thinking like a Reiver.'

'Anything that speeds this up,' Kastor said, unlocking his crozius and bolt pistol.

'I will take point,' Severus said. 'After I have eliminated the gretchin guarding this side of the gorge, hold position along its edge. We strike together.'

They moved, keeping back from the edge of the cliff face. Kastor, third in line behind Stryx, didn't see Severus bring down the diminutive greenskins watching over the camp below, but his hearing detected the clicking sound of a flurry of silenced bolt pistol shots.

'Stay low,' murmured the Reiver. Kastor brought himself once more to the edge of the gorge, the sound of ceramite grating on dirt and stone unbearably loud. He could sense Severus' silent displeasure, and the unwanted attention served to stoke his rage even further. He was the Battle-Chaplain of the Fulminata, not some sneaking assassin. He forced himself to take a breath and calm his thoughts, focusing on the greenskins below.

His anger would find a home soon enough.

'On my mark,' Severus breathed, his long knife whispering from its sheath.

'Hold,' Fobus said, his voice cutting through the tension. 'The auspex is picking up fresh readings.'

Severus consulted his own display, wired to his left vambrace. Kastor's grip around Salve Imperator tightened fractionally. The desire to release the after-effects of the battle stimms and combat adrenaline was almost overwhelming.

'Closing from the east and west,' Severus confirmed. 'Skirmish formation. They're less than a hundred paces from our position. Stay prone.'

The Reiver had barely issued the instruction before Kastor became aware of figures moving in the darkness out beyond the gorge edge. They were hunched over and furtive, and his night vision picked up heavy wasteland capes drawn close, ash goggles and the outlines of autoguns and lasrifles.

'Don't move,' Severus murmured, apparently sensing Kastor's tension. The four Primaris remained pressed to the ground on the edge of the gorge, as across from them the new arrivals, over fifty in number, dropped to their bellies and began to crawl forwards to its edge.

Below, the greenskins remained oblivious, the rock space resounding with the clang of wrenches and the angry bark and growl of squabbling xenos. Kastor looked from the unsuspecting aliens back towards the figures – definitely human – who were silently taking up firing positions above them.

'We do not compromise our cover,' Severus said over the vox. 'No matter what happens, you wait for my orders, Chaplain.'

Kastor didn't reply. He could see a heavily robed figure crouched barely two dozen paces to his left, priming a clutch of stick grenades. Another was carefully setting up a heavy stubber bipod on a flat rock directly above the two broken trucks at the centre of the greenskin encampment.

'They're about to discover the gretchin,' Stryx said, meaning the diminutive xenos guards Severus had silently terminated.

'When they open fire we move back from the gorge edge, fast and silent,' the sergeant replied. 'While they're focused on the greenskins we head for the adjacent valley floor and carry on north. Understood?'

'No,' Kastor said. 'These men are about to attack the xenos filth. I will not abandon them. An Adeptus Astartes never allows another man to fight his battles for him.'

'There are no Imperial forces currently operating in the Tombstones,' Severus hissed. 'They could be anyone – waste nomads, deserters, renegades. Our only certainty is that they are not operating alongside us.'

'If they have abandoned their faith in the Emperor then they will recant soon enough,' Kastor growled.

'And you will waste precious time ensuring that. If you have prayed recently, I suggest these men are your answer. Their assault will provide the perfect opportunity for us to carry on north without breaking our own cover. The faster we reach Shebat, the faster we reach your blood brother. Remember why you are here, Chaplain Kastor. Remember the blood of Iax.'

As though to punctuate the Reiver's words, a detonation tore through the gorge below, its thunderclap rebounding from the cliff faces and juddering through the stones beneath Kastor. The human attacker had thrown his stick grenade bundle.

The night lit up. Las-bolts and hard rounds rained down like a sudden hailstorm on the greenskin camp, blazing from both sides of the gorge. Kastor saw dozens of xenos go down within seconds, twitching back and forth as they were struck from multiple angles, riddled with bullets and las. Others dived for cover within or beneath their vehicles, or snatched up sluggas and shootas, blazing away into the night.

'Move,' Severus ordered tersely, already backing away from the edge of the gorge. Kastor forced himself to follow, teeth gritted. To be denied righteous combat was one thing, but to actively avoid it when men were risking their lives to put down xenos filth was nigh-unbearable. He sought out the words of the Catechism of Limitation as he moved after Severus, keeping low, the sounds of power armour crunching off dry stone and grit lost in the sudden thunder of the ambush.

None of the Primaris made it far. Kastor had barely gone a dozen yards before he picked up a voice over the sounds of the firefight, detected by his Lyman's Ear.

'Contacts right! By the cliff edge!'

'They've seen us,' he said, just before the first las-bolt cracked into a boulder half a dozen yards to his left, scorching a black mark in the yellow stone.

More shots followed, las and hard rounds both, snapping at the earth around the Primaris. In the darkness, it was impossible to say whether the humans had mistaken their bulky forms for orks, or whether they truly were renegades. Regardless, it could only be a matter of seconds before they began priming grenades or, worse, before Severus and his death-brethren began shooting back.

'Enough!' Kastor barked. He stood. Shots filled the air around him, striking and sparking from his black battle-plate. He ignored them. In one fist, he raised Salve Imperator and activated it. With a crack of discharged power, lightning wreathed the skull-tipped mace and illuminated the Primaris, towering in all his grim, power-armoured might.

'In the name of the immortal Emperor of Mankind, cease fire!'

His words boomed out, amplified by his vox-vocaliser, resounding over the reports of gunfire and the crack of ricochets.

The shooting stopped almost immediately.

'Stop firing!' he heard one man screaming. 'For Throne's sake, cease fire!'

'Soldiers of the Emperor,' Kastor intoned, lowering Salve Imperator so it pointed towards the gorge. 'Strike them down!'

CHAPTER NINE ANTHROPOPHAGITE

POLIXIS

The beast left Polixis to struggle for much of the day, the corpses of his battle-brothers laid out before him. Only with the onset of night did it summon more of its minions, among them a clanking greenskin that seemed to be composed of crude, rusting bionics more than green flesh. The thing was lugging a heavy industrial saw in its wake, and attended by a train of hook-nosed gretchin hefting spanners and other work tools.

'Dis 'ere's my big mek,' Urgork said to Polixis. He'd witnessed the warlord take three injections from its medicae throughout the day, each time apparently reliant on the foul concoction to arrest the seizures that would intermittently grip it. A part of the Apothecary felt a morbid sense of fascination towards the unnatural alien and his apparently numerous afflictions. There was no medical precedent for the existence of such a freak experiment, and yet here it was, seemingly kept alive as much by its own schizophrenic willpower as by the dark potions of its creator.

'Cogkrusha 'ere l-likes all your beakie gubbins,' Urgork was saying, indicating to the greenskin mechanic that was peering at Polixis from behind grubby bionic lenses. 'All dem armour bits and dakka, and especially ya big truck. Told him he c-can tinka wiv it all he wants once I've got ya helpin' me.'

Polixis swallowed his retort, knowing it was pointless. The idea that the xenos wanted to experiment on such blessed armour was as sickening as the thought of them defiling the flesh of the dead Primaris. Urgork waved the thing he'd addressed as Cogkrusha over to the remains of Demeter, Skyrus and Squad Tiro. The thing's gretchin slaves scurried and scampered over the fallen Primaris, grimy little hands tugging at armour plates and helmets, squabbling among themselves. Urgork seemed to grow impatient as his mechanic prevaricated over the bodies, apparently overwhelmed by the choices on display.

'Cogkrusha,' the warlord barked, singling out the body of one of the Aggressors, Brother Uxis, with a claw. 'C-c-cut dat git open!'

The mechanic hefted its heavy saw, its augmented limbs grating, and the basilica filled with an ear-splitting scream as the wicked blade seared into Brother Uxis' Gravis armour. Polixis gritted his teeth so hard that the metallic tang of blood filled his mouth, trying not to think about the brutal defilement of the hallowed battleplate. Trying not to think about what the greenskins were going to do when they finally cracked it open.

Fat sparks burst across the flagstones, ceramite then plasteel then adamantium giving way with a slow, grim reluctance. It took long minutes to break the will of the Gravis plate. The gretchin scurried about the feet of their mechanical master, tugging away the scraps of twisted blue metal hacked apart by the saw's relentless work. Eventually, Uxis was reduced to his under-armour and black carapace, the greenskins tugging away dermal nodes and connector ports with gleeful, savage abandon. The Ultramarine's dead flesh was left exposed, his breastplate cleft in half, his helmet dragged off, his heraldry split and defiled.

'Dat's enough!' Urgork snapped, pointing once more at the body. 'Bring it over 'ere.'

A trio of orks dragged the heavy corpse and what little remained of its armour before Polixis' rack, grating it over the flagstones.

The Apothecary found himself looking down into Uxis' dead eyes. Even in death the slain Aggressor appeared stoic, jaw set, expression unwavering. He looked away.

'Squeamish, is ya?' Urgork demanded, planting a boot on Uxis' torso. The ork's hobnails dug into the pale flesh of the Ultramarine's chest. Polixis met the thing's gaze, his eyes burning.

'Dat's more like it,' Urgork snarled. 'Dat's da face of a propa humie git lookin' for a scrap. Never understood why youse get so angry sometimes – us lads just want a good fight. No point gettin' all worked up about it. Still, 'ere we is. Doc, get over 'ere.'

The ork medicae scampered to its master's side. It was grinning up at Polixis in its leering manner, clearly delighting in what was about to take place. Polixis felt his anger mount as he began to realise what was happening.

'You i-is about to witness a medical first,' Urgork said proudly, planting his balled fists on his hips. 'Doc Grok 'ere is about ta perform da first ever removative surgery on a h-humie beakie in front of anuvva human beakie. Doc, we awaits your pleasure.'

The warlord took his boot off Uxis and stepped away. The

medicae crouched over the corpse, like some sort of hideous carrion creature. After a brief inspection, it laid out a leather strip on the floor, scattered with various rusting blades. The vile parody of the surgeon's fine art turned Polixis' stomach, and he found himself straining once more at his bonds. The servos shuddered slightly, grating but going no further. None of the greenskins seemed to notice – they were all staring with bated excitement at their hunched-over painboy.

The ork's fingers moved over the instruments of its supposed profession, apparently pondering which one it wanted to employ first. Eventually it snatched up what appeared to be a small, rusting power saw. The buzz of the cutting tool, like a miniature version of the industrial rotor used by the ork mechanic, filled Polixis' ears.

'Stop.'

He realised he had barked the word involuntarily. The greenskin medicae looked up, clearly startled, saw still in its hand. Urgork emitted a hacking laugh that devolved into another bout of coughing. He inhaled noisily and spat, before his grin returned.

'C-c-can't stop da march of science, b-beakie boy. Da good doc here has been itchin' ta carve up these gubbins for days n-now. Wouldn't be right or propa for him or his patients ta cancel da operation now. It'd take somethin' big ta do that, say maybe...' He paused. 'You givin' me what I want. Tell me your s-secrets, beakie. Tell me how I can be free of all dis.' The ork jabbed his claw in the direction of the medicae's syringe satchel.

Polixis stayed silently. Inwardly, he was snarling a string of enraged blasphemies that would have risked a blow from Kastor. He damned himself for his own weakness, damned himself for being drawn by Urgork's defilement. Brother

Uxis would not have wanted him to yield, no matter what cruelties were heaped on his corpse. He would not converse with the xenos, would not justify its existence even with words of hatred.

'Lost your tongue again?' Urgork grunted, looking disappointed. 'Fine den, 'ave it your way. Grok...'

The smaller greenskin's expression was the opposite of its master's. Smiling manically, it raised its saw blade.

'Gonna need this to chop through dat thick bone stuff,' the xenos said, its tone full of relish. It cranked the saw to maximum output and pressed it down against Uxis' bare chest.

For a second, the flesh of the Primaris resisted. Then it gave way beneath the buzzing blade, and blood, dark with age, splattered along the saw's edge, hitting the ork's face and stained overalls. The alien licked the blood from its lips, grinning wickedly, but its joyous expression turned to a strained rictus as it put all of its scrawny strength behind the cutting tool, pressing down as it sought to split the Primaris' toughened rib bone. There was a hideous, juddering shriek as rusting metal fought through the breastplate beneath the black carapace, and Polixis thought the saw was going to shatter. Suddenly, there was a sickening crunch. Polixis knew he had just heard Uxis' fused ribs caving in.

'Been wonderin' what makes you beakies so big an' strong,' Urgork growled at Polixis, eyes on the Apothecary while his minion continued to crack the rib cavity open. 'And we reckon we's found what it is.'

The medicae ork let out a yelp of satisfaction and dragged its saw back out of the Space Marine's torso, deactivating the tool as blood and viscera sprayed from it. It swapped it for a flat planing knife, not unlike the two long blades carried by Urgork. As the greenskin began to slice back the Aggressor's flesh, it used wicked meat hooks to further widen the chest cavity incision. Polixis realised just what it was doing.

It was carving out one of the Space Marine's twin hearts.

The medicae abandoned its blade when most of Uxis' chest had been reduced to raw, flensed muscle. The wound running along his breastbone was now gaping. The ork took up a smaller, hook-tipped knife, clumsily cuffing blood and spittle from its mouth as it crouched over the Ultramarine. Polixis tried to put his mind elsewhere, to think about anything other than what was about to happen. Anything to take his mind off the fury that felt as though it were going to burst his own hearts and tear his muscles apart.

The ork reached into the raw cavity with its knife and began to cut. It was not the sickening, straining work of the bone saw, or the cruel slicing of the flensing blade – the little nicks were almost incongruous, but they were the most sacrilegious cuts of all. Eventually, warty tongue jutting from between its tusks in concentration, the greenskin plunged its grubby glove down into the incision. There was a squelching sound before it ripped its hand back out, holding something aloft.

'I gots it, boss,' it said excitedly to Urgork. The warlord held out his hand to receive his underling's trophy, before turning to Polixis and holding it up – the dripping, glistening mass of muscle and flesh that was Uxis' primary heart.

'I told you, beakie, I knows a fing or two about you. We's seen how hard you fight ta get bits outta ya boys when they gets chopped. I knows how much you gits in da white armour want dem.'

The ork held the torn heart close to Polixis' face, grinning, his yellow eyes full of madness.

'Don't know why ya needs it so bad – don't care either. All dat matters to me is dat it matters to you.'

'You know nothing,' Polixis snarled.

'We's been watchin' you lads,' the warlord said, his eyes still on Polixis as he turned the gristly organ over in his palm. The medicae's crude butchery had only removed part of it. 'Besides, you think you was da first beakie I've had strapped up here? He wouldn't tell us much at first, but den we hooked ol' Slyboy up to his brain. We can do the same ta you, but for now I just wants you to know what I know. What I can do.'

As the greenskin finished speaking he clenched his fist. There was a wet squelch, and Urgork opened his hand once again to reveal the crushed remains of the heart, spread against his palm.

'The Emperor is with me,' Polixis began to say, seeking out the words of the Rite of Intonation, familiar to all Ultramarines Apothecaries, in an effort to suppress his fury. 'He is around me and within me, in my words and in my heart, in my deeds and in my sinews.'

'Angry git, aren't ya?' Urgork mocked, taking a step closer, so that the ork and the Primaris were only separated by a narrow, charged space. 'Once I gets you g-goin', anyway. It's good to see dat sometimes. You and I, beakie, we ain't so different.'

'You are an abomination,' Polixis spat.

'Big word,' Urgork said, nodding slowly. 'A-bommin-nation. I knows it though. I've heard it plenty times before. Other big humie words too. Monstros-itty. Aberrance. I understands them, beakie. It's cos I'm different from these other gits.' The beast paused to encompass the rest of the basilica and its greenskin occupiers, speaking as though none of them could hear him.

'I'm bigga and betta than dem, so they call me fings.

Even some of da lads used ta say fings. Freak. Deadboy. Stitchy-skin. Then I crumped 'em, and they stopped sayin' those w-words. I'm b-bigga and I'm b-betta because I was made ta be. And dat's how we is the same, beakie.'

'You are an insane xenos monster. We have *nothing* in common.'

'You was made to be da best,' Urgork continued, as though Polixis hadn't spoken. 'You was put togetha. You didn't grow like da lads or normal humies. You was designed. Made to be a boss, like me. Dat's why I want you, beakie. Dat's why you is here. Even more than da smaller beakie boys, you was made to beat everyone else. I reckon da secret to dat is here, and here.'

The ork pressed a claw against Polixis' breastplate, and then his throat, singling out his progenoids. The Space Marine shuddered with revulsion, turning his face away from the monster and its hideous gaze.

'There is nothing the organs of the Adeptus Astartes can do to preserve your rotting flesh,' he said. 'Cut apart all these bodies, do likewise to me and you will still be beyond salvation. You were born a monster, and you will die one.'

'We'll see,' Urgork said slowly, then, without warning, snatched Polixis by the jaw, yanking his head back round.

He tried to resist, but bound as he was there was nothing he could do to fight the warlord's nightmarish strength. The ork forced a claw into his mouth, holding his jaw in a vice-grip, threatening to crush bone and break his teeth. As Polixis struggled to draw breath while simultaneously biting down on the foul digit, Urgork gripped the torn remains of Uxis' heart in his other hand and rammed it against the Primaris' mouth.

Polixis's eyes widened with horror as he realised what was

happening. He tried to close his jaw, tried to spit out the alien's filthy fingers, tried to tear them off, but the stinking, unyielding grip of the brutish creature was irresistible. He tasted the coppery tang of blood, followed by a greasy, choking morass.

'G-g-gonna t-t-take your medicine, b-b-beakie,' Urgork snarled, thick strings of drool dangling from his tusks, his butcher's breath engulfing the Apothecary. The flesh of the heart made Polixis heave, but he could not halt its passage, couldn't stop the stifling, horrifying realisation of what was happening. It slid thickly down his throat, until it passed the point of no return. He found his breath, and screamed with outrage, but it did no good. Urgork let go and stepped back, allowing Polixis' head to fall. The Primaris remained still, breathing heavily, his mouth full of a foul, greasy aftertaste, his genhanced body keeping him from retching.

'Tastes g-g-good, don't it?' Urgork leered, gesturing for his medicae's syringe as his body started shaking. 'P-p-plenty m-more where dat came from.'

Polixis threw his head back and roared. The sound, full of fury and despair, filled the basilica, reverberating from the vaults and cloisters, taking on a life of its own, until it sounded like a hundred battle-brothers, giving vent to a pain that was beyond words. Even the most raucous greenskins filling the nave and balconies were silenced by the terrible sound, and all stopped and stared at the captive Primaris, some fingering their weapons nervously, others casting glances at the pillars and annexes and the high ceiling, as though expecting to see a host of vengeful warriors materialise at the sound of their brother's agony.

But none did. Polixis' cry trailed away to a long, low moan, and the sounds bouncing around the basilica faded, until there was nothing but silence.

The medicae jabbed its syringe into Urgork's flank. The warlord grunted and went rigid, his eyes never leaving Polixis. The Space Marine looked up at the beast, held its gaze, his expression one of purest, most unadulterated hatred.

'Cogkrusha,' Urgork said as his medicines took effect once more. 'Bring da doc here anuvva body.'

KASTOR

The commander's name was Davik. He was a Kelestani colonel, shaven-headed, short and stocky, like most Stormers. At some point since the fall of Shebat he'd broken his arm – it was bound against his breast by a sling made from a torn-up Namarian camo cape. The injury made making the sign of the aquila impossible, but he bowed his head reverentially to Kastor as best he could.

'My apologies again, lord,' he said. 'My men thought you were too large to be anything other than greenskins. The last thing we expected to find out here were the champions of Ultramar.'

'In the future, be sure to run through proper target identification drills with your men, colonel,' Kastor said.

The Chaplain knew his chastening tone was perhaps unjust. They were a ragtag collection of Guard outfits – Kelestani, Voitekans, Namarians, a few Faeburn. That their discipline was shaken could hardly be held against them. But Kastor was still coming down from an unfulfilled combat high and that made him acerbic at best. The urge to purge still sang through his veins, battered out by his slowly decelerating heartbeats.

He focused his attention on the men before him. When

the rok had come down, it had struck the southern end of Shebat. The forces there had been decimated, but a few units holding the most southerly extent of the slums had avoided annihilation. A scattering of survivors had managed to retreat southwards into the mountains. Davik told the Primaris how he had initially been the second ranking officer of the ragged group.

'There was a dispute with a Zoishen colonel, yesterday afternoon,' Davik said. 'He wanted to make a break eastwards, for Imperial lines. He thought we could use the trucks we took in the first few ambushes. I told him the trucks would break down, and we'd find ourselves stranded out in the wastes and at the mercy of their damn air cover.'

'How many men do you have remaining?' Severus asked the colonel. He'd been interrogating Davik in the bottom of the gorge when Kastor had joined them, absent initially while he had been blessing the bodies of the three Guardsmen killed during the ambush. The colonel glanced from the Chaplain to the Reiver, clearly uncertain about which of the two skull-faced giants held seniority. Eventually, he addressed Severus.

'Following the latest roll call, sixty-eight combat effective, eleven wounded.'

'Do you count yourself among that last number, colonel?'

'A laspistol only takes one hand, lord.'

Kastor turned his gaze to the nearest Guardsmen as Davik spoke. A composite team in the mismatching gear of Voitekan and Namarian infantrymen were heaping the greenskins killed in the ambush, preparing the bodies for torching so as to destroy the spores given off by their corpses. A few kept casting worried glances towards the Primaris, as though afraid the hulking warriors were about to suddenly attack them. They were a weary, demoralised-looking band, caked in dust and dirt. It was not the attitude Kastor would have expected from an outfit that had only just conducted a successful ambush against a superior force. Their morale was all-but broken.

'This is the third column we've successfully destroyed,' Davik was saying, tapping his boot against the thick tyre of the ork truck beside him.

'And the third coming up from the south?' Severus asked.

'The south?' Davik asked, a look of uncertainty crossing his stolid expression.

'These greenskins were coming through the southern passes? From the direction of Baspyre?'

'No,' Davik said. 'No, they've all come from Shebat. They were turning back. Look.'

The colonel moved to the rear of the open truck and dragged away a stained covering. Immediately the stink of opened innards and the buzzing of hungry, fat-bellied rotwings assailed Kastor's auto-senses. The back of the truck was heaped with the butchered remains of a brace of slope tuskers and smaller, unidentifiable beasts, their blood congealed in long rivulets towards the trailer's edge.

'They weren't reinforcements,' Davik said. 'They were a foraging party. They've been coming up into the Tombstones ever since they took Shebat. There isn't enough food for them down there, at least not until their vile spores have taken root.'

'Lieutenant Tyranus must be informed of this,' Kastor said. 'If we can confine the xenos to the city, we may be able to starve them out.'

'I will send word to the lieutenant as soon as we are able to establish a connection,' Severus said. 'In the meantime, I am going to requisition one of these trucks, along with its contents.'

'Why?' Davik asked. 'I was going to have them burned with the bodies.'

'Not this one,' Severus said, gesturing to the nearest truck with his long blade. 'I have a use for it. Bring me half a dozen xenos corpses as well.'

To his credit, Davik didn't hesitate, snapping a string of orders to his weary men. Kastor could sense his desire to know more, though. As six greenskin bodies were hauled in front of Severus, the colonel spoke.

'Lords, with all due respect... May I ask what it is you're doing out here? Are there more of you coming?'

Kastor looked to Severus, partly disapproving of the man's boldness, partly impressed by his bravery. The Reiver responded.

'No. We are conducting a covert operation. We aim to infiltrate Shebat.'

'Assassination?' Davik wondered aloud. 'Sabotage?'

'It is not your place to ask us such things,' Severus said. 'If you are as wise as you are courageous, colonel, you will hold your tongue.'

'Of course. I would not presume to question the objectives of the Adeptus Astartes, my lord, but it would be remiss of me not to offer the services of myself and my men. If there is anything we can do to further your mission, just say the word.'

Kastor expected the usual cold rebuke from the Reiver. Instead, the skull-faced killer nodded.

'There is in fact some assistance your men may be able to provide me with, colonel. How much in the way of explosive material were you able to evacuate out of Shebat?'

* * *

SKREWITT

Mek Drok's workshop seemed to be getting busier every night. The greenskin mechanic had secured the collapsed remnants of a manufactorum block on the south side of town the day the lads had stormed the humie city. A new roof of scavenged corrugated iron had been installed, and the rubble had been heaped high enough to give some semblance of structure. Since then the workshop's floor, cleared of debris by the efforts of Drok's gaggle of gretchin slaves, had seen lots of fixin' and tinkerin', and played host to the wheels of over a dozen different speed-mobs, all eager to get their battered war machines back into the fight as quickly as possible. Drok was certainly doing better business than either of his two biggest rivals, meks Fixta and Grugg. Cogkrusha himself would've been proud, or so Drok kept insisting.

Skrewitt made an obscene gesture at the mek's back as he rifled through his gubbins, searching for a bigger spanner. The other grots around Skrewitt snickered with ill-concealed humour, clustered around the engine block of the truck they were supposed to be fixing. Drok spun at the sound, eyes blazing.

'Skrewitt, ya little squig-munch!' the ork bellowed, lunging for the gretchin. Skrewitt yelped and flung himself over the engine, his scrawny frame narrowly avoiding his master's grasping claws. He tumbled down on the other side of the broken-down vehicle, intent on making a run for the workshop's open door.

Skrag, of course, stuck a leg out in time to trip him. The gretchin tumbled over his fellow oiler's limb, a flailing hand snagging Drok's work tarpaulin draped over the engine's flank and hauling a mound of the mek's tools down with him.

Skrag's plot didn't go as planned – most of the rusting pieces of equipment came down directly on top of him, knocking him unconscious. Skrewitt scrabbled through the dirt as the clang of falling metal resounded in his ears, expecting to feel Drok's claws closing around his skinny throat.

They didn't. He realised that, far from the cackles of laughter and excitement that would usually fill the workshop when Drok attempted to snag one of his underlings, a hushed silence had fallen. He stayed on his stomach, hands clasped over his head, eyes screwed shut. Still, neither wrench nor fist fell. He opened one eye.

Drok was standing over him, but the mek's eyes weren't on his wayward oiler. The scrap-armoured greenskin was staring out of the warehouse entrance, towards the foothills of the mountains that loomed over the ruined city. There, just beyond the edge of the broken slums, a great fireball was rising up out of the darkness, its thunderclap detonation – initially masked by the clatter of falling tools – rolling back from the dry, dead hills.

'What da–' Drok began to say, but a further burst of light out in the darkness stopped him. Flashes of colour darted through the night, dozens of little tracers quickly swallowed up by the blackness. They were describing a pattern down the hillside towards the city's edge.

Another explosion burst into life, nearer this time, its report sounding clear across the ruins away to the edge of the rok's crater. Bellows filled the night as the greenskins nesting in the southern slums began to react to the unexpected activity.

'Humies!' shouted Krunk, the boss of the truck currently being tinkered with in Drok's workshop. The nob waved his axe in the direction of the lightshow, which appeared to be steadily descending towards the city. 'Let's go, lads!'

'Scabrot, shut up shop!' Drok bellowed to his apprentice welder as he snatched up his kustom blasta. He jogged out into the night, Skrewitt's antics apparently forgotten, the grots scrambling to follow him. Skrewitt managed to get to his feet in time to join them, aiming a vicious kick at the still-unconscious Skrag as he went.

Outside, the night had descended into chaos. Boys were scrambling in from all sides, hefting choppas and blazing indiscriminately into the darkness with their shootas. Most were headed for the city's outskirts, towards the bolts of light that Skrewitt now recognised as belonging to the humies' pew-guns.

The gretchin attending the mobs knew better than to try to follow their masters – whatever was going on, it wasn't worth a trampling. Instead they scampered to the tops of the biggest rubble heaps they could find, craning for a better look at the excitement that was waking up the city. Skrewitt hiked up his breeches and scrambled to keep up, mounting the rubble of the nearest hab block's remains, arm over arm. He used his elbows to force his way close to the highest point – only fat Choppa and Drok's chief bootlicker, Rench, remained above him. The perch afforded them a view of the city's southern limits, and the column approaching from out of the darkness.

It was one of the food grubbin' mobs, sent up into the hills by the big boss to get more scran for the lads. Skrewitt recognised the headlights bobbing through the dark, winding a precarious route down into the slum ruins. It was obvious, however, that not all the approaching trucks belonged to the grubbers and scran lads any more. Bolts of light were spraying from the rear of the three speeding transports, shooting towards the two trucks in front, and as they drew nearer the roar of engines and the crack of gunfire became audible.

'What's goin' on?' demanded one of the grots further down the rubble heap, unable to get a good view of the rapidly approaching action. Rench, eager as ever to be the centre of attention, began to provide a commentary.

'Looks like some humies have jumped da scran lads somewhere in da foothills. Gots hold of one of da mob's trucks and now they is chasin' da uvva two wiv it.'

'One truck of humies is chasin' two trucks of da lads?' another gretchin demanded incredulously. Rench's angry retort was cut out by another explosion, bursting into fiery existence just to the left of one of the fleeing trucks. It looked as though the humies were lobbing bombs too.

'They is gonna get right crumped,' Choppa squealed excitedly, pointing a claw at the mobs now mobilising out into the slums. Dozens of trucks and warbuggies roared through the rubble, headlights playing over the ruins as they bounced along, greenskins holding on to every surface while bellowing and blazing away with their sidearms. The two scran trucks fleeing from the hills were only a few hundred yards from the safety of the orks rushing to meet them, searing bolts of energy continuing to perforate the air around them as the humies kept up their pursuit. As the distance closed, some of the hijackers switched to targeting the oncoming mobs, their energy bolts spitting out to lance buggies and open-topped wartracks. Return fire lit up the night, blazing away inaccurately in all directions.

'They're gonna hit!' Rench said excitedly. Skrewitt craned his neck as the gretchin around and below him jostled for a better view of the unfolding drama. The two trucks fleeing from the humies shot past the lead vehicles of their rescuers, bouncing along the debris-clogged remnants of the city's streets, while behind the humie truck came up short. It took a hard right and, to loud jeers, began to race back towards the looming darkness of the Tombstones. The dozens of rickety greenskin vehicles tearing towards them accelerated, their occupants furious that the humies would consider offering a scrap only to turn tail at the last moment.

Choppa grunted, cuffing a smaller gretchin beneath him around the back of the head. 'Da big 'uns need a scrap, else they'll take it out on us when dey gets back!'

There was a chorus of groans from the assembled grots as they contemplated orks left without anything to crump. Skrewitt was too busy watching the approaching trucks to join in. The two that had come down from the hills hadn't turned at bay when they'd reached the rest of the lads, but had instead carried on into the city, thundering past the mound of rubble being used by the gretchin. It looked like they'd been hit hard by the humies – only two boys were left, one at the steering wheel of each of the vehicles, wrapped up good in the ragged capes and goggles the speed boys used when they were out in the ash wastes. Skrewitt was only afforded a split-second view as the trucks thundered past, kicking out dirt and rubble from their heavy tyres, and then they were gone, careering deeper into the ruined city's heart.

The rest of the gretchin were still watching the ongoing pursuit as the humies fled back up the hillside and into the darkness. Shots pursued them and another explosion rocked the night air, catching one of the trucks that had been gaining on the humies. It tipped it over in a gout of flames, sending it crashing into a wartrack that had been pulling up alongside and immolating them both. The grots let out a loud gasp followed by a few cheers as the pyrotechnics continued, touching off another buggy and sending flames licking along the hillside. Despite all the excitement, it looked as though the humies were getting away.

'You got lucky,' Skrewitt heard Rench saying as he dropped down from the rubble pile. 'Boss Drok was gonna crump you good before all dis kicked off. Skrewitt?'

Skrewitt didn't respond. He'd noticed something, something that wasn't right at all. Something that was just begging to be snooped on. Before the other gretchin had realised that he was gone, he was heading into the darkness of the city's ruins, in the wake of the two scran-waggons.

GROTSNOG

Something was happening further south, out in the slums and along the hillsides. Nob Grotsnog had been roused from his sleep beneath the squighide covering that his mob had draped over the ruined alleyway, jerked awake by the excited bickering of a gang of nearby gretchin.

'What's happenin'?' he demanded groggily as he rolled out from beneath the hide, scrabbling for his axe. Grulk, the mob's big shoota, was stumbling back down from the nearest mound of rubble, his hulking weapon strapped across his back.

'Humies!' he bellowed as he came, rousing more of the boys scattered along the alleyway. Most of the mob were out scrapping with Morgath's lads, angry that their rivals had got closer to the humie positions on the ridgeline the day before. Those who remained behind were half-intoxicated with fungal beer, but the promise of a real fight got them awake and alert quickly enough.

'What's goin' on?' Grotsnog demanded once more, half snatching, half catching Grulk as he tumbled down the last few feet of rubble and into the alleyway.

'Humies chasin' da scran lads,' the big shoota boy panted, pointing a claw southwards. 'Back down from da hills. All da boys down dat way is headed out to crump 'em.'

'Gork's droppings,' Grotsnog snapped. He could hear the commotion further south – bellowing, the roar of engines and the clatter of gunfire. There were already dozens of mobs, most of them bigger or faster, between them and the south side of the city. Grotsnog had been inordinately pleased with himself when he'd managed to claim the alley close to the big spikey humie building for his lads early in the occupation, but having a base of operations near the ruin-city's heart suddenly didn't seem so smart. Being far from the edges meant far from the fight.

'Don't just stand there!' the nob bellowed at those around him. 'Get sloggin'!'

'What about da other lads?' Dunf demanded.

'It's their loss,' Grotsnog said, shoving Dunf towards the end of the alleyway. 'Now move it!'

The assorted mob didn't get far – no more than a dozen paces. The mounting howl of an abused engine and the squeal of tyres, followed by the shriek of poorly applied brakes, heralded the arrival of a truck, careering around the remains of a tumbled-down refinery smokestack. The vehicle made straight for the semi-clear space of the alleyway, forcing Grotsnog and his lads to throw themselves against the rubble on either side to avoid getting flattened by the oncoming truck.

Grotsnog's angry protestations were lost in the shriek of a second vehicle as it came screeching around the corner to join the first, black smoke billowing from its exhaust vents.

'Watch where you's drivin'!' Grotsnog bellowed, banging the flat of his axe head against the nearest truck's runners as it finally came to a halt beside him. The git driving it was alone, wrapped up good in a scabby dune cape and goggles. Grotsnog recognised the paint job on the truck as belonging to one of the scran mobs that had been sent up into the hills to help supplement the diet of the hundreds of mobs now assembling in the city.

'Oi, you see da humies while youse was up there?' he demanded. The driver didn't seem to have heard him, exiting from the other side of the truck's drive compartment. Urzog, on the opposite side of the truck from Grotsnog, made to get out of the big greenskin's way, but tripped and stumbled against the vehicle's chassis. It was only as he hit the dirt that Grotsnog's sluggish brain registered that there was something very, very wrong about the scran boys.

They were big, bigger even than Grotsnog, and none of the lads who'd gone up into the hills had been particularly fine examples of ork might. Even as he realised the disparity, he also realised that blood was jetting from Urzog's severed throat – he hadn't tripped at all.

He began to bellow incoherently, reaching for his slugga, at the same time as Dunf dragged back one of the coverings protecting the slaughtered beasts heaped in the back of the first truck. Even as he did so, a body rose up from the bloody remains, its heavy armour smeared with viscera, a mace in one fist lashing out to crack the greenskin's skull open.

Grotsnog opened fire. The shattered alleyway resounded with the bark of his pistol, shots spraying inaccurately into the rubble, while around him everything descended into chaos. Grulk, slower on the uptake, was struggling to bring his big shoota to bear on the thing that had been driving the first truck – it leapt from the open drive seat straight over the vehicle's bonnet, hideously fast for something so large, a long blade sliding from its ragged cape. Grotsnog was only barely aware of a decapitating blow taking Grulk's head off. He managed just five shots before more wicked silver flashed in the firelit darkness. It took him a few seconds to realise why his slugga wasn't firing any more; by the time he'd accepted the fact that his severed arm was lying at his feet, fist still clenched around his pistol's grip, a second blow had laid his throat open to the bone.

The remains of the mob died quickly, their bellows cut short, their inaccurate gunfire eliminated. Silence fell over the alleyway, sinister and surreal amid the uproarious city. Grotsnog tried to get up, tried to fight, but all he could do was keep his hands clamped around his opened throat as he bled to death. He was half-aware of one of the murderous giants quickly shattering the headlights of both trucks, bringing darkness to the scene as the two drivers tugged away their capes and goggles, revealing blue armour and leering skull masks.

'The bodies?' one asked.

'No time,' the other replied. 'Move.'

KASTOR

The Primaris advanced to the head of the alleyway, low and fast.

'Stay close,' Severus ordered Kastor over the vox. He did so, trying to quell the natural dislike he felt towards infiltration techniques. It had been difficult enough out in the Tombstones, surrounded by nothing but the soaring vastness of the mountains, but now that he was in the midst of a city overrun by xenos scum, the urge to carry righteous death to them was almost overwhelming. He overcame his urges by fixing his mind on the *Lectato* and its Codex-led teachings about the importance of flexibility and adaptability in all of war's many aspects.

He was a Battle-Chaplain, not a blind zealot. He had already managed to countenance concealing himself amidst the rancid meat collected by the greenskins in the back of their rickety waggons. Doing so had been a necessary evil, part of Severus' bold plan to infiltrate Shebat under the cover of a distraction led by Colonel Davik. Kastor had no idea whether the Guardsmen in the third commandeered truck had managed to break away from the greenskin pursuit and make it back to the foothills before being caught. Concealed in the waggon's rear, he'd been blind until an ork had pulled back the covering and felt the sudden heat of his wrath.

'There are more contacts closing from the north and north-east,' Stryx said, consulting the bulky auspex-primary as they came to the end of the alley. The other two Reivers were crouched behind him, knives sheathed, the crude disguises that had allowed them to race through the ork lines cast off.

'Do they approach with purpose?' Severus demanded.

'No, but they will likely stumble across this location in a matter of minutes.'

'And has the device concluded its subterranean scans?'

'Yes, sergeant. The original locator beacon is correct.'

Stryx pointed with his own blade beyond the end of the alley, towards the street the trucks had come down.

'Take point,' Severus ordered. They hadn't got far before Kastor's visor pinged with a lit-up transmission sigil.

'Vox contact,' he said. 'We're back in signal range.'

'Still no fix, though,' Severus replied. 'It will take longer for a proper connection to become established. We carry on.'

The Reivers and the Chaplain moved out into the street. The darkness surrounding them was riven with the howling of greenskin mobs and the battering reports of their crude firearms, flares of light illuminating the rubble that towered all around like the great, dark barrows of long-dead warrior kings. It seemed that Davik's gambit had been too successful – it felt as though the entire city were awake, the initial disruption spreading from mob to mob all the way to Shebat's heart.

They reached the exfiltration point without meeting opposition. It was a sub-street storage hangar, marked out on the powerful auspex array carried by Stryx as having survived the rok's impact. The tremors caused by the collision had not only brought down almost the entirety of the city, it had also split and ruptured Shebat Alpha's underworld – sub-surface storage bays, the sewer system, basements and the subway mag-lev had all been broken and reformed, and while most of the tunnels had simply collapsed in their entirety, some had remained open. The scans picked up by the auspex were incomplete, but they offered the best hope of navigating below ground, away from the mobs infesting the surface ruins.

Task Force Marilus descended, moving aside the girders and rubble to expose the hangar's entrance. It had once been a vast storage space for a printing business, and its survival was a curious juxtaposition to the devastation of the workshop it had once serviced. Though the lumens had failed, the wide room below remained in an orderly state, packed with sealed plastek containers. A door led to a service corridor, rusting and abandoned, which carried on through to a half-collapsed smelting pit.

'What's the likelihood of the xenos pursuing us down there?' Kastor asked.

'There is no evidence that they have accessed the underground,' Severus replied. 'That may change as we move deeper into the city, but for now it offers us the best chance of avoiding detection, and allows us to scan for the largest concentrations of xenos without putting ourselves at risk. Wherever they are, that is almost certainly where we will find Helix.'

There were two possible routes beyond the smelter pit. One was from a section of the mag-lev line that had collapsed in on itself, providing access from the adjacent rooms and basements. The other was a waste chute that led to the sewage systems. According to the readings on the auspex, it was still open at the far end.

'Fobus, take the subway line,' Severus ordered. 'Stryx, the chute. Reconnaissance pattern, maintain vox contact if possible. Report back here within the hour. Synchronise your chrono countdown.'

'I can accompany one of them,' Kastor said.

'No need,' Severus responded brusquely. 'We have to find our bearings and establish just how accurate these readings are before moving any further. They don't need your help to do that.'

'So what will I do instead?'

'You will do the same thing as me, Brother-Chaplain. You will review the tactical log and mission briefings, and you will wait.'

POLIXIS

The heart had choked his throat. It had made him gag and retch. But the memories were worse. The memories choked his mind. They came on unbidden as Polixis remained bound to the rack, a sudden flood, stifling in their clarity and overwhelming in their intensity.

He was going to die. They all were. Still, on they fought.

Uxis' flamestorm gauntlets had nearly bled dry, the promethium wells stuttering as what had once been twin spears of flame were reduced to flaring bursts. It hardly seemed to matter any more – everything around him was a sheet of fire, aliens stumbling and writhing about, blinded by ash and smoke, burning alive in the fury of the Fulminata unleashed. It was like a scene from one of Chaplain Kastor's sermons, the coming of the Emperor's righteous judgement, when the heretic and the xenos would be purged by unending, divine fire.

Uxis only wished he had more to give. He slammed his ignited fists forwards, pulverising an ork's torso as it came charging through the fires, ignited from head to foot.

Tiro and Torr were both dead, their Gravis plate hacked open, half buried by a mound of ork corpses. Ancient Skyrus had fallen too, still holding his standard aloft even in death. Extremis was immobilised, one side of its grav-lift wrecked by the endless barrage of greenskin rockets and stick grenades. Only Uxis and Captain Demeter still fought.

A huge brute of a greenskin hammered two long blades time and again against the captain's Gravis armour as Demeter battled to protect the standard of the Fulminata. Uxis was trying to reach the captain's side, but the big ork's kindred were swarming him. Another leapt at the sole surviving Aggressor, clutching at him, trying to wrestle him to the ground with a terrible strength. His heavy gauntlet pulverised the skull of another even as it drove a two-handed chainblade into his midriff. Pain surged as the roaring blades bit deep.

A backhand swipe of his gauntlet smashed the ork's head from its shoulders, but it was too late. Another was digging a knife through the armour joints beneath his backpack. He felt his legs growing weak as his Belisarian Furnace kicked in, demanding one last bout of slaughter in the name of the Chapter and the primarch.

He crushed skulls and broke bones, choking on his own blood, given over to mindless fury now as he sought to kill as many xenos as he could before they took him. Beyond, he was vaguely aware of the captain. The ork he was fighting had cleaved away one arm with a huge swing of one of its blades, and now it was bellowing with laughter as it stepped away from the crackling arcs of Demeter's boltstorm gauntlet. It was toying with him. The realisation sent a fresh surge of hate jolting through Uxis.

He tried once more to reach the captain, but something hammered into his flank, causing him to stumble. A squig had leapt clear through the flames and was now clamping its huge, slavering jaws around his right arm, sawing its teeth through ceramite and plasteel. He smashed his other fist into it, causing it to burst in a huge wave of stinking gore and meat, but the effort of the blow forced him to his knees. He could feel his strength ebbing, the pain from his wounds too much to ignore any more.

Demeter had fallen as well, his armour buckled in half a dozen places. Uxis saw him framed against the blue and white of the Fulminata's standard, the beastly alien warlord looming over him, burning bodies heaped all about. The captain's blood-splattered white helm turned, and Uxis realised they were looking at each other.

Demeter's voice clicked over the vox, somehow still so calm, even at the end.

'Courage and honour, Brother Uxis.'

Then the green tide fell upon them both, and they were gone.

As suddenly as the vision appeared, it shattered. Polixis' eyes focused again, and his breathing returned. The dead lay before Polixis, silent, the judgement of their glassy helmet lenses damning. Where were you, Brother-Apothecary? Where were you when we gave our lives, that others might live?

Polixis had seen it. In a half-sleep he had seen Uxis' final moments and, alongside him, those of Captain Demeter. His omophagea, the eighth organ implanted in all Space Marines, had made sure he was not spared his brothers' dying moments. Normally the implant allowed an Adeptus Astartes to gain a degree of recollection by consuming the flesh of another. Polixis had never heard of it occurring thanks to the forced consumption of gene-seed before. It only added to the horror, choking Polixis as surely as the gland had itself, cold and clammy, like Uxis' death grip from beyond the grave.

In the longest, darkest hours of the night, Polixis realised that what little emotions he possessed had been bled dry. The calculating part of his mind told him as much, continuing to narrate his situation in its surgical tone, removed from the reality of his predicament. That reality, he now understood, was that the meaning of his existence had been reduced to nothingness. He had sundered his sacred duty to his Chapter and the Imperium. He had failed to protect the lives, bodies and wargear of those in his charge. Worse than that, he had disgraced them, dishonoured them with abject defeat. He was trapped, his soul bound forever to the oblivion of regret, locked in the darkness of a body unable to so much as move a single arm.

He would die here, he had no doubt. It would be slow, probably butchery. That knowledge did not concern him. His life was forfeit regardless. He had no means to resist his fate, and thus all other considerations became academical.

And then, abruptly, the situation changed. He heard a faint, metallic groan. It took a second to draw his thoughts up out of the despair that had nearly drowned them. He realised that his whole body had been tense for hours, and that both his arms were now actively pressing against the metal bent crudely round his wrists.

That meant the servos were responding.

His thoughts quickened. The shame remained, but now there was something more, something that had deserted him as night had fallen and shadows had wrapped up the bodies at his feet – anger. The urge to immediately rip himself free from the rack and set about the greenskins slumbering around him was almost overwhelming. He forced himself to steady his breathing and slow his heart rate. He had to test his systems. The majority of his armour could still be incapacitated.

He relaxed both arms and tried to slowly raise one foot. As he had feared, the servos in both legs were still unresponsive. His armour was gradually recharging after the ministrations of the xenos prong. It had been days since he had last been struck by it – in that time, he realised, his battleplate had been returning itself to full functionality. If he could avoid another shock, he might eventually be capable of full movement.

A grunt nearby made him go still, worried that his sudden degree of freedom had been spotted. There was a thud of boots on flagstones, a few snarled words in the darkness. He moved his head slightly, eyes adjusting to pick out several figures on the steps leading to the apse. One was an ork, and it was holding a squirming gretchin by the scruff of its neck. They had disturbed one of Polixis' captors, who now seemed to be demanding some sort of explanation from them. Their tongue was too guttural for him to make out, but judging by the pointing and the gretchin's high-pitched squealing it seemed like they were reporting something that had occurred out in the city. The ork turned and kicked two of its sleeping underlings awake, barking orders and gesticulating at their weapons. Other orks around them stirred drowsily, disturbed by the sudden commotion.

The beast snatched the two it had woken and thrust them down the apse, sending them after the first greenskin and his gretchin, towards the basilica's doors. It made to follow but paused, glancing back at Polixis. He stayed perfectly still, watching the greenskin, wondering how much it could discern in the darkness. After a while it grunted and turned away, hastening after its kin.

Something was happening out in Shebat. Polixis didn't intend to remain in the basilica long enough to find out what.

GRIMTOOF

Grimtoof had told the git he'd let the big boss skin him alive if he was lying. They'd come in the middle of the night, some zogger from Zagby's mob, hauling along a gretchin he'd snatched from Mek Drok. Grimtoof had almost cracked him on the jaw for waking him, but the boy's story had eventually penetrated the angry fug of the kommando's tiredness.

There were humies in the south of the city. According to the grot's excited, stammering report, some scran-waggons had been snatched by some gits hiding up in the mountains. They'd chased the rest of the scran lads back to the edge of town before turning and legging it. That in itself was only moderately interesting, but Grimtoof had managed to restrain himself long enough for the story to start getting better.

The grot claimed that there had only been a few boys in the escaped scran-waggons, and they'd been wrapped up tight. They'd not stopped when they reached the city but kept going, on past the mobs rushing after the humies. Then Zagby's mob had stumbled across a bunch of bodies – the greenskin seemed vague on the number, probably due to his inability to count – all from Grotsnog's mob, including the deviant nob himself. According to Zagby's lad, they'd been 'cut up real good'.

Even more importantly, they'd been littered around the two scran trucks, now abandoned.

All told, it constituted what Stabskar would've called a 'situashun'.

Grimtoof had kicked Krulkil and Urgin awake, and told them to follow. Both had known better than to complain. The kommandos trailed Zagby's lad and the grot out into the city.

The git wasn't lying about one thing at least – something had certainly stirred up Shebat's new greenskin inhabitants. The mobs occupying the square beyond the spikey building's doors were rousing, arguing and scrapping among them-selves as distant bellows and gunfire resounded through the night. Grimtoof shoved his way through the press, the sight of his cape cowing any protest. They'd all heard about Stab-skar's skinning, and how Grimtoof had succeeded where the previous nob had failed. Now his boys guarded the beakie prisoner, beneath the very eyes of the big boss.

Despite the prestige being close to Urgork brought with it, Grimtoof realised that it felt good to be back out again. For all the idea that the kommandos were a cut above the footslogga mobs, boys would be boys – they hadn't had a proper scrap for days, kept in while other lads had attacked the humie ridgeline over and over. The boys were getting fractious, and Grimtoof could threaten to crump them only so many times. Word about the mysterious trucks and Grotsnog's corpses was just what they needed – it had set the kommando nob's instincts on edge. There was a hunt in the offing, and he wanted to get stuck right in.

The guides led them through Shebat's night-shrouded ruins, south towards the city limits. In the remnants of a dark alleyway they came across the rest of Zagby's mob. They were gathered around two idling trucks, grunting and restless, clearly eager to fully claim the abandoned vehicles for themselves and roar south towards all the commotion.

'Definitely scran-waggons,' Grimtoof said as he surveyed the bloody contents in the open rear of both trucks, using a torch carried by one of Zagby's lads. He turned to the bodies of Grotsnog and his boys, scattered around the vehicles.

'They ain't been touched,' Zagby promised. Grimtoof grunted, not believing for a second that the mob hadn't already pillaged the corpses. He picked his way from one to another, turning them over with his boot. Their wounds were all clear and sharp, made by long blades and a great deal of strength. All except one. One of the boys had received a crushing blow to its skull, staving it in and leaving the ork lifeless against the wheel of one of the trucks.

Just as he was about to move on to the next body, he noticed something abandoned beside the truck's tyre. He sniffed and picked it up, turning it over in his hands – it was a ragged cape, like the ones used by the footsloggas out in the ash wastes or up in the high hills. There was blood on it, crusted and dark.

'You seen this before?' he demanded, holding the threadbare cloth up in front of Drok's grot.

'Yeah, boss,' the runty thing squeaked. 'S-seen them scran boys wearin' 'em. Them's what da drivers had on.'

Grimtoof held the rags close to his face, hawked and spat, then inhaled deeply. There was no mistaking it. He turned to Zagby, bearing his tusks in a wicked grin.

'Send your boys out to all da nearest mobs. Get 'em 'ere right now, and tell 'em to keep a sharp eye. There's beakie boys around, and we is gonna find 'em.'

CHAPTER TEN   SKULL MASKS

KASTOR

Fobus and Stryx had yet to return. Kastor remained in the smelter pit with Severus. It had been quiet since they had descended underground, the greenskins seemingly unaware that so many of Shebat Alpha's deep-sunk storage containment blocks and access tunnels had remained open despite the rok's devastation. The smelter pit itself was a good example – with space in the industrial sprawl at a premium, it was a workshop that had been sunken down into the city's bedrock, its fume and waste flumes and ventilation shafts keeping the metal presses and bench lines from being shrouded in toxic smoke. A hundred labourers would once have filled the subterranean space with the pounding of hammers and steel, but now it was deserted, tools gathered neatly, great sheets of plate stacked awaiting the pressers and moulds. Like the print shop, the everyday orderliness was a surreal counterpoint to the ruination that Kastor knew was heaped just above.

Severus sat down beside the broken-down entrance to the mag-lev subway line. Kastor took a seat on one of the solid metal workbenches across from him, the frame groaning beneath his weight. Time seemed to pass with infuriating slowness, defying the Chaplain's attempts to ease it along with a string of murmured prayers from the *Lectato*'s psalter. Even disregarding the desire to find Polixis, to be so deep in enemy-infested territory without being able to strike was anathema to Kastor. In the silence of the pit, he found his thoughts straying, doubts materialising like one of Severus' death-brothers from the shadows.

He should not be here. He should not have abandoned the Fulminata. The entire venture was almost certainly hopeless, and was going to cost the Chapter not only his own life but the lives of the Reivers as well.

Polixis would have stopped him. He could almost hear his older brother's words, as stern as the Chaplain's when he wished them to be.

'The Chapter comes before your personal quest for honour, Kastor. It must come before everything, even before you and me. You know that, yet I must be the one to repeat it to you?'

He realised one hand had strayed to Salve Imperator's mag-locked haft, as it so often did when darkness surrounded him. He forced himself to set the rising doubts aside – he had considered his course, decided upon it, and now had no choice other than to maintain it. The fruits of the seeds of doubt were death, defeat and dishonour.

He turned to Severus. The Reiver hadn't moved since taking his seat, a dire, death's head shadow on Kastor's optic enhancers. After considering him, the Chaplain spoke.

'When Lieutenant Tyranus gave you this assignment, what were your immediate thoughts?'

Severus' eyes darted up. He said nothing for a while before responding. 'I was pleased. I considered it a challenge.'

'A challenge because it is unlikely to succeed?'

'Because it offers numerous operational difficulties that will push both my own abilities and those of my death-brethren.'

'I suspect you would get on well with my brother if you conversed with him more often. You are both adept at avoiding questions.'

'You mean we are both more analytic in our responses than you, Brother-Chaplain.'

'I suppose it's a matter of perspective,' Kastor said, allowing himself a tight smile.

'Is perspective something you permit yourself to indulge in often?'

'It's usually an unwholesome luxury,' he admitted.

The pit lapsed into silence once more. Kastor resisted the urge to unchain his copy of the *Lectato* again – he'd insisted on bringing it, despite its unwieldy nature and the covert status of their mission. It was chained about his waist along with Polixis' gladius. The two items were the only concessions Severus had allowed.

Kastor found himself reflecting on how unnatural it felt to be under strict orders. It had been a long time since he had been subjected to the barked commands and stinging rod of his Reclusiam Superior, and his rank as Chaplain afforded him numerous privileges beyond the command structure of regular battle companies – privileges that he now realised he had come to take for granted. His current situation exemplified his own presumptions. He had allowed his arrogance to deceive him into breaking with the letter of the Codex Astartes. The realisation sent a pulse of anger through his thoughts, and that in turn left a cold, bitter wake of shame.

His reflexive response to any difficulty had become one of fiery rage. He understood that now, understood that at times he was too close to becoming just another deranged zealot, one who justified his own increasingly radical actions by measuring them against a false belief in his own high standing.

This was the consequence of breaking the letter of the Codex Astartes. These were the seeds of pride and arrogance. The realisation haunted him. He spoke to Severus once more, seeking release through idle words.

'Were you disappointed to be drawn away from the front line?'

'I am a Reiver. I do not belong on the front line,' the death-brother said tersely. 'I belong behind the enemy's, or in their midst. The skills of my brotherhood are not fully realised if they are fighting the Emperor's enemies face-to-face. We are better employed elsewhere.'

'And what about your two brothers, Stryx and Fobus?'

'You need not concern yourself, Chaplain Kastor. None of the death-brethren required any urging to volunteer for this operation. In fact, Scaris wanted to knife-fight for the honour. An undertaking such as this is the very purpose we exist for. Besides, it is for Helix. Any of us would die for him.'

There was emotion behind the statement, even though it was delivered with Severus' usual cold inflection. It made Kastor's heart beat faster as his mind turned once more to Polixis. That even the Reiver, seemingly so cold, so removed from the rest of the brotherhood, held such respect for the Apothecary reaffirmed everything Kastor believed. Bringing Polixis back was something worth dying for.

'We must find him, my death-brother,' he said quietly. 'For all our sakes.'

* * *

POLIXIS

Whatever form of patience Urgork possessed, it seemed to have run out. The warlord appeared to be in a foul mood as Polixis jolted from his catalepsean node rest, weak sunlight filtering in through the basilica's broken windows and the gaps smashed in its walls and roof.

'Doc!' the warlord bellowed as he mounted the apse, his small eyes fixed on Polixis. The medicae ork hurried to attend its master, fumbling with its satchel of syringes and tools. Urgork stopped before the rack and cast around, mismatched eyes raving with a hint of mania.

'Where's dat git Grimtoof?' he bellowed. One of the kommandos was shoved to the front of those who'd been guarding Polixis. Frozen before the hulking patchwork monstrosity, it managed to stammer some sort of explanation in a tongue too guttural for Polixis to comprehend. Urgork let out a snort of pure frustration and thrust a hand out towards the medicae. After a few seconds of fumbling, the runty greenskin passed a syringe to the warlord. The beast rounded back on Polixis, drool from his distended tusks splattering the Primaris.

'You is forcin' me ta take d-desperate measures,' Urgork spat. 'But I always wanted ta see what da good stuff does to you big humies.'

Urgork held the syringe up for Polixis to see, the foul-looking yellow liquid it contained bubbling dangerously.

'Youse might feel a little prick,' the ork said, and plunged the needle into the Apothecary's left tasset port.

The effect was immediate. Polixis felt a pain like nothing he had ever experienced before shoot from the entry point, immediately diffusing his left thigh, hip and groin. Usually even the worst agony would only flare for a few seconds before a Space Marine's enhanced physiology overcame it. A three-part process of deadened nerves, hyper-potent stimms and cranial surgery meant that there was almost no chance of a member of the Adeptus Astartes being incapacitated by his injuries.

This pain, however, did not go away. It grew.

Polixis gritted his teeth against it, muscles taut, trying to focus through the agony he could feel spreading through his body. He was sure the substance he'd been injected with was the same one Urgork used to control his fits, yet it acted more like a poison than any stimulant or suppressive – he could feel it burning through his body, travelling along his A delta and C fibre network, burning out flesh and nerve endings, and sending pain sizzling to parts of his brain that should have remained dormant.

A cry escaped his lips, and he realised his limbs were straining at their bonds, threatening to buckle the metal. Urgork hadn't noticed, attention focused on Polixis' features as the Primaris fought against the anguish.

Eventually, it lessened. The pain, which had spread all the way up his abdominal muscles and down past his left knee, began to recede. Polixis mastered himself, driving out the horrific ache the substance had left behind as it burned itself out. Normally, his diagnostor helmet would have been screaming warnings at him, reading vitae signs ravaged by the ork's vile concoctions. Instead, he had only Urgork's hacking laughter as the beast yanked the syringe from his thigh.

'Good medicine, ain't it, doc?' the beast demanded. 'Makes ya feel right as rain. But you see why I don't want ta take it no more. You is gonna fix me up.'

'You will suffer in agony,' Polixis snarled, spittle flecking his lips. 'For the rest of your days, short though they may be.'

'Still mouthin', ya git,' Urgork snarled, his dark mood returning. He leaned in close.

'We've been zoggin' about togetha for too long. The l-lads is restless. Can't have da big boss sittin' about playin' with some humie while there's loads of crumpin' dat still needs doin'.'

'So kill me,' Polixis spat, defiance surging through his mind, fists clenching as he prepared to wrench them from their restraints. 'For I will never aid you.'

'I kn-nows dat,' Urgork said, rancid breath washing over the Ultramarine. 'Known dat from da start. We coulda done this da easy way, but da truth is I wanted t-ta see what you could take. Now I'm just gonna rip all I need to know right outta your skull.'

The warlord turned and shouted something into the mob of greenskins crowding the basilica. Those nearest the front parted, pushing and shoving to get out of the way of the fig-ure that limped up the apse steps in response to Urgork's summons. It was stunted, a runt not dissimilar to the med-icae, but this one's green skull was lumpen and distended, ringed by thin white hair. It carried a totemic staff in one bony hand. Strangest of all, it was blind, tapping its way ahead with the staff. Polixis had never heard of a creature without sight surviving in the barbaric environment that passed for greenskin society.

The thing came to a halt before Urgork, cringing in the huge shadow of its misshapen master.

'Dis here is da beakie,' Urgork said, pointing at Polixis, as though the smaller xenos would be aware of the gesture.

'And dis h-here is my boss weirdboy, Sly,' Urgork said to Polixis, smacking the creature on the shoulder and making it twitch and groan. 'He's seen you before, beakie, in a big dream while we was in mad-space. Dis da one, ain't it, Sly?'

The greenskin tapped its way closer to Polixis, staff outstretched, the bits of bone, trophies and fetishes tied to it rattling. It sniffed and grimaced, milky eyes staring up at Polixis, and the Apothecary found himself shuddering beneath its sightless gaze – he remembered the medicae describing an ork psyker it hated, and he had encountered the crude, shamanic warp-users of the xenos race before. The taint of witchcraft filled his senses.

'Dis one's trouble,' the ork shaman said, growling like a small hound around a larger, caged predator. 'He's gonna cause a lot a crumpin' real soon, boss.'

'But h-he's da one,' Urgork reiterated. 'He's g-gonna make me even bigga and stronga, ain't he?'

'He'll make ya more killy,' the psyker said, squinting up at Polixis, cuffing drool from its tusks with a spotted green hand. 'But it won't be easy, boss. His mates is comin' for him.'

'Good,' Urgork said bluntly. 'More crumpin' to do. Now get ta work, Sly. Wasted enough time softening him up for ya.'

The ork psyker raised its hand and planted it on Polixis' breastplate. At first, nothing happened, but then the greenskin began muttering under its breath. Its eyes started to glow, suffused by an ethereal green energy. There was a crack, and verdant lightning ignited around its swollen cranium.

Its thoughts came for Polixis, and he screamed once more.

KASTOR

The vox came back online fully just under half an hour before Stryx and Fobus returned. Kastor was still seated in the smelter pit when the sigil on his visor lit up again. He blinked the transmission icon without hesitation.

'Prime Alpha, this is Salve. Do you copy?' he said. He'd tried half a dozen times since the signifier had first indicated they were once again within effective communications range, but the link had only just been fully established when the first response came back, brutally chopped by static.

'Salve, this is Prime Alpha.' It was Lieutenant Tyranus. *'Confirm your location and status immediately. You are with the death-brothers?'*

'I am,' Kastor answered.

'Their operation is progressing as planned?'

'It is, brother-lieutenant. We hope to make contact with the target in a matter of hours.'

'Then at least some good has come from your disobedience, Salve.'

'Alpha–' Kastor began to say but, for once, realised he had no words. He knew he had broken the chain of command and, in doing so, sundered the teachings of the Codex. No amount of explanation could hope to change that, and he would not disgrace himself further by trying.

'You disobeyed my orders,' Tyranus said, the ice in his voice audible even over the channel's interference. *'You sundered your sacred charge and abandoned your battle-brothers when they were in dire need.'*

'I broke from your directives,' Kastor admitted, trying to keep his voice level, the pain the lieutenant's words brought causing his fists to clench and his hearts to pound harder in his breast. 'If the Emperor's grace is sufficient to see me survive this venture, I will stand before your judgement.'

'No, you shall not,' Tyranus responded. *'This matter is now beyond the Fulminata. I will be reporting it to the Chapter*

Reclusiam. You will stand trial before the Master of Sanctity on holy Macragge, when the time allows.'

The words sent a chill through Kastor, but he mastered himself quickly, forcing his voice to remain level.

'As you wish. I pray to the Emperor and the primarch that I survive to answer with all honesty.'

'I pray you do, Salve,' Tyranus said.

'Prime Alpha,' Kastor said before Tyranus switched the link to address Severus. 'Have there been losses among the brotherhood since I left?'

Tyranus said nothing, the line's static crackling in Kastor's ear. Eventually, he responded.

'This link is not secure. May the Emperor guide you, brother.'

The line went dead.

Severus relayed what information the Reivers had gathered back to Tyranus. Fobus and Stryx added their own with their return. Both had bloodied blades – it seemed Shebat's broken underworld was not as devoid of the green menace as they had first thought.

'Word from Ridge One too,' Kastor said, reviewing the data-link that had finally been established, however briefly, with the rest of the Fulminata. 'There have been three full-scale xenos assaults since we departed. The line holds, though reinforcements are still being brought in from Kroten. There have been three fatalities since we departed. The conflict is entering a new phase of attrition.'

Kastor knew that it was a phase he likely wouldn't live to see. Even if he did, Tyranus' pronouncements had left little doubt about his future. Assuming he didn't perish on Ikara first, he would be summoned to blessed Macragge, where he would stand before the Chapter's assembled Chaplains,

Reclusiarchs and the Master of Sanctity, assuming the tides of war had carried enough of them home to form a council. That was the measure of Kastor's disobedience – he was to be put on trial before his peers as a battle-brother who had disgraced both his rank and the Codex Astartes. It was difficult to conceive of a greater shame.

He had already failed. All he had left was the desire to find Polixis. A dark ennui gripped the Chaplain's thoughts as he moved out with the Reivers once again, following the mag-lev subway line. It seemed fitting that this mission should cost him his life. He found himself praying for the opportunity to not only free Helix but also give himself honourably in the act. That was the only way he could conceive of amending his disgrace.

Such a possibility at least seemed attainable. The Reivers had done well, even by the usual standards of the death-brotherhood – Stryx had traced the mag-lev line close to the undercroft of the basilica. Its foundations still stood strong, as much a part of Ikara as the bedrock it was buried into. While he didn't have direct access, Stryx hadn't detected any greenskins within the crypt after scanning it. Besides the rok itself, the basilica remained the most likely focal point of ork leadership, as well as the location of any prisoners they still held. Reaching it from underground would be considerably easier than doing so on the surface – none of the strike force's members needed the auspex to tell them that the area around the basilica was infested with xenos.

They pressed on at a rapid pace, even the cold Reivers seemingly invigorated now that their hunt was nearing an end. It took less than twenty minutes to reach the point in the curving tunnel map-locked by Stryx.

'Here,' the Reiver said, halting at an unassuming section of the subway and tapping the stonework with the tip of his long knife. The sound seemed no different from any other part of the line to Kastor, yet the auspex confirmed whatever Stryx had detected – thanks to the shifting of the earth beneath the city, they were now separated from the basilica's crypts by only a narrow section of cracked tunnel wall.

'Melta charge,' Severus ordered, gesturing to the base of the wall.

'And if the xenos hear us entering?' Kastor asked.

'We have to gain access to the basilica. It's either this way, or through the front doors, Brother-Chaplain. As much as I suspect you'd prefer the latter, this is our best option. We must act now, before the greenskins pick up our trail and follow us down here.'

Fobus clamped a shaped melta charge to the base of the section of tunnel indicated by Stryx. Kastor unlocked Salve Imperator, sensing his doubts fall away as he felt the familiar, skull-tipped weight of the blessed mace in his gauntlet.

'Breaching,' Fobus said. There was a shriek of pyrum charge, a whoosh as a section of stonework was seared through and a crack of tumbling masonry as the mag-lev wall gave way.

The Primaris swept into the dust and smoke beyond, weapons ready.

POLIXIS

The xenos was in his mind.

Polixis convulsed as green lightning suffused his body. It was not the crackling charge that harmed him, though, it was the presence of the alien psyker driving itself against his mental barriers. Its skinny, deformed body hid a potency far beyond the usual abilities of the greenskin race. Its intrusion was the most horrific, most violating thing the Apothecary had ever experienced – Polixis could feel it ripping through his thoughts, laughing as it defiled memories, tearing and discarding them like a gleeful child.

He could have crushed it in an instant, with one hand, as could most of the greenskins in the basilica. When its powers were unleashed, however, the runty creature had dominion over all. The servos in Polixis armour were now fully operational once again, but his mind was completely impaired, forced into a state of pain-fuelled paralysis by the thing's unnatural talents.

After what felt like an eternity, it stopped. It drew its hand away from Polixis and its lightning shorted out, though energy continued to crackle around its staff. Smoke was visibly rising from its cranium, and its tongue was lolling out from between its tusks as it panted for breath. It shook its head before turning to Urgork and the medicae. It uttered something in its guttural tongue and pointed at Polixis.

'Again,' Urgork snapped. 'Zap 'im again.'

Polixis didn't have a chance to spit his defiance before the lightning struck once more.

KASTOR

Kastor found himself in a dark, stony space, his auto-senses picking out and highlighting features already logged previously by his armour. He realised he was back amongst the vaults and effigies of Saint Albarak the Smelter's crypts.

The place had changed since he and his older brother had last stood in the dusty shadows. The crates of munitions the Guard had been stockpiling had gone, looted by the greenskins. They'd left behind pallets, ripped plastek, dung and indiscernible debris littered throughout the tombs and statuary alcoves. Some had started smashing and defiling the effigies of the fallen or prising open their resting places, leaving bones and mouldering scraps of funerary shroud scattered around.

Given the cruelties heaped on so much that Kastor held sacred, it might have been assumed there was only so much anger the Chaplain could harbour. Still though, he found his spirit ignite as he took in the crude blasphemies inflicted by the xenos scum, the desolation they had caused in the sacred resting place of honoured Imperial servants.

The Reivers didn't pause to consider the state of the basilica's crypts. Silently, they spread out through the darkness, bolt pistols and combat knives unclamped, hunting for anything that might have been aware of their entrance into the tombs. There was nothing, though – the place seemed deserted.

'They are nesting down here,' Severus said, indicating the refuse piles filling the alcoves and corners. 'We cannot stay for long.'

'I didn't intend to,' Kastor growled softly. Fobus took point as the four Primaris advanced to the crypt's primary stairway, weapons bared and ready for the smallest hint of discovery. As they began to climb, a sound reached Kastor, echoing down from the basilica. It was the noise of someone in immense suffering.

It only took Kastor a few seconds to recognise that the sound was being made by his brother.

'Polixis,' he snarled, instinctively throwing himself up the stairs. Severus halted him, physically blocking the narrow stone passage. The black plate almost collided with the blue, and for a second two skulls glared at one another, inches apart.

'You will remain here,' Severus said, voice clicking over the vox.

'He's alive,' Kastor replied. The words rasped over the helmet vox like embers that had been kicked back to life, sudden fire amidst red-edged ash. The heat in them would have given even fellow Adeptus Astartes pause. Severus didn't move.

'He is,' the Reiver agreed, his voice a frigid counterpoint to the heat of the Chaplain's words. 'And you will remain here until Fobus has ascertained what waits for us above.'

'I cannot!' Kastor made to thrust the Reiver to one side, but froze a second before contact. Severus' blade had twitched towards his gorget, its steel a sliver of light in the dark.

'I will not allow you to compromise this operation,' the Reiver said. 'Not my life, the lives of my death-brothers, nor even that of Helix will be put at risk because you cannot control your passions.'

'I am in control,' Kastor said, forcing himself to back away a step.

'You are not,' Severus said bluntly. 'You will go up there, and you will attack the first xenos you lay eyes on. Even if you do reach Polixis and are able to free him, you will not be able to escape before being overwhelmed.'

A scream pierced the air once more.

'He needs us,' Kastor snapped.

'And you will not help him by storming up there alone,' Severus said. 'The truth is that it's more than likely a trap. What other reason would they have for seizing and torturing him, beyond luring more of us into their lair? Come to your senses, Brother-Chaplain. There is no worse a time for your faith and fury than here and now.'

Kastor stifled an exclamation of pure rage. He held his ground on the stairs, neither pushing forwards nor retreating.

Ahead, behind Severus, Stryx had knelt, weapons ready once more as he faced up the stairwell. Fobus had vanished.

'Patience,' Severus urged. 'Trust in the Emperor, Kastor.'

The Chaplain forced himself to loosen his grip fraction-ally on Salve Imperator. He did not seek out prayers or catechisms – the screams ringing down to him were prayers enough. Instead, he focused on rooting himself to the spot, denying his taut muscles the imperative to move. Control. It was his only saving grace now.

It seemed to take an age for Fobus to return. Kastor remained perfectly still, head bowed with the effort of restraint. Mem-ories came back to him, like a sudden wind to whip up the flames once more. He was standing in the rough-hewn tim-ber agri stead his birth-family called home, outside the door of his brother's bedroom. The sallow, hook-nosed figure of Doctor Martel, the agri collective's medicae practitioner, had entered twenty minutes earlier, casting a dismissive glance at Kastor as he passed. Since then he had heard little coming from his brother's room other than soft sobs. The pitiable sounds made Kastor's small hands clench into fists. Accord-ing to their father, Polixis was feverish. Kastor had remained there, by the closed door, too afraid to enter but unable to abandon his brother, hoping that his presence and his loy-alty somehow communicated itself to the older boy. The feeling of helplessness was one that, even at his young age, Kastor had realised would never leave him. It was the sort of memory long wiped from Polixis' mind, but cruelly embed-ded in Kastor's, seemingly for eternity.

He had sworn he would never leave his brother helpless in the hands of another again. He had broken that vow, just one of many now. He was tired, sick to the core of what he had done in the past few days. It was time to end it.

He realised Severus was no longer standing before him. He'd moved slightly further up the crypt stairs, and Fobus had reappeared at their top. The Reivers were relaying a hushed conversation between themselves.

Polixis' screaming had stopped.

'He is up there,' Severus said, turning back to Kastor. 'As is the alpha-level target.'

'The warlord?' Kastor asked.

'Yes. Fobus has positively identified Urgork and a number of other xenos believed to be in his inner circle.'

'What are they doing to my brother? How badly is he injured?'

'Physically, he appears almost unharmed,' Fobus said. 'But a greenskin witch is performing some foul rite over him.'

Kastor again moved towards the stairs, and again was firmly checked by Severus.

'This is an opportunity,' the Reiver said, a hand planted firmly on Kastor's ribbed breastplate. 'All of your prayers could not have delivered us a better one, Chaplain. We have a chance here to not only remove your brother from the clutches of the xenos, but also strike off the head of the monster.'

'I do not see how that will bring back the Fulminata's Apothecary,' Kastor responded. 'Eliminating the warlord and freeing my brother at the same time would make exfiltration almost impossible. We would be surrounded and cut off.'

'And Urgork would be dead. At the very least, the greenskins' effort on Ikara would suffer a fatal blow. Shebat would be completely retaken in a matter of weeks. The Waaagh! across the neighbouring systems might even collapse.'

'You would make martyrs of us,' Kastor said, struggling to keep his voice in check.

'I would have us do our *duty*.'

'If I could give my life to slay the beast I would, without hesitation. You know that. But I came here to ensure that my brother lives. Even with Urgork dead, the Fulminata will need Helix. The *Chapter* needs him.'

'Then the Chapter will have him,' Severus said, and for once Kastor got the impression that there was a hint of a smile behind the grim death mask. 'I am a sergeant of the Reivers, Brother-Chaplain. There is a far better way to bring down the beast than with our own lives. Do you still have vox contact with the lieutenant?'

CHEVIK

General Chevik brushed forefinger and thumb along the tip of his moustache, eyes wandering from the holo display to Field Marshal Klos' indicator marker, lighting up the salient parts of the battle map being beamed into the centre of the command dome. It was the sixth or seventh full staff briefing in the past day, and the Vostroyan was dead on his feet. Damned if he would admit it, though – there were a gaggle of faces gathered around the display not from his corps, all new arrivals from Kroten. Throne take him if he showed more than the most grudging of thanks at the arrival of their reinforcements, let alone hint at his own exhaustion.

He forced his mind to focus on what Klos was saying, running through the details of logistical military minutiae. There were delays in moving up munitions from the main artillery park to the emplacements along sectors one through three on the ridgeline, and the field marshal wanted to know why. These were the things that battles turned on, Chevik reminded himself for what must have been the sixth or seventh time in the last hour.

Raised voices came from beyond the dome's main entrance flap. A few of the staff officers glanced towards it. Klos carried on, apparently oblivious, holding up a data-slate report from a Kelestani Earthshaker commander who claimed in the event of another full-frontal greenskin attack, his batteries wouldn't have enough ordnance to adequately support his sector.

The commotion outside rose. Chevik recognised the voice of the commander of the headquarters' Scion security detail. More eyes turned, and Klos faltered, a look of anger crossing his scarred face. The flap snatched back, and the expression vanished – filling the entrance was a Primaris Space Marine. A few of the new arrivals gasped audibly, and it took what little remained of Chevik's concentration to maintain his bluff, uncaring aura.

'Field Marshal Klos,' the warrior said, ducking into the space. Chevik realised it was the same one he had briefed immediately after the withdrawal from Shebat, though it was difficult to be certain – from what little he had seen of the Ultramarines, they all seemed to share the same strong, broad features and short, curling blond hair.

'My lord,' Klos said, making the sign of the aquila. The other Guard officers clustered around the holo hastened to do likewise.

'I come bearing vital news,' the Ultramarine said. 'But first, you must issue a front-wide command directive. Prepare all forward battalions to advance.'

CHAPTER ELEVEN   GAMBITS

HANLON

The Space Marines had left. Word filtered down the line as dawn broke, whispered whenever the officers or commissars were absent. It was said that they'd withdrawn, that companies in the rear echelons had seen them moving east, away from the front line. Others said massive, armoured flyers had swooped down to extract them from the landing zones being laid out in the direction of Kroten. No one seemed to know anyone who'd seen any of it first-hand.

Vorn asked Lieutenant Hanlon about it directly while the Namarians were cooking up ration packs and tins of recaff in a section of the reserve dugouts north-east of General Chevik's command post. It was the first hot meal they'd had in days, and Hanlon was loath to let anything spoil it. She sent Vorn back to his stove-unit with orders not to spread hearsay. If the Space Marines had left, it was good news – it could only mean the worst of the fighting was now happening elsewhere.

Hanlon closed her eyes and inhaled the recaff cooling in the tin cupped between her fingers, trying her best to put the memory of her first encounter with the giant warriors to the back of her mind. She was sitting on the firestep near the edge of the redoubt, drinking in the scents of cooking, relishing the relative solitude of her seat away from the rest of the platoon. They'd been rotated off the front line the night before, trudging back under the thunder of the guns to sleep the sleep of the dead in their new reserve position. Tarpaulins and gas flaps had been strung over the parapets which, when combined with a chugging air recyc-unit, had allowed them to finally remove their respirator masks, if only for a while. Being free of the sweat-stinking, rubbery suffocation felt a little like salvation.

It had been hellish since the first ork assault. Reinforcements from Kroten had been coming in from the second day, but the logistical difficulties of rotating troops in between frontal assaults and while under near-constant artillery bombardment had meant that the new units hadn't simply taken over the old positions en masse.

'Sir.' The voice of Krevin interrupted Hanlon's thoughts. She opened her eyes, blinking, wondering how long the vox-operator had been standing there. He was Wylk's replacement. The memory of Wylk going down, cut apart by ork shots out in the wasteland, flashed through Hanlon's mind. She forced it aside, and took the message chit offered by Krevin.

'From battalion, sir. All company commanders have been called to a snap-briefing at Colonel Ruther's headquarters. Anticipation of fresh orders.'

'Throne give me strength,' Hanlon said, scanning the message transcribed by the vox-operator and closing her eyes again, tilting her head back against the flakboard behind her. They'd only just got here.

She took a breath and mastered herself. Duty and honour.

'Prepare yourself, Krev,' she said, handing the chit back to the vox-man. She drained the last of the recaff, stretched her back and stood, refusing to acknowledge the aching in her legs and the pain in her feet.

'Eat up quickly,' she ordered the platoon. 'Full equipment check in ten minutes. I want everyone ready to move immediately after.'

Most of the men were too tired to even voice their dismay.

'We going back up there, sir?' Private Shara asked. 'Back up to the front?'

'Your guess is as good as mine,' Hanlon said. 'All I know is that the company commander is with the colonel right now, and we've been told to anticipate new orders.'

'Maybe they're going to have us lead the withdrawal to Kroten,' Vorn quipped. 'And give us first pick of the thankful female populace of the capital.'

'Or maybe we'll be leading the bayonet charge into Shebat,' Hanlon responded. 'Either way, hurry up and eat. It may be the last food we get for a while.'

GRIMTOOF

Grimtoof shoved his way through the basilica, bellowing at those in front of him to shift or face a beating. It seemed like every git in the city had packed himself into the spikey old building, come to see the final moments of the captured beakie.

A captured beakie that Grimtoof now realised was not alone. He'd picked up tracks in the rubble – one clumsy one, and probably several more. The trail had stopped suddenly, the hunt interrupted, but the kommando nob was convinced he knew why.

'Boss!' he bellowed, kicking his way past the last few of Urgork's big nob bodyguards that surrounded the altar throne. 'Boss, I gots somethin' you gotta hear!'

Urgork shifted, blinking and grimacing angrily at Grimtoof. The weirdboy Sly and the doc, Grok, were both gathered around the beakie prisoner, who was still lashed to the upright rack. He looked worse for wear, his white armour blackened by Sly's mad-bolts, his features twisted with raw, deep-set pain.

'Grim, where you been?' Urgork barked.

'Huntin', boss,' the nob said hastily, drawing back his cape and averting his eyes reverentially. 'Some grots found something out in da city. I reckon there's beakies 'ere, somewhere with us.'

'He's right here, you stupid g-git,' Urgork snapped, gesturing at the humie on the rack.

'No, boss,' Grimtoof exclaimed. 'More of 'em! They snuck in with a scran-waggon last night. They is here to spring 'im free.'

'So why ain't you crumped 'em?' Urgork demanded. 'Dat's your job, ain't it?'

'I reckon they is underground, boss,' Grimtoof said. 'They be using tunnels and all dis and dat to move under da lads.'

'Tunnels,' Urgork said, eyes narrowing. 'Dis place got tunnels, don't it, Grim?'

'Yeah, boss,' Grimtoof went on, more enthusiastic now he realised he was getting somewhere. 'They could be down there right now!'

'Huh,' Urgork said, gaze going from Grimtoof to the beakie, then to Sly and Grok. 'Maybe dat's why da squigs have been goin' wild and chompin' all da lads. Well, only one w-way to find out. Let 'em loose.'

* * *

KASTOR

Stryx had been on lookout since dawn, near the top of the crypt's primary stairway. The Reivers had secured all three stair routes down in the undercroft, besides the entrance blast. They'd killed the seven xenos that had so far wandered down, silencing each one before it could raise the alarm.

Kastor remained apart from the death-brothers. He spent most of the time standing silent and still before a mortuary icon of the Emperor in His form as the reaper, cloaked and skull-faced. The statue was human-sized but dwarfed by the Primaris. It was a juxtaposition of two deathly figures, one the living, breathing legacy of the other's graven image, both wreathed in shadow.

Word had been sent back to Tyranus. They waited. It was burning Kastor, burning him through, his own fires eating him alive while in the shadows the two figures of death regarded one another, one carved stone, the other black-and-bone armour bearing within it nothing but anger. The Chaplain's thoughts had been seared away by the white heat housed within those scarred, black plates – reduced to ash, to bitter embers that choked the back of his throat and made his hands twitch.

Occasionally, the sounds of Polixis' pain would drift down to the subterranean chamber. When that happened, Kastor's fists would clench and the breath scraping from his skull helm would shorten. Severus, crouched at the bottom of one of the two secondary stairways, would glance back at him over the tombstones and plinths. But the Chaplain didn't move. He stayed locked before the statue, as silent as the representation of death before him.

'*What's that sound?*' clicked Fobus' voice over the vox. It reached Kastor's ears a few seconds later – high-pitched, ugly squealing, and the scrabble of what appeared to be claws on stone. Stryx's answer came back over the net.

'Maw beasts. They've unchained them.'

'Prepare yourself,' Severus said, the externalised order echoing faintly through the dark, cold space. Kastor moved, armour whirring as its servos came to life, the clack of a fresh bolt pistol round being chambered mirroring Severus' words.

'They're coming,' Stryx voxed. The declaration was followed by the clicking reports of a silenced bolt pistol. The squealing, scraping sounds intensified.

'Let them,' Kastor snarled, moving to Severus' side as the Reiver stood up. Fobus engaged at the third stairwell, his bolter joining that of Stryx's at the second. Above Kastor and Severus, the light filtering into the crypt from the basilica was abruptly obscured. Something came bouncing down the dank stone steps like an inflated ball, if the ball had been half slavering, teeth-filled maw.

Severus shot the squig first, a trio of tightly spaced rounds bursting it apart in a shower of stinking fungal viscera. The next two after it died in the same manner, the third ripped open like a flesh-sac by Kastor's bolt-rounds.

The next one sprung from the stairwell's top step with such power that it hurtled all the way to the bottom in a single stride. Severus impaled it on his long knife as it slammed into him, the silver vibrosteel jamming up into the bridge of its abnormally huge mouth and stabbing through whatever passed for its brain. Kastor finished it with a crunching blow of his crozius, spraying both of the Ultramarines with its exploded innards.

'They know we're here,' Severus said, leaving his knife lodged in the squig's remains while he reloaded. 'Tyranus is inbound…'

'But won't be here in time,' Kastor said, finishing the thought. Up in the basilica, the greenskins had started to roar, their bestial excitement drowning out all else.

'Our window of opportunity is about to close,' Severus said. 'We strike now. Stryx, Fobus, on me. Brother-Chaplain –' He turned to Kastor, and nodded.

'Now is the time for your fury.'

POLIXIS

The basilica was in uproar. The slavering, yapping squig beasts unleashed by the greenskins had all flung themselves at the stone entrances to the undercroft, and the shrieks of their deaths had been all the confirmation the xenos needed – there were enemies in their midst, and the realisation had driven them into an excitable frenzy.

'Burnas!' Urgork was bellowing. 'Get da burna boys in 'ere and flame 'em out!' The warlord had turned away from Polixis, as had his retinue. Even the blind psyker had stepped back and was cringing on its haunches, disorientated by the sudden furore. Polixis felt his mind clear, the xenos' probing gone from his thoughts. He drew a shuddering breath, forcing his aching limbs to respond, testing them against the restraints while all around him greenskins surged to the apse and the undercroft stairs beyond.

If any of the mobs packed into the basilica had heard Urgork's orders, they didn't get the opportunity to obey them. There was a flash and a bang from behind the apse's partition, and Polixis recognised the detonation of stun grenades just before a ferocious howl filled the air. It pierced even the combined ruckus of the aliens, a teeth-juddering, ear-pounding shriek of vox-amplified battle rage so potent it could send human combatants fleeing or paralyse them with raw fear. It was the sound of Reivers on the attack, and amidst it all Polixis recognised the voice of his brother.

'In the Emperor's name, *die!*'

'Salve.' Polixis breathed the name without meaning to. His secondary heart surged. His brother was here, with him. For better or for worse, they would be together again.

He tasted an acidic tang at the back of his throat. He focused on it, seeking to build it up.

The chaos in the basilica became even more pronounced. The reports of gunfire rebounded from the vaults overhead and the amplified, disorienting vox roars of the Reivers were joined by the familiar crackle of Salve Imperator. Polixis could see nothing of the assault, though, shielded as it was by the rear walling and piled trophies around the back of the apse, and the angle at which he was held by the rack. The orks immediately around him, a mixture of kommandos and Urgork's hulking bodyguards, were milling around in apparent confusion while Urgork, driven wild by the interruption of his experiments, was bellowing incoherently and smashing anything that came in reach. The ork shaman dropped its staff and writhed on its knees in front of Polixis and the rack. Its hands clamped around its throbbing, distended skull, seemingly unable to deal with the psychic backlash of so much sudden, concentrated excitement from the hordes of greenskins surrounding it.

Polixis tensed one more time, about to wrench himself free, when a new figure wormed its way through the churning green mass before him. It was the medicae creature. It reached the shaman's side and knelt close to it, one arm on its shoulder, as though to help it stand. Instead, a dark splatter of arterial blood hit the flagstones, and Polixis realised it had slashed a scalpel across the psyker's throat. The blind ork vainly tried to clamp its hands around the wound, gagging, its milky eyes wide. The medicae kicked the psyker over, leaving it to scrabble and bleed out on the floor.

'Told ya I'd get 'im, one way or anuvva,' the medicae cackled, approaching Polixis. 'That git was ripping all sorts from your 'ead, humie. Couldn't be havin' dat! I'm the only one dat can help da boss! *Me!*'

The manic creature once more mounted Polixis' armour, foot on his knee guard and a claw gripping his pauldron while it brought its bloody scalpel up to his face.

'Looks like your lads is here to spring ya,' the creature said, sneering at him, face inches from his own. 'Shame they is too late. Let's see how tough your eyeballs is, shall we?'

'There's one aspect of Adeptus Astartes biology that you appear to be unaware of,' Polixis responded, offering the ork a smile. The thing frowned, frozen in place by the unexpected expression.

'What?'

'The Betcher's Gland,' Polixis replied, and spat.

He had been clenching the organs located in his hard palate and salivary glands for the past few minutes, causing them to begin emitting the corrosive substance they stored up to aid a Space Marine's enhanced digestion. The two glands worked his saliva up to toxic levels, leaving a bitter, burning taste in his mouth.

The greenskin was just inches from Polixis when the Apothecary spat the acidic load directly into its face. The ork recoiled with a shriek, dropping its scalpel, hands going up to its eyes as the deadly substance ate its way towards the alien's skull.

Polixis roared and ripped his arms free from their restraints.

Metal buckled, then bent. Razor wire snapped as the Primaris unleashed every last ounce of strength in muscles and servos alike, channelling the pain, frustration and despair of the past few days into his efforts. The rack came apart and he thumped onto the basilica's floor.

He was in motion the moment he hit, a hand shooting out to send the screaming medicae flying back into the press. The orks around him turned as one, finally roused from their frenzied confusion, reaching for their weapons. Polixis flung himself into them, fists clenched.

'Don't kill 'im!' he could hear Urgork roaring, the warlord trying to force his way through to the Apothecary. 'Don't zoggin' kill 'im!'

The orders gave the first greenskins the briefest moment's hesitation. Polixis used it. He caved in the face of a kommando with a single, furious blow, his gauntlet cracking tusks and bone and driving the creature's thick skull back into its brain. He snatched up the thing's axe, lifting the brute weapon with servo-enhanced ease, and swung it, the force behind the strike lopping through a limb before burying the axe head in a torso.

The rest of the aliens rushed him before he could wrench it free. Blows struck his left pauldron and the right side of his body, and he was forced to twist down and away to protect his bare head. He kept moving, using what little space he could force amongst the press, trying to get past Urgork's throne and get his back to the rear wall ringing the apse. A greenskin wrapped its thick arms around his waist, attempting to bring him down, while a trio of gretchin snatched at his heels – he grasped the head of the former and twisted savagely, cracking its neck, while stamping down on the smaller greenskins. The blessings of Primaris physiology meant he was as large as any of Urgork's nobs, and even faster and more durable in his battleplate. They couldn't lay a hand on him.

He had almost made it to the wall, impeded only by the remains of Squad Tiro and Captain Demeter, which still lay littered around Urgork's blasphemous throne. A flash of steel met his eye amidst the bloodied blue power armour. It was Justicier, Demeter's ancient power sword, lying abandoned at the feet of the slain captain.

'I will avenge you, brother-captain,' Polixis snarled. 'And free your blade with the blood of your killers.'

Polixis bent for the weapon, turning his body as he did so to throw the ork lunging for him onto the spikes adorning Urgork's throne. His fingers closed around the worn hilt, and with a prayer to the blade's sorrowful spirit he swung it upwards and clenched the ignition rune. The sword sprang to life, lightning crackling across its length, the smell of ozone filling Polixis' nostrils. The greenskins coming at him faltered.

Before either he or the xenos could react, there was a crash from the Apothecary's left. A greenskin's body had slammed through a crumbling section of the apse's rear wall, rubble tumbling down around it, its skull caved in. A figure punched its way through the jagged gap, wreathed in dust and lightning of its own. The actinic flashes picked out bloodied armour black as pitch, and the grim spectacle of a leering death's head helmet.

He had never found the nightmare vision of his brother so welcoming.

'Polixis!' Kastor shouted, and tossed the blade he held in his free gauntlet. Polixis caught it in his left hand, Justicier in his right, immediately recognising the familiar balance of his gladius.

There was no time for any further exchange. The greenskin horde charged, roaring their bestial fury, pushing and trampling one another in their need to reach the Primaris. Side by side, the two brothers met them.

HANLON

The war returned to Shebat Alpha from the air. As the day approached its peak, the greater part of the Imperial Navy's remaining forces on Ikara IX reached the outskirts of the capital. The orks responded in force, alerted not long after the wings had left their airfields around Kroten. Lieutenant Hanlon saw the dogfights break out amidst the ash clouds directly above, tight formations of fighters breaking and scattering across the heavens as they were lit up by streamers of hard rounds and pearly darts of las-fire. The noise was incredible, rising even further when a flight of two dozen ochre-painted Harakoni Valkyrie airborne assault carriers and attendant Vulture gunships growled overhead, heading in the direction of Shebat. In the midst of the protective flock were two monstrosities – gigantic armour-plated flyers, bearing the blue-and-white heraldry of the Ultramarines and bristling with weapons. Besides the mass conveyance lighters used to ferry the Guard planetside, Hanlon had never seen such large and heavily armoured aerial transports.

'This really must be it,' Vorn said over the roar of the aircraft's passing.

'Our throw of the dice,' Hanlon replied, putting her finger to her ear as her microbead clicked. 'This is it. Up and over, Second Platoon.'

She slung her rifle and gripped the redoubt's parapet ladder, climbing the short distance over the crest of sandbags and flakboards. The slope opened up before her, a vista of carnage after the repeated greenskin assaults, stretching away to the grey ruins of Shebat and the great mountain peaks that framed them on the horizon. She found her feet, looking left and right as the rest of her ragged command joined her on the slope. In both directions, for as far as she could see, Imperial Guard units were clambering from their defensive works out into the corpse-choked no-man's-land, shouldering rifles and spreading out down the ridgeline. A hundred yards to her right a trio of Zoishen Leman Russ tanks were moving in single file between two defensive works, treads kicking up a fine cloud of ash dust as they grumbled out beyond the static line. Further left, the rest of Hanlon's own battalion were advancing, the colonel snapping orders about spacing and advance-to-contact protocols over the command channel.

'Don't bunch up,' Hanlon ordered as they began to move downhill, picking their way between the bloody, ash-heaped remains of the greenskin dead. As though to underline her words an ork fighter, wreathed in flame, came hammering down at the foot of the slope a few hundred yards to the right, metal shrieking and bending as it tumbled through the dirt. Above, the battle for control of Shebat's airspace continued. Hanlon watched the Valkyries and the great Space Marine flyers receding over the city's shattered skyline.

'Give them hell,' she found himself murmuring.

The advance resumed.

TYRANUS

Tyranus led the Fulminata in with the first wave, vengeful and eager. The Harakoni Warhawks were with them, a battalion of heavy drop-troops clad in ochre carapace armour and black fatigues. They hit the square outside the basilica from above, their assault preceded by the murderous work of their Valkyries and Vulture gunships, heavy bolters, lascannons and missile pods ripping apart the mobs of greenskins packed into the open space. The updates on Tyranus' command channel reported that the xenos' own air support was nowhere to be found, caught flat-footed by the sudden massed aerial drive on the heart of Shebat – while the airborne carriers came in low over the ruins and rubble, Thunderbolts and Lightning air superiority fighters kept the ramshackle greenskin aircraft at bay, the sky over the industrial city dotted and dashed with contrails and the bursts of explosions.

The Ultramarines and the Warhawks assaulted the square well before it had been cleared by the firepower of the gunships. There was no time – Tyranus knew that if they hesitated, the orks would reassert control of the air and bring reinforcements flooding in from elsewhere in the city. Urgork would slip away. The Fulminata would be wiped out, sacrificed for no gain. So they struck, Guardsmen and Space Marines rappelling down directly into the bloody, shredded remains of the greenskins below, bolt rifles and lascarbines raining down a pounding hail of fire.

Tyranus was with Squad Nerva as they alighted from the Overlord *Sicarius*, the engines of the huge Primaris gunship shuddering the air around it. The steps leading to the basilica's shattered doors lay directly ahead. Between them, however, was a sea of green carnage. Hundreds of orks had been ripped apart by the barrage of the incoming air wings, and their bloody remains formed a thick, twitching carpet before the Ultramarines. Others had only been wounded or had avoided the downpour altogether, and were now dragging themselves from the slaughter yard remains with bellows of angry bloodlust.

Tyranus glanced at the tactical display. The Warhawks were coming down around the square's edges, securing it from the mobs trying to rush in from the adjacent streets. The Fulminata stormed the square itself, the concentrated firepower of the Intercessors and Hellblasters decimating the broken remains of the ork horde.

The lieutenant keyed the company-wide command channel, highlighting the basilica towering over them with a blink-click.

'Ultramarines, advance.'

CHAPTER TWELVE   BLOOD BROTHERS

POLIXIS/KASTOR

The brothers from Iax fought as one. The black and the white, retribution and salvation, avatars of their respective purposes united in the purging of mankind's enemies.

Polixis battled on with a fury he had never known before. It was not the same anger that had gripped him when he had fought in Shebat's ruins for the body of Brother Lorens, or in the redoubts on Ridge 1. Then, a part of him had still been detached, distant, analytical. That part was gone now. He killed the xenos with Justicier in one fist and his gladius in the other, twin-bladed death, sawing through everything that came at him. His muscles burned with the exultant release as he parried a hit with one weapon and gutted the xenos with the other, turned the motion into a beheading stroke with the power sword before letting the backhand swing bring his gladius up to block a buzzing chainblade. The teeth locked against the vibrosteel and left its wielder open to an impaling strike. Polixis recovered his guard, plunging his power sword through thick skin and ribs, and jarring it off the alien's spine. He ripped the weapon free, relishing the destructive energies of its ancient disruptor field as it pulver-ised flesh and bone.

Kastor killed with no less brutality than his brother, but he did so without the mindless, furious hatred that powered each of the Apothecary's blows. Though the Chaplain's fire burned as brightly as ever, within was a measure of peace he had never before known in the white heat of combat. The melee was too vicious and too desperate to ponder it, but there were two things that Kastor knew with complete surety. He was back alongside his brother and, regardless of what happened now, he would not leave him again.

'It's like Elipax all over again,' the Chaplain exclaimed as he slammed Salve Imperator down through an alien's skull, pulping it into the cracked flagstones underfoot. 'You remem-ber our third ever assignment together?'

'In Sergeant Scaro's squad?' Polixis asked.

'See, you do recall some things, Helix!'

Polixis grunted as he caught the downward swing of a cleaver and locked it between both his blades, before sever-ing it entirely with Justicier.

'That was after our induction, you fool,' he snarled, in no mood for his brother's amusement.

'Still, it was a glorious purging, was it not? Do you remem-ber how we butchered our way through that hrud's nest, above the star port?'

'I remember you pushing too far ahead, as ever, and the rest of us having to drag you out,' Polixis said, parrying an axe haft with his power sword and thumping his gladius home through the alien's stomach. 'As usual.'

Kastor didn't respond, but he was smiling. The brothers killed and killed, Polixis venting his pain and Kastor his relief, their lightning-clad weapons combining to create an elemental force of destruction that eviscerated and crushed everything that came for them. Both knew the chances of survival were slender. Neither cared any more.

Iax was united and they would stay that way, in life or in death.

HANLON

Second Platoon pressed forwards.

Coren was down, so Corporal Sern had taken charge of what was left of his squad. The rest of the company were on the flanks of Hanlon's platoon, leapfrogging from one position to the next amidst the desolation of Shebat's eastern outskirts, lasrifles and autoguns cracking and snapping.

'Incline right,' Hanlon barked into her comm-link, cursing as a spray of hard rounds battered at the broken remnants of the wall she was crouched behind. An ork wartrack was bedded down in a shallow shell crater just to the north-east, its guns threatening to stall the platoon's advance.

'Verik, hit it!' Hanlon demanded as dust from the crumbling wall burst around her. A second later there was the whoosh of a missile launcher, followed by the echoing report of a detonation. The hard round impacts stopped, and Hanlon risked a glance over the ruins to see that a krak rocket had reduced the ork machine to a wreck, belching black flames.

'Forward,' she shouted, rising once more and vaulting the riddled wall. To her left and right her squads pressed on, the recon team at her back. It was almost impossible to tell what was going on beyond the sphere of her own platoon – the jagged mounds of rubble and the tumbled-down remains of the shacks that had once constituted the city's slums obscured visibility, aided by the smoke and dust being kicked up by the battle. It seemed the battalion was on the attack, and she could hear the grumbling engines and teeth-juddering discharges of the Zoishen tanks somewhere off to the right. Beyond that Hanlon felt as though she were operating alone. The fog of war had descended, riven with screams and explosions, and all they could do was what they always did – press forwards.

'More contacts front!' Sergeant Tarn shouted from Hanlon's left. She'd already heard the howls – the debris directly ahead dropped into a shallow slope, and the dead ground held more xenos. She was afforded a view of the city's edge as she mounted the brief rise – not just the mob rushing her, but also the desolate sprawl ahead and, distantly, the spires of the Basilica of Saint Albarak the Smelter, standing lonely in the wilderness that had once been an industrial heartland.

'Open fire! *Open fire!*'

The Namarians poured las and hard rounds down into the onrushing orks. Hanlon knelt in the dirt and loosed a trio of shots, trying to ignore the return fire whipping the air around her; trying to ignore the churning fear in her stomach and the adrenaline thundering through her system; trying to ignore everything except her shooting drills. In that moment, with life and death reduced to her iron sights and the thump of recoil into her shoulder plate, it was easy to lose herself.

Her target went down, upper torso and throat lacerated. Another filled its place, bounding up the slope like an enraged simian. They were huge, and their tough hides soaked up bullets and las-bolts alike – they weren't going to stop them.

'Bayonets!' Hanlon shouted, sliding her blade free. 'Hold your ground!'

She lunged down with her rifle into the first ork to mount

the rise in front of her, just as Vorn did likewise from her right. The two bayonets impaled the alien through the torso, punching through its stinking leather armour, but still it came on, running itself through and forcing both soldiers to dig their heels in and brace themselves. Finally, they were able to bring it down onto its knees, and Vorn finished it with a burst of shots directly into its gut. Hanlon planted her boot on its shoulder and twisted her bayonet free, snarling.

'There's too many!' Vorn shouted over the thunder of gunfire and alien roars. He was right – another mob was scrambling to engage, more pouring eastwards from the city's ruins. They needed support. Armour. Artillery. *Anything*. Before she could shout a reply, she heard a sharp zipping sound, followed by a crunch, and felt something warm and wet splatter her face. She half turned in time to catch Vorn as he toppled backwards, his face hideously torn, skull burst open by a slug round.

'Damn it!' Hanlon shouted, caught for a second between holding up the twitching corpse and reloading, more of Vorn's blood drenching her. Another round hit a piece of masonry at her feet and ricocheted up between her legs, twitching her fatigues with a near miss.

'Stand firm!' she shouted, letting go of Vorn and reaching for a fresh magazine. To her left she could see Krevin grappling with another greenskin, the big alien wrestling him to the dirt and choking the life from him. Markel was already dead, laid out by an ork cudgel, sniper rifle broken. She couldn't even see the rest of her recon team, let alone the rest of the platoon.

'Throne take you!' she screamed, and again opened fire into the beasts rushing her. Another one fell, a primed stick grenade tumbling from its fingers, bouncing a few feet down the slope.

'Grenade!' Hanlon managed to shout, before the blast engulfed her. Her ears burst and she felt herself being lifted, battered by a hail of dirt and debris. The impact with the ground drove the air from her lungs and caused stars to burst across her vision. She tried to move, to breathe, smoke and wreckage engulfing her. Throne damn whoever had ordered this assault. Throne damn them all.

She managed to bring herself up into a sitting position, gasping for breath, just in time for something to slam into her chest and throw her back down. It was a boot, its wicked studs grating against her flak-plate, and as she struggled to prize it off she found herself looking up at a greenskin, the beast keeping her pinned effortlessly.

Hanlon tried to reach for her rifle, but she had no idea where it had fallen. The ork raised its boot, and she just had time to spit at it before it came slamming down into her face. Pain exploded, and darkness overtook her.

GRIMTOOF

Grimtoof managed to prise himself from the press long enough to reach the edge of the basilica's nave. The whole building was in turmoil – not only had the beakies burst up from the tombs, their flash-bangs and howls zogging up the lads around them, but it seemed more of them were coming down from the skies outside. It had been a trap all along, and Grimtoof had been the only one to sniff it out.

'Zoggin' beakie gits,' Grimtoof growled. The white beakie had broken free, and now a black one had joined him beside the big boss' throne, smashing up every git that went for them. The big boss himself was trying to reach them, driven mad with rage, but Grimtoof knew better than to join the hundreds of lads trying to mob those gits from the front.

Contrary to the thinking of most boys, a big knife in the back was always the best option.

The kommando nob had worked his way out to the walls, where the pressure of surging greenskin bodies was lessened. The humies were holding the narrow space of the apse, so Grimtoof was going to go around, get in behind them and finish the madness before it got any madder.

He turned a corner into the narrow stone channel that ran in a semicircle behind the apse partition. Just as he did, something smacked into the flagstones at his boots, splattering his legs and feet with blood – it was the severed head of one of Gobinz's boys, tongue lolling out, eyes wide.

Grimtoof glanced up, and found himself looking into the grinning face of death. Other beakies were still back behind the apse, holding the stairwells going down into the crypts. They had skull masks on, and their form-fitting blue armour was smeared and dripping with the remains of dozens of boys and squigs.

'I am your death, xenos,' the beakie said.

'Come get some then, ya git,' Grimtoof spat back.

The death-face in front of Grimtoof raised the long stabba it carried, blood running from its blade, and let out a howl. The ork didn't cringe back from the humie's amplified fury – instead, he let loose a bellow of his own and lunged, axe hurtling for the beakie's grinning bone-mask.

With a crash the knife met the axe's haft.

* * *

SEVERUS

Severus put his weight behind his knife, trying to saw it through the handle of the cape-clad ork's axe. This one was bigger than the others, a leader-beast with the equipment to match. Its instinctive reaction to Severus' vox-roar hadn't been to flinch away in the same manner that its lesser kin had, but to throw itself at him.

That nearly caught the Reiver off guard. He parried the thing's first strike, but it recovered quickly, slamming a fist into Severus' right pauldron and attempting to drag him off balance. He spun his knife point-down and tried to punch it into the greenskin's guts, but it flung itself up hard against him, getting in his face, its ugly alien stink and the sweating pressure of its grimy, green skin invading the Reiver's poised stance before he could strike. He was forced to give ground, and still it kept coming on, another blow from its axe jarring from the Ultramarine's blade.

There were more orks with it, trying to work their way round behind him. He could still hear Stryx and Fobos fighting, their vox-amplified bellowing interspersed with grunts and the butcher's sounds of metal on meat. They couldn't support him, though – there was too many of the xenos. Kastor had gone, breaking through to the apse and his brother. They were running out of time.

The ork grappled with Severus, his knife locked beneath the axe's head, their free hands both grasping at torsos as each sought the purchase that would allow them to angle a killing blow. The ork snapped its tusks at him and snarled something indecipherable in its savage tongue, its eyes wild with alien battle-lust.

There was a little click, barely audible over the ork's grunts and the rasping of Severus' own breath. Both the Primaris and the greenskin glanced down, and realised the arming pin from one of the crude stick grenades strapped to the ork's front had been yanked loose in the tussle. Their eyes met, and Severus experienced the closest thing he ever could to a moment's understanding with an alien beast.

He flung himself backwards just as the thunderclap of the detonation engulfed him.

KASTOR

It seemed as though Kastor and Polixis would live. From beyond the walls of the basilica, the thunder of the Fulminata's assault was audible.

'*We are inbound, my brethren,*' Tyranus' voice clicked over the vox-net. '*Hold firm, for Guilliman and the Emperor.*'

Kastor felt his spirit soar further, and his tired body blazed with fresh vigour as he struck down one greenskin after another. The Emperor did not abandon the righteous, and he swore in that moment that he would honour the reprieve he and his brother had been granted, many times over.

Then *Extremis* hit. The mighty Repulsor grav-tank had been defiled and cannibalised, its noble machine-spirit tortured as cruelly as Polixis had been. Now some insane greenskin creatures had managed to get one of the tank's engines up and running again.

The hulking vehicle lurched forwards, only its right side raised up by the gravitic motor-blocks, its left flank shrieking and kicking up a shower of sparks as it was dragged across the basilica's floor. Orks who were too slow to get out of the way were crushed or pulverised. It rammed into the wall along the rear of the apse, sending masonry tumbling. The whole building shook.

Kastor was closest to the Repulsor's impact. He tried to step away from the wall at his back as the stonework started to give, but an ork nob used the opportunity to fling itself against him, slamming him back into the bricks. Its defiance didn't last long – the collapse crushed its skull and broke its back. The impact caused Kastor to stumble, then fall, Salve Imperator slipping from his grip.

He looked up and realised that the wall's demise had split them apart. Polixis had managed to avoid the worse of the debris, but he had been forced left, and the green-skins were on him again before he could rejoin his brother. Kastor let out a bellow and heaved the rubble off himself, power armour grating. He snatched up Salve Imperator and smashed its inactive head into the first ork to come at him from out of the dust shroud that had blanketed the apse.

The second beast that emerged was Urgork.

The ork warlord roared, the primal, savage noise of his race's might reverberating around the defiled space. Its skinning blades were out, and they came for Kastor in a hail of blows, driven with a brute force even his Mark X armour couldn't withstand. One carved through his left pauldron, splitting its heraldry and hitting bone, while another overhead swing bit into the top of his backpack, causing him to stumble.

He recovered with a snarl, his own rage reigniting. This was the monstrosity that had tried to tear his brother apart, the beast of patchwork, discoloured flesh and swollen muscle that sought dominion over mankind's realm. The Chaplain rammed Salve Imperator forwards, smashing it against the beast's chest, hearing ribs crack. Urgork showed no sign of having even registered the blow – he came on, his small, mismatched eyes wide with a maniacal frenzy, foam bubbling from between his thick tusks.

'I will break you, xenos,' Kastor snarled as he met it. 'For what you did to my brother, I will destroy you utterly.'

'Salve!' he heard Polixis shout from his left, but he had time only to glance in his direction – the Apothecary was beset by more orks, the hulking brutes of Urgork's bodyguard, gladius lodged in one nob's throat and discarded, Justicier wielded now in both hands.

'Your unholy existence is at an end!' Kastor shouted as he turned back to Urgork, slamming Salve Imperator down once more.

The crozius arcanum's disruptor field wouldn't reignite, but the Chaplain wielded it nonetheless, limbs burning with the destructive energies of a genhanced Primaris as he rained blows on the towering greenskin. Urgork simply soaked them up, the crunch of muscle and tendon seemingly neither inhibiting nor discomforting him. When the ork struck back, it did so with a force not even Kastor could match. The skinning blades thumped through ceramite, shattering the stylised ribcage encasing the Chaplain's breastplate and scoring a wicked groove down the left temple of his helmet. It laid open his right thigh and sent blood pattering down onto black ceramite. Still the Ultramarine fought, his wounds nothing more than a dull ache, his body immune to the stunning impacts that rang from his helmet.

The two giants stood and traded blows, almost too fast to follow, neither taking a backward step. Kastor's fury only mounted as his armour registered more damage and his body bled.

'I will smash your unholy form apart, beast,' the Chaplain

growled, taking another hit to his pauldron. 'And immolate your foul remains.'

One of them had to fall. Kastor heard his brother's cry once more, and stole a glance long enough to see him being borne to the floor by two nobs, Justicier impaled through the torso of one of them.

'Helix!' Kastor bellowed, but the moment's distraction was enough for Urgork. One of the ork's blades cracked into Salve Imperator's haft, and the crozius was sent spinning away, clattering against the rubble at the Chaplain's feet. Kastor barely had time to right himself before the warlord surged forwards with a roar, slamming his scarred head directly into the skull helm.

There was a hideous crunch and half of Kastor's visor display blinked offline, the left lens crushed. The jarring impact forced him back a single step, and he found himself tripping amidst the rubble, his battered armour unable to fully support him any more. He fell, trying to roll with the impact, reaching for the crozius, but Urgork's iron-shod boot struck him the moment he landed, slamming him back against the broken remnants of the apse with a horrid crunch.

'T-too late, l-little black b-beakie,' the warlord snarled, spittle and dark blood pattering down onto the Chaplain. 'Your mate is mine now. See?'

Kastor managed to turn his head. Polixis had been dragged down like his brother. The Apothecary bellowed with desperate fury as he slammed the drill of his activated narthecium into the skull of one nob, Justicier and his gladius already impaled in the other two. He was still fighting, still howling with a blood-fury Kastor had never seen in him, but any chance for finesse was gone in the crushing press of bodies.

'You won't take him,' he snarled up at Urgork. 'Death is coming for you, beast. Can't you hear it?'

'Be l-l-long gone by the time th-they is here,' the monster snapped back. 'Maybe they can put your bits b-back t-t-togetha after I've chopped 'em up.'

The ork struck. Kastor brought his arms up in a protective cross just in time to stop the blow caving in his skull. He grunted as the metal cut through his vambrace, severing sinew coils and biting to the bone.

The hits kept coming, Urgork's frenzy insatiable, until blood was pouring from Kastor's elbows and his forearms were a mess of bloody ruin and hacked ceramite. He tried to push himself back up, to find the half-second to unleash his fury once again, but Urgork was relentless, his animalistic strength unfaltering.

And then, suddenly, the beast stopped. For a second, Kastor thought the ork was trying to trick him into lowering his guard. Then he realised that, trick or not, this was his last chance. Teeth gritted, he dropped his arms.

Urgork stood over him, transfixed. The madness had gone from his eyes, replaced by a glazed, unblinking expression. His maw began to foam, and his whole body became rigid.

Slowly, the warlord started to shake. The spasms started as a tick in his left eye that spread rapidly, until his whole form was shuddering. A low, unnatural whining sound erupted from his throat, and his jaw locked, the froth now overspilling and pattering down on Kastor.

The Chaplain regained his feet, taking a step back in the rubble as he tried to decide whether to make a move for Salve Imperator, and whether his brutalised arms were still capable of lifting the blessed weapon. Urgork's eyes refocused, but now instead of hate-fuelled madness, they were filled with emotions Kastor had rarely seen in a greenskin before.

Fear.

Pain.

Understanding.

Urgork tried to cast about, gaze roving as though he were seeking someone or something. Whatever it was, there was no sign of it. The rigidity in his body snapped and he went down abruptly onto both knees, the whining noise replaced by a violent, hacking cough that quickly became retching and then full-fledged choking. Kastor moved further back as whatever seizure was gripping the warlord worsened, the ork's whole body spasming. He was sick, a thick, noxious, stinking stream of yellow bile splattering across the splintered flagstones and rubble at Kastor's feet. The vile-looking liquid darkened as blood discoloured it, followed by chunks of what looked like liquefied organs.

The ork warlord managed to draw enough of a breath to spit out a word, blood and bile now pouring from his nose as well as his mouth.

'G-g-gr... Grok...'

Then, with a last shuddering exhalation of gory vomit, he collapsed forwards and was still.

Silence gripped the basilica, but then the howls of the orks around Kastor and his brother redoubled. Many were staring at the body of their warlord, slumped unceremoniously in a spreading pool of its own effluvium. Others cast looks back towards the basilica's main doors, where the searing light of plasma was now visible, accompanied by the click-boom of bolt rifles on full auto. Some of the aliens abruptly turned on those around them, fists flying as the larger greenskins realised that the command of the entire Waaagh! was on offer to the strongest.

Kastor snatched up Salve Imperator with the one hand that was still responding, his genhancements failing to fully block the agony of his torn and broken limbs. He smashed the mace against the head of the last nob still pinning Polixis to the ground, sending a sudden splatter of cranial matter across the Apothecary's battered armour. Polixis kicked the twitching corpse off him and rose once more to his feet, his gladius back in one fist.

Back-to-back, Kastor and Polixis stood their ground and surveyed the carnage around them, then each other.

'Good of you to join me, little brother,' Polixis said. Kastor smiled.

'I couldn't let you have all the glory, Helix. What would the rest of the Chapter say of the Fulminata if our Apothecary finished a campaign with the highest kill tally of all of us?'

The fight had gone out of the orks. Those not locked in their sudden struggle for supremacy with one another were panicking, realising that more humans were storming the front of the basilica. They turned on one another in the sudden rush to escape, the Space Marines still at the back of the apse completely forgotten.

Polixis turned and looked down at his brother's forearms, at the bent and broken black ceramite and the blood that still oozed from between the rent metal.

'What is your armour reading?' he asked.

'Left arm is shattered,' Kastor admitted, glancing at the remaining auto-sense readouts on his damaged visor display. 'I can still use the right.'

Polixis didn't respond, and the Chaplain looked at him. He sensed a sudden tension in his brother's stance, and saw his grey eyes widen as they focused on something behind Kastor.

'Move!' the Apothecary shouted, thrusting his brother to

one side. A green limb slammed through the suddenly empty space, cracking its fist against Polixis' breastplate and shattering one of the empty reserve cryo-vials hanging from around his neck.

Kastor spun, and found himself confronted once more by Urgork. The foul monster had resurrected, blood and bile pouring from its eyes, ears, nose and mouth.

'Impossible,' the Chaplain breathed.

A keening noise escaped from the warlord's slack jaw as his whole body shook violently. He reached towards the two Space Marines with claws that clenched and unclenched with bone-crushing force.

'Back,' Kastor shouted as the huge ork lunged for him. Polixis, however, wasn't going back. He thrust past his brother, driving him to one side. Knocking him from the path of Urgork's fist.

Polixis, the older brother. Polixis, the protector. Polixis, who would rather charge a starved crophound than abandon his sibling even for a moment. Kastor cried out in anger and horror, even as he stumbled. It had all been for nothing. He had failed.

But Urgork's blow never fell. Silver steel flashed, and the ork's head flew from his shoulders, the hideous noise he had been making cut short by a jet of black blood and yellowing fluids. He crunched to his knees and then, finally, slumped onto his side at the feet of the remains of Squad Tiro and Captain Demeter, his head bouncing away down the apse. The decapitated body twitched one more time, then was still.

Behind it stood Severus. The Reiver was almost unrecognisable – much of his bare head was raw or blackened by burns. Blood stained the white grin of his skull mask, and his larger left pauldron had been ripped away to reveal a shoulder that was little more than a mess of muscle and cartilage. Kastor realised that the Reiver's left arm now ended at the elbow. In his remaining fist, he carried a combat knife that dripped with Urgork's blood.

'All objectives achieved,' the Reiver said, voice tight with pain. He stayed on his feet a moment longer, then collapsed.

COGKRUSHA

The Basilica of Saint Albarak the Smelter resounded with the howls of dying greenskins.

The humies were long gone, evacuated on their flyers, to where the battle in the slums still rumbled on. Greenskins had flooded in from all over the city, at first to crump the beakies and then, when they realised they'd slipped away, to contend for the new position of big boss.

Cogkrusha had seen it all before. When a warboss went down, chaos ensued. It was just the way of things. Eventually a new leader would emerge, usually bigger and stronger than the one before, and the clans and mobs would rally to him. Until then, though, there was nothing but disunity. Orks fought, grots cowered and the squigs feasted on those not strong enough to survive the new status quo.

The big mek knew better than to stick around through it all. He'd managed to get the big floaty tank fired up, at least – both sides were working now, and the grots on the shootas he'd welded to the sides had specific orders to gun down any git that got too close to the technological wonder. A few minutes more and they'd be out of the basilica and laying low until a new boss came forward deserving Cogkrusha's services.

That, or Cogkrusha would make a boss for himself.

He found Grok crouched behind the ruins of Urgork's throne, the warboss' body lying trampled and forgotten nearby while his former nobs beat the snot out of each other over the defiled altar. Cogkrusha approached as fast as his clanking body would permit, careful not to make eye contact with anyone. The painboy looked up as the mek loomed over him, blinking his one remaining eye, his face a hideous, melted morass of acid-eaten flesh.

'C-cog,' he slurred. Cogkrusha looked down at the thing the pathetic little runt was cradling – it was Urgork's severed head, eyes glassy, tongue hanging out, the blood from the ex-warboss' orifices slowly congealing.

'You's comin' wiv me,' Cogkrusha rasped, a metallic claw snagging the disfigured painboy before he could run. 'And you's bringin' dat head wiv you.'

EPILOGUE

POLIXIS

The medicae bay on the *Spear of Macragge* felt like an alien place to Polixis. It had been a Terran month since the Apothecary had last stood within its white-tiled walls, lit by the harsh illumination of the surgical lamps, the air thrumming softly with active vitae monitors and health systems. It felt like it had been a lifetime.

This was his domain, and yet he had never been comfortable in it, not the way Kastor was with the Chapel of the Dioskuri, the *Spear of Macragge*'s primary place of worship. The medicae ward was a workplace to Polixis, nothing more and nothing less. The location he thought of as home – the green and golden fields of Iax – was long lost to him.

Kastor sat on one of the metal examination plates near the bay's centre, his legs over the side, clad in a simple black chiton. He was looking down at his exposed forearms – the thick muscles were criss-crossed with dozens of deep, raw lacerations, made lumpen and discoloured by the synth-skin plasts Polixis had applied. His left arm was bound in ferroplate splints, kept in place by a cast of fibremesh that was still setting. The air was heavy with the chemical stink of counterseptics.

'You can't stop me from returning,' the Chaplain said, still looking at his injuries.

'Is there anyone who can? Certainly not Lieutenant Tyranus, nor even the Codex Astartes, it seems.'

Kastor looked up, and there was a fire in his eyes, but it died quickly when it met with Polixis' cool gaze. He looked back down again, speaking slowly.

'As soon as I have confirmation from Artificer Frenn that my battleplate is functional once more, I am rejoining the demi-company.'

'I know,' Polixis allowed. 'So long as you don't mind fighting single-handed for the week it will take your bones to set.'

'The Emperor will be my shield.'

The two lapsed into silence. Polixis turned away, washing his hands in a surgical scrub bowl beside the plate. Like his brother he was unarmoured, clad now in the white robes of the apothecarion, the stylised red helix tattoo of his position laid bare on his right arm. As he scrubbed his brother's blood from his palms, his thoughts strayed back to Shebat.

The Fulminata had lost a single brother during the insertion into the city, Otho of Squad Domitian, whose plasma weapon had finally overheated during the storming of the basilica and seared away much of his upper body.

Another life lost for him. He'd spent every day telling himself that was not the case – the reason for the massed mobilisation across the front had been the chance to kill Urgork. That plan had succeeded. Yet he feared the numbers of the slain would continue to rise. In the cryo unit next to the bay lay Severus, his broken body suspended in a hibernation state by his sus-an membrane. When Polixis had seen the Reiver, just after killing Urgork, he had suspected he was only functioning thanks to his Belasarian Furnace, the implant unique to Primaris that drove a warrior into a hyper-aggressive state following a fatal wound. Severus, however, did not yet seem ready to pass over. Polixis had asked Kastor to pray for him – he had endured enough loss as it was.

'You should not have come,' the Apothecary said, almost without meaning to. He turned off the bowl's water pump and looked back at his brother. Kastor did not return his gaze, though he had lowered his scarred forearms to his lap.

'I know,' he said. 'But you would have. For me.'

'That does not make it right.'

'I do not regret my decision, brother.'

'What will they do to you?'

'A council of the Reclusiam will be convened, once they have processed Tyranus' report,' Kastor said, finally looking up at his brother. His scarred expression was heavy with disappointment. 'If practical, I will be removed to blessed Macragge to stand trial. If not I will do so via hololithic attendance. I suspect it will be within the month.'

'It seems… unjust,' Polixis said.

Kastor smiled sadly. 'I broke the tenets of the Codex. I will be judged by those same tenets now. That is as it should be.'

'True enough,' Polixis allowed. He moved to check the containment seal of the mortuary casks that lay in a data-locked vault beneath the bay, the salvaged organs of recovered Primaris corpses stored in the heavy, hoarfrost-coated ice crates in the sub-zero chamber. Among them were the harvested remains of the bodies of Squad Tiro and Captain Demeter, or at least what Polixis had been able to retrieve. The Fulminata had removed Urgork's trophies when they evacuated, and the armour plates were now being tended to by the *Spear of Macragge*'s tech-savants and repair teams in the lower decks. The company banner had also been returned, its tattered, bloody folds hung reverently within the Chapel of the Dioskuri. They would be borne into battle once more in only a few hours – the Fulminata would be returning to Ikara IX, ready to prosecute the greenskin menace once again.

'Will your battleplate be repaired in time for an immediate return to the surface?' Polixis asked as he stepped back out of the containment vault, seeking to ease the events of the past few days with simple words.

'I await Frenn's assessment,' Kastor said. 'That will have to be enough. If the xenos fleet was to return now I would have to don it, regardless of its state.'

Polixis nodded in agreement. The most vital blow of all following Urgork's death had fallen against the ork ship assets. When it became apparent the warlord really was dead, the xenos vessels anchored in high orbit had turned on one another, each captain desperate to ensure control over its most prized assets. Broadsides, ramming runs and boarding actions had decimated the alien fleet as a full-scale civil war took hold. Rear Admiral Corran hadn't hesitated. Supported by the *Spear of Macragge*, his ships had returned from the system's edge and wrested control of Ikara's orbital anchorages from the scattering xenos fleet.

The arrival of their flagship had afforded the Fulminata the chance to resupply fully for the first time since the campaign had begun. Tyranus had authorised twenty-four hours aboard the strike cruiser – the demi-company's Overlords had extracted them from the edge of Shebat while Guard forces were still mustering for a renewed offensive, and the greenskins continued to show no sign of a counter-attack.

While Tyranus himself had expressed displeasure at the Ful-minata's withdrawal, however brief, it was apparent that the Primaris needed it – ammunition was short, and not a single warrior hadn't suffered injuries or sustained damage to his wargear. When the Ultramarines returned, it would be in full force.

'This cannot happen again,' Polixis said. 'Swear that, when we strike upon the anvil once more, you will not risk your all, let alone the lives of others, for my sake.'

'I have broken enough oaths,' Kastor said, holding his brother's gaze. 'I will not make another that could further shame me. I did not set out to find you for oaths or prom-ises. I did it for a memory. For Iax. For a home that no longer exists but will not die so long as we both live.'

'You are too sentimental by half,' Polixis said. 'What use have we for memories of home, brother?'

'If you saw the men and women I speak to on the eve of battle, you would not ask me that, Helix. You would not ask them. They know what purpose those memories serve. They bring hope on cold, dark nights and courage in the heat of battle. Without my own memories, how could I ever address them, put steel in their bellies and fire in their throats? My words would be lies, sowing only dead ash.'

Polixis paused, his head dipping briefly. 'Forgive me, brother,' he said, approaching the slab once more and sit-ting down beside Kastor. 'It has been a long campaign, or it has at least felt like one.'

'What did they do, Polixis?' Kastor asked. 'The greenskins and their witch?'

The memory of the shaman forcing itself into his mind made the Apothecary's skin crawl. Even the hideous defile-ment of his brother's corpses had paled in comparison to the violation of feeling an alien presence in his own thoughts. He answered without looking at his brother.

'Perhaps I will tell you one day. Perhaps not.'

It seemed as though Kastor would press the matter, but then he looked down and tapped the splints on his broken arm.

'A week, you say?' he asked.

'If you rest it.'

'And how much chance is there of that, Brother-Apothecary?' Kastor asked. Polixis realised he was smiling for the first time since Shebat.

'Probably none, unless I accompany you personally to make sure you don't do anything more reckless.'

Kastor's smile widened. Polixis nodded towards the chrono display on the medicae bay's wall.

'Fifteen minutes until Captain Tyranus' insertion briefing. We had best be on our way.'

The Apothecary checked Severus' vitae monitor and left him in the care of the serf attendants, while he and his brother departed for the *Spear of Macragge*'s bridge, side by side once again.

ABOUT THE AUTHOR

Robbie MacNiven is a Highlands-born History graduate from the University of Edinburgh. He has written the Warhammer 40,000 novels *Blood of Iax*, *The Last Hunt*, *Carcharodons: Red Tithe*, *Carcharodons: Outer Dark* and *Legacy of Russ* as well as the short stories 'Redblade', 'A Song for the Lost' and 'Blood and Iron'. His hobbies include re-enacting, football and obsessing over Warhammer 40,000.

WARHAMMER
40,000

DAN ABNETT

ANARCH

A GAUNT'S GHOSTS NOVEL

ANARCH
by Dan Abnett

The battle for Urdesh has begun – and the outcome will determine the fate of the Sabbat Worlds Crusade. Ibram Gaunt is right hand to the Warmaster, and his Ghosts hold the key to victory – but can they defeat the sinister Anarch and his Sons of Sek?

YOUR NEXT READ

CIAPHAS CAIN: CHOOSE YOUR ENEMIES
by Sandy Mitchel

Commissar Ciaphas Cain returns! After putting down an uprising on a mining world, he finds evidence that the corruption might have spread to other planets, and the forge world of Ironfound could now be at risk…